50
TALES OF VALOUR, VICTORY AND THE VANQUISHED

50 TALES OF VALOUR, VICTORY AND THE VANQUISHED

RUPA

Published by
Rupa Publications India Pvt. Ltd 2023
7/16, Ansari Road, Daryaganj
New Delhi 110002

Sales Centres:

Prayagraj Bengaluru Chennai
Hyderabad Jaipur Kathmandu
Kolkata Mumbai

Edition copyright © Rupa Publications India Pvt. Ltd 2023

All rights reserved.
No part of this publication may be reproduced, transmitted, or stored in a retrieval system, in any form or by any means, electronic, mechanical, photocopying, recording or otherwise, without the prior permission of the publisher.

P-ISBN: 978-93-5702-454-9
E-ISBN: 978-93-5702-471-6

First impression 2023

10 9 8 7 6 5 4 3 2 1

Printed in India

This book is sold subject to the condition that it shall not,
by way of trade or otherwise, be lent, resold, hired out, or otherwise circulated, without the publisher's prior consent, in any form of binding or cover other than that in which it is published.

CONTENTS

Introduction — ix

1. AN OCCURRENCE AT OWL CREEK BRIDGE — 1
   Ambrose Bierce
2. THE MAN WITHOUT A COUNTRY — 12
   Edward Everett Hale
3. CHRISTMAS EVE IN WAR TIMES — 41
   Edward Payson Roe
4. THE NAMESAKE — 61
   Willa Cather
5. THE AFFAIR AT COULTER'S NOTCH — 75
   Ambrose Bierce
6. THE SERGEANT'S PRIVATE MADHOUSE — 85
   Stephen Crane
7. A DUEL — 94
   Guy de Maupassant
8. THE REVOLUTIONIST — 100
   Michaïl P. Artzybashev
9. THE SHOT — 112
   Alexander Pushkin
10. EPIPHANY — 127
    Guy de Maupassant
11. THE STORY OF YOSHITSUNE — 140
    Yei Theodora Ozaki
12. THE GLORY OF WAR — 156
    M.B. Levick
13. THE COUP DE GRÂCE — 160
    Ambrose Bierce

14. THE FORCED MARCH — 167
Hornell Hart

15. THE BLACK DOOR — 170
Gordon Seagrove

16. THE OLD MAN AT THE BRIDGE — 172
Ernest Hemingway

17. THE LONE CHARGE OF WILLIAM B. PERKINS — 175
Stephen Crane

18. EDITHA — 181
William D. Howells

19. WAR — 198
Luigi Pirandello

20. WHY THE TRENCH WAS LOST — 203
Charles F. Pietsch

21. THE QUEST OF THE V.C. — 205
A. Byers Fletcher

22. SOMEWHERE IN BELGIUM — 210
Percy Godfrey Savage

23. SOLDIER'S HOME — 212
Ernest Hemingway

24. THE SOUL OF A REGIMENT — 221
Talbot Mundy

25. A CURIOUS EXPERIENCE — 236
Mark Twain

26. ROGER MALVIN'S BURIAL — 268
Nathaniel Hawthorne

27. ONE OFFICER, ONE MAN — 291
Ambrose Bierce

28. TWO LITTLE SOLDIERS — 298
Guy de Maupassant

29.	LUCK *Mark Twain*	305
30.	THE DOG OF TITHWAL *Saadat Hasan Manto*	311
31.	MARINES SIGNALLING UNDER FIRE AT GUANTANAMO *Stephen Crane*	318
32.	GUESTS OF THE NATION *Frank O'Connor*	326
33.	A LATE ENCOUNTER WITH THE ENEMY *Flannery O'Connor*	340
34.	WEE WILLIE WINKIE *Rudyard Kipling*	352
35.	WHAT THE WOUNDED SAY AND DO *Ira L. Reeves*	364
36.	THE WORST MAN IN THE TROOP *Charles King*	368
37.	THE FATE OF 'NANA SAHIB'S ENGLISHMAN' *Archibald Forbes*	395
38.	A BAFFLED AMBUSCADE *Ambrose Bierce*	413
39.	WAR *Jack London*	416
40.	AN EPISODE OF WAR *Stephen Crane*	423
41.	THE GENTLEMAN PRIVATE OF THE 'SKILAMALINKS' *Archibald Forbes*	428
42.	A WAY YOU'LL NEVER BE *Ernest Hemingway*	440

43. THE FLY 454
    Katherine Mansfield
44. DALYRIMPLE GOES WRONG 461
    F. Scott Fitzgerald
45. THE BOWMEN 481
    Arthur Machen
46. MARY POSTGATE 485
    Rudyard Kipling
47. DAGON 502
    H.P. Lovecraft
48. MIXING WAR, ART AND DANCING 509
    Ernest Hemingway
49. THE LOCKET 511
    Kate Chopin
50. TWO FRIENDS 518
    Guy de Maupassant

INTRODUCTION

Stories of battles, gallantry and sacrifice have been at the forefront of our historical imagination and cultural upbringing irrespective of our language, region and religion. War has helped define our culture, its extent and our conception of ourselves. Even today, there is valorization of a mythical past where one group were the victors or one where they were victims and persecuted. Fighting out differences and the tribalism that breeds war is a story as old as humanity itself.

It is therefore no wonder that we enjoy reading about the exploits of soldiers, their acts of bravery that immortalize them and their battles. They become a repository of icons that define our culture and how we define ourselves. War heroes since ancient times, from Homer's Achilles to Mallory's King Arthur, have been constructed to serve as models of masculinity and tradition. The ideal soldier serves as a model for an ideal citizen within these old and new tales that valorize not just individuals, but entire sets of beliefs and ideas.

In the past two centuries, however, the horrors of war have hit closer to home. No longer contained to simply remote spaces that are agreed upon by the warring sides to fight in, the horrifying Napoleonic Wars, the Civil War, and two World Wars, have demystified the aura of war for a lot of people, showing it up for what it really is—terrible, destructive and merciless. The advent of even more wars in the twentieth century, along with their coverage, has disillusioned a lot of us as to what war and weaponry means and the implicit nobility of these concepts.

This collection presents to you fifty stories of war and what it does to people near it. These are tales of bravery, of valour and of strength, but also of the futility of the enterprise, and how innocent bystanders get caught up in it. They look at the effects of war, some which last for years after the event. Featuring stories by some of the most famous writers, from Maupassant, to Bierce, to Hemingway, these stories cover the length and breadth of the experience of war, its glory, its horrors, heroes and victims.

1

AN OCCURRENCE AT OWL CREEK BRIDGE

Ambrose Bierce

I

A man stood upon a railroad bridge in northern Alabama, looking down into the swift water 20 feet below. The man's hands were behind his back, the wrists bound with a cord. A rope closely encircled his neck. It was attached to a stout cross-timber above his head and the slack fell to the level of his knees. Some loose boards laid upon the sleepers supporting the metals of the railway supplied a footing for him and his executioners—two private soldiers of the Federal Army, directed by a sergeant who in civil life may have been a deputy sheriff. At a short remove upon the same temporary platform was an officer in the uniform of his rank, armed. He was a captain. A sentinel at each end of the bridge stood with his rifle in the position known as 'support,' that is to say, vertical in front of the left shoulder, the hammer resting on the forearm thrown straight across the chest—a formal and unnatural position, enforcing an erect carriage of the body. It did not appear to be the duty of these two men to know what was occurring at the centre of the bridge; they merely blockaded the two ends of the foot planking that traversed it.

Beyond one of the sentinels nobody was in sight; the railroad ran straight away into a forest for a hundred yards, then, curving, was lost to view. Doubtless there was an outpost farther along. The other bank of the stream was open ground—a gentle acclivity topped with a stockade of vertical tree trunks, loop-holed for rifles, with a single embrasure through which protruded the muzzle of a brass cannon commanding the bridge. Midway of the slope between bridge and fort were the spectators—a single company of infantry in line, at 'parade rest,' the butts of the rifles on the ground, the barrels inclining slightly backwards against the right shoulder, the hands crossed upon the stock. A lieutenant stood at the right of the line, the point of his sword upon the ground, his left hand resting upon his right. Excepting the group of four at the centre of the bridge, not a man moved. The company faced the bridge, staring stonily, motionless. The sentinels, facing the banks of the stream, might have been statues to adorn the bridge. The captain stood with folded arms, silent, observing the work of his subordinates, but making no sign. Death is a dignitary who when he comes announced is to be received with formal manifestations of respect, even by those most familiar with him. In the code of military etiquette silence and fixity are forms of deference.

The man who was engaged in being hanged was apparently about thirty-five years of age. He was a civilian, if one might judge from his habit, which was that of a planter. His features were good—a straight nose, firm mouth, broad forehead, from which his long, dark hair was combed straight back, falling behind his ears to the collar of his well-fitting frock-coat. He wore a moustache and pointed beard, but no whiskers; his eyes were large and dark grey, and had a kindly expression which one would hardly have expected in one whose neck was in the hemp. Evidently this was no vulgar assassin. The liberal military code makes provision for hanging many kinds of persons, and gentlemen are not excluded.

The preparations being complete, the two private soldiers stepped aside and each drew away the plank upon which he had been standing. The sergeant turned to the captain, saluted and placed himself immediately behind that officer, who in turn moved apart one pace. These movements left the condemned man and the sergeant standing on the two ends of the same plank, which spanned three of the cross-ties of the bridge. The end upon which the civilian stood almost, but not quite, reached a fourth. This plank had been held in place by the weight of the captain; it was now held by that of the sergeant. At a signal from the former the latter would step aside, the plank would tilt and the condemned man go down between two ties. The arrangement commended itself to his judgement as simple and effective. His face had not been covered nor his eyes bandaged. He looked a moment at his 'unsteadfast footing,' then let his gaze wander to the swirling water of the stream racing madly beneath his feet. A piece of dancing driftwood caught his attention and his eyes followed it down the current. How slowly it appeared to move! What a sluggish stream!

He closed his eyes in order to fix his last thoughts upon his wife and children. The water, touched to gold by the early sun, the brooding mists under the banks at some distance down the stream, the fort, the soldiers, the piece of drift—all had distracted him. And now he became conscious of a new disturbance. Striking through the thought of his dear ones was a sound which he could neither ignore nor understand, a sharp, distinct, metallic percussion like the stroke of a blacksmith's hammer upon the anvil; it had the same ringing quality. He wondered what it was, and whether immeasurably distant or near by—it seemed both. Its recurrence was regular, but as slow as the tolling of a death knell. He awaited each stroke with impatience and—he knew not why—apprehension. The intervals of silence grew progressively longer; the delays became maddening. With their greater infrequency the sounds increased in strength and sharpness. They hurt his ear like the thrust of a knife; he feared he would shriek. What he heard was the ticking of his watch.

He unclosed his eyes and saw again the water below him. 'If I could free my hands,' he thought, 'I might throw off the noose and spring into the stream. By diving I could evade the bullets and, swimming vigorously, reach the bank, take to the woods and get away home. My home, thank God, is as yet outside their lines; my wife and little ones are still beyond the invader's farthest advance.'

As these thoughts, which have here to be set down in words, were flashed into the doomed man's brain rather than evolved from it the captain nodded to the sergeant. The sergeant stepped aside.

II

Peyton Farquhar was a well-to-do planter, of an old and highly respected Alabama family. Being a slave owner and like other slave owners a politician he was naturally an original secessionist and ardently devoted to the Southern cause. Circumstances of an imperious nature, which it is unnecessary to relate here, had prevented him from taking service with the gallant army that had fought the disastrous campaigns ending with the fall of Corinth, and he chafed under the inglorious restraint, longing for the release of his energies, the larger life of the soldier, the opportunity for distinction. That opportunity, he felt, would come, as it comes to all in war time. Meanwhile, he did what he could. No service was too humble for him to perform in aid of the South, no adventure too perilous for him to undertake if consistent with the character of a civilian who was at heart a soldier, and who in good faith and without too much qualification assented to at least a part of the frankly villainous dictum that all is fair in love and war.

One evening while Farquhar and his wife were sitting on a rustic bench near the entrance to his grounds, a grey-clad soldier rode up to the gate and asked for a drink of water. Mrs Farquhar was only too happy to serve him with her own white hands. While she was fetching the water her husband approached the dusty horseman and inquired eagerly for news from the front.

'The Yanks are repairing the railroads,' said the man, 'and are getting ready for another advance. They have reached the Owl Creek Bridge, put it in order and built a stockade on the north bank. The commandant has issued an order, which is posted everywhere, declaring that any civilian caught interfering with the railroad, its bridges, tunnels or trains will be summarily hanged. I saw the order.'

'How far is it to the Owl Creek Bridge?' Farquhar asked.

'About thirty miles.'

'Is there no force on this side the creek?'

'Only a picket post half a mile out, on the railroad, and a single sentinel at this end of the bridge.'

'Suppose a man—a civilian and student of hanging—should elude the picket post and perhaps get the better of the sentinel,' said Farquhar, smiling, 'what could he accomplish?'

The soldier reflected. 'I was there a month ago,' he replied. 'I observed that the flood of last winter had lodged a great quantity of driftwood against the wooden pier at this end of the bridge. It is now dry and would burn like tow.'

The lady had now brought the water, which the soldier drank. He thanked her ceremoniously, bowed to her husband and rode away. An hour later, after nightfall, he repassed the plantation, going northwards in the direction from which he had come. He was a Federal scout.

III

As Peyton Farquhar fell straight downwards through the bridge he lost consciousness and was as one already dead. From this state he was awakened—ages later, it seemed to him—by the pain of a sharp pressure upon his throat, followed by a sense of suffocation. Keen, poignant agonies seemed to shoot from his neck downwards through every fibre of his body and limbs. These pains appeared to flash along well-defined lines of ramification and to beat with an inconceivably rapid periodicity. They seemed like streams of pulsating fire heating him to an intolerable temperature. As to his head, he was conscious of nothing but a feeling of fullness—of congestion. These sensations were unaccompanied by thought. The intellectual part of his nature was already effaced; he had power only to feel, and feeling was torment. He was conscious of motion. Encompassed in a luminous cloud, of which he was now merely the fiery heart, without material substance, he swung through unthinkable arcs of oscillation, like a vast pendulum. Then all at once, with terrible suddenness, the light about him shot upwards with the noise of a loud plash; a frightful roaring was in his ears, and all was cold and dark. The power of thought was restored; he knew that the rope had broken and he had fallen into the stream. There was no additional strangulation; the noose about his neck was already suffocating him and kept the water from his lungs. To die of hanging at the bottom of a river!—the idea seemed to him ludicrous. He opened his eyes in the darkness and saw above him a gleam of light, but how distant, how inaccessible! He was still sinking, for the light became fainter and fainter until it was a mere glimmer. Then it began to grow and brighten, and he knew that he was rising towards the surface—knew it with reluctance, for he was now very comfortable. 'To be hanged and drowned,' he thought, 'that is not so bad; but I do not wish to be shot. No; I will not be shot; that is not fair.'

He was not conscious of an effort, but a sharp pain in his wrist apprised him that he was trying to free his hands. He gave the struggle his attention, as an idler might observe the feat of a juggler, without interest in the outcome. What splendid effort!—what magnificent, what superhuman strength! Ah, that was a fine endeavour! Bravo! The cord fell away; his arms parted and floated upwards, the hands dimly seen on each side in the growing light. He watched them with a new interest as first one and then the other pounced upon the noose at his neck. They tore it away and thrust it fiercely aside, its undulations resembling those of a water-snake. 'Put it back, put it back!' He thought he shouted these words to his hands, for the undoing of the noose had been succeeded by the direst pang that he had yet experienced. His neck ached horribly; his brain was on fire; his heart, which had been fluttering faintly, gave a great leap, trying to force itself out at his mouth. His whole body was racked and wrenched with an insupportable anguish! But his disobedient hands gave no heed to the command. They beat the water vigorously with quick, downwards strokes, forcing him to the surface. He felt his head emerge; his eyes were blinded by the sunlight; his chest expanded convulsively, and with a supreme and crowning agony his lungs engulfed a great draught of air, which instantly he expelled in a shriek!

He was now in full possession of his physical senses. They were, indeed, preternaturally keen and alert. Something in the awful disturbance of his organic system had so exalted and refined them that they made record of things never before perceived. He felt the ripples upon his face and heard their separate sounds as they struck. He looked at the forest on the bank of the stream, saw the individual trees, the leaves and the veining of each leaf— saw the very insects upon them: the locusts, the brilliant-bodied flies, the grey spiders stretching their webs from twig to twig. He noted the prismatic colours in all the dewdrops upon a million blades of grass. The humming of the gnats that danced above the eddies of the stream, the beating of the dragon-flies' wings, the strokes of the water-spiders' legs, like oars which had lifted their boat—all these made audible music. A fish slid along beneath his eyes and he heard the rush of its body parting the water.

He had come to the surface facing down the stream; in a moment the visible world seemed to wheel slowly round, himself the pivotal point, and he saw the bridge, the fort, the soldiers upon the bridge, the captain, the sergeant, the two privates, his executioners. They were in silhouette against the blue sky. They shouted and gesticulated, pointing at him. The captain had drawn his pistol, but did not fire; the others were unarmed. Their movements were grotesque and horrible, their forms gigantic.

Suddenly he heard a sharp report and something struck the water smartly within a few inches of his head, spattering his face with spray. He heard a second report, and saw one of the sentinels with his rifle at his shoulder, a light cloud of blue smoke rising from the muzzle. The man in the water saw the eye of the man on the bridge gazing into his own through the sights of the rifle. He observed that it was a grey eye and remembered having read that grey eyes were keenest, and that all famous markmen had them. Nevertheless, this one had missed.

A counter-swirl had caught Farquhar and turned him half round; he was again looking into the forest on the bank opposite the fort. The sound of a clear, high voice in a monotonous singsong now rang out behind him and came across the water with a distinctness that pierced and subdued all other sounds, even the beating of the ripples in his ears. Although no soldier, he had frequented camps enough to know the dread significance of that deliberate, drawling, aspirated chant; the lieutenant on shore was taking a part in the morning's work. How coldly and pitilessly—with what an even, calm intonation, presaging and enforcing tranquillity in the men—with what accurately measured intervals fell those cruel words:

'Attention, company!... Shoulder arms!... Ready!... Aim!... Fire!'

Farquhar dived—dived as deeply as he could. The water roared in his ears like the voice of Niagara, yet he heard the dulled thunder of the volley and, rising again towards the surface, met shining bits of metal, singularly flattened, oscillating slowly downwards. Some of them touched him on the face and hands, then fell away, continuing their descent. One lodged between his collar and neck; it was uncomfortably warm and he snatched it out.

As he rose to the surface, gasping for breath, he saw that he had been a long time under water; he was perceptibly farther down stream—nearer to safety. The soldiers had almost finished reloading; the metal ramrods flashed all at once in the sunshine as they were drawn from the barrels, turned in the air, and thrust into their sockets. The two sentinels fired again, independently and ineffectually.

The hunted man saw all this over his shoulder; he was now swimming vigorously with the current. His brain was as energetic as his arms and legs; he thought with the rapidity of lightning.

'The officer,' he reasoned, 'will not make that martinet's error a second time. It is as easy to dodge a volley as a single shot. He has probably already given the command to fire at will. God help me, I cannot dodge them all!'

An appalling plash within two yards of him was followed by a loud, rushing sound, *diminuendo*, which seemed to travel back through the air to the fort and died in an explosion which stirred the very river to its deeps! A rising sheet of water curved over him, fell down upon him, blinded him, strangled him! The cannon had taken a hand in the game. As he shook his head free from the commotion of the smitten water he heard the deflected shot humming through the air ahead, and in an instant it was cracking and smashing the branches in the forest beyond.

'They will not do that again,' he thought; 'the next time they will use a charge of grape. I must keep my eye upon the gun; the smoke will apprise me—the report arrives too late; it lags behind the missile. That is a good gun.'

Suddenly he felt himself whirled round and round—spinning

like a top. The water, the banks, the forests, the now distant bridge, fort and men—all were commingled and blurred. Objects were represented by their colours only; circular horizontal streaks of colour—that was all he saw. He had been caught in a vortex and was being whirled on with a velocity of advance and gyration that made him giddy and sick. In a few moments he was flung upon the gravel at the foot of the left bank of the stream—the southern bank—and behind a projecting point which concealed him from his enemies. The sudden arrest of his motion, the abrasion of one of his hands on the gravel, restored him, and he wept with delight. He dug his fingers into the sand, threw it over himself in handfuls and audibly blessed it. It looked like diamonds, rubies, emeralds; he could think of nothing beautiful which it did not resemble. The trees upon the bank were giant garden plants; he noted a definite order in their arrangement, inhaled the fragrance of their blooms. A strange, roseate light shone through the spaces among their trunks and the wind made in their branches the music of æolian harps. He had no wish to perfect his escape—was content to remain in that enchanting spot until retaken.

A whiz and rattle of grapeshot among the branches high above his head roused him from his dream. The baffled cannoneer had fired him a random farewell. He sprang to his feet, rushed up the sloping bank, and plunged into the forest.

All that day he travelled, laying his course by the rounding sun. The forest seemed interminable; nowhere did he discover a break in it, not even a woodman's road. He had not known that he lived in so wild a region. There was something uncanny in the revelation.

By nightfall he was fatigued, footsore, famishing. The thought of his wife and children urged him on. At last he found a road which led him in what he knew to be the right direction. It was as wide and straight as a city street, yet it seemed untravelled. No fields bordered it, no dwelling anywhere. Not so much as the barking of a dog suggested human habitation. The black bodies of the trees formed a straight wall on both sides, terminating on the horizon in a point, like a diagram in a lesson in perspective. Overhead, as he looked up through this rift in the wood, shone great golden stars looking unfamiliar and grouped in strange constellations. He was sure they were arranged in some order which had a secret and malign significance. The wood on either side was full of singular noises, among which—once, twice, and again—he distinctly heard whispers in an unknown tongue.

His neck was in pain and lifting his hand to it he found it horribly swollen. He knew that it had a circle of black where the rope had bruised it. His eyes felt congested; he could no longer close them. His tongue was swollen with thirst; he relieved its fever by thrusting it forward from between his teeth into the cold air. How softly the turf had carpeted the untravelled avenue—he could no longer feel the roadway beneath his feet!

Doubtless, despite his suffering, he had fallen asleep while walking, for now he sees another scene—perhaps he has merely recovered from a delirium. He stands at the gate of his own home. All is as he left it, and all bright and beautiful in the morning sunshine. He must have travelled the entire night. As he pushes open the gate and passes up the wide white walk, he sees a flutter of female garments; his wife, looking fresh and cool and sweet, steps down from the veranda to meet him. At the bottom of the steps she stands waiting, with a smile of ineffable joy, an attitude of matchless grace and dignity. Ah, how beautiful she is! He springs forward with extended arms. As he is about to clasp her he feels a stunning blow upon the back of the neck; a blinding white light blazes all about him with a sound like the shock of a cannon—then all is darkness and silence!

Peyton Farquhar was dead; his body, with a broken neck, swung gently from side to side beneath the timbers of the Owl Creek Bridge.

2

THE MAN WITHOUT A COUNTRY

Edward Everett Hale

I supposed that very few casual readers of the 'New York Herald' of August 13th observed, in an obscure corner, among the 'Deaths,' the announcement,

'NOLAN. Died, on board U.S. Corvette Levant, Lat. 2° 11' S., Long. 131° W., on the 11th of May, PHILIP NOLAN.'

I happened to observe it, because I was stranded at the old Mission-House in Mackinaw, waiting for a Lake Superior steamer which did not choose to come, and I was devouring to the very stubble all the current literature I could get hold of, even down to the deaths and marriages in the 'Herald'. My memory for names and people is good, and the reader will see, as he goes on, that I had reason enough to remember Philip Nolan. There are hundreds of readers who would have paused at that announcement, if the officer of the Levant who reported it had chosen to make it thus:—'Died, May 11th, THE MAN WITHOUT A COUNTRY.' For it was as 'The Man without a Country' that poor Philip Nolan had generally been known by the officers who had him in charge during some fifty years, as, indeed, by all the men who sailed under them. I dare say there is many a man who has taken wine with him once a fortnight, in a three years' cruise, who never knew that his name was 'Nolan,' or whether the poor wretch had any name at all.

There can now be no possible harm in telling this poor creature's story. Reason enough there has been till now, ever since Madison's administration went out in 1817, for very strict secrecy, the secrecy of honour itself, among the gentlemen of the navy who have had Nolan in successive charge. And certainly it speaks well for the *esprit de corps* of the profession, and the personal honour of its members, that to the press this man's story has been wholly unknown,—and, I think, to the country at large also. I have reason to think, from some investigations I made in the Naval Archives when I was attached to the Bureau of Construction, that every official report relating to him was burned when Ross burned the public buildings at Washington. One of the Tuckers, or possibly one of the Watsons, had Nolan in charge at the end of the war; and when, on returning from his cruise, he reported at Washington to one of the Crowninshields,—who was in the Navy Department when he came home,—he found that the department ignored the whole business. Whether they really knew nothing about it or whether it was a '*Non mi ricordo*,' determined on as a piece of policy, I do not know. But this I do know, that since 1817, and possibly before, no naval officer has mentioned Nolan in his report of a cruise.

But, as I say, there is no need for secrecy any longer. And now the poor creature is dead, it seems to me worth while to tell a little of his story, by way of showing young Americans of to-day what it is to be

A MAN WITHOUT A COUNTRY.

Philip Nolan was as fine a young officer as there was in the 'Legion of the West,' as the Western division of our army was then called. When Aaron Burr made his first dashing expedition down to New Orleans in 1805, at Fort Massac, or somewhere above on the river, he met, as the Devil would have it, this gay, dashing, bright young fellow, at some dinner-party, I think. Burr marked him, talked to him, walked with him, took him a day or two's voyage in his flat-boat, and, in short, fascinated him.

For the next year, barrack-life was very tame to poor Nolan. He occasionally availed himself of the permission the great man had given him to write to him. Long, high-worded, stilted letters the poor boy wrote and rewrote and copied. But never a line did he have in reply from the gay deceiver. The other boys in the garrison sneered at him, because he sacrificed in this unrequited affection for a politician the time which they devoted to Monongahela, hazard, and high-low-jack. Bourbon, euchre, and poker were still unknown. But one day Nolan had his revenge. This time Burr came down the river, not as an attorney seeking a place for his office, but as a disguised conqueror. He had defeated I know not how many district-attorneys; he had dined at I know not how many public dinners; he had been heralded in I know not how many Weekly Arguses, and it was rumoured that he had an army behind him and an empire before him. It was a great day—his arrival—to poor Nolan. Burr had not been at the fort an hour before he sent for him. That evening he asked Nolan to take him out in his skiff, to show him a canebrake or a cotton-wood tree, as he said,—really to seduce him; and by the time the sail was over, Nolan was enlisted body and soul. From that time, though he did not yet know it, he lived as A MAN WITHOUT A COUNTRY.

What Burr meant to do I know no more than you, dear reader. It is none of our business just now. Only, when the grand catastrophe came, and Jefferson and the House of Virginia of that day undertook to break on the wheel all the possible Clarences of the then House of York, by the great treason-trial at Richmond, some of the lesser fry in that distant Mississippi Valley, which was farther from us than Puget's Sound is to-day, introduced the like novelty on their provincial stage, and, to while away the monotony of the summer at Fort Adams, got up, for *spectacles*, a string of court-martials on the officers there. One and another of the colonels and majors were tried, and, to fill out the list, little Nolan, against whom, Heaven knows, there was evidence enough,—that he was sick of the service, had been willing to be false to it, and would have obeyed any order to march anywhither with any one who would follow him had the order been signed, 'By command of His Exc. A. Burr.' The courts dragged on. The big flies escaped,—rightly for all I know. Nolan was proved guilty enough, as I say; yet you and I would never have heard of him, reader, but that, when the president of the court asked him at the close, whether he wished to say anything to show that he had always been faithful to the United States, he cried out, in a fit of frenzy,—

'D—n the United States! I wish I may never hear of the United States again!'

I suppose he did not know how the words shocked old Colonel Morgan, who was holding the court. Half the officers who sat in it had served through the Revolution, and their lives, not to say their necks, had been risked for the very idea which he so cavalierly cursed in his madness. He, on his part, had grown up in the West of those days, in the midst of 'Spanish plot,' 'Orleans plot,' and all the rest. He had been educated on a plantation where the finest company was a Spanish officer or a French merchant from Orleans. His education, such as it was, had been perfected in commercial expeditions to Vera Cruz, and I think he told me his father once hired an Englishman to be a private tutor for a winter on the plantation. He had spent half his youth with an older brother, hunting horses in Texas; and, in a word, to him 'United States' was scarcely a reality. Yet he had been fed by 'United States' for all the years since he had been in the army. He had sworn on his faith as a Christian to be true to 'United States.' It was 'United States' which gave him the uniform he wore, and the sword by his side. Nay, my poor Nolan, it was only because 'United States' had picked you out first as one of her own confidential men of honour that 'A. Burr' cared for you a straw more than for the flat-boat men who sailed his ark for him. I do not excuse Nolan; I only explain to the reader why he damned his country, and wished he might never hear her name again.

He never did hear her name but once again. From that moment, September 23, 1807, till the day he died, May 11, 1863, he never heard her name again. For that half-century and more he was a man without a country.

Old Morgan, as I said, was terribly shocked. If Nolan had compared George Washington to Benedict Arnold, or had cried, 'God save King George,' Morgan would not have felt worse. He called the court into his private room, and returned in fifteen minutes, with a face like a sheet, to say,—

'Prisoner, hear the sentence of the Court! The Court decides, subject to the approval of the President, that you never hear the name of the United States again.'

Nolan laughed. But nobody else laughed. Old Morgan was too solemn, and the whole room was hushed dead as night for a minute. Even Nolan lost his swagger in a moment. Then Morgan added,—

'Mr Marshal, take the prisoner to Orleans in an armed boat, and deliver him to the naval commander there.'

The Marshal gave his orders and the prisoner was taken out of court.

'Mr Marshal,' continued old Morgan, 'see that no one mentions the United States to the prisoner. Mr Marshal, make my respects to Lieutenant Mitchell at Orleans, and request him to order that no one shall mention the United States to the prisoner while he is on board ship. You will receive your written orders from the officer on duty here this evening. The court is adjourned without day.'

I have always supposed that Colonel Morgan himself took the proceedings of the court to Washington City, and explained them to Mr Jefferson. Certain it is that the President approved them,—

certain, that is, if I may believe the men who say they have seen his signature. Before the Nautilus got round from New Orleans to the Northern Atlantic coast with the prisoner on board the sentence had been approved, and he was a man without a country.

The plan then adopted was substantially the same which was necessarily followed ever after. Perhaps it was suggested by the necessity of sending him by water from Fort Adams and Orleans. The Secretary of the Navy—it must have been the first Crowninshield, though he is a man I do not remember—was requested to put Nolan on board a government vessel bound on a long cruise, and to direct that he should be only so far confined there as to make it certain that he never saw or heard of the country. We had few long cruises then, and the navy was very much out of favour; and as almost all of this story is traditional, as I have explained, I do not know certainly what his first cruise was. But the commander to whom he was intrusted,—perhaps it was Tingey or Shaw, though I think it was one of the younger men,—we are all old enough now,—regulated the etiquette and the precautions of the affair, and according to his scheme they were carried out, I suppose, till Nolan died.

When I was second officer of the Intrepid, some thirty years after, I saw the original paper of instructions. I have been sorry ever since that I did not copy the whole of it. It ran, however, much in this way:—

> '*Washington*,' (with a date, which must have been late in 1807).

'SIR,—You will receive from Lieutenant Neale the person of Philip Nolan, late a Lieutenant in the United States Army.

'This person on his trial by court-martial expressed with an oath the wish that he might 'never hear of the United States again.'

'The Court sentenced him to have his wish fulfilled.

'For the present, the execution of the order is intrusted by the President to this Department.

'You will take the prisoner on board your ship, and keep him there with such precautions as shall prevent his escape.

'You will provide him with such quarters, rations, and clothing as would be proper for an officer of his late rank, if he were a passenger on your vessel on the business of his Government.

'The gentlemen on board will make any arrangements agreeable to themselves regarding his society. He is to be exposed to no indignity of any kind, nor is he ever unnecessarily to be reminded that he is a prisoner.

'But under no circumstances is he ever to hear of his country or to see any information regarding it, and you will specially caution all the officers under your command to take care, that, in the various indulgences which may be granted, this rule, in which his punishment is involved, shall not be broken.

'It is the intention of the Government that he shall never again see the country which he has disowned. Before the end of your cruise you will receive orders which will give effect to this intention.

'Respe'y yours,
'W. SOUTHARD, for the
Sec'y of the Navy.'

If I had only preserved the whole of this paper, there would be no break in the beginning of my sketch of this story. For Captain Shaw, if it were he, handed it to his successor in the charge, and he to his, and I suppose the commander of the Levant has it to-day as his authority for keeping this man in this mild custody.

The rule adopted on board the ships on which I have met 'the man without a country' was, I think, transmitted from the beginning. No mess liked to have him permanently, because his presence cut off all talk of home or of the prospect of return, of politics or letters, of peace or of war,—cut off more than half the talk men liked to have at sea. But it was always thought too hard that he should never meet the rest of us, except to touch hats, and we finally sank into one system. He was not permitted to talk with the men, unless an officer was by. With officers he had unrestrained intercourse, as far as they and he chose. But he grew shy, though he had favourites: I was one. Then the captain always asked him to dinner on Monday. Every mess in succession took up the invitation in its turn. According to the size of the ship, you had him at your mess more or less often at dinner. His breakfast he ate in his own state-room,—he always had a state-room,—which was where a sentinel or somebody on the watch could see the door. And whatever else he ate or drank, he ate or drank alone. Sometimes, when the marines or sailors had any special jollification, they were permitted to invite 'Plain-Buttons,' as they called him. Then Nolan was sent with some officer, and the men were forbidden to speak of home while he was there. I believe the theory that the sight of his punishment did them good. They called him 'Plain-Buttons,' because, while he always chose to wear a regulation army-uniform, he was not permitted to wear the army-button, for the reason that it bore either the initials or the insignia of the country he had disowned.

I remember, soon after I joined the navy, I was on shore with some of the older officers from our ship and from the Brandywine, which we had met at Alexandria. We had leave to make a party and go up to Cairo and the Pyramids. As we jogged along (you went on donkeys then), some of the gentlemen (we boys called them 'Dons,' but the phrase was long since changed) fell to talking about Nolan, and someone told the system which was adopted from the first about his books and other reading. As he was almost never permitted to go on shore, even though the vessel lay in port for months, his time at the best hung heavy;

and everybody was permitted to lend him books, if they were not published in America and made no allusion to it. These were common enough in the old days, when people in the other hemisphere talked of the United States as little as we do of Paraguay. He had almost all the foreign papers that came into the ship, sooner or later; only somebody must go over them first, and cut out any advertisement or stray paragraph that alluded to America. This was a little cruel sometimes, when the back of what was cut out might be as innocent as Hesiod. Right in the midst of one of Napoleon's battles, or one of Canning's speeches, poor Nolan would find a great hole, because on the back of the page of that paper there had been an advertisement of a packet for New York, or a scrap from the President's message. I say this was the first time I ever heard of this plan, which afterwards I had enough and more than enough to do with. I remember it, because poor Phillips, who was of the party, as soon as the allusion to reading was made, told a story of something which happened at the Cape of Good Hope on Nolan's first voyage; and it is the only thing I ever knew of that voyage. They had touched at the Cape, and had done the civil thing with the English Admiral and the fleet, and then, leaving for a long cruise up the Indian Ocean, Phillips had borrowed a lot of English books from an officer, which, in those days, as indeed in these, was quite a windfall. Among them, as the Devil would order, was the 'Lay of the Last Minstrel,' which they had all of them heard of, but which most of them had never seen. I think it could not have been published long. Well, nobody thought there could be any risk of anything national in that, though Phillips swore old Shaw had cut out the 'Tempest' from Shakespeare before he let Nolan have it, because he said 'the Bermudas ought to be ours, and, by Jove, should be one day.' So Nolan was permitted to join the circle one afternoon when a lot of them sat on deck smoking and reading aloud. People do not do such things so often now, but when I was young we got rid of a great deal of time so. Well, so it happened that in his turn Nolan took the book and read to the others; and he read very well, as I know. Nobody in the circle knew a line of the poem, only it was all magic and Border chivalry, and was ten thousand years ago. Poor Nolan read steadily through the fifth canto, stopped a minute and drank something, and then began, without a thought of what was coming,—

> 'Breathes there the man, with soul so dead,
> Who never to himself hath said,'—

It seems impossible to us that anybody ever heard this for the first time; but all these fellows did then, and poor Nolan himself went on, still unconsciously or mechanically,—

> 'This is my own, my native land!'

Then they all saw something was to pay; but he expected to get through, I suppose, turned a little pale, but plunged on,—

> 'Whose heart hath ne'er within him burned,
> As home his footsteps he hath turned
> From wandering on a foreign strand?—
> If such there breathe, go, mark him well,'—

By this time the men were all beside themselves, wishing there was any way to make him turn over two pages; but he had not quite presence of mind for that; he gagged a little, coloured crimson, and staggered on,—

> 'For him no minstrel raptures swell;
> High though his titles, proud his name,
> Boundless his wealth as wish can claim,
> Despite these titles, power, and pelf,
> The wretch, concentred all in self,'—

and here the poor fellow choked, could not go on, but started up, swung the book into the sea, vanished into his state-room, 'And by Jove,' said Phillips, 'we did not see him for two months again. And I had to make up some beggarly story to that English surgeon why I did not return his Walter Scott to him.'

That story shows about the time when Nolan's braggadocio must have broken down. At first, they said, he took a very high tone, considered his imprisonment a mere farce, affected to enjoy the voyage, and all that; but Phillips said that after he came out of his state-room he never was the same man again. He never read aloud again, unless it was the Bible or Shakespeare, or something else he was sure of. But it was not that merely. He never entered in with the other young men exactly as a companion again. He was always shy afterwards, when I knew him,—very seldom spoke, unless he was spoken to, except to a very few friends. He lighted up occasionally,—I remember late in his life hearing him fairly eloquent on something which had been suggested to him by one of Fléchier's sermons,—but generally he had the nervous, tired look of a heart-wounded man.

When Captain Shaw was coming home,—if, as I say, it was Shaw,—rather to the surprise of everybody they made one of the Windward Islands, and lay off and on for nearly a week. The boys said the officers were sick of salt-junk, and meant to have turtle-soup before they came home. But after several days the Warren came to the same rendezvous; they exchanged signals; she sent to Phillips and these homewards-bound men letters and papers, and told them she was outwards-bound, perhaps to the Mediterranean, and took poor Nolan and his traps on the boat back to try his second cruise. He looked very blank when he was told to get ready to join her. He had known enough of the signs of the sky to know that till that moment he was going 'home.' But this was a distinct evidence of something he had not thought of, perhaps,—that there was no going home for him, even to a prison. And this was the first of some twenty such transfers, which brought him sooner or later into half our best vessels, but which kept him all his life at least some hundred miles from the country he had hoped he might never hear of again.

It may have been on that second cruise,—it was once when he was up the Mediterranean,—that Mrs Graff, the celebrated Southern beauty of those days, danced with him. They had been lying a long time in the Bay of Naples, and the officers were very intimate in the English fleet, and there had been great festivities, and our men thought they must give a great ball on board the ship. How they ever did it on board the 'Warren' I am sure I do not know. Perhaps it was not the 'Warren,' or perhaps ladies did not take up so much room as they do now. They wanted to use Nolan's state-room for something, and they hated to do it without asking him to the ball; so the captain said they might ask him, if they would be responsible that he did not talk with the wrong people, 'who would give him intelligence.' So the dance went on, the finest party that had ever been known, I dare say; for I never heard of a man-of-war ball that was not. For ladies they had the family of the American consul, one or two travellers who had adventured so far, and a nice bevy of English girls and matrons, perhaps Lady Hamilton herself.

Well, different officers relieved each other in standing and talking with Nolan in a friendly way, so as to be sure that nobody else spoke to him. The dancing went on with spirit, and after a while even the fellows who took this honourary guard of Nolan ceased to fear any contretemps. Only when some English lady— Lady Hamilton, as I said, perhaps—called for a set of 'American dances,' an odd thing happened. Everybody then danced contra-dances. The black band, nothing loath, conferred as to what 'American dances' were, and started off with a 'Virginia Reel,' which they followed with 'Money-Musk,' which, in its turn in those days, should have been followed by 'The Old Thirteen.' But just as Dick, the leader, tapped for his fiddles to begin, and bent forward, about to say, in true negro state, "The Old Thirteen,' gentlemen and ladies!' as he had said "Virginny Reel,' if you please!' and "Money-Musk,' if you please!' the captain's boy tapped him on the shoulder, whispered to him, and he did not announce the name of the dance; he merely bowed, began on the air, and they all fell to,—the officers teaching the English girls the figure, but not telling them why it had no name.

But that is not the story I started to tell.—As the dancing went on, Nolan and our fellows all got at ease, as I said,—so much so, that it seemed quite natural for him to bow to that splendid Mrs Graff, and say,—

'I hope you have not forgotten me, Miss Rutledge. Shall I have the honour of dancing?'

He did it so quickly, that Fellows, who was by him, could not hinder him. She laughed and said,—

'I am not Miss Rutledge any longer, Mr Nolan; but I will dance all the same,' just nodded to Fellows, as if to say he must leave Mr Nolan to her, and led him off to the place where the dance was forming.

Nolan thought he had got his chance. He had known her at Philadelphia, and at other places had met her, and this was a Godsend. You could not talk in contra-dances, as you do in cotillons, or even in the pauses of waltzing; but there were chances for tongues and sounds, as well as for eyes and blushes. He began with her travels, and Europe, and Vesuvius, and the French; and then, when they had worked down, and had that long talking-time at the bottom of the set, he said, boldly,—a little pale, she said, as she told me the story, years after,—

'And what do you hear from home, Mrs Graff?'

And that splendid creature looked through him. Jove! how she must have looked through him!

'Home!! Mr Nolan!!! I thought you were the man who never wanted to hear of home again!'—and she walked directly up the deck to her husband, and left poor Nolan alone, as he always was.—He did not dance again.

I cannot give any history of him in order; nobody can now; and, indeed, I am not trying to. These are the traditions, which I sort out, as I believe them, from the myths which have been told about this man for forty years. The lies that have been told about him are legion. The fellows used to say he was the 'Iron Mask'; and poor George Pons went to his grave in the belief that this was the author of 'Junius,' who was being punished for his celebrated libel on Thomas Jefferson. Pons was not very strong in the historical line. A happier story than either of these I have told is of the War. That came along soon after. I have heard this affair told in three or four ways,—and, indeed, it may have happened more than once. But which ship it was on I cannot tell. However, in one, at least, of the great frigate-duels with the English, in which the navy was really baptized, it happened that a round-shot from the enemy entered one of our ports square, and took right down the officer of the gun himself, and almost every man of the gun's crew. Now you may say what you choose about courage, but that is not a nice thing to see. But, as the men who were not killed picked themselves up, and as they and the surgeon's people were carrying off the bodies, there appeared Nolan, in his shirt-sleeves, with the rammer in his hand, and, just as if he had been the officer, told them off with authority,—who should go to the cockpit with the wounded men, who should stay with him,—perfectly cheery, and with that way which makes men feel sure all is right and is going to be right. And he finished loading the gun with his own hands, aimed it, and bade the men fire. And there he stayed, captain of that gun, keeping those fellows in spirits, till the enemy struck,—sitting on the carriage while the gun was cooling, though he was exposed all the time,—showing them easier ways to handle heavy shot,—making the raw hands laugh at their own blunders,—and when the gun cooled again, getting it loaded and fired twice as often as any other gun on the ship. The captain walked forward by way of encouraging the men, and Nolan touched his hat and said,—

'I am showing them how we do this in the artillery, sir.'

And this is the part of the story where all the legends agree; and the Commodore said,—

'I see you do, and I thank you, sir; and I shall never forget this day, sir, and you never shall, sir.'

And after the whole thing was over, and he had the Englishman's sword, in the midst of the state and ceremony of the quarter-deck, he said,—

'Where is Mr Nolan? Ask Mr Nolan to come here.'

And when Nolan came, the captain said,—

'Mr Nolan, we are all very grateful to you to-day; you are one of us to-day; you will be named in the despatches.'

And then the old man took off his own sword of ceremony, and gave it to Nolan, and made him put it on. The man told me this who saw it. Nolan cried like a baby, and well he might. He had not worn a sword since that infernal day at Fort Adams. But always afterwards on occasions of ceremony, he wore that quaint old French sword of the Commodore's.

The captain did mention him in the despatches. It was always said he asked that he might be pardoned. He wrote a special letter to the Secretary of War. But nothing ever came of it. As I said, that was about the time when they began to ignore the whole transaction at Washington, and when Nolan's imprisonment began to carry itself on because there was nobody to stop it without any new orders from home.

I have heard it said that he was with Porter when he took possession of the Nukahiwa Islands. Not this Porter, you know, but old Porter, his father, Essex Porter,—that is, the old Essex Porter, not this Essex. As an artillery officer, who had seen service in the West, Nolan knew more about fortifications, embrasures, ravelins, stockades, and all that, than any of them did; and he worked with a right good-will in fixing that battery all right. I have always thought it was a pity Porter did not leave him in command there with Gamble. That would have settled all the question about his punishment. We should have kept the islands, and at this moment we should have one station in the Pacific Ocean. Our French friends, too, when they wanted this little watering-place, would have found it was preoccupied. But Madison and the Virginians, of course, flung all that away.

All that was near fifty years ago. If Nolan was thirty then, he must have been near eighty when he died. He looked sixty when he was forty. But he never seemed to me to change a hair afterwards. As I imagine his life, from what I have seen and heard of it, he must have been in every sea, and yet almost never on land. He must have known, in a formal way, more officers in our service than any man living knows. He told me once, with a grave smile, that no man in the world lived so methodical a life as he. 'You know the boys say I am the Iron Mask, and you know how busy he was.' He said it did not do for anyone to try to read all the time, more than to do anything else all the time; but that he read just five hours a day. 'Then,' he said, 'I keep up my note-books, writing in them at such and such hours from what I have been reading; and I include in these my scrap-books.' These were very curious indeed. He had six or eight, of different subjects. There was one of History, one of Natural Science, one which he called 'Odds and Ends.' But they were not merely books of extracts from newspapers. They had bits of plants and ribbons, shells tied on, and carved scraps of bone and wood, which he had taught the men to cut for him, and they were beautifully illustrated. He drew admirably. He had some of the funniest drawings there, and some of the most pathetic, that I have ever seen in my life. I wonder who will have Nolan's scrap-books.

Well, he said his reading and his notes were his profession, and that they took five hours and two hours respectively of each day. 'Then,' said he, 'every man should have a diversion as well as a profession. My Natural History is my diversion.' That took two hours a day more. The men used to bring him birds and fish, but on a long cruise he had to satisfy himself with centipedes and cockroaches and such small game. He was the only naturalist I ever met who knew anything about the habits of the house-fly and the mosquito. All those people can tell you whether they are *Lepidoptera* or *Steptopotera*; but as for telling how you can get rid of them, or how they get away from you when you strike them,—why Linnæus knew as little of that as John Foy the idiot did. These nine hours made Nolan's regular daily 'occupation.' The rest of the time he talked or walked. Till he grew very old, he went aloft a great deal. He always kept up his exercise; and I never heard that he was ill. If any other man was ill, he was the kindest nurse in the world; and he knew more than half the surgeons do. Then if anybody was sick or died, or if the captain wanted him to, on any other occasion, he was always ready to read prayers. I have said that he read beautifully.

My own acquaintance with Philip Nolan began six or eight years after the War, on my first voyage after I was appointed a midshipman. It was in the first days after our Slave-Trade treaty, while the Reigning House, which was still the House of Virginia, had still a sort of sentimentalism about the suppression of the horrors of the Middle Passage, and something was sometimes done that way. We were in the South Atlantic on that business. From the time I joined, I believe I thought Nolan was a sort of lay chaplain,—a chaplain with a blue coat. I never asked about him. Everything in the ship was strange to me. I knew it was green to ask questions, and I suppose I thought there was a 'Plain-Buttons' on every ship. We had him to dine in our mess once a week, and the caution was given that on that day nothing was to be said about home. But if they had told us not to say anything about the planet Mars or the Book of Deuteronomy, I should not have asked why; there were a great many things which seemed to me to have as little reason. I first came to understand anything about 'the man without a country' one day when we overhauled a dirty little schooner which had slaves on board. An officer was sent to take charge of her, and, after a few minutes, he sent back his boat to ask that someone might be sent him who could speak Portuguese. We were all looking over the rail when the message came, and we all wished we could interpret, when the captain asked who spoke Portuguese. But none of the officers did; and just as the captain was sending forward to ask if any of the people could, Nolan stepped out and said he should be glad to interpret, if the captain wished, as he understood the language. The captain thanked him, fitted out another boat with him, and in this boat it was my luck to go.

When we got there, it was such a scene as you seldom see, and never want to. Nastiness beyond account, and chaos run loose in the midst of the nastiness. There were not a great many of the negroes; but by way of making what there were understand that they were free, Vaughan had had their hand-cuffs and ankle-cuffs knocked off, and, for convenience' sake, was putting them upon the rascals of the schooner's crew. The negroes were, most of them, out of the hold, and swarming all round the dirty deck, with a central throng surrounding Vaughan and addressing him in every dialect, and *patois* of a dialect, from the Zulu click up to the Parisian of Beledeljereed.

As we came on deck, Vaughan looked down from a hogshead, on which he had mounted in desperation, and said,—

'For God's love, is there anybody who can make these wretches understand something? The men gave them rum, and that did not quiet them. I knocked that big fellow down twice, and that did not soothe him. And then I talked Choctaw to all of them together; and I'll be hanged if they understood that as well as they understood the English.'

Nolan said he could speak Portuguese, and one or two fine-looking Kroomen were dragged out, who, as it had been found already, had worked for the Portuguese on the coast at Fernando Po.

'Tell them they are free,' said Vaughan; 'and tell them that these rascals are to be hanged as soon as we can get rope enough.'

Nolan 'put that into Spanish,'—that is, he explained it in such Portuguese as the Kroomen could understand, and they in turn to such of the negroes as could understand them. Then there was such a yell of delight, clinching of fists, leaping and dancing, kissing of Nolan's feet, and a general rush made to the hogshead by way of spontaneous worship of Vaughan, as the deus ex machina of the occasion.

'Tell them,' said Vaughan, well pleased, 'that I will take them all to Cape Palmas.'

This did not answer so well. Cape Palmas was practically as far from the homes of most of them as New Orleans or Rio Janeiro was; that is, they would be eternally separated from home there. And their interpreters, as we could understand, instantly said, 'Ah, non Palmas' and began to propose infinite other expedients in most voluble language. Vaughan was rather disappointed at this result of his liberality, and asked Nolan eagerly what they said. The drops stood on poor Nolan's white forehead, as he hushed the men down, and said,—

'He says, 'Not Palmas.' He says, 'Take us home, take us to our own country, take us to our own house, take us to our own pickaninnies and our own women.' He says he has an old father and mother who will die if they do not see him. And this one says he left his people all sick, and paddled down to Fernando to beg the white doctor to come and help them, and that these devils caught him in the bay just in sight of home, and that he has never seen anybody from home since then. And this one says,' choked out Nolan, 'that he has not heard a word from his home in six months, while he has been locked up in an infernal barracoon.'

Vaughan always said he grew grey himself while Nolan struggled through this interpretation. I, who did not understand anything of the passion involved in it, saw that the very elements were melting with fervent heat, and that something was to pay somewhere. Even the negroes themselves stopped howling, as they saw Nolan's agony, and Vaughan's almost equal agony of sympathy. As quick as he could get words, he said,—

'Tell them yes, yes, yes; tell them they shall go to the Mountains of the Moon, if they will. If I sail the schooner through the Great White Desert, they shall go home!'

And after some fashion Nolan said so. And then they all fell to kissing him again, and wanted to rub his nose with theirs.

But he could not stand it long; and getting Vaughan to say he might go back, he beckoned me down into our boat. As we lay back in the stern-sheets and the men gave way, he said to me: 'Youngster, let that show you what it is to be without a family, without a home, and without a country. And if you are ever tempted to say a word or to do a thing that shall put a bar between you and your family, your home, and your country, pray God in his mercy to take you that instant home to his own heaven. Stick by your family, boy; forget you have a self, while you do everything for them. Think of your home, boy; write and send, and talk about it. Let it be nearer and nearer to your thought, the farther you have to travel from it; and rush back to it, when you are free, as that poor black slave is doing now. And for your country, boy,' and the words rattled in his throat, 'and for that flag,' and he pointed to the ship, 'never dream a dream but of serving her as she bids you, though the service carry you through a thousand hells. No matter what happens to you, no matter who flatters you or who abuses you, never look at another flag, never let a night pass but you pray God to bless that flag. Remember, boy, that behind all these men you have to do with, behind officers, and government, and people even, there is the Country Herself, your Country, and that you belong to Her as you belong to your own mother. Stand by Her, boy, as you would stand by your mother, if those devils there had got hold of her to-day!'

I was frightened to death by his calm, hard passion, but I blundered out, that I would, by all that was holy, and that I had never thought of doing anything else. He hardly seemed to hear me; but he did, almost in a whisper, say: 'O, if anybody had said so to me when I was of your age!'

I think it was this half-confidence of his, which I never abused, for I never told this story till now, which afterwards made us great friends. He was very kind to me. Often he sat up, or even got up, at night, to walk the deck with me, when it was my watch. He explained to me a great deal of my mathematics, and I owe to him my taste for mathematics. He lent me books, and helped me about my reading. He never alluded so directly to his story again; but from one and another officer I have learned, in thirty years, what I am telling. When we parted from him in St Thomas harbor, at the end of our cruise, I was more sorry than I can tell. I was very glad to meet him again in 1830; and later in life, when I thought I had some influence in Washington, I moved heaven and earth to have him discharged. But it was like getting a ghost out of prison. They pretended there was no such man, and never was such a man. They will say so at the Department now! Perhaps they do not know. It will not be the first thing in the service of which the Department appears to know nothing!

There is a story that Nolan met Burr once on one of our vessels, when a party of Americans came on board in the Mediterranean. But this I believe to be a lie; or, rather, it is a myth, ben trovato, involving a tremendous blowing-up with which he sunk Burr,—asking him how he liked to be 'without a country.' But it is clear from Burr's life, that nothing of the sort could have happened;

and I mention this only as an illustration of the stories which get a-going where there is the least mystery at bottom.

So poor Philip Nolan had his wish fulfilled. I know but one fate more dreadful; it is the fate reserved for those men who shall have one day to exile themselves from their country because they have attempted her ruin, and shall have at the same time to see the prosperity and honour to which she rises when she has rid herself of them and their iniquities. The wish of poor Nolan, as we all learned to call him, not because his punishment was too great, but because his repentance was so clear, was precisely the wish of every Bragg and Beauregard who broke a soldier's oath two years ago, and of every Maury and Barron who broke a sailor's. I do not know how often they have repented. I do know that they have done all that in them lay that they might have no country,—that all the honours, associations, memories, and hopes which belong to 'country' might be broken up into little shreds and distributed to the winds. I know, too, that their punishment, as they vegetate through what is left of life to them in wretched Boulognes and Leicester Squares, where they are destined to upbraid each other till they die, will have all the agony of Nolan's, with the added pang that every one who sees them will see them to despise and to execrate them. They will have their wish, like him.

For him, poor fellow, he repented of his folly, and then, like a man, submitted to the fate he had asked for. He never intentionally added to the difficulty or delicacy of the charge of those who had him in hold. Accidents would happen; but they never happened from his fault. Lieutenant Truxton told me, that, when Texas was annexed, there was a careful discussion among the officers, whether they should get hold of Nolan's handsome set of maps, and cut Texas out of it,—from the map of the world and the map of Mexico. The United States had been cut out when the atlas was bought for him. But it was voted, rightly enough, that to do this would be virtually to reveal to him what had happened, or, as Harry Cole said, to make him think Old Burr had succeeded. So it was from no fault of Nolan's that a great botch happened at my own table, when, for a short time, I was in command of the George Washington corvette, on the South American station. We were lying in the La Plata, and some of the officers, who had been on shore, and had just joined again, were entertaining us with accounts of their misadventures in riding the half-wild horses of Buenos Ayres. Nolan was at table, and was in an unusually bright and talkative mood. Some story of a tumble reminded him of an adventure of his own, when he was catching wild horses in Texas with his adventurous cousin, at a time when he must have been quite a boy. He told the story with a good deal of spirit,—so much so, that the silence which often follows a good story hung over the table for an instant, to be broken by Nolan himself. For he asked perfectly unconsciously,—

'Pray, what has become of Texas? After the Mexicans got their independence, I thought that province of Texas would come forward very fast. It is really one of the finest regions on earth; it is the Italy of this continent. But I have not seen or heard a word of Texas for near twenty years.'

There were two Texan officers at the table. The reason he had never heard of Texas was that Texas and her affairs had been painfully cut out of his newspapers since Austin began his settlements; so that, while he read of Honduras and Tamaulipas, and, till quite lately, of California,—this virgin province, in which his brother had travelled so far, and, I believe, had died, had ceased to be to him. Waters and Williams, the two Texas men, looked grimly at each other, and tried not to laugh. Edward Morris had his attention attracted by the third link in the chain of the captain's chandelier. Watrous was seized with a convulsion of sneezing. Nolan himself saw that something was to pay, he did not know what. And I, as master of the feast, had to say,—

'Texas is out of the map, Mr Nolan. Have you seen Captain

Back's curious account of Sir Thomas Roe's Welcome?'

After that cruise I never saw Nolan again. I wrote to him at least twice a year, for in that voyage we became even confidentially intimate; but he never wrote to me. The other men tell me that in those fifteen years he *aged* very fast, as well he might indeed, but that he was still the same gentle, uncomplaining, silent sufferer that he ever was, bearing as best he could his self-appointed punishment,—rather less social, perhaps, with new men whom he did not know, but more anxious, apparently, than ever to serve and befriend and teach the boys, some of whom fairly seemed to worship him. And now it seems the dear old fellow is dead. He has found a home at last, and a country.

Since writing this, and while considering whether or no I would print it, as a warning to the young Nolans and Vallandighams and Tatnalls of to-day of what it is to throw away a country, I have received from Danforth, who is on board the Levant, a letter which gives an account of Nolan's last hours. It removes all my doubts about telling this story.

To understand the first words of the letter, the non-professional reader should remember that after 1817, the position of every officer who had Nolan in charge was one of the greatest delicacy. The government had failed to renew the order of 1807 regarding him. What was a man to do? Should he let him go? What, then, if he were called to account by the Department for violating the order of 1807? Should he keep him? What, then, if Nolan should be liberated some day, and should bring an action for false imprisonment or kidnapping against every man who had had him in charge? I urged and pressed this upon Southard, and I have reason to think that other officers did the same thing. But the Secretary always said, as they so often do at Washington, that there were no special orders to give, and that we must act on our own judgement. That means, 'If you succeed, you will be sustained; if you fail, you will be disavowed.' Well, as Danforth says, all that is over now, though I do not know but I expose myself to a criminal prosecution on the evidence of the very revelation I am making.

Here is the letter:—

'*Levant*, 2° 2' S. @ 131° W.

'DEAR FRED,—I try to find heart and life to tell you that it is all over with dear old Nolan. I have been with him on this voyage more than I ever was, and I can understand wholly now the way in which you used to speak of the dear old fellow. I could see that he was not strong, but I had no idea the end was so near. The doctor has been watching him very carefully, and yesterday morning came to me and told me that Nolan was not so well, and had not left his state-room,—a thing I never remember before. He had let the doctor come and see him as he lay there,—the first time the doctor had been in the state-room,—and he said he should like to see me. Oh, dear! do you remember the mysteries we boys used to invent about his room, in the old Intrepid days? Well, I went in, and there, to be sure, the poor fellow lay in his berth, smiling pleasantly as he gave me his hand, but looking very frail. I could not help a glance round, which showed me what a little shrine he had made of the box he was lying in. The stars and stripes were triced up above and around a picture of Washington, and he had painted a majestic eagle, with lightnings blazing from his beak and his foot just clasping the whole globe, which his wings overshadowed. The dear old boy saw my glance, and said, with a sad smile, 'Here, you see, I have a country!' And then he pointed to the foot of his bed, where I had not seen before a great map of the United States, as he had drawn it from memory, and which he had there to look upon as he lay. Quaint, queer old names were on it, in large letters: 'Indiana Territory,'

'Mississippi Territory,' and 'Louisiana Territory,' as I suppose our fathers learned such things: but the old fellow had patched in Texas, too; he had carried his western boundary all the way to the Pacific, but on that shore he had defined nothing.

"Oh, Danforth,' he said, 'I know I am dying. I cannot get home. Surely you will tell me something now?—Stop! stop! Do not speak till I say what I am sure you know, that there is not in this ship, that there is not in America,—God bless her!—a more loyal man than I. There cannot be a man who loves the old flag as I do, or prays for it as I do, or hopes for it as I do. There are thirty-four stars in it now, Danforth. I thank God for that, though I do not know what their names are. There has never been one taken away: I thank God for that. I know by that that there has never been any successful Burr. Oh! Danforth, Danforth,' he sighed out, 'how like a wretched night's dream a boy's idea of personal fame or of separate sovereignty seems, when one looks back on it after such a life as mine! But tell me,—tell me something,—tell me everything, Danforth, before I die!'

'Ingham, I swear to you that I felt like a monster that I had not told him everything before. Danger or no danger, delicacy or no delicacy, who was I, that I should have been acting the tyrant all this time over this dear, sainted old man, who had years ago expiated, in his whole manhood's life, the madness of a boy's treason? 'Mr Nolan,' said I, 'I will tell you every thing you ask about. Only, where shall I begin?'

'Oh, the blessed smile that crept over his white face! and he pressed my hand and said, 'God bless you!' 'Tell me their names,' he said, and he pointed to the stars on the flag. 'The last I know is Ohio. My father lived in Kentucky. But I have guessed Michigan and Indiana and Mississippi,—that was where Fort Adams is,—they make twenty. But where are your other fourteen? You have not cut up any of the old ones, I hope?'

'Well, that was not a bad text, and I told him the names in

as good order as I could, and he bade me take down his beautiful map and draw them in as I best could with my pencil. He was wild with delight about Texas, told me how his cousin died there; he had marked a gold cross near where he supposed his grave was; and he had guessed at Texas. Then he was delighted as he saw California and Oregon;—that, he said, he had suspected partly, because he had never been permitted to land on that shore, though the ships were there so much. 'And the men,' said he, laughing, 'brought off a good deal besides furs.' Then he went back—heavens, how far!—to ask about the Chesapeake, and what was done to Barron for surrendering her to the Leopard, and whether Burr ever tried again,—and he ground his teeth with the only passion he showed. But in a moment that was over, and he said, 'God forgive me, for I am sure I forgive him.' Then he asked about the old war,—told me the true story of his serving the gun the day we took the Java,—asked about dear old David Porter, as he called him. Then he settled down more quietly, and very happily, to hear me tell in an hour the history of fifty years.

'How I wished it had been somebody who knew something! But I did as well as I could. I told him of the English war. I told him about Fulton and the steamboat beginning. I told him about old Scott, and Jackson; told him all I could think of about the Mississippi, and New Orleans, and Texas, and his own old Kentucky. And do you think, he asked who was in command of the 'Legion of the West.' I told him it was a very gallant officer named Grant, and that, by our last news, he was about to establish his head-quarters at Vicksburg. Then, 'Where was Vicksburg?' I worked that out on the map; it was about a hundred miles, more or less, above his old Fort Adams; and I thought Fort Adams must he a ruin now. 'It must be at old Vick's plantation,' at Walnut Hills, said he: 'well, that is a change!'

'I tell you, Ingham, it was a hard thing to condense the history of half a century into that talk with a sick man. And

I do not now know what I told him,—of emigration, and the means of it,—of steamboats, and railroads, and telegraphs,—of inventions, and books, and literature,—of the colleges, and West Point, and the Naval School,—but with the queerest interruptions that ever you heard. You see it was Robinson Crusoe asking all the accumulated questions of fifty-six years!

'I remember he asked, all of a sudden, who was President now; and when I told him, he asked if Old Abe was General Benjamin Lincoln's son. He said he met old General Lincoln, when he was quite a boy himself, at some Indian treaty. I said no, that Old Abe was a Kentuckian like himself, but I could not tell him of what family; he had worked up from the ranks. 'Good for him!' cried Nolan; 'I am glad of that. As I have brooded and wondered, I have thought our danger was in keeping up those regular successions in the first families.' Then I got talking about my visit to Washington. I told him of meeting the Oregon Congressman, Harding; I told him about the Smithsonian, and the Exploring Expedition; I told him about the Capitol, and the statues for the pediment, and Crawford's Liberty, and Greenough's Washington: Ingham, I told him everything I could think of that would show the grandeur of his country and its prosperity; but I could not make up my mouth to tell him a word about this infernal Rebellion!

'And he drank it in, and enjoyed it as I cannot tell you. He grew more and more silent, yet I never thought he was tired or faint. I gave him a glass of water, but he just wet his lips, and told me not to go away. Then he asked me to bring the Presbyterian 'Book of Public Prayer,' which lay there, and said, with a smile, that it would open at the right place,—and so it did. There was his double red mark down the page; and I knelt down and read, and he repeated with me, 'For ourselves and our country, O gracious God, we thank Thee, that, notwithstanding our manifold transgressions of Thy holy laws, Thou hast continued to us Thy marvellous kindness,'—and so to the end of that thanksgiving.

Then he turned to the end of the same book, and I read the words more familiar to me: 'Most heartily we beseech Thee with Thy favour to behold and bless Thy servant, the President of the United States, and all others in authority,'—and the rest of the Episcopal collect. 'Danforth,' said he, 'I have repeated those prayers night and morning, it is now fifty-five years.' And then he said he would go to sleep. He bent me down over him and kissed me; and he said, 'Look in my Bible, Danforth, when I am gone.' And I went away.

'But I had no thought it was the end. I thought he was tired and would sleep. I knew he was happy and I wanted him to be alone.

'But in an hour, when the doctor went in gently he found Nolan had breathed his life away with a smile. He had something pressed close to his lips. It was his father's badge of the Order of the Cincinnati.

'We looked in his Bible, and there was a slip of paper at the place where he had marked the text,—

'"They desire a country, even a heavenly: wherefore God is not ashamed to be called their God: for he hath prepared for them a city."

'On this slip of paper he had written,—

'"Bury me in the sea; it has been my home, and I love it. But will not some one set up a stone for my memory at Fort Adams or at Orleans, that my disgrace may not be more than I ought to bear? Say on it,—

'"In Memory of
'"PHILIP NOLAN,
'"Lieutenant in the Army of the United States.

'"He loved his country as no other man has loved her; but no man deserved less at her hands."'

3

CHRISTMAS EVE IN WAR TIMES

Edward Payson Roe

It was the beginning of a battle. The skirmish line of the Union advance was sweeping rapidly over a rough mountainous region in the South, and in his place on the extreme left of this line was Private Anson Marlow. Tall trees rising from underbrush, rocks, bowlders, gulches worn by spring torrents, were the characteristics of the field, which was in wild contrast with the parade-grounds on which the combatants had first learned the tactics of war. The majority, however, of those now in the ranks had since been drilled too often under like circumstances, and with lead and iron shotted guns, not to know their duty, and the lines of battle were as regular as the broken country allowed. So far as many obstacles permitted, Marlow kept his proper distance from the others on the line and fired coolly when he caught glimpses of the retreating Confederate skirmishers. They were retiring with ominous readiness towards a wooded height which the enemy occupied with a force of unknown strength. That strength was soon manifested in temporary disaster to the Union forces, which were driven back with heavy loss.

Neither the battle nor its fortunes are the objects of our present concern, but rather the fate of Private Marlow. The tide of battle drifted away and left the soldier desperately wounded in a narrow ravine, through which babbled a small stream. Excepting the voices of his wife and children no music had ever sounded so sweetly in his ears. With great difficulty he crawled to a little bubbling pool formed by a tiny cascade and encircling stones, and partially slaked his intolerable thirst.

He believed he was dying—bleeding to death. The very thought blunted his faculties for a time; and he was conscious of little beyond a dull wonder. Could it be possible that the tragedy of his death was enacting in that peaceful, secluded nook? Could Nature be so indifferent or so unconscious if it were true that he was soon to lie there dead? He saw the speckled trout lying motionless at the bottom of the pool, the grey squirrels sporting in the boughs over his head. The sunlight shimmered and glinted through the leaves, flecking with light his prostrate form. He dipped his hand in the blood that had welled from his side, and it fell in rubies from his fingers. Could that be his blood—his life-blood; and would it soon all ooze away? Could it be that death was coming through all the brightness of that summer afternoon?

From a shadowed tree further up the glen, a wood-thrush suddenly began its almost unrivalled song. The familiar melody, heard so often from his cottage-porch in the June twilight, awoke him to the bitter truth. His wife had then sat beside him, while his little ones played here and there among the trees and shrubbery. They would hear the same song to-day; he would never hear it again. That counted for little; but the thought of their sitting behind the vines and listening to their favourite bird, spring after spring and summer after summer, and he ever absent, overwhelmed him.

'Oh, Gertrude, my wife, my wife! Oh, my children!' he groaned.

His breast heaved with a great sigh; the blood welled afresh from his wound; what seemed a mortal weakness crept over him; and he thought he died.

'Say, Eb, is he done gone?'

''Clar to grashus if I know. 'Pears mighty like it.' These

words were spoken by two stout negroes, who had stolen to the battlefield as the sounds of conflict died away.

'I'm doggoned if I tink dat he's dead. He's only swoonded,' asserted the man addressed as Eb. "Twon't do to lebe 'im here to die, Zack.'

'Sartin not; we'd hab bad luck all our days.'

'I reckon ole man Pearson will keep him; and his wife's a po'ful nuss.'

'Pearson orter; he's a Unioner.'

'S'pose we try him; 'tain't so bery fur off.'

On the morning of the 24th of December, Mrs Anson Marlow sat in the living-room of her cottage, that stood well out in the suburbs of a Northern town. Her eyes were hollow and full of trouble that seemed almost beyond tears, and the bare room, that had been stripped of nearly every appliance and suggestion of comfort, but too plainly indicated one of the causes. Want was stamped on her thin face, that once had been so full and pretty; poverty in its bitter extremity was unmistakably shown by the uncarpeted floor, the meagre fire, and scanty furniture. It was a period of depression; work had been scarce, and much of the time she had been too ill and feeble to do more than care for her children. Away back in August her resources had been running low; but she had daily expected the long arrears of pay which her husband would receive as soon as the exigencies of the campaign permitted. Instead of these funds, so greatly needed, came the tidings of a Union defeat, with her husband's name down among the missing. Beyond that brief mention, so horrible in its vagueness, she had never heard a word from the one who not only sustained her home, but also her heart. Was he languishing in a Southern prison, or, mortally wounded, had he lingered out some terrible hours on that wild battlefield, a brief description of which had been so dwelt upon by her morbid fancy that it had become like one of the scenes in Dante's 'Inferno'? For a long time she could not and would not believe that such an overwhelming disaster had befallen her and her children, although she knew that similar losses had come to thousands of others. Events that the world regards as not only possible but probable are often so terrible in their personal consequences that we shrink from even the bare thought of their occurrence.

If Mrs Marlow had been told from the first that her husband was dead, the shock resulting would not have been so injurious as the suspense that robbed her of rest for days, weeks, and months. She haunted the post office, and if a stranger was seen coming up the street towards her cottage she watched feverishly for his turning in at her gate with the tidings of her husband's safety. Night after night she lay awake, hoping, praying that she might hear his step returning on a furlough to which wounds or sickness had entitled him. The natural and inevitable result was illness and nervous prostration.

Practical neighbours had told her that her course was all wrong; that she should be resigned and even cheerful for her children's sake; that she needed to sleep well and live well, in order that she might have strength to provide for them. She would make pathetic attempts to follow this sound and thrifty advice, but suddenly when at her work or in her troubled sleep, that awful word 'missing' would pierce her heart like an arrow, and she would moan, and at times in the depths of her anguish cry out, 'Oh, where is he? Shall I ever see him again?'

But the unrelenting demands of life are made as surely upon the breaking as upon the happy heart. She and her children must have food, clothing, and shelter. Her illness and feebleness at last taught her that she must not yield to her grief, except so far as she was unable to suppress it; that for the sake of those now seemingly dependent upon her, she must rally every shattered nerve and every relaxed muscle. With a heroism far beyond that of her husband and his comrades in the field, she sought to fight the wolf from the door, or at least to keep him at bay. Although the struggle seemed a hopeless one, she patiently did her best from day to day, eking out her scanty earnings by the sale or pawning of such of her household goods as she could best spare. She felt that she would do anything rather than reveal her poverty or accept charity. Some help was more or less kindly offered, but beyond such aid as one neighbour may receive of another, she had said gently but firmly, 'Not yet.'

The Marlows were comparative strangers in the city where they had resided. Her husband had been a teacher in one of its public schools, and his salary small. Patriotism had been his motive for entering the army, and while it had cost him a mighty struggle to leave his family, he felt that he had no more reason to hold back than thousands of others. He believed that he could still provide for those dependent upon him, and if he fell, those for whom he died would not permit his widow and children to suffer. But the first popular enthusiasm for the war had largely died out; the city was full of widows and orphans; there was depression of spirit, stagnation in business, and a very general disposition on the part of those who had means, to take care of themselves, and provide for darker days that might be in the immediate future. Sensitive, retiring Mrs Marlow was not the one to push her claims or reveal her need. Moreover, she could never give up the hope that tidings from her husband might at any time bring relief and safety.

But the crisis had come at last; and on this dreary December day she was face to face with absolute want. The wolf, with his gaunt eyes, was crouched beside her cold hearth. A pittance owed to her for work had not been paid. The little food left in the house had furnished the children an unsatisfying breakfast; she had eaten nothing. On the table beside her lay a note from the agent of the estate of which her home was a part, bidding her call that morning. She knew why—the rent was two months in arrears. It seemed like death to leave the house in which her husband had placed her, and wherein she had spent her happiest days. It stood well away from the crowded town. The little yard and garden, with their trees, vines, and shrubbery, some of which her husband had planted, were all dear from association. In the rear there was a grove and open fields, which, though not belonging to the cottage, were not forbidden to the children; and they formed a wonderland of delight in spring, summer, and fall. Must she take her active, restless boy Jamie, the image of his father, into a crowded tenement? Must golden-haired Susie, with her dower of beauty, be imprisoned in one close room, or else be exposed to the evil of corrupt association just beyond the threshold?

Moreover, her retired home had become a refuge. Here she could hide her sorrow and poverty. Here she could touch what he had touched, and sit during the long winter evenings in his favourite corner by the fire. Around her, within and without, were the little appliances for her comfort which his hands had made, how could she leave all this and live? Deep in her heart also the hope would linger that he would come again and seek her where he had left her.

'O God!' she cried suddenly. 'Thou wouldst not, couldst not permit him to die without one farewell word,' and she buried her face in her hands and rocked back and forth, while hard, dry sobs shook her slight, famine-pinched form.

The children stopped their play and came and leaned upon her lap.

'Don't cry, mother,' said Jamie, a little boy of ten. 'I'll soon be big enough to work for you; and I'll get rich, and you shall have the biggest house in town. I'll take care of you if papa don't come back.'

Little Sue knew not what to say, but the impulse of her love was her best guide. She threw her arms around her mother's neck with such an impetuous and childlike outburst of affection that the poor woman's bitter and despairing thoughts were banished for a time. The deepest chord of her nature, mother love, was touched; and for her children's sake she rose up once more and faced the hard problems of her life. Putting on her bonnet and thin shawl (she had parted with much that she now so sorely needed), she went out into the cold December wind. The sky was clouded like her hopes, and the light, even in the morning hours, was dim and leaden-hued.

She first called on Mr Jackson, the agent from whom she rented her home, and besought him to give her a little more time.

'I will beg for work from door to door,' she said. 'Surely in this Christian city there must be those who will give me work; and that is all I ask.'

The sleek, comfortable man, in his well-appointed office, was touched slightly, and said in a voice that was not so gruff as he at first had intended it should be:

'Well, I will wait a week or two longer. If then you cannot pay something on what is already due, my duty to my employers will compel me to take the usual course. You have told me all along that your husband would surely return, and I have hated to say a word to discourage you; but I fear you will have to bring yourself to face the truth and act accordingly, as so many others have done. I know it's very hard for you, but I am held responsible by my employer, and at my intercession he has been lenient, as you must admit. You could get a room or two in town for half what you must pay where you are. Good-morning.'

She went out again into the street, which the shrouded sky made sombre in spite of preparations seen on every side for the chief festival of the year. The fear was growing strong that like Him in whose memory the day was honoured, she and her little ones might soon not know where to lay their heads. She succeeded in getting the small sum owed to her and payment also for some sewing just finished. More work she could not readily obtain, for every one was busy and preoccupied by the coming day of gladness.

'Call again,' some said kindly or carelessly, according to their nature. 'After the holidays are over we will try to have or make some work for you.'

'But I need—I must have work now,' she ventured to say whenever she had the chance.

In response to this appeal there were a few offers of charity, small indeed, but from which she drew back with an instinct so strong that it could not be overcome. On every side she heard the same story. The times were very hard; requests for work and aid had been so frequent that purses and patience were exhausted. Moreover, people had spent their Christmas money on their households and friends, and were already beginning to feel poor.

At last she obtained a little work, and having made a few purchases of that which was absolutely essential, she was about to drag her weary feet homewards when the thought occurred to her that the children would want to hang up their stockings at night; and she murmured: 'It may be the last chance I shall ever have to put a Christmas gift in them. Oh, that I were stronger! Oh, that I could take my sorrow more as others seem to take theirs! But I cannot, I cannot! My burden is greater than I can bear. The cold of this awful day is chilling my very heart, and my grief, as hope dies, is crushing my soul. Oh, he must be dead, he must be dead! That is what they all think. God help my little ones! Oh, what will become of them if I sink, as I fear I shall! If it were not for them I feel as if I would fall and die here in the street. Well, be our fate what it may, they shall owe to me one more gleam of happiness;' and she went into a confectioner's shop and bought a few ornamented cakes. These were the only gifts she could afford, and they must be in the form of food.

Before she reached home the snow was whirling in the frosty air, and the shadows of the brief winter day deepening fast. With a smile far more pathetic than tears she greeted the children, who were cold, hungry, and frightened at her long absence; and they, children-like, saw only the smile, and not the grief it masked. They saw also the basket which she had placed on the table, and were quick to note that it seemed a little fuller than of late.

'Jamie,' she said, 'run to the store down the street for some coal and kindlings that I bought, and then we will have a good fire and a nice supper;' and the boy, at such a prospect, eagerly obeyed.

She was glad to have him gone, that she might hide her weakness. She sank into a chair, so white and faint that even little Susie left off peering into the basket, and came to her with a troubled face.

'It's nothing, dearie,' the poor creature said. 'Mamma's only a little tired. See,' she added, tottering to the table, 'I have brought you a great piece of gingerbread.'

The hungry child grasped it, and was oblivious and happy.

By the time Jamie returned with his first basket of kindling and coal, the mother had so far rallied from her exhaustion as to meet him smilingly again and help him replenish the dying fire.

'Now you shall rest and have your gingerbread before going for your second load,' she said cheerily; and the boy took what was ambrosia to him, and danced around the room in joyous reaction from the depression of the long weary day, during which, lonely and hungry, he had wondered why his mother did not return.

'So little could make them happy, and yet I cannot seem to obtain even that little,' she sighed. 'I fear—indeed, I fear—I cannot be with them another Christmas; therefore they shall remember that I tried to make them happy once more, and the recollection may survive the long sad days before them, and become a part of my memory.'

The room was now growing dark, and she lighted the lamp. Then she cowered shiveringly over the reviving fire, feeling as if she could never be warm again.

The street-lamps were lighted early on that clouded, stormy evening, and they were a signal to Mr Jackson, the agent, to leave his office. He remembered that he had ordered a holiday dinner, and now found himself in a mood to enjoy it. He had scarcely left his door before a man, coming up the street with great strides and head bent down to the snow-laden blast, brushed roughly against him. The stranger's cap was drawn over his eyes, and the raised collar of his blue army overcoat nearly concealed his face. The man hurriedly begged pardon, and was hastening on when Mr Jackson's exclamation of surprise caused him to stop and look at the person he had jostled.

'Why, Mr Marlow,' the agent began, 'I'm glad to see you. It's a pleasure I feared I should never have again.'

'My wife,' the man almost gasped, 'she's still in the house I rented of you?'

'Oh, certainly,' was the hasty reply. 'It'll be all right now.'

'What do you mean? Has it not been all right?'

'Well, you see,' said Mr Jackson, apologetically, 'we have been very lenient to your wife, but the rent has not been paid for over two months, and—'

'And you were about to turn her and her children out-of-doors in midwinter,' broke in the soldier, wrathfully. 'That is the way you sleek, comfortable stay-at-home people care for those fighting your battles. After you concluded that I was dead, and that the rent might not be forthcoming, you decided to put my wife into the street. Open your office, sir, and you shall have your rent.'

'Now, Mr Marlow, there's no cause for pitching into me in this way. You know that I am but an agent, and—'

'Tell your rich employer, then, what I have said, and ask

him what he would be worth to-day were there not men like myself, who are willing to risk everything and suffer everything for the Union. But I've no time to bandy words. Have you seen my wife lately?'

'Yes,' was the hesitating reply; 'she was here to-day, and I—'

'How is she? What did you say to her?'

'Well, she doesn't look very strong. I felt sorry for her, and gave her more time, taking the responsibility myself—'

'How much time?'

'I said two weeks, but no doubt I could have had the time extended.'

'I have *my* doubts. Will you and your employer please accept my humble gratitude that you had the grace not to turn her out-of-doors during the holiday season? It might have caused remark; but that consideration and some others that I might name are not to be weighed against a few dollars and cents. I shall now remove the strain upon your patriotism at once, and will not only pay arrears, but also for two months in advance.'

'Oh, there's no need of that to-day.'

'Yes, there is. My wife shall feel to-night that she has a home. She evidently has not received the letter I wrote as soon as I reached our lines, or you would not have been talking to her about two weeks more of shelter.'

The agent reopened his office and saw a roll of bills extracted from Marlow's pocket that left no doubt of the soldier's ability to provide for his family. He gave his receipt in silence, feeling that words would not mend matters, and then trudged off to his dinner with a nagging appetite.

As Marlow strode away he came to a sudden resolution—he would look upon his wife and children before they saw him; he would feast his eyes while they were unconscious of the love that was beaming upon them. The darkness and storm favoured his project, and in brief time he saw the light in his window.

Unlatching the gate softly, and with his steps muffled by the snow that already carpeted the frozen ground, he reached the window, the blinds of which were but partially closed. His children frolicking about the room were the first objects that caught his eye, and he almost laughed aloud in his joy. Then, by turning another blind slightly, he saw his wife shivering over the fire.

'Great God!' he muttered, 'how she has suffered!' and he was about to rush in and take her into his arms. On the threshold he restrained himself, paused, and said, 'No, not yet; I'll break the news of my return in my own way. The shock of my sudden appearance might be too great for her;' and he went back to the window. The wife's eyes were following her children with such a wistful tenderness that the boy, catching her gaze, stopped his sport, came to her side, and began to speak. They were but a few feet away, and Marlow caught every word.

'Mamma,' the child said, 'you didn't eat any breakfast, and I don't believe you have eaten anything to-day. You are always giving everything to us. Now I declare I won't eat another bit unless you take half of my cake;' and he broke off a piece and laid it in her lap.

'Oh, Jamie,' cried the poor woman, 'you looked so like your father when you spoke that I could almost see him;' and she caught him in her arms and covered him with kisses.

'I'll soon be big enough to take care of you. I'm going to grow up just like papa and do everything for you,' the boy said proudly as she released him.

Little Susie also came and placed what was left of her cake in her mother's lap, saying:

'I'll work for you, too, mamma; and to-morrow I'll sell the doll Santa Claus gave me last Christmas, and then we'll all have plenty to eat.'

Anson Marlow was sobbing outside the window as only a man weeps; and his tears in the bitter cold became drops of ice before they reached the ground.

'My darlings!' the mother cried. 'Oh, God spare me to you and provide some way for us! Your love should make me rich though I lack all else. There, I won't cry any more, and you shall have as happy a Christmas as I can give you. Perhaps He who knew what it was to be homeless and shelterless will provide for our need; so we'll try to trust Him and keep His birthday. And now, Jamie, go and bring the rest of the coal, and then we will make the dear home that papa gave us cheery and warm once more. If he were only with us we wouldn't mind hunger or cold, would we? Oh, my husband!' she broke out afresh, 'if you could only come back, even though crippled and helpless, I feel that I could live and grow strong from simple gladness.'

'Don't you think, mamma,' Jamie asked, 'that God will let papa come down from heaven and spend Christmas with us? He might be here like the angels, and we not see him.'

'I'm afraid not,' the sad woman replied, shaking her head and speaking more to herself than to the child. 'I don't see how he could go back to heaven and be happy if he knew all. No, we must be patient and try to do our best, so that we can go to him. Go now, Jamie, before it gets too late. I'll get supper, and then we'll sing a Christmas hymn; and you and Susie shall hang up your stockings, just as you did last Christmas, when dear papa was with us. We'll try to do everything he would wish, and then by and by we shall see him again.'

As the boy started on his errand his father stepped back out of the light of the window, then followed the child with a great yearning in his heart. He would make sure the boy was safe at home again before he carried out his plan. From a distance he saw the little fellow receive the coal and start slowly homewards with the burden, and he followed to a point where the light of the street-lamps ceased, then joined the child, and said in a gruff voice, 'Here, little man, I'm going your way. Let me carry your basket;' and he took it and strode on so fast that the boy had to run to keep pace with him. Jamie shuffled along through the snow as well as he could, but his little legs were so short in comparison with those of the kindly stranger that he found himself gradually falling behind. So he put on an extra burst of speed and managed to lay hold of the long blue skirt of the army overcoat.

'Please, sir, don't go quite so fast,' he panted.

The stranger slackened his pace, and in a constrained tone of voice, asked:

'How far are you going, little man?'

'Only to our house—mamma's. She's Mrs Marlow, you know.'

'Yes, I know—that is, I reckon I do. How much further is it?'

'Oh, not much; we're most halfway now. I say, you're a soldier, aren't you?'

'Yes, my boy,' said Marlow, with a lump in his throat. 'Why?'

'Well, you see, my papa is a soldier, too, and I thought you might know him. We haven't heard from him for a good while, and'—choking a bit—'mamma's afraid he is hurt, or taken prisoner or something.' He could not bring himself to say 'killed.'

Jamie let go the overcoat to draw his sleeve across his eyes, and the big man once more strode on faster than ever, and Jamie began to fear lest the dusky form might disappear in the snow and darkness with both basket and coal; but the apparent stranger so far forgot his part that he put down the basket at Mrs Marlow's gate, and then passed on so quickly that the panting boy had not time to thank him. Indeed, Anson Marlow knew that if he lingered but a moment he would have the child in his arms.

'Why, Jamie,' exclaimed his mother, 'how could you get back so soon with that heavy basket? It was too heavy for you, but you will have to be mamma's little man now.'

'A big man caught up with me and carried it. I don't care if he did have a gruff voice, I'm sure he was a good kind man.

He knew where we lived too, for he put the basket down at our gate before I could say a word, I was so out of breath, and then he was out of sight in a minute.' Some instinct kept him from saying anything about the army overcoat.

'It's some neighbour that lives further up the street, I suppose, and saw you getting the coal at the store,' Mrs Marlow said, 'Yes, Jamie, it was a good, kind act to help a little boy, and I think he'll have a happier Christmas for doing it.'

'Do you really think he'll have a happier Christmas, mamma?'

'Yes, I truly think so. We are so made that we cannot do a kind act without feeling the better for it.'

'Well, I think he was a queer sort of a man if he was kind. I never knew any one to walk so fast. I spoke to him once, but he did not answer. Perhaps the wind roared so he couldn't hear me.'

'No doubt he was hurrying home to his wife and children,' she said with a deep sigh.

When his boy disappeared within the door of the cottage, Marlow turned and walked rapidly towards the city, first going to the grocery at which he had been in the habit of purchasing his supplies. The merchant stared for a moment, then stepped forward and greeted his customer warmly.

'Well,' he said, after his first exclamations of surprise were over, 'the snow has made you almost as white as a ghost; but I'm glad you're not one. We scarce ever thought to see you again.'

'Has my wife an open account here now?' was the brief response.

'Yes, and it might have been much larger. I've told her so too. She stopped taking credit some time ago, and when she's had a dollar or two to spare she's paid it on the old score. She bought so little that I said to her once that she need not go elsewhere to buy; that I'd sell to her as cheap as any one: that I believed you'd come back all right, and if you didn't she could pay me when she could. What do you think she did? Why, she burst out crying, and said, 'God bless you, sir, for saying my husband will come back! So many have discouraged me.' I declare to you her feeling was so right down genuine that I had to mop my own eyes. But she wouldn't take any more credit, and she bought so little that I've been troubled. I'd have sent her something, but your wife somehow ain't one of them kind that you can give things to, and—'

Marlow interrupted the good-hearted, garrulous shopman by saying significantly, 'Come with me to your back office'; for the soldier feared that some one might enter who would recognize him and carry the tidings to his home prematurely.

'Mr Wilkins,' he said rapidly, 'I wanted to find out if you too had thriftily shut down on a soldier's wife. You shall not regret your kindness.'

'Hang it all!' broke in Wilkins, with compunction, 'I haven't been very kind. I ought to have gone and seen your wife and found out how things were; and I meant to, but I've been so confoundedly busy—'

'No matter now; I've not a moment to spare. You must help me to break the news of my return in my own way. I mean they shall have such a Christmas in the little cottage as was never known in this town. You could send a load right over there, couldn't you?'

'Certainly, certainly,' said Wilkins, under the impulse of both business thrift and goodwill; and a list of tea, coffee, sugar, flour, bread, cakes, apples, etc., was dashed off rapidly; and Marlow had the satisfaction of seeing the errand-boy, the two clerks, and the proprietor himself busily working to fill the order in the shortest possible space of time.

He next went to a restaurant, a little further down the street, where he had taken his meals for a short time before he brought his family to town, and was greeted with almost equal surprise and warmth. Marlow cut short all words by his almost feverish haste. A huge turkey had just been roasted for the needs of the coming holiday, and this with a cold ham and a pot of coffee was ordered to be sent in a covered tray within a quarter of an hour. Then a toy shop was visited, and such a doll purchased! for tears came into Marlow's eyes whenever he thought of his child's offer to sell her dolly for her mother's sake.

After selecting a sled for Jamie, and directing that they should be sent at once, he could restrain his impatience no longer, and almost tore back to his station at the cottage window. His wife was placing the meagre little supper on the table, and how poor and scanty it was!

'Is that the best the dear soul can do on Christmas Eve?' he groaned. 'Why, there's scarcely enough for little Sue. Thank God, my darling, I will sit down with you to a rather different supper before long!'

He bowed his head reverently with his wife as she asked God's blessing, and wondered at her faith. Then he looked and listened again with a heart-hunger which had been growing for months.

'Do you really think Santa Claus will fill our stockings tonight?' Sue asked.

'I think he'll have something for you,' she replied. 'There are so many poor little boys and girls in the city that he may not be able to bring very much to you.'

'Who is Santa Claus, anyway?' questioned Jamie.

Tears came into the wife's eyes as she thought of the one who had always remembered them so kindly as far as his modest means permitted.

She hesitated in her reply; and before she could decide upon an answer there was a knock at the door. Jamie ran to open it, and started back as a man entered with cap, eyebrows, beard, and shaggy coat all white with the falling snow. He placed two great baskets of provisions on the floor, and said they were for Mrs Anson Marlow.

'There is some mistake,' Mrs Marlow began; but the children, after staring a moment, shouted, 'Santa Claus! Santa Claus!'

The grocer's man took the unexpected cue instantly, and said, 'No mistake, ma'am. They are from Santa Claus;' and before another word could be spoken he was gone. The face of the grocer's man was not very familiar to Mrs Marlow, and the snow had disguised him completely. The children had no misgivings and pounced upon the baskets and with, exclamations of delight drew out such articles as they could lift.

'I can't understand it,' said the mother, bewildered and almost frightened.

'Why, mamma, it's as plain as day,' cried Jamie. 'Didn't he look just like the pictures of Santa Claus—white beard and white eyebrows? Oh, mamma, mamma, here is a great paper of red-cheeked apples!' and he and Susie tugged at it until they dragged it over the side of the basket, when the bottom of the bag came out, and the fruit flecked the floor with red and gold. Oh, the bliss of picking up those apples; of comparing one with another; of running to the mother and asking which was the biggest and which the reddest and most beautifully streaked!

'There must have been some mistake,' the poor woman kept murmuring as she examined the baskets and found how liberal and varied was the supply, 'for who could or would have been so kind?'

'Why, mommie,' said little Sue, reproachfully, 'Santa Claus brought 'em. Haven't you always told us that Santa Claus liked to make us happy?'

The long-exiled father felt that he could restrain himself but a few moments longer, and he was glad to see that the rest of his purchases were at the door. With a look so intent, and yearning concentration of thought so intense that it was strange that they could not feel his presence, he bent his eyes once more upon a scene that would imprint itself upon his memory forever.

But while he stood there, another scene came before his mental vision. Oddly enough his thought went back to that far-off Southern brookside, where he had lain with his hands in the cool water. He leaned against the window casing, with the Northern snow whirling about his head; but he breathed the balmy breath of a Southern forest, the wood thrush sang in the trees overhead, and he could—so it seemed to him—actually feel the water-worn pebbles under his palms as he watched the life-blood ebbing from his side. Then there was a dim consciousness of rough but kindly arms bearing him through the underbrush, and more distinctly the memory of weary weeks of convalescence in a mountaineer's cabin. All these scenes of peril, before he finally reached the Union lines, passed before him as he stood in a species of trance beside the window of his home.

The half-grown boys sent from the restaurant and toy shop could not be mistaken for Santa Claus even by the credulous fancy of the children, and Mrs Marlow stepped forward eagerly and said:

'I am sure there is some mistake. You are certainly leaving these articles at the wrong house.' The faces of the children began to grow anxious and troubled also, for even their faith could not accept such marvellous good-fortune. Jamie looked at the sled with a kind of awe, and saw at a glance that it was handsomer than any in the street 'Mr Lansing, a wealthy man, lives a little further on,' Mrs Marlow began to urge; 'and these things must be meant—'

'Isn't your name Mrs Anson Marlow?' asked the boy from the restaurant.

'Yes.'

'Then I must do as I've been told;' and he opened his tray and placed the turkey, the ham, and the coffee on the table.

'If he's right, I'm right too,' said he of the toy shop. 'Them was my directions;' and they were both about to depart when the woman sprang forward and gasped: 'Stay!'

She clasped her hands and trembled violently.

'Who sent these things?' she faltered.

'Our bosses, mum,' replied the boy from the restaurant, hesitatingly.

She sprang towards him, seized his arm, and looked imploringly into his face. 'Who ordered them sent?' she asked in a low, passionate voice.

The young fellow began to smile, and stammered awkwardly, 'I don't think I'm to tell.'

She released his arm and glanced around with a look of intense expectation.

'Oh, oh!' she gasped with quick short sobs, 'can it be—' Then she sprang to the door, opened it, and looked out into the black, stormy night. What seemed a shadow rushed towards her; she felt herself falling, but strong arms caught and bore her, half fainting, to a lounge within the room.

Many have died from sorrow, but few from joy. With her husband's arms around her Mrs Marlow's weakness soon passed. In response to his deep, earnest tones of soothing and entreaty, she speedily opened her eyes and gave him a smile so full of content and unutterable joy that all anxiety in her behalf began to pass from his mind.

'Yes,' she said softly, 'I can live now. It seems as if a new and stronger life were coming back with every breath.'

The young fellows who had been the bearers of the gifts were so touched that they drew their rough sleeves across their eyes as they hastened away, closing the door on the happiest family in the city.

4

THE NAMESAKE

Willa Cather

Seven of us, students, sat one evening in Hartwell's studio on the Boulevard St Michel. We were all fellow countrymen; one from New Hampshire, one from Colorado, another from Nevada, several from the farm lands of the Middle West, and I myself from California. Lyon Hartwell, though born abroad, was simply, as every one knew, 'from America.' He seemed, almost more than any other one living man, to mean all of it—from ocean to ocean. When he was in Paris, his studio was always open to the seven of us who were there that evening, and we intruded upon his leisure as often as we thought permissible.

Although we were within the terms of the easiest of all intimacies, and although the great sculptor, even when he was more than usually silent, was at all times the most gravely cordial of hosts, yet, on that long remembered evening, as the sunlight died on the burnished brown of the horse-chestnuts below the windows, a perceptible dullness yawned through our conversation.

We were, indeed, somewhat low in spirit, for one of our number, Charley Bentley, was leaving us indefinitely, in response to an imperative summons from home. To-morrow his studio, just across the hall from Hartwell's, was to pass into other hands, and Bentley's luggage was even now piled in discouraged resignation before his door. The various bales and boxes seemed literally to weigh upon us as we sat in his neighbour's hospitable rooms, drearily putting in the time until he should leave us to catch the ten o'clock express for Dieppe.

The day we had got through very comfortably, for Bentley made it the occasion of a somewhat pretentious luncheon at Maxim's. There had been twelve of us at table, and the two young Poles were so thirsty, the Gascon so fabulously entertaining, that it was near upon five o'clock when we put down our liqueur glasses for the last time, and the red, perspiring waiter, having pocketed the reward of his arduous and protracted services, bowed us affably to the door, flourishing his napkin and brushing back the streaks of wet, black hair from his rosy forehead. Our guests having betaken themselves belated to their respective engagements, the rest of us returned with Bentley—only to be confronted by the depressing array before his door. A glance about his denuded rooms had sufficed to chill the glow of the afternoon, and we fled across the hall in a body and begged Lyon Hartwell to take us in.

Bentley had said very little about it, but we all knew what it meant to him to be called home. Each of us knew what it would mean to himself, and each had felt something of that quickened sense of opportunity which comes at seeing another man in any way counted out of the race. Never had the game seemed so enchanting, the chance to play it such a piece of unmerited, unbelievable good fortune.

It must have been, I think, about the middle of October, for I remember that the sycamores were almost bare in the Luxembourg Gardens that morning, and the terraces about the queens of France were strewn with crackling brown leaves. The fat red roses, out the summer long on the stand of the old flower woman at the corner, had given place to dahlias and purple asters. First glimpses of autumn toilettes flashed from the carriages; wonderful little bonnets nodded at one along the Champs-Elysées; and in the Quarter an occasional feather boa, red or black or white, brushed one's coat sleeve in the gay twilight of the early evening. The crisp, sunny autumn air was all day full of the stir of people and carriages and of the cheer of salutations; greetings of the students, returned brown and bearded from their holiday, gossip of people come back from Trouville, from St Valery, from Dieppe, from all over Brittany and the Norman coast. Everywhere was the joyousness of return, the taking up again of life and work and play.

I had felt ever since early morning that this was the saddest of all possible seasons for saying good-bye to that old, old city of youth, and to that little corner of it on the south shore which since the Dark Ages themselves—yes, and before—has been so peculiarly the land of the young.

I can recall our very postures as we lounged about Hartwell's rooms that evening, with Bentley making occasional hurried trips to his desolated workrooms across the hall—as if haunted by a feeling of having forgotten something—or stopping to poke nervously at his *perroquets*, which he had bequeathed to Hartwell, gilt cage and all. Our host himself sat on the couch, his big, bronze-like shoulders backed up against the window, his shaggy head, beaked nose, and long chin cut clean against the grey light.

Our drowsing interest, in so far as it could be said to be fixed upon anything, was centred upon Hartwell's new figure, which stood on the block ready to be cast in bronze, intended as a monument for some American battlefield. He called it 'The Color Sergeant.' It was the figure of a young soldier running, clutching the folds of a flag, the staff of which had been shot away. We had known it in all the stages of its growth, and the splendid action and feeling of the thing had come to have a kind of special significance for the half dozen of us who often gathered at Hartwell's rooms—though, in truth, there was as much to dishearten one as to inflame, in the case of a man who had done so much in a field so amazingly difficult; who had thrown up in bronze all the restless, teeming force of that adventurous wave still climbing westwards in our own land across the waters. We recalled his 'Scout,' his 'Pioneer,' his 'Gold Seekers,' and those monuments in which he had invested one and another of the heroes of the Civil War with such convincing dignity and power.

'Where in the world does he get the heat to make an idea like that carry?' Bentley remarked morosely, scowling at the clay figure. 'Hang me, Hartwell, if I don't think it's just because you're not really an American at all, that you can look at it like that.'

The big man shifted uneasily against the window. 'Yes,' he replied smiling, 'perhaps there is something in that. My citizenship was somewhat belated and emotional in its flowering. I've half a mind to tell you about it, Bentley.' He rose uncertainly, and, after hesitating a moment, went back into his workroom, where he began fumbling among the litter in the corners.

At the prospect of any sort of personal expression from Hartwell, we glanced questioningly at one another; for although he made us feel that he liked to have us about, we were always held at a distance by a certain diffidence of his. There were rare occasions—when he was in the heat of work or of ideas—when he forgot to be shy, but they were so exceptional that no flattery was quite so seductive as being taken for a moment into Hartwell's confidence. Even in the matter of opinions—the commonest of currency in our circle—he was niggardly and prone to qualify. No man ever guarded his mystery more effectually. There was a singular, intense spell, therefore, about those few evenings when he had broken through this excessive modesty, or shyness, or melancholy, and had, as it were, committed himself.

When Hartwell returned from the back room, he brought with him an unframed canvas which he put on an easel near his clay figure. We drew close about it, for the darkness was rapidly coming on. Despite the dullness of the light, we instantly recognized the boy of Hartwell's 'Color Sergeant.' It was the portrait of a very handsome lad in uniform, standing beside a charger impossibly rearing. Not only in his radiant countenance and flashing eyes, but in every line of his young body there was an energy, a gallantry, a joy of life, that arrested and challenged one.

'Yes, that's where I got the notion,' Hartwell remarked, wandering back to his seat in the window. 'I've wanted to do it for years, but I've never felt quite sure of myself. I was afraid of missing it. He was an uncle of mine, my father's half-brother, and I was named for him. He was killed in one of the big battles of Sixty-four, when I was a child. I never saw him—never knew him until he had been dead for twenty years. And then, one night, I came to know him as we sometimes do living persons—intimately, in a single moment.'

He paused to knock the ashes out of his short pipe, refilled it, and puffed at it thoughtfully for a few moments with his hands on his knees. Then, settling back heavily among the cushions and looking absently out of the window, he began his story. As he proceeded further and further into the experience which he was trying to convey to us, his voice sank so low and was sometimes so charged with feeling, that I almost thought he had forgotten our presence and was remembering aloud. Even Bentley forgot his nervousness in astonishment and sat breathless under the spell of the man's thus breathing his memories out into the dusk.

'It was just fifteen years ago this last spring that I first went home, and Bentley's having to cut away like this brings it all back to me.

'I was born, you know, in Italy. My father was a sculptor, though I dare say you've not heard of him. He was one of those first fellows who went over after Story and Powers,—went to Italy for 'Art,' quite simply; to lift from its native bough the willing, iridescent bird. Their story is told, informingly enough, by some of those ingenuous marble things at the Metropolitan. My father came over some time before the outbreak of the Civil War, and was regarded as a renegade by his family because he did not go home to enter the army. His half-brother, the only child of my grandfather's second marriage, enlisted at fifteen and was killed the next year. I was ten years old when the news of his death reached us. My mother died the following winter, and I was sent away to a Jesuit school, while my father, already ill himself, stayed on at Rome, chipping away at his Indian maidens and marble goddesses, still gloomily seeking the thing for which he had made himself the most unhappy of exiles.

'He died when I was fourteen, but even before that I had been put to work under an Italian sculptor. He had an almost morbid desire that I should carry on his work, under, as he often pointed out to me, conditions so much more auspicious. He left me in the charge of his one intimate friend, an American gentleman in the consulate at Rome, and his instructions were that I was to be educated there and to live there until I was twenty-one. After I was of age, I came to Paris and studied under one master after another until I was nearly thirty. Then, almost for the first time, I was confronted by a duty which was not my pleasure.

'My grandfather's death, at an advanced age, left an invalid maiden sister of my father's quite alone in the world. She had suffered for years from a cerebral disease, a slow decay of the faculties which rendered her almost helpless. I decided to go to America and, if possible, bring her back to Paris, where I seemed on my way towards what my poor father had wished for me.

'On my arrival at my father's birthplace, however, I found that this was not to be thought of. To tear this timid, feeble, shrinking creature, doubly aged by years and illness, from the spot where she had been rooted for a lifetime, would have been little short of brutality. To leave her to the care of strangers seemed equally heartless. There was clearly nothing for me to do but to remain and wait for that slow and painless malady to run its course. I was there something over two years.

'My grandfather's home, his father's homestead before him,

lay on the high banks of a river in Western Pennsylvania. The little town twelve miles down the stream, whither my great-grandfather used to drive his ox-wagon on market days, had become, in two generations, one of the largest manufacturing cities in the world. For hundreds of miles about us the gentle hill slopes were honey-combed with gas wells and coal shafts; oil derricks creaked in every valley and meadow; the brooks were sluggish and discoloured with crude petroleum, and the air was impregnated by its searching odour. The great glass and iron manufactories had come up and up the river almost to our very door; their smoky exhalations brooded over us, and their crashing was always in our ears. I was plunged into the very incandescence of human energy. But, though my nerves tingled with the feverish, passionate endeavour which snapped in the very air about me, none of these great arteries seemed to feed me; this tumultuous life did not warm me. On every side were the great muddy rivers, the ragged mountains from which the timber was being ruthlessly torn away, the vast tracts of wild country, and the gulches that were like wounds in the earth; everywhere the glare of that relentless energy which followed me like a searchlight and seemed to scorch and consume me. I could only hide myself in the tangled garden, where the dropping of a leaf or the whistle of a bird was the only incident.

'The Hartwell homestead had been sold away little by little, until all that remained of it was garden and orchard. The house, a square brick structure, stood in the midst of a great garden which sloped towards the river, ending in a grassy bank which fell some forty feet to the water's edge. The garden was now little more than a tangle of neglected shrubbery; damp, rank, and of that intense blue-green peculiar to vegetation in smoky places where the sun shines but rarely, and the mists form early in the evening and hang late in the morning.

'I shall never forget it as I saw it first, when I arrived there in the chill of a backwards June. The long, rank grass, thick and soft and falling in billows, was always wet until midday. The gravel walks were bordered with great lilac-bushes, mock-orange, and bridal-wreath. Back of the house was a neglected rose garden, surrounded by a low stone wall over which the long suckers trailed and matted. They had wound their pink, thorny tentacles, layer upon layer, about the lock and the hinges of the rusty iron gate. Even the porches of the house, and the very windows, were damp and heavy with growth: wistaria, clematis, honeysuckle, and trumpet vine. The garden was grown up with trees, especially that part of it which lay above the river. The bark of the old locusts was blackened by the smoke that crept continually up the valley, and their feathery foliage, so merry in its movement and so yellow and joyous in its colour, seemed peculiarly precious under that sombre sky. There were sycamores and copper beeches; gnarled apple trees, too old to bear; and fall pear trees, hung with a sharp, hard fruit in October; all with a leafage singularly rich and luxuriant, and peculiarly vivid in colour. The oaks about the house had been old trees when my great-grandfather built his cabin there, more than a century before, and this garden was almost the only spot for miles along the river where any of the original forest growth still survived. The smoke from the mills was fatal to trees of the larger sort, and even these had the look of doomed things—bent a little towards the town and seemed to wait with head inclined before that oncoming, shrieking force.

'About the river, too, there was a strange hush, a tragic submission—it was so leaden and sullen in its colour, and it flowed so soundlessly forever past our door.

'I sat there every evening, on the high veranda overlooking it, watching the dim outlines of the steep hills on the other shore, the flicker of the lights on the island, where there was a boat-house, and listening to the call of the boatmen through the mist. The mist came as certainly as night, whitened by moonshine or starshine. The tin water-pipes went splash, splash, with it all evening, and the wind, when it rose at all, was little more than a sighing of the old boughs and a troubled breath in the heavy grasses.

'At first it was to think of my distant friends and my old life that I used to sit there; but after a while it was simply to watch the days and weeks go by, like the river which seemed to carry them away.

'Within the house I was never at home. Month followed month, and yet I could feel no sense of kinship with anything there. Under the roof where my father and grandfather were born, I remained utterly detached. The somber rooms never spoke to me, the old furniture never seemed tinctured with race. This portrait of my boy uncle was the only thing to which I could draw near, the only link with anything I had ever known before.

'There is a good deal of my father in the face, but it is my father transformed and glorified; his hesitating discontent drowned in a kind of triumph. From my first day in that house, I continually turned to this handsome kinsman of mine, wondering in what terms he had lived and had his hope; what he had found there to look like that, to bound at one, after all those years, so joyously out of the canvas.

'From the timid, clouded old woman over whose life I had come to watch, I learned that in the backyard, near the old rose garden, there was a locust tree which my uncle had planted. After his death, while it was still a slender sapling, his mother had a seat built round it, and she used to sit there on summer evenings. His grave was under the apple trees in the old orchard.

'My aunt could tell me little more than this. There were days when she seemed not to remember him at all.

'It was from an old soldier in the village that I learned the boy's story. Lyon was, the old man told me, but fourteen when the first enlistment occurred, but was even then eager to go. He was in the courthouse square every evening to watch the recruits at their drill, and when the home company was ordered off he rode into the city on his pony to see the men board the train and to wave them good-by. The next year he spent at home with a tutor, but when he was fifteen he held his parents to their promise and went into the army. He was colour sergeant of his regiment and fell in a charge upon the breastworks of a fort about a year after his enlistment.

'The veteran showed me an account of this charge which had been written for the village paper by one of my uncle's comrades who had seen his part in the engagement, it seems that as his company were running at full speed across the bottom lands towards the fortified hill, a shell burst over them. This comrade, running beside my uncle, saw the colours waver and sink as if falling, and looked to see that the boy's hand and forearm had been torn away by the exploding shrapnel. The boy, he thought, did not realize the extent of his injury, for he laughed, shouted something which his comrade did not catch, caught the flag in his left hand, and ran on up the hill. They went splendidly up over the breastworks, but just as my uncle, his colours flying, reached the top of the embankment, a second shell carried away his left arm at the armpit, and he fell over the wall with the flag settling about him.

'It was because this story was ever present with me, because I was unable to shake it off, that I began to read such books as my grandfather had collected upon the Civil War. I found that this war was fought largely by boys, that more men enlisted at eighteen than at any other age. When I thought of those battlefields—and I thought of them much in those days—there was always that glory of youth above them, that impetuous, generous passion stirring the long lines on the march, the blue battalions in the plain. The bugle, whenever I have heard it since, has always seemed to me the very golden throat of that boyhood which spent itself so gaily, so incredibly.

'I used often to wonder how it was that this uncle of mine, who seemed to have possessed all the charm and brilliancy allotted to his family and to have lived up its vitality in one splendid hour, had left so little trace in the house where he was born and where he had awaited his destiny. Look as I would, I could find no letters from him, no clothing or books that might have been his. He had been dead but twenty years, and yet nothing seemed to have survived except the tree he had planted. It seemed incredible and cruel that no physical memory of him should linger to be cherished among his kindred,—nothing but the dull image in the brain of that aged sister. I used to pace the garden walks in the evening, wondering that no breath of his, no echo of his laugh, of his call to his pony or his whistle to his dogs, should linger about those shaded paths where the pale roses exhaled their dewy, country smell. Sometimes, in the dim starlight, I have thought that I heard on the grasses beside me the stir of a footfall lighter than my own, and under the black arch of the lilacs I have fancied that he bore me company.

'There was, I found, one day in the year for which my old aunt waited, and which stood out from the months that were all of a sameness to her. On the thirtieth of May she insisted that I should bring down the big flag from the attic and run it up upon the tall flagstaff beside Lyon's tree in the garden. Later in the morning she went with me to carry some of the garden flowers to the grave in the orchard,—a grave scarcely larger than a child's.

'I had noticed, when I was hunting for the flag in the attic, a leather trunk with my own name stamped upon it, but was unable to find the key. My aunt was all day less apathetic than usual; she seemed to realize more clearly who I was, and to wish me to be with her. I did not have an opportunity to return to the attic until after dinner that evening, when I carried a lamp upstairs and easily forced the lock of the trunk. I found all the things that I had looked for; put away, doubtless, by his mother, and still smelling faintly of lavender and rose leaves; his clothes, his exercise books, his letters from the army, his first boots, his riding-whip, some of his toys, even. I took them out and replaced them gently. As I was about to shut the lid, I picked up a copy of the Æneid, on the fly-leaf of which was written in a slanting, boyish hand, 'Lyon Hartwell, January, 1862.' He had gone to the wars in Sixty-three, I remembered.

'My uncle, I gathered, was none too apt at his Latin, for the pages were dog-eared and rubbed and interlined, the margins mottled with pencil sketches—bugles, stacked bayonets, and artillery carriages. In the act of putting the book down, I happened to run over the pages to the end, and on the flyleaf at the back I saw his name again, and a drawing—with his initials and a date—of the Federal flag; above it, written in a kind of arch and in the same unformed:

'Oh, say, can you see by the dawn's early light
What so proudly we hailed at the twilight's last gleaming?'

It was a stiff, wooden sketch, not unlike a detail from some Egyptian inscription, but, the moment I saw it, wind and colour seemed to touch it. I caught up the book, blew out the lamp, and rushed down into the garden.

'I seemed, somehow, at last to have known him; to have been with him in that careless, unconscious moment and to have known him as he was then.

'As I sat there in the rush of this realization, the wind began to rise, stirring the light foliage of the locust over my head and bringing, fresher than before, the woody odour of the pale roses that overran the little neglected garden. Then, as it grew stronger, it brought the sound of something sighing and stirring over my head in the perfumed darkness.

'I thought of that sad one of the Destinies who, as the Greeks believed, watched from birth over those marked for a violent or untimely death. Oh, I could see him, there in the shine of the morning, his book idly on his knee, his flashing eyes looking straight before him, and at his side that grave figure, hidden in her draperies, her eyes following his, but seeing so much farther—seeing what he never saw, that great moment at the end, when he swayed above his comrades on the earthen wall.

'All the while, the bunting I had run up in the morning flapped fold against fold, heaving and tossing softly in the dark—against a sky so black with rain clouds that I could see above me only the blur of something in soft, troubled motion.

'The experience of that night, coming so overwhelmingly to a man so dead, almost rent me in pieces. It was the same feeling that artists know when we, rarely, achieve truth in our work; the feeling of union with some great force, of purpose and security, of being glad that we have lived. For the first time I felt the pull of race and blood and kindred, and felt beating within me things that had not begun with me. It was as if the earth under my feet had grasped and rooted me, and were pouring its essence into me. I sat there until the dawn of morning, and all night long my life seemed to be pouring out of me and running into the ground.'

Hartwell drew a long breath that lifted his heavy shoulders, and then let them fall again. He shifted a little and faced more squarely the scattered, silent company before him. The darkness had made us almost invisible to each other, and, except for the occasional red circuit of a cigarette end travelling upwards from the arm of a chair, he might have supposed us all asleep.

'And so,' Hartwell added thoughtfully, 'I naturally feel an interest in fellows who are going home. It's always an experience.'

No one said anything, and in a moment there was a loud rap at the door,—the concierge, came to take down Bentley's luggage and to announce that the cab was below. Bentley got his hat and coat, enjoined Hartwell to take good care of his *perroquets*, gave each of us a grip of the hand, and went briskly down the long flights of stairs. We followed him into the street, calling our good wishes, and saw him start on his drive across the lighted city to the Gare St Lazare.

5

THE AFFAIR AT COULTER'S NOTCH

Ambrose Bierce

'Do you think, Colonel, that your brave Coulter would like to put one of his guns in here?' the general asked.

He was apparently not altogether serious; it certainly did not seem a place where any artillerist, however brave, would like to put a gun. The colonel thought that possibly his division commander meant good-humouredly to intimate that in a recent conversation between them Captain Coulter's courage had been too highly extolled.

'General,' he replied warmly, 'Coulter would like to put a gun anywhere within reach of those people,' with a motion of his hand in the direction of the enemy.

'It is the only place,' said the general. He was serious, then.

The place was a depression, a 'notch,' in the sharp crest of a hill. It was a pass, and through it ran a turnpike, which reaching this highest point in its course by a sinuous ascent through a thin forest made a similar, though less steep, descent towards the enemy. For a mile to the left and a mile to the right, the ridge, though occupied by Federal infantry lying close behind the sharp crest and appearing as if held in place by atmospheric pressure, was inaccessible to artillery. There was no place but the bottom of the notch, and that was barely wide enough for the roadbed. From the Confederate side this point was commanded by two batteries posted on a slightly lower elevation beyond a creek, and a half-mile away. All the guns but one were masked by the trees of an orchard; that one—it seemed a bit of impudence—was on an open lawn directly in front of a rather grandiose building, the planter's dwelling. The gun was safe enough in its exposure—but only because the Federal infantry had been forbidden to fire. Coulter's Notch—it came to be called so—was not, that pleasant summer afternoon, a place where one would 'like to put a gun.'

Three or four dead horses lay there sprawling in the road, three or four dead men in a trim row at one side of it, and a little back, down the hill. All but one were cavalrymen belonging to the Federal advance. One was a quartermaster. The general commanding the division and the colonel commanding the brigade, with their staffs and escorts, had ridden into the notch to have a look at the enemy's guns—which had straightway obscured themselves in towering clouds of smoke. It was hardly profitable to be curious about guns which had the trick of the cuttlefish, and the season of observation had been brief. At its conclusion—a short remove backwards from where it began—occurred the conversation already partly reported. 'It is the only place,' the general repeated thoughtfully, 'to get at them.'

The colonel looked at him gravely. 'There is room for only one gun, General—one against twelve.'

'That is true—for only one at a time,' said the commander with something like, yet not altogether like, a smile. 'But then, your brave Coulter—a whole battery in himself.'

The tone of irony was now unmistakable. It angered the colonel, but he did not know what to say. The spirit of military subordination is not favourable to retort, nor even to deprecation.

At this moment a young officer of artillery came riding slowly up the road attended by his bugler. It was Captain Coulter. He could not have been more than twenty-three years of age. He was of medium height, but very slender and lithe, and sat his horse with something of the air of a civilian. In face he was of a type singularly unlike the men about him; thin, high-nosed, grey-eyed, with a slight blond moustache, and long, rather straggling hair of the same colour. There was an apparent negligence in his attire. His cap was worn with the visor a trifle askew; his coat was buttoned only at the sword-belt, showing a considerable expanse of white shirt, tolerably clean for that stage of the campaign. But the negligence was all in his dress and bearing; in his face was a look of intense interest in his surroundings. His grey eyes, which seemed occasionally to strike right and left across the landscape, like searchlights, were for the most part fixed upon the sky beyond the Notch; until he should arrive at the summit of the road there was nothing else in that direction to see. As he came opposite his division and brigade commanders at the roadside he saluted mechanically and was about to pass on. The colonel signed to him to halt.

'Captain Coulter,' he said, 'the enemy has twelve pieces over there on the next ridge. If I rightly understand the general, he directs that you bring up a gun and engage them.'

There was a blank silence; the general looked stolidly at a distant regiment swarming slowly up the hill through rough undergrowth, like a torn and draggled cloud of blue smoke; the captain appeared not to have observed him. Presently the captain spoke, slowly and with apparent effort:

'On the next ridge, did you say, sir? Are the guns near the house?'

'Ah, you have been over this road before. Directly at the house.'

'And it is—necessary—to engage them? The order is imperative?'

His voice was husky and broken. He was visibly paler. The colonel was astonished and mortified. He stole a glance at the commander. In that set, immobile face was no sign; it was as hard as bronze. A moment later the general rode away, followed by his staff and escort. The colonel, humiliated and indignant, was about to order Captain Coulter in arrest, when the latter spoke a few words in a low tone to his bugler, saluted, and rode straight forward into the Notch, where, presently, at the summit of the road, his field glass at his eyes, he showed against the sky, he and his horse, sharply defined and statuesque. The bugler had dashed down the speed and disappeared behind a wood. Presently his bugle was heard singing in the cedars, and in an incredibly short time a single gun with its caisson, each drawn by six horses and manned by its full complement of gunners, came bounding and banging up the grade in a storm of dust, unlimbered under cover, and was run forward by hand to the fatal crest among the dead horses. A gesture of the captain's arm, some strangely agile movements of the men in loading, and almost before the troops along the way had ceased to hear the rattle of the wheels, a great white cloud sprang forward down the slope, and with a deafening report the affair at Coulter's Notch had begun.

It is not intended to relate in detail the progress and incidents of that ghastly contest—a contest without vicissitudes, its alternations only different degrees of despair. Almost at the instant when Captain Coulter's gun blew its challenging cloud twelve answering clouds rolled upwards from among the trees about the plantation house, a deep multiple report roared back like a broken echo, and thenceforth to the end the Federal cannoneers fought their hopeless battle in an atmosphere of living iron whose thoughts were lightnings and whose deeds were death.

Unwilling to see the efforts which he could not aid and the slaughter which he could not stay, the colonel ascended the ridge at a point a quarter of a mile to the left, whence the Notch, itself invisible, but pushing up successive masses of smoke, seemed the crater of a volcano in thundering eruption. With his glass he watched the enemy's guns, noting as he could the effects of Coulter's fire—if Coulter still lived to direct it. He saw that the Federal gunners, ignoring those of the enemy's pieces whose positions could be determined by their smoke only, gave their whole attention to the one that maintained its place in the open—the lawn in front of the house. Over and about that hardy piece the shells exploded at intervals of a few seconds. Some exploded in the house, as could be seen by thin ascensions of smoke from the breached roof. Figures of prostrate men and horses were plainly visible.

'If our fellows are doing so good work with a single gun,' said the colonel to an aide who happened to be nearest, 'they must be suffering like the devil from twelve. Go down and present the commander of that piece with my congratulations on the accuracy of his fire.'

Turning to his adjutant-general he said, 'Did you observe Coulter's damned reluctance to obey orders?'

'Yes, sir, I did.'

'Well, say nothing about it, please. I don't think the general will care to make any accusations. He will probably have enough to do in explaining his own connection with this uncommon way of amusing the rear-guard of a retreating enemy.'

A young officer approached from below, climbing breathless up the acclivity. Almost before he had saluted, he gasped out:

'Colonel, I am directed by Colonel Harmon to say that the enemy's guns are within easy reach of our rifles, and most of them visible from several points along the ridge.'

The brigade commander looked at him without a trace of interest in his expression. 'I know it,' he said quietly.

The young adjutant was visibly embarrassed. 'Colonel Harmon would like to have permission to silence those guns,' he stammered.

'So should I,' the colonel said in the same tone. 'Present my compliments to Colonel Harmon and say to him that the general's orders for the infantry not to fire are still in force.'

The adjutant saluted and retired. The colonel ground his heel into the earth and turned to look again at the enemy's guns.

'Colonel,' said the adjutant-general, 'I don't know that I ought to say anything, but there is something wrong in all this. Do you happen to know that Captain Coulter is from the South?'

'No; *was* he, indeed?'

'I heard that last summer the division which the general then commanded was in the vicinity of Coulter's home—camped there for weeks, and—'

'Listen!' said the colonel, interrupting with an upwards gesture. 'Do you hear *that*?'

'That' was the silence of the Federal gun. The staff, the orderlies, the lines of infantry behind the crest—all had 'heard', and were looking curiously in the direction of the crater, whence no smoke now ascended except desultory cloudlets from the enemy's shells. Then came the blare of a bugle, a faint rattle of wheels; a minute later the sharp reports recommenced with double activity. The demolished gun had been replaced with a sound one.

'Yes,' said the adjutant-general, resuming his narrative, 'the general made the acquaintance of Coulter's family. There was trouble—I don't know the exact nature of it—something about Coulter's wife. She is a red-hot Secessionist, as they all are, except Coulter himself, but she is a good wife and high-bred lady. There was a complaint to army headquarters. The general was transferred to this division. It is odd that Coulter's battery should afterwards have been assigned to it.'

The colonel had risen from the rock upon which they had been sitting. His eyes were blazing with a generous indignation.

'See here, Morrison,' said he, looking his gossiping staff officer straight in the face, 'did you get that story from a gentleman or a liar?'

'I don't want to say how I got it, Colonel, unless it is necessary'—he was blushing a trifle—'but I'll stake my life upon its truth in the main.'

The colonel turned towards a small knot of officers some distance away. 'Lieutenant Williams!' he shouted.

One of the officers detached himself from the group and coming forward saluted, saying: 'Pardon me, Colonel, I thought you had been informed. Williams is dead down there by the gun. What can I do, sir?'

Lieutenant Williams was the aide who had had the pleasure of conveying to the officer in charge of the gun his brigade commander's congratulations.

'Go,' said the colonel, 'and direct the withdrawal of that gun instantly. No—I'll go myself.'

He strode down the declivity towards the rear of the Notch at a breakneck pace, over rocks and through brambles, followed by his little retinue in tumultuous disorder. At the foot of the declivity they mounted their waiting animals and took to the road at a lively trot, round a bend and into the Notch. The spectacle which they encountered there was appalling!

Within that defile, barely broad enough for a single gun, were piled the wrecks of no fewer than four. They had noted the silencing of only the last one disabled—there had been a lack of men to replace it quickly with another. The débris lay on both sides of the road; the men had managed to keep an open way between, through which the fifth piece was now firing. The men?—they looked like demons of the pit! All were hatless, all stripped to the waist, their reeking skins black with blotches of powder and spattered with gouts of blood. They worked like madmen, with rammer and cartridge, lever and lanyard. They set their swollen shoulders and bleeding hands against the wheels at each recoil and heaved the heavy gun back to its place. There were no commands; in that awful environment of whooping shot, exploding shells, shrieking fragments of iron, and flying splinters of wood, none could have been heard. Officers, if officers there were, were indistinguishable; all worked together—each while he lasted—governed by the eye. When the gun was sponged, it was loaded; when loaded, aimed and fired. The colonel observed something new to his military experience—something horrible and unnatural: the gun was bleeding at the mouth! In temporary default of water, the man sponging had dipped his sponge into a pool of comrade's blood. In all this work there was no clashing; the duty of the instant was obvious. When one fell, another, looking a trifle cleaner, seemed to rise from the earth in the dead man's tracks, to fall in his turn.

With the ruined guns lay the ruined men—alongside the wreckage, under it and atop of it; and back down the road—a ghastly procession!—crept on hands and knees such of the wounded as were able to move. The colonel—he had compassionately sent his cavalcade to the right about—had to ride over those who were entirely dead in order not to crush those who were partly alive. Into that hell he tranquilly held his way, rode up alongside the gun, and, in the obscurity of the last discharge, tapped upon the cheek the man holding the rammer—who straightway fell, thinking himself killed. A fiend seven times damned sprang out of the smoke to take his place, but paused and gazed up at the mounted officer with an unearthly regard, his teeth flashing between his black lips, his eyes, fierce and expanded, burning like coals beneath his bloody brow. The colonel made an authoritative gesture and pointed to the rear. The fiend bowed in token of obedience. It was Captain Coulter.

Simultaneously with the colonel's arresting sign, silence fell upon the whole field of action. The procession of missiles no longer streamed into that defile of death, for the enemy also had ceased firing. His army had been gone for hours, and the commander of his rear guard, who had held his position perilously long in hope to silence the Federal fire, at that strange moment had silenced his own. 'I was not aware of the breadth of my authority,' said the colonel to anybody, riding forward to the crest to see what had really happened.

An hour later his brigade was in bivouac on the enemy's ground, and its idlers were examining, with something of awe, as the faithful inspect a saint's relics, a score of straddling dead horses and three disabled guns, all spiked. The fallen men had been carried away; their torn and broken bodies would have given too great satisfaction.

Naturally, the colonel established himself and his military family in the plantation house. It was somewhat shattered, but it was better than the open air. The furniture was greatly deranged and broken. Walls and ceilings were knocked away here and there, and a lingering odour of powder smoke was everywhere. The beds, the closets of women's clothing, the cupboards were not greatly damaged. The new tenants for a night made themselves comfortable, and the virtual effacement of Coulter's battery supplied them with an interesting topic.

During supper an orderly of the escort showed himself into the dining-room and asked permission to speak to the colonel.

'What is it, Barbour?' said that officer pleasantly, having overheard the request.

'Colonel, there is something wrong in the cellar; I don't know what—somebody there. I was down there rummaging about.'

'I will go down and see,' said a staff officer, rising.

'So will I,' the colonel said; 'let the others remain. Lead on, orderly.'

They took a candle from the table and descended the cellar stairs, the orderly in visible trepidation. The candle made but a feeble light, but presently, as they advanced, its narrow circle of illumination revealed a human figure seated on the ground against the black stone wall which they were skirting, its knees elevated, its head bowed sharply forward. The face, which should have been seen in profile, was invisible, for the man was bent so far forward that his long hair concealed it; and, strange to relate, the beard, of a much darker hue, fell in a great tangled mass and lay along the ground at his side. They involuntarily paused; then the colonel, taking the candle from the orderly's shaking hand, approached the man and attentively considered him. The long dark beard was the hair of a woman—dead. The dead woman clasped in her arms a dead babe. Both were clasped in the arms of the man, pressed against his breast, against his lips. There was blood in the hair of the woman; there was blood in the hair of the man. A yard away, near an irregular depression in the beaten earth which formed the cellar's floor—fresh excavation with a convex bit of iron, having jagged edges, visible in one of the sides—lay an infant's foot. The colonel held the light as high as he could. The floor of the room above was broken through, the splinters pointing at all angles downwards. 'This casemate is not bomb-proof,' said the colonel gravely. It did not occur to him that his summing up of the matter had any levity in it.

They stood about the group awhile in silence; the staff officer was thinking of his unfinished supper, the orderly of what might possibly be in one of the casks on the other side of the cellar. Suddenly the man whom they had thought dead raised his head and gazed tranquilly into their faces. His complexion was coal black; the cheeks were apparently tattooed in irregular sinuous lines from the eyes downwards. The lips, too, were white, like those of a stage negro. There was blood upon his forehead.

The staff officer drew back a pace, the orderly two paces.

'What are you doing here, my man?' said the colonel, unmoved.

'This house belongs to me, sir,' was the reply, civilly delivered.

'To you? Ah, I see! And these?'

'My wife and child. I am Captain Coulter.'

6

THE SERGEANT'S PRIVATE MADHOUSE

Stephen Crane

The moonlight was almost steady blue flame and all this radiance was lavished out upon a still lifeless wilderness of stunted trees and cactus plants. The shadows lay upon the ground, pools of black and sharply outlined, resembling substances, fabrics, and not shadows at all. From afar came the sound of the sea coughing among the hollows in the coral rock.

The land was very empty; one could easily imagine that Cuba was a simple vast solitude; one could wonder at the moon taking all the trouble of this splendid illumination. There was no wind; nothing seemed to live.

But in a particular large group of shadows lay an outpost of some forty United States marines. If it had been possible to approach them from any direction without encountering one of their sentries, one could have gone stumbling among sleeping men and men who sat waiting, their blankets tented over their heads; one would have been in among them before one's mind could have decided whether they were men or devils. If a marine moved, he took the care and the time of one who walks across a death-chamber. The lieutenant in command reached for his watch and the nickel chain gave forth the faintest tinkling sound. He could see the glistening five or six pairs of eyes that slowly turned to regard him. His sergeant lay near him and he bent his face down to whisper. 'Who's on post behind the big cactus plant?'

'Dryden,' rejoined the sergeant just over his breath.

After a pause the lieutenant murmured: 'He's got too many

nerves. I shouldn't have put him there.' The sergeant asked if he should crawl down and look into affairs at Dryden's post. The young officer nodded assent and the sergeant, softly cocking his rifle, went away on his hands and knees. The lieutenant with his back to a dwarf tree, sat watching the sergeant's progress for the few moments that he could see him moving from one shadow to another. Afterwards, the officer waited to hear Dryden's quick but low-voiced challenge, but time passed and no sound came from the direction of the post behind the cactus bush.

The sergeant, as he came nearer and nearer to this cactus bush—a number of peculiarly dignified columns throwing shadows of inky darkness—had slowed his pace, for he did not wish to trifle with the feelings of the sentry, and he was expecting the stern hail and was ready with the immediate answer which turns away wrath. He was not made anxious by the fact that he could not yet see Dryden, for he knew that the man would be hidden in a way practised by sentry marines since the time when two men had been killed by a disease of excessive confidence on picket. Indeed, as the sergeant went still nearer, he became more and more angry. Dryden was evidently a most proper sentry.

Finally he arrived at a point where he could see Dryden seated in the shadow, staring into the bushes ahead of him, his rifle ready on his knee. The sergeant in his rage longed for the peaceful precincts of the Washington Marine Barracks where there would have been no situation to prevent the most complete non-commissioned oratory. He felt indecent in his capacity of a man able to creep up to the back of a G Company member on guard duty. Never mind; in the morning back at camp—

But, suddenly, he felt afraid. There was something wrong with Dryden. He remembered old tales of comrades creeping out to find a picket seated against a tree perhaps, upright enough but stone dead. The sergeant paused and gave the inscrutable back of the sentry a long stare. Dubious he again moved forward. At three paces, he hissed like a little snake. Dryden did not show a sign of hearing. At last, the sergeant was in a position from which he was able to reach out and touch Dryden on the arm. Whereupon was turned to him the face of a man livid with mad fright. The sergeant grabbed him by the wrist and with discreet fury shook him. 'Here! Pull yourself together!'

Dryden paid no heed but turned his wild face from the newcomer to the ground in front. 'Don't you see 'em, sergeant? Don't you see 'em?'

'Where?' whispered the sergeant.

'Ahead, and a little on the right flank. A reg'lar skirmish line. Don't you see 'em?'

'Naw,' whispered the sergeant. Dryden began to shake. He began moving one hand from his head to his knee and from his knee to his head rapidly, in a way that is without explanation. 'I don't dare fire,' he wept. 'If I do they'll see me, and oh, how they'll pepper me!'

The sergeant lying on his belly, understood one thing. Dryden had gone mad. Dryden was the March Hare. The old man gulped down his uproarious emotions as well as he was able and used the most simple device. 'Go,' he said, 'and tell the lieutenant while I cover your post for you.'

'No! They'd see me! They'd see me! And then they'd pepper me! O, how they'd pepper me!'

The sergeant was face to face with the biggest situation of his life. In the first place he knew that at night a large or small force of Spanish guerillas was never more than easy rifle range from any marine outpost, both sides maintaining a secrecy as absolute as possible in regard to their real position and strength. Everything was on a watch-spring foundation. A loud word might be paid for by a night-attack which would involve five hundred men who needed their earned sleep, not to speak of some of them who would need their lives. The slip of a foot and the rolling of a pint of gravel might go from consequence to consequence until various crews went to general quarters on their ships in the harbour, their batteries booming as the swift search-light flashes tore through the foliage. Men would get killed—notably the sergeant and Dryden—and outposts would be cut off and the whole night would be one pitiless turmoil. And so Sergeant George H. Peasley began to run his private madhouse behind the cactus-bush.

'Dryden,' said the sergeant, 'you do as I tell you and go tell the lieutenant.'

'I don't dare move,' shivered the man. 'They'll see me if I move. They'll see me. They're almost up now. Let's hide—'

'Well, then you stay here a moment and I'll go and—'

Dryden turned upon him a look so tigerish that the old man felt his hair move. 'Don't you stir,' he hissed. 'You want to give me away. You want them to see me. Don't you stir.' The sergeant decided not to stir.

He became aware of the slow wheeling of eternity, its majestic incomprehensibility of movement. Seconds, minutes, were quaint little things, tangible as toys, and there were billions of them, all alike. 'Dryden,' he whispered at the end of a century in which, curiously, he had never joined the marine corps at all but had taken to another walk of life and prospered greatly in it. 'Dryden, this is all foolishness.' He thought of the expedient of smashing the man over the head with his rifle, but Dryden was so supernaturally alert that there surely would issue some small scuffle and there could be not even the fraction of a scuffle. The sergeant relapsed into the contemplation of another century.

His patient had one fine virtue. He was in such terror of the phantom skirmish line that his voice never went above a whisper, whereas his delusion might have expressed itself in hyena yells and shots from his rifle. The sergeant, shuddering, had visions of how it might have been—the mad private leaping into the air and howling and shooting at his friends and making them the centre of the enemy's eager attention. This, to his mind, would have been conventional conduct for a maniac. The trembling victim of an idea was somewhat puzzling. The sergeant decided that from time to time he would reason with his patient. 'Look here, Dryden, you don't see any real Spaniards. You've been drinking or—something. Now—'

But Dryden only glared him into silence. Dryden was inspired with such a profound contempt of him that it was become hatred. 'Don't you stir!' And it was clear that if the sergeant did stir, the mad private would introduce calamity. 'Now,' said Peasley to himself, 'if those guerillas *should* take a crack at us to-night, they'd find a lunatic asylum right in the front and it would be astonishing.'

The silence of the night was broken by the quick low voice of a sentry to the left some distance. The breathless stillness brought an effect to the words as if they had been spoken in one's ear.

'*Halt—who's there—halt or I'll fire!*' Bang!

At the moment of sudden attack particularly at night, it is improbable that a man registers much detail of either thought or action. He may afterwards say: 'I was here.' He may say: 'I was there.' 'I did this.' 'I did that.' But there remains a great incoherency because of the tumultuous thought which seethes through the head. 'Is this defeat?' At night in a wilderness and against skilful foes half-seen, one does not trouble to ask if it is also Death. Defeat is Death, then, save for the miraculous. But the exaggerating magnifying first thought subsides in the ordered mind of the soldier and he knows, soon, what he is doing and how much of it. The sergeant's immediate impulse had been to squeeze close to the ground and listen—listen—above all else, listen. But the next moment he grabbed his private asylum by the scruff of its neck, jerked it to its feet and started to retreat upon the main outpost.

To the left, rifle-flashes were bursting from the shadows. To the rear, the lieutenant was giving some hoarse order or admonition. Through the air swept some Spanish bullets, very high, as if they had been fired at a man in a tree. The private asylum came on so hastily that the sergeant found he could remove his grip, and soon they were in the midst of the men of the outpost. Here there was no occasion for enlightening the lieutenant. In the first place such surprises required statement, question and answer. It is impossible to get a grossly original and fantastic idea through a man's head in less than one minute of rapid talk, and the sergeant knew the lieutenant could not spare the minute. He himself had no minutes to devote to anything but the business of the outpost. And the madman disappeared from his pen and he forgot about him.

It was a long night and the little fight was as long as the night. It was heartbreaking work. The forty marines lay in an irregular oval. From all sides, the Mauser bullets sang low and hard. Their occupation was to prevent a rush, and to this end they potted carefully at the flash of a Mauser—save when they got excited for a moment, in which case their magazines rattled like a great Waterbury watch. Then they settled again to a systematic potting.

The enemy were not of the regular Spanish forces. They were of a corps of guerillas, native-born Cubans, who preferred the flag of Spain. They were all men who knew the craft of the woods and were all recruited from the district. They fought more like red Indians than any people but the red Indians themselves. Each seemed to possess an individuality, a fighting individuality, which is only found in the highest order of irregular soldiers. Personally they were as distinct as possible, but through equality of knowledge and experience, they arrived at concert of action. So long as they operated in the wilderness, they were formidable troops. It mattered little whether it was daylight or dark; they were mainly invisible. They had schooled from the Cubans insurgent to Spain. As the Cubans fought the Spanish troops, so would these particular Spanish troops fight the Americans. It was wisdom.

The marines thoroughly understood the game. They must lie close and fight until daylight when the guerillas promptly would go away. They had withstood other nights of this kind, and now their principal emotion was probably a sort of frantic annoyance.

Back at the main camp, whenever the roaring volleys lulled, the men in the trenches could hear their comrades of the outpost, and the guerillas pattering away interminably. The moonlight faded and left an equal darkness upon the wilderness. A man could barely see the comrade at his side. Sometimes guerillas crept so close that the flame from their rifles seemed to scorch the faces of the marines, and the reports sounded as if from two or three inches of their very noses. If a pause came, one could hear the guerillas gabbling to each other in a kind of drunken delirium. The lieutenant was praying that the ammunition would last. Everybody was praying for daybreak.

A black hour came finally, when the men were not fit to have their troubles increased. The enemy made a wild attack on one portion of the oval, which was held by about fifteen men. The remainder of the force was busy enough, and the fifteen were naturally left to their devices. Amid the whirl of it, a loud voice suddenly broke out in song:

> 'When shepherds guard their flocks by night,
> All seated on the ground,
> An angel of the Lord came down
> And glory shone around.'

'Who the hell is that?' demanded the lieutenant from a throat full of smoke. There was almost a full stop of the firing. The Americans were somewhat puzzled. Practical ones muttered that the fool should have a bayonet-hilt shoved down his throat.

Others felt a thrill at the strangeness of the thing. Perhaps it was a sign!

> 'The minstrel boy to the war has gone,
> In the ranks of death you'll find him,
> His father's sword he has girded on
> And his wild harp slung behind him.'

This croak was as lugubrious as a coffin. 'Who is it? Who is it?' snapped the lieutenant. 'Stop him, somebody.'

'It's Dryden, sir,' said old Sergeant Peasley, as he felt around in the darkness for his madhouse. 'I can't find him—yet.'

> 'Please, O, please, O, do not let me fall;
> You're—gurgh—ugh—'

The sergeant had pounced upon him.

This singing had had an effect upon the Spaniards. At first they had fired frenziedly at the voice, but they soon ceased, perhaps from sheer amazement. Both sides took a spell of meditation.

The sergeant was having some difficulty with his charge. 'Here, you, grab 'im. Take 'im by the throat. Be quiet, you devil.'

One of the fifteen men, who had been hard-pressed, called out, 'We've only got about one clip apiece, Lieutenant. If they come again—'

The lieutenant crawled to and fro among his men, taking clips of cartridges from those who had many. He came upon the sergeant and his madhouse. He felt Dryden's belt and found it simply stuffed with ammunition. He examined Dryden's rifle and found in it a full clip. The madhouse had not fired a shot. The lieutenant distributed these valuable prizes among the fifteen men. As the men gratefully took them, one said: 'If they had come again hard enough, they would have had us, sir,—maybe.'

But the Spaniards did not come again. At the first indication of daybreak, they fired their customary goodbye volley. The marines lay tight while the slow dawn crept over the land. Finally the lieutenant arose among them, and he was a bewildered man, but very angry. 'Now where is that idiot, Sergeant?'

'Here he is, sir,' said the old man cheerfully. He was seated on the ground beside the recumbent Dryden who, with an innocent smile on his face, was sound asleep.

'Wake him up,' said the lieutenant briefly.

The sergeant shook the sleeper. 'Here, Minstrel Boy, turn out. The lieutenant wants you.'

Dryden climbed to his feet and saluted the officer with a dazed and childish air. 'Yes, sir.'

The lieutenant was obviously having difficulty in governing his feelings, but he managed to say with calmness, 'You seem to be fond of singing, Dryden? Sergeant, see if he has any whisky on him.'

'Sir?' said the madhouse stupefied. 'Singing—fond of singing?'

Here the sergeant interposed gently, and he and the lieutenant held palaver apart from the others. The marines, hitching more comfortably their almost empty belts, spoke with grins of the madhouse. 'Well, the Minstrel Boy made 'em clear out. They couldn't stand it. But—I wouldn't want to be in his boots. He'll see fireworks when the old man interviews him on the uses of grand opera in modern warfare. How do you think he managed to smuggle a bottle along without us finding it out?'

When the weary outpost was relieved and marched back to camp, the men could not rest until they had told a tale of the voice in the wilderness. In the meantime the sergeant took Dryden aboard a ship, and to those who took charge of the man, he defined him as 'the most useful crazy man in the service of the United States.'

7

A DUEL

Guy de Maupassant

The war was over. The Germans occupied France. The whole country was pulsating like a conquered wrestler beneath the knee of his victorious opponent.

The first trains from Paris, distracted, starving, despairing Paris, were making their way to the new frontiers, slowly passing through the country districts and the villages. The passengers gazed through the windows at the ravaged fields and burned hamlets. Prussian soldiers, in their black helmets with brass spikes, were smoking their pipes astride their chairs in front of the houses which were still left standing. Others were working or talking just as if they were members of the families. As you passed through the different towns you saw entire regiments drilling in the squares, and, in spite of the rumble of the carriage-wheels, you could every moment hear the hoarse words of command.

M. Dubuis, who during the entire siege had served as one of the National Guard in Paris, was going to join his wife and daughter, whom he had prudently sent away to Switzerland before the invasion.

Famine and hardship had not diminished his big paunch so characteristic of the rich, peace-loving merchant. He had gone through the terrible events of the past year with sorrowful resignation and bitter complaints at the savagery of men. Now that he was journeying to the frontier at the close of the war, he saw the Prussians for the first time, although he had done his duty on the ramparts and mounted guard on many a cold night.

He stared with mingled fear and anger at those bearded armed men, installed all over French soil as if they were at home, and he felt in his soul a kind of fever of impotent patriotism, at the same time also the great need of that new instinct of prudence which since then has, never left us. In the same railway carriage were two Englishmen, who had come to the country as sightseers and were gazing about them with looks of quiet curiosity. They were both also stout, and kept chatting in their own language, sometimes referring to their guidebook, and reading aloud the names of the places indicated.

Suddenly the train stopped at a little village station, and a Prussian officer jumped up with a great clatter of his sabre on the double footboard of the railway carriage. He was tall, wore a tight-fitting uniform, and had whiskers up to his eyes. His red hair seemed to be on fire, and his long moustache, of a paler hue, stuck out on both sides of his face, which it seemed to cut in two.

The Englishmen at once began staring at him, with smiles of newly awakened interest, while M. Dubuis made a show of reading a newspaper. He sat concealed in his corner like a thief in presence of a gendarme.

The train started again. The Englishmen went on chatting and looking out for the exact scene of different battles; and all of a sudden, as one of them stretched out his arm towards the horizon as he pointed out a village, the Prussian officer remarked in French, extending his long legs and lolling backwards:

'I killed a dozen Frenchmen in that village and took more than a hundred prisoners.'

The Englishmen, quite interested, immediately asked:

'Ha! and what is the name of this village?'

The Prussian replied:

'Pharsbourg.' He added: 'We caught those French scoundrels by the ears.'

And he glanced towards M. Dubuis, laughing conceitedly

into his moustache.

The train rolled on, still passing through hamlets occupied by the victorious army. German soldiers could be seen along the roads, on the edges of fields, standing in front of gates or chatting outside cafes. They covered the soil like African locusts.

The officer said, with a wave of his hand:

'If I had been in command, I'd have taken Paris, burned everything, killed everybody. No more France!'

The Englishman, through politeness, replied simply:

'Ah! yes.'

He went on:

'In twenty years all Europe, all of it, will belong to us. Prussia is more than a match for all of them.'

The Englishmen, getting uneasy, no longer replied. Their faces, which had become impassive, seemed made of wax behind their long whiskers. Then the Prussian officer began to laugh. And still, lolling back, he began to sneer. He sneered at the downfall of France, insulted the prostrate enemy; he sneered at Austria, which had been recently conquered; he sneered at the valiant but fruitless defence of the departments; he sneered at the Garde Mobile and at the useless artillery. He announced that Bismarck was going to build a city of iron with the captured cannon. And suddenly he placed his boots against the thigh of M. Dubuis, who turned away his eyes, reddening to the roots of his hair.

The Englishmen seemed to have become indifferent to all that was going on, as if they were suddenly shut up in their own island, far from the din of the world.

The officer took out his pipe, and looking fixedly at the Frenchman, said:

'You haven't any tobacco—have you?'

M. Dubuis replied:

'No, monsieur.'

The German resumed:

'You might go and buy some for me when the train stops.'

And he began laughing afresh as he added:

'I'll give you the price of a drink.'

The train whistled, and slackened its pace. They passed a station that had been burned down; and then they stopped altogether.

The German opened the carriage door, and, catching M. Dubuis by the arm, said:

'Go and do what I told you—quick, quick!'

A Prussian detachment occupied the station. Other soldiers were standing behind wooden gratings, looking on. The engine was getting up steam before starting off again. Then M. Dubuis hurriedly jumped on the platform, and, in spite of the warnings of the station master, dashed into the adjoining compartment.

He was alone! He tore open his waistcoat, his heart was beating so rapidly, and, gasping for breath, he wiped the perspiration from his forehead.

The train drew up at another station. And suddenly the officer appeared at the carriage door and jumped in, followed close behind by the two Englishmen, who were impelled by curiosity. The German sat facing the Frenchman, and, laughing still, said:

'You did not want to do what I asked you?'

M. Dubuis replied:

'No, monsieur.'

The train had just left the station.

The officer said:

'I'll cut off your moustache to fill my pipe with.'

And he put out his hand towards the Frenchman's face.

The Englishmen stared at them, retaining their previous impassive manner.

The German had already pulled out a few hairs, and was still tugging at the moustache, when M. Dubuis, with a back stroke of his hand, flung aside the officer's arm, and, seizing him by the collar, threw him down on the seat. Then, excited to a pitch of fury, his temples swollen and his eyes glaring, he kept throttling the officer with one hand, while with the other clenched he began to strike him violent blows in the face. The Prussian struggled, tried to draw his sword, to clinch with his adversary, who was on top of him. But M. Dubuis crushed him with his enormous weight and kept punching him without taking breath or knowing where his blows fell. Blood flowed down the face of the German, who, choking and with a rattling in his throat, spat out his broken teeth and vainly strove to shake off this infuriated man who was killing him.

The Englishmen had got on their feet and came closer in order to see better. They remained standing, full of mirth and curiosity, ready to bet for, or against, either combatant.

Suddenly M. Dubuis, exhausted by his violent efforts, rose and resumed his seat without uttering a word.

The Prussian did not attack him, for the savage assault had terrified and astonished the officer as well as causing him suffering. When he was able to breathe freely, he said:

'Unless you give me satisfaction with pistols I will kill you.'

M. Dubuis replied:

'Whenever you like. I'm quite ready.'

The German said:

'Here is the town of Strasbourg. I'll get two officers to be my seconds, and there will be time before the train leaves the station.'

M. Dubuis, who was puffing as hard as the engine, said to the Englishmen:

'Will you be my seconds?' They both answered together:

'Oh, yes!'

And the train stopped.

In a minute the Prussian had found two comrades, who brought pistols, and they made their way towards the ramparts.

The Englishmen were continually looking at their watches, shuffling their feet and hurrying on with the preparations, uneasy lest they should be too late for the train.

M. Dubuis had never fired a pistol in his life.

They made him stand twenty paces away from his enemy. He was asked:

'Are you ready?'

While he was answering, 'Yes, monsieur,' he noticed that one of the Englishmen had opened his umbrella in order to keep off the rays of the sun.

A voice gave the signal:

'Fire!'

M. Dubuis fired at random without delay, and he was amazed to see the Prussian opposite him stagger, lift up his arms and fall forward, dead. He had killed the officer.

One of the Englishmen exclaimed: 'Ah!' He was quivering with delight, with satisfied curiosity and joyous impatience. The other, who still kept his watch in his hand, seized M. Dubuis' arm and hurried him in double-quick time towards the station, his fellow-countryman marking time as he ran beside them, with closed fists, his elbows at his sides, 'One, two; one, two!'

And all three, running abreast rapidly, made their way to the station like three grotesque figures in a comic newspaper.

The train was on the point of starting. They sprang into their carriage. Then the Englishmen, taking off their travelling caps, waved them three times over their heads, exclaiming:

'Hip! hip! hip! hurrah!'

And gravely, one after the other, they extended their right hands to M. Dubuis and then went back and sat down in their own corner.

8

THE REVOLUTIONIST

Michaïl P. Artzybashev

I

Gabriel Andersen, the teacher, walked to the edge of the school garden, where he paused, undecided what to do. Off in the distance, two miles away, the woods hung like bluish lace over a field of pure snow. It was a brilliant day. A hundred tints glistened on the white ground and the iron bars of the garden railing. There was a lightness and transparency in the air that only the days of early spring possess. Gabriel Andersen turned his steps towards the fringe of blue lace for a tramp in the woods.

'Another spring in my life,' he said, breathing deep and peering up at the heavens through his spectacles. Andersen was rather given to sentimental poetising. He walked with his hands folded behind him, dangling his cane.

He had gone but a few paces when he noticed a group of soldiers and horses on the road beyond the garden rail. Their drab uniforms stood out dully against the white of the snow, but their swords and horses' coats tossed back the light. Their bowed cavalry legs moved awkwardly on the snow. Andersen wondered what they were doing there. Suddenly the nature of their business flashed upon him. It was an ugly errand they were upon, an instinct rather that his reason told him. Something unusual and terrible was to happen. And the same instinct told him he must conceal himself from the soldiers. He turned to the left quickly, dropped on his knees, and crawled on the soft, thawing, crackling snow to a low haystack, from behind which, by craning his neck, he could watch what the soldiers were doing.

There were twelve of them, one a stocky young officer in a grey cloak caught in prettily at the waist by a silver belt. His face was so red that even at that distance Andersen caught the odd, whitish gleam of his light protruding moustache and eyebrows against the vivid colour of his skin. The broken tones of his raucous voice reached distinctly to where the teacher, listening intently, lay hidden.

'I know what I am about. I don't need anybody's advice,' the officer cried. He clapped his arms akimbo and looked down at some one among the group of bustling soldiers. 'I'll show you how to be a rebel, you damned skunk.'

Andersen's heart beat fast. 'Good heavens!' he thought. 'Is it possible?' His head grew chill as if struck by a cold wave.

'Officer,' a quiet, restrained, yet distinct voice came from among the soldiers, 'you have no right—It's for the court to decide—you aren't a judge—it's plain murder, not—' 'Silence!' thundered the officer, his voice choking with rage. 'I'll give you a court. Ivanov, go ahead.'

He put the spurs to his horse and rode away. Gabriel Andersen mechanically observed how carefully the horse picked its way, placing its feet daintily as if for the steps of a minuet. Its ears were pricked to catch every sound. There was momentary bustle and excitement among the soldiers. Then they dispersed in different directions, leaving three persons in black behind, two tall men and one very short and frail. Andersen could see the hair of the short one's head. It was very light. And he saw his rosy ears sticking out on each side.

Now he fully understood what was to happen. But it was a thing so out of the ordinary, so horrible, that he fancied he was dreaming.

'It's so bright, so beautiful—the snow, the field, the woods, the sky. The breath of spring is upon everything. Yet people are going to be killed. How can it be? Impossible!' So his thoughts ran in confusion. He had the sensation of a man suddenly gone insane, who finds he sees, hears and feels what he is not accustomed to, and ought not hear, see and feel.

The three men in black stood next to one another hard by the railing, two quite close together, the short one some distance away.

'Officer!' one of them cried in a desperate voice—Andersen could not see which it was—'God sees us! Officer!'

Eight soldiers dismounted quickly, their spurs and sabres catching awkwardly. Evidently they were in a hurry, as if doing a thief's job.

Several seconds passed in silence until the soldiers placed themselves in a row a few feet from the black figures and levelled their guns. In doing so one soldier knocked his cap from his head. He picked it up and put it on again without brushing off the wet snow.

The officer's mount still kept dancing on one spot with his ears pricked, while the other horses, also with sharp ears erect to catch every sound, stood motionless looking at the men in black, their long wise heads inclined to one side.

'Spare the boy at least!' another voice suddenly pierced the air. 'Why kill a child, damn you! What has the child done?'

'Ivanov, do what I told you to do,' thundered the officer, drowning the other voice. His face turned as scarlet as a piece of red flannel.

There followed a scene savage and repulsive in its gruesomeness. The short figure in black, with the light hair and the rosy ears, uttered a wild shriek in a shrill child's tones and reeled to one side. Instantly it was caught up by two or three soldiers. But the boy began to struggle, and two more soldiers ran up.

'Ow-ow-ow-ow!' the boy cried. 'Let me go, let me go! Ow-ow!'

His shrill voice cut the air like the yell of a stuck porkling not quite done to death. Suddenly he grew quiet. Some one must have struck him. An unexpected, oppressive silence ensued. The boy was being pushed forward. Then there came a deafening report. Andersen started back all in a tremble. He saw distinctly, yet vaguely as in a dream, the dropping of two dark bodies, the flash of pale sparks, and a light smoke rising in the clean, bright atmosphere. He saw the soldiers hastily mounting their horses without even glancing at the bodies. He saw them galloping along the muddy road, their arms clanking, their horses' hoofs clattering.

He saw all this, himself now standing in the middle of the road, not knowing when and why he had jumped from behind the haystack. He was deathly pale. His face was covered with dank sweat, his body was aquiver. A physical sadness smote and tortured him. He could not make out the nature of the feeling. It was akin to extreme sickness, though far more nauseating and terrible.

After the soldiers had disappeared beyond the bend towards the woods, people came hurrying to the spot of the shooting, though till then not a soul had been in sight.

The bodies lay at the roadside on the other side of the railing, where the snow was clean, brittle and untrampled and glistened cheerfully in the bright atmosphere. There were three dead bodies, two men and a boy. The boy lay with his long soft neck stretched on the snow. The face of the man next to the boy was invisible. He had fallen face downwards in a pool of blood. The third was a big man with a black beard and huge, muscular arms. He lay stretched out to the full length of his big body, his arms extended over a large area of blood-stained snow.

The three men who had been shot lay black against the white snow, motionless. From afar no one could have told the terror that was in their immobility as they lay there at the edge of the narrow road crowded with people.

That night Gabriel Andersen in his little room in the schoolhouse did not write poems as usual. He stood at the window and looked at the distant pale disk of the moon in the misty blue sky, and thought. And his thoughts were confused, gloomy, and heavy as if a cloud had descended upon his brain.

Indistinctly outlined in the dull moonlight he saw the dark railing, the trees, the empty garden. It seemed to him that he beheld them—the three men who had been shot, two grown up, one a child. They were lying there now at the roadside, in the empty, silent field, looking at the far-off cold moon with their dead, white eyes as he with his living eyes.

'The time will come some day,' he thought, 'when the killing of people by others will be an utter impossibility. The time will come when even the soldiers and officers who killed these three men will realize what they have done and will understand that what they killed them for is just as necessary, important, and dear to them—to the officers and soldiers—as to those whom they killed.'

'Yes,' he said aloud and solemnly, his eyes moistening, 'that time will come. They will understand.' And the pale disk of the moon was blotted out by the moisture in his eyes.

A large pity pierced his heart for the three victims whose eyes looked at the moon, sad and unseeing. A feeling of rage cut him as with a sharp knife and took possession of him.

But Gabriel Andersen quieted his heart, whispering softly, 'They know not what they do.' And this old and ready phrase gave him the strength to stifle his rage and indignation.

II

The day was as bright and white, but the spring was already advanced. The wet soil smelt of spring. Clear cold water ran everywhere from under the loose, thawing snow. The branches of the trees were springy and elastic. For miles and miles around, the country opened up in clear azure stretches.

Yet the clearness and the joy of the spring day were not in the village. They were somewhere outside the village, where there were no people—in the fields, the woods and the mountains. In the village the air was stifling, heavy and terrible as in a nightmare.

Gabriel Andersen stood in the road near a crowd of dark, sad, absent-minded people and craned his neck to see the preparations for the flogging of seven peasants.

They stood in the thawing snow, and Gabriel Andersen could not persuade himself that they were people whom he had long known and understood. By that which was about to happen to them, the shameful, terrible, ineradicable thing that was to happen to them, they were separated from all the rest of the world, and so were unable to feel what he, Gabriel Andersen, felt, just as he was unable to feel what they felt. Round them were the soldiers, confidently and beautifully mounted on high upon their large steeds, who tossed their wise heads and turned their dappled wooden faces slowly from side to side, looking contemptuously at him, Gabriel Andersen, who was soon to behold this horror, this disgrace, and would do nothing, would not dare to do anything. So it seemed to Gabriel Andersen; and a sense of cold, intolerable shame gripped him as between two clamps of ice through which he could see everything without being able to move, cry out or utter a groan.

They took the first peasant. Gabriel Andersen saw his strange, imploring, hopeless look. His lips moved, but no sound was heard, and his eyes wandered. There was a bright gleam in them as in the eyes of a madman. His mind, it was evident, was no longer able to comprehend what was happening.

And so terrible was that face, at once full of reason and of madness, that Andersen felt relieved when they put him face downwards on the snow and, instead of the fiery eyes, he saw his bare back glistening—a senseless, shameful, horrible sight.

The large, red-faced soldier in a red cap pushed towards him, looked down at his body with seeming delight, and then cried in a clear voice:

'Well, let her go, with God's blessing!'

Andersen seemed not to see the soldiers, the sky, the horses or the crowd. He did not feel the cold, the terror or the shame. He did not hear the swish of the knout in the air or the savage howl of pain and despair. He only saw the bare back of a man's body swelling up and covered over evenly with white and purple stripes. Gradually the bare back lost the semblance of human flesh. The blood oozed and squirted, forming patches, drops and rivulets, which ran down on the white, thawing snow.

Terror gripped the soul of Gabriel Andersen as he thought of the moment when the man would rise and face all the people who had seen his body bared out in the open and reduced to a bloody pulp. He closed his eyes. When he opened them, he saw four soldiers in uniform and red hats forcing another man down on the snow, his back bared just as shamefully, terribly and absurdly—a ludicrously tragic sight.

Then came the third, the fourth, and so on, to the end.

And Gabriel Andersen stood on the wet, thawing snow, craning his neck, trembling and stuttering, though he did not say a word. Dank sweat poured from his body. A sense of shame permeated his whole being. It was a humiliating feeling, having to escape being noticed so that they should not catch him and lay him there on the snow and strip him bare—him, Gabriel Andersen.

The soldiers pressed and crowded, the horses tossed their heads, the knout swished in the air, and the bare, shamed human flesh swelled up, tore, ran over with blood, and curled like a snake. Oaths, wild shrieks rained upon the village through the clean white air of that spring day.

Andersen now saw five men's faces at the steps of the town hall, the faces of those men who had already undergone their shame. He quickly turned his eyes away. After seeing this a man must die, he thought.

III

There were seventeen of them, fifteen soldiers, a subaltern and a young beardless officer. The officer lay in front of the fire looking intently into the flames. The soldiers were tinkering with the firearms in the wagon.

Their grey figures moved about quietly on the black thawing ground, and occasionally stumbled across the logs sticking out from the blazing fire.

Gabriel Andersen, wearing an overcoat and carrying his cane behind his back, approached them. The subaltern, a stout fellow with a moustache, jumped up, turned from the fire, and looked at him.

'Who are you? What do you want?' he asked excitedly. From his tone it was evident that the soldiers feared everybody in that district, through which they went scattering death, destruction and torture.

'Officer,' he said, 'there is a man here I don't know.'

The officer looked at Andersen without speaking.

'Officer,' said Andersen in a thin, strained voice, 'my name is Michelson. I am a business man here, and I am going to the village on business. I was afraid I might be mistaken for some one else—you know.'

'Then what are you nosing about here for?' the officer said angrily, and turned away.

'A business man,' sneered a soldier. 'He ought to be searched, this business man ought, so as not to be knocking about at night. A good one in the jaw is what he needs.'

'He's a suspicious character, officer,' said the subaltern. 'Don't you think we'd better arrest him, what?'

'Don't,' answered the officer lazily. 'I'm sick of them, damn 'em.'

Gabriel Andersen stood there without saying anything. His eyes flashed strangely in the dark by the firelight. And it was strange to see his short, substantial, clean, neat figure in the field at night among the soldiers, with his overcoat and cane and glasses glistening in the firelight.

The soldiers left him and walked away. Gabriel Andersen remained standing for a while. Then he turned and left, rapidly disappearing in the darkness.

The night was drawing to a close. The air turned chilly, and the tops of the bushes defined themselves more clearly in the dark. Gabriel Andersen went again to the military post. But this time he hid, crouching low as he made his way under the cover of the bushes. Behind him people moved about quietly and carefully, bending the bushes, silent as shadows. Next to Gabriel, on his right, walked a tall man with a revolver in his hand.

The figure of a soldier on the hill outlined itself strangely, unexpectedly, not where they had been looking for it. It was faintly illumined by the gleam from the dying fire. Gabriel Andersen recognized the soldier. It was the one who had proposed that he should be searched. Nothing stirred in Andersen's heart. His face was cold and motionless, as of a man who is asleep. Round the fire the soldiers lay stretched out sleeping, all except the subaltern, who sat with his head drooping over his knees.

The tall thin man on Andersen's right raised the revolver and pulled the trigger. A momentary blinding flash, a deafening report.

Andersen saw the guard lift his hands and then sit down

on the ground clasping his bosom. From all directions short, crackling sparks flashed up which combined into one riving roar. The subaltern jumped up and dropped straight into the fire. Grey soldiers' figures moved about in all directions like apparitions, throwing up their hands and falling and writhing on the black earth. The young officer ran past Andersen, fluttering his hands like some strange, frightened bird. Andersen, as if he were thinking of something else, raised his cane. With all his strength he hit the officer on the head, each blow descending with a dull, ugly thud. The officer reeled in a circle, struck a bush, and sat down after the second blow, covering his head with both hands, as children do. Some one ran up and discharged a revolver as if from Andersen's own hand. The officer sank together in a heap and lunged with great force head foremost on the ground. His legs twitched for a while, then he curled up quietly.

The shots ceased. Black men with white faces, ghostly grey in the dark, moved about the dead bodies of the soldiers, taking away their arms and ammunition.

Andersen watched all this with a cold, attentive stare. When all was over, he went up, took hold of the burned subaltern's legs, and tried to remove the body from the fire. But it was too heavy for him, and he let it go.

IV

Andersen sat motionless on the steps of the town hall, and thought. He thought of how he, Gabriel Andersen, with his spectacles, cane, overcoat and poems, had lied and betrayed fifteen men. He thought it was terrible, yet there was neither pity, shame nor regret in his heart. Were he to be set free, he knew that he, Gabriel Andersen, with the spectacles and poems, would go straightway and do it again. He tried to examine himself, to see what was going on inside his soul. But his thoughts were heavy and confused. For some reason it was more painful for him to think of the three men lying on the snow, looking at the pale disk of the far-off moon with their dead, unseeing eyes, than of the murdered officer whom he had struck two dry, ugly blows on the head. Of his own death he did not think. It seemed to him that he had done with everything long, long ago. Something had died, had gone out and left him empty, and he must not think about it.

And when they grabbed him by the shoulder and he rose, and they quickly led him through the garden where the cabbages raised their dry heads, he could not formulate a single thought.

He was conducted to the road and placed at the railing with his back to one of the iron bars. He fixed his spectacles, put his hands behind him, and stood there with his neat, stocky body, his head slightly inclined to one side.

At the last moment he looked in front of him and saw rifle barrels pointing at his head, chest and stomach, and pale faces with trembling lips. He distinctly saw how one barrel levelled at his forehead suddenly dropped.

Something strange and incomprehensible, as if no longer of this world, no longer earthly, passed through Andersen's mind. He straightened himself to the full height of his short body and threw back his head in simple pride. A strange indistinct sense of cleanness, strength and pride filled his soul, and everything—the sun and the sky and the people and the field and death—seemed to him insignificant, remote and useless.

The bullets hit him in the chest, in the left eye, in the stomach, went through his clean coat buttoned all the way up. His glasses shivered into bits. He uttered a shriek, circled round, and fell with his face against one of the iron bars, his one remaining eye wide open. He clawed the ground with his outstretched hands as if trying to support himself.

The officer, who had turned green, rushed towards him, and

senselessly thrust the revolver against his neck, and fired twice. Andersen stretched out on the ground.

The soldiers left quickly. But Andersen remained pressed flat to the ground. The index finger of his left hand continued to quiver for about ten seconds.

9

THE SHOT

Alexander Pushkin

I

We were stationed in the little town of N—. The life of an officer in the army is well known. In the morning, drill and the riding-school; dinner with the Colonel or at a Jewish restaurant; in the evening, punch and cards. In N— there was not one open house, not a single marriageable girl. We used to meet in each other's rooms, where, except our uniforms, we never saw anything.

One civilian only was admitted into our society. He was about thirty-five years of age, and therefore we looked upon him as an old fellow. His experience gave him great advantage over us, and his habitual taciturnity, stern disposition, and caustic tongue produced a deep impression upon our young minds. Some mystery surrounded his existence; he had the appearance of a Russian, although his name was a foreign one. He had formerly served in the Hussars, and with distinction. Nobody knew the cause that had induced him to retire from the service and settle in a wretched little village, where he lived poorly and, at the same time, extravagantly. He always went on foot, and constantly wore a shabby black overcoat, but the officers of our regiment were ever welcome at his table. His dinners, it is true, never consisted of more than two or three dishes, prepared by a retired soldier, but the champagne flowed like water. Nobody knew what his circumstances were, or what his income was, and nobody dared to question him about them. He had a collection of books, consisting chiefly of works on military matters and a few novels. He willingly lent them to us to read, and never asked for them back; on the other hand, he never returned to the owner the books that were lent to him. His principal amusement was shooting with a pistol. The walls of his room were riddled with bullets, and were as full of holes as a honeycomb. A rich collection of pistols was the only luxury in the humble cottage where he lived. The skill which he had acquired with his favourite weapon was simply incredible; and if he had offered to shoot a pear off somebody's forage-cap, not a man in our regiment would have hesitated to place the object upon his head.

Our conversation often turned upon duels. Silvio—so I will call him—never joined in it. When asked if he had ever fought, he dryly replied that he had; but he entered into no particulars, and it was evident that such questions were not to his liking. We came to the conclusion that he had upon his conscience the memory of some unhappy victim of his terrible skill. Moreover, it never entered into the head of any of us to suspect him of anything like cowardice. There are persons whose mere look is sufficient to repel such a suspicion. But an unexpected incident occurred which astounded us all.

One day, about ten of our officers dined with Silvio. They drank as usual, that is to say, a great deal. After dinner we asked our host to hold the bank for a game at faro. For a long time he refused, for he hardly ever played, but at last he ordered cards to be brought, placed half a hundred ducats upon the table, and sat down to deal. We took our places round him, and the play began. It was Silvio's custom to preserve a complete silence when playing. He never disputed, and never entered into explanations. If the punter made a mistake in calculating, he immediately paid him the difference or noted down the surplus. We were acquainted with this habit of his, and we always allowed him to have his own way; but among us on this occasion was an officer who had only recently been transferred to our regiment. During the course of the game, this officer absently scored one point too many. Silvio took the chalk and noted down the correct account according to his usual custom. The officer, thinking that he had made a mistake, began to enter into explanations. Silvio continued dealing in silence. The officer, losing patience, took the brush and rubbed out what he considered was wrong. Silvio took the chalk and corrected the score again. The officer, heated with wine, play, and the laughter of his comrades, considered himself grossly insulted, and in his rage he seized a brass candlestick from the table, and hurled it at Silvio, who barely succeeded in avoiding the missile. We were filled with consternation. Silvio rose, white with rage, and with gleaming eyes, said:

'My dear sir, have the goodness to withdraw, and thank God that this has happened in my house.'

None of us entertained the slightest doubt as to what the result would be, and we already looked upon our new comrade as a dead man. The officer withdrew, saying that he was ready to answer for his offence in whatever way the banker liked. The play went on for a few minutes longer, but feeling that our host was no longer interested in the game, we withdrew one after the other, and repaired to our respective quarters, after having exchanged a few words upon the probability of there soon being a vacancy in the regiment.

The next day, at the riding-school, we were already asking each other if the poor lieutenant was still alive, when he himself appeared among us. We put the same question to him, and he replied that he had not yet heard from Silvio. This astonished us. We went to Silvio's house and found him in the courtyard shooting bullet after bullet into an ace pasted upon the gate. He received us as usual, but did not utter a word about the event of the previous evening. Three days passed, and the lieutenant was still alive. We asked each other in astonishment: 'Can it be possible that Silvio is not going to fight?'

Silvio did not fight. He was satisfied with a very lame explanation, and became reconciled to his assailant.

This lowered him very much in the opinion of all our young fellows. Want of courage is the last thing to be pardoned by young men, who usually look upon bravery as the chief of all human virtues, and the excuse for every possible fault. But, by degrees, everything became forgotten, and Silvio regained his former influence.

I alone could not approach him on the old footing. Being endowed by nature with a romantic imagination, I had become attached more than all the others to the man whose life was an enigma, and who seemed to me the hero of some mysterious drama. He was fond of me; at least, with me alone did he drop his customary sarcastic tone, and converse on different subjects in a simple and unusually agreeable manner. But after this unlucky evening, the thought that his honour had been tarnished, and that the stain had been allowed to remain upon it in accordance with his own wish, was ever present in my mind, and prevented me treating him as before. I was ashamed to look at him. Silvio was too intelligent and experienced not to observe this and guess the cause of it. This seemed to vex him; at least I observed once or twice a desire on his part to enter into an explanation with me, but I avoided such opportunities, and Silvio gave up the attempt. From that time forward I saw him only in the presence of my comrades, and our confidential conversations came to an end.

The inhabitants of the capital, with minds occupied by so many matters of business and pleasure, have no idea of the many sensations so familiar to the inhabitants of villages and small towns, as, for instance, the awaiting the arrival of the post. On Tuesdays and Fridays our regimental bureau used to be filled with officers: some expecting money, some letters, and others newspapers. The packets were usually opened on the spot, items of news were communicated from one to another, and the bureau used to present a very animated picture. Silvio used to have his letters addressed to our regiment, and he was generally there to receive them.

One day he received a letter, the seal of which he broke with a look of great impatience. As he read the contents, his eyes sparkled. The officers, each occupied with his own letters, did not observe anything.

'Gentlemen,' said Silvio, 'circumstances demand my immediate departure; I leave to-night. I hope that you will not refuse to dine with me for the last time. I shall expect you, too,' he added, turning towards me. 'I shall expect you without fail.'

With these words he hastily departed, and we, after agreeing to meet at Silvio's, dispersed to our various quarters.

I arrived at Silvio's house at the appointed time, and found nearly the whole regiment there. All his things were already packed; nothing remained but the bare, bullet-riddled walls. We sat down to table. Our host was in an excellent humour, and his gayety was quickly communicated to the rest. Corks popped every moment, glasses foamed incessantly, and, with the utmost warmth, we wished our departing friend a pleasant journey and every happiness. When we rose from the table it was already late in the evening. After having wished everybody good-bye, Silvio took me by the hand and detained me just at the moment when I was preparing to depart.

'I want to speak to you,' he said in a low voice.

I stopped behind.

The guests had departed, and we two were left alone. Sitting down opposite each other, we silently lit our pipes. Silvio seemed greatly troubled; not a trace remained of his former convulsive gayety. The intense pallor of his face, his sparkling eyes, and the thick smoke issuing from his mouth, gave him a truly diabolical appearance. Several minutes elapsed, and then Silvio broke the silence.

'Perhaps we shall never see each other again' said he; 'before we part, I should like to have an explanation with you. You may have observed that I care very little for the opinion of other people, but I like you, and I feel that it would be painful to me to leave you with a wrong impression upon your mind.'

He paused, and began to knock the ashes out of his pipe. I sat gazing silently at the ground.

'You thought it strange,' he continued, 'that I did not demand satisfaction from that drunken idiot R——. You will admit, however, that having the choice of weapons, his life was in my hands, while my own was in no great danger. I could ascribe my forbearance to generosity alone, but I will not tell a lie. If I could have chastised R——without the least risk to my own life, I should never have pardoned him.'

I looked at Silvio with astonishment. Such a confession completely astounded me. Silvio continued:

'Exactly so: I have no right to expose myself to death. Six years ago I received a slap in the face, and my enemy still lives.'

My curiosity was greatly excited.

'Did you not fight with him?' I asked. 'Circumstances probably separated you.'

'I did fight with him,' replied Silvio; 'and here is a souvenir of our duel.'

Silvio rose and took from a cardboard box a red cap with a gold tassel and embroidery (what the French call a *bonnet de police*); he put it on—a bullet had passed through it about an inch above the forehead.

'You know,' continued Silvio, 'that I served in one of the Hussar regiments. My character is well known to you: I am accustomed to taking the lead. From my youth this has been my passion. In our time dissoluteness was the fashion, and I was the most outrageous man in the army. We used to boast of our drunkenness; I beat in a drinking bout the famous Bourtsoff, of whom Denis Davidoff has sung. Duels in our regiment were constantly taking place, and in all of them I was either second or principal. My comrades adored me, while the regimental commanders, who were constantly being changed, looked upon me as a necessary evil.

'I was calmly enjoying my reputation, when a young man belonging to a wealthy and distinguished family—I will not mention his name—joined our regiment. Never in my life have I met with such a fortunate fellow! Imagine to yourself youth, wit, beauty, unbounded gayety, the most reckless bravery, a famous name, untold wealth imagine all these, and you can form some idea of the effect that he would be sure to produce among us. My supremacy was shaken. Dazzled by my reputation, he began to seek my friendship, but I received him coldly, and without the least regret he held aloof from me. I took a hatred to him. His success in the regiment and in the society of ladies brought me to the verge of despair. I began to seek a quarrel with him; to my epigrams he replied with epigrams which always seemed to me more spontaneous and more cutting than mine, and which were decidedly more amusing, for he joked while I fumed. At last, at a ball given by a Polish landed proprietor, seeing him the object of the attention of all the ladies, and especially of the mistress of the house, with whom I was upon very good terms, I whispered some grossly insulting remark in his ear. He flamed up and gave me a slap in the face. We grasped our swords; the ladies fainted; we were separated; and that same night we set out to fight.

'The dawn was just breaking. I was standing at the appointed place with my three seconds. With inexplicable impatience I awaited my opponent. The spring sun rose, and it was already growing hot. I saw him coming in the distance. He was walking on foot, accompanied by one second. We advanced to meet him.

He approached, holding his cap filled with black cherries. The seconds measured twelve paces for us. I had to fire first, but my agitation was so great, that I could not depend upon the steadiness of my hand; and in order to give myself time to become calm, I ceded to him the first shot. My adversary would not agree to this. It was decided that we should cast lots. The first number fell to him, the constant favourite of fortune. He took aim, and his bullet went through my cap. It was now my turn. His life at last was in my hands; I looked at him eagerly, endeavouring to detect if only the faintest shadow of uneasiness. But he stood in front of my pistol, picking out the ripest cherries from his cap and spitting out the stones, which flew almost as far as my feet. His indifference annoyed me beyond measure. 'What is the use,' thought I, 'of depriving him of life, when he attaches no value whatever to it?' A malicious thought flashed through my mind. I lowered my pistol.

"'You don't seem to be ready for death just at present," I said to him: "you wish to have your breakfast; I do not wish to hinder you."

"'You are not hindering me in the least," replied he. "Have the goodness to fire, or just as you please—the shot remains yours; I shall always be ready at your service."

'I turned to the seconds, informing them that I had no intention of firing that day, and with that the duel came to an end.

'I resigned my commission and retired to this little place. Since then not a day has passed that I have not thought of revenge. And now my hour has arrived.'

Silvio took from his pocket the letter that he had received that morning, and gave it to me to read. Some one (it seemed to be his business agent) wrote to him from Moscow, that *a certain person* was going to be married to a young and beautiful girl.

'You can guess,' said Silvio, 'who the certain person is. I am going to Moscow. We shall see if he will look death in the face with as much indifference now, when he is on the eve of being married, as he did once with his cherries!'

With these words, Silvio rose, threw his cap upon the floor, and began pacing up and down the room like a tiger in his cage. I had listened to him in silence; strange conflicting feelings agitated me.

The servant entered and announced that the horses were ready. Silvio grasped my hand tightly, and we embraced each other. He seated himself in his *telega*, in which lay two trunks, one containing his pistols, the other his effects. We said goodbye once more, and the horses galloped off.

II

Several years passed, and family circumstances compelled me to settle in the poor little village of M—. Occupied with agricultural pursuits, I ceased not to sigh in secret for my former noisy and careless life. The most difficult thing of all was having to accustom myself to passing the spring and winter evenings in perfect solitude. Until the hour for dinner I managed to pass away the time somehow or other, talking with the bailiff, riding about to inspect the work, or going round to look at the new buildings; but as soon as it began to get dark, I positively did not know what to do with myself. The few books that I had found in the cupboards and storerooms I already knew by heart. All the stories that my housekeeper Kirilovna could remember I had heard over and over again. The songs of the peasant women made me feel depressed. I tried drinking spirits, but it made my headache; and moreover, I confess I was afraid of becoming a drunkard from mere chagrin, that is to say, the saddest kind of drunkard, of which I had seen many examples in our district.

I had no near neighbours, except two or three topers, whose

conversation consisted for the most part of hiccups and sighs. Solitude was preferable to their society. At last I decided to go to bed as early as possible, and to dine as late as possible; in this way I shortened the evening and lengthened out the day, and I found that the plan answered very well.

Four versts from my house was a rich estate belonging to the Countess B——; but nobody lived there except the steward. The Countess had only visited her estate once, in the first year of her married life, and then she had remained there no longer than a month. But in the second spring of my hermitical life a report was circulated that the Countess, with her husband, was coming to spend the summer on her estate. The report turned out to be true, for they arrived at the beginning of June.

The arrival of a rich neighbour is an important event in the lives of country people. The landed proprietors and the people of their households talk about it for two months beforehand and for three years afterwards. As for me, I must confess that the news of the arrival of a young and beautiful neighbour affected me strongly. I burned with impatience to see her, and the first Sunday after her arrival I set out after dinner for the village of A——, to pay my respects to the Countess and her husband, as their nearest neighbour and most humble servant.

A lackey conducted me into the Count's study, and then went to announce me. The spacious apartment was furnished with every possible luxury. Around the walls were cases filled with books and surmounted by bronze busts; over the marble mantelpiece was a large mirror; on the floor was a green cloth covered with carpets. Unaccustomed to luxury in my own poor corner, and not having seen the wealth of other people for a long time, I awaited the appearance of the Count with some little trepidation, as a suppliant from the provinces awaits the arrival of the minister. The door opened, and a handsome-looking man, of about thirty-two years of age, entered the room. The Count approached me with a frank and friendly air; I endeavoured to be self-possessed and began to introduce myself, but he anticipated me. We sat down. His conversation, which was easy and agreeable, soon dissipated my awkward bashfulness; and I was already beginning to recover my usual composure, when the Countess suddenly entered, and I became more confused than ever. She was indeed beautiful. The Count presented me. I wished to appear at ease, but the more I tried to assume an air of unconstraint, the more awkward I felt. They, in order to give me time to recover myself and to become accustomed to my new acquaintances, began to talk to each other, treating me as a good neighbour, and without ceremony. Meanwhile, I walked about the room, examining the books and pictures. I am no judge of pictures, but one of them attracted my attention. It represented some view in Switzerland, but it was not the painting that struck me, but the circumstance that the canvas was shot through by two bullets, one planted just above the other.

'A good shot that!' said I, turning to the Count.

'Yes,' replied he, 'a very remarkable shot... Do you shoot well?' he continued.

'Tolerably,' replied I, rejoicing that the conversation had turned at last upon a subject that was familiar to me. 'At thirty paces I can manage to hit a card without fail,—I mean, of course, with a pistol that I am used to.'

'Really?' said the Countess, with a look of the greatest interest. 'And you, my dear, could you hit a card at thirty paces?'

'Some day,' replied the Count, 'we will try. In my time I did not shoot badly, but it is now four years since I touched a pistol.'

'Oh!' I observed, 'in that case, I don't mind laying a wager that Your Excellency will not hit the card at twenty paces; the pistol demands practice every day. I know that from experience. In our regiment I was reckoned one of the best shots. It once happened that I did not touch a pistol for a whole month, as

I had sent mine to be mended; and would you believe it, Your Excellency, the first time I began to shoot again, I missed a bottle four times in succession at twenty paces. Our captain, a witty and amusing fellow, happened to be standing by, and he said to me: 'It is evident, my friend, that your hand will not lift itself against the bottle.' No, Your Excellency, you must not neglect to practise, or your hand will soon lose its cunning. The best shot that I ever met used to shoot at least three times every day before dinner. It was as much his custom to do this as it was to drink his daily glass of brandy.'

The Count and Countess seemed pleased that I had begun to talk.

'And what sort of a shot was he?' asked the Count.

'Well, it was this way with him, Your Excellency: if he saw a fly settle on the wall—you smile, Countess, but, before Heaven, it is the truth—if he saw a fly, he would call out: 'Kouzka, my pistol!' Kouzka would bring him a loaded pistol—bang! and the fly would be crushed against the wall.'

'Wonderful!' said the Count. 'And what was his name?'

'Silvio, Your Excellency.'

'Silvio!' exclaimed the Count, starting up. 'Did you know Silvio?'

'How could I help knowing him, Your Excellency: we were intimate friends; he was received in our regiment like a brother officer, but it is now five years since I had any tidings of him. Then Your Excellency also knew him?'

'Oh, yes, I knew him very well. Did he ever tell you of one very strange incident in his life?'

'Does Your Excellency refer to the slap in the face that he received from some blackguard at a ball?'

'Did he tell you the name of this blackguard?'

'No, Your Excellency, he never mentioned his name... Ah! Your Excellency!' I continued, guessing the the truth: 'pardon me... I did not know...could it really have been you?'

'Yes, I myself,' replied the Count, with a look of extraordinary agitation;' and that bullet-pierced picture is a memento of our last meeting.'

'Ah, my dear,' said the Countess, 'for Heaven's sake, do not speak about that; it would be too terrible for me to listen to.'

'No,' replied the Count: 'I will relate everything. He knows how I insulted his friend, and it is only right that he should know how Silvio revenged himself.

The Count pushed a chair towards me, and with the liveliest interest I listened to the following story:

'Five years ago I got married. The first month—the honeymoon—I spent here, in this village. To this house I am indebted for the happiest moments of my life, as well as for one of its most painful recollections.

'One evening we went out together for a ride on horseback. My wife's horse became restive; she grew frightened, gave the reins to me, and returned home on foot. I rode on before. In the courtyard I saw a travelling carriage, and I was told that in my study sat waiting for me a man, who would not give his name, but who merely said that he had business with me. I entered the room and saw in the darkness a man, covered with dust and wearing a beard of several days' growth. He was standing there, near the fireplace. I approached him, trying to remember his features.

'"You do not recognize me, Count?" said he, in a quivering voice.

'"Silvio!" I cried, and I confess that I felt as if my hair had suddenly stood on end.

'"Exactly," continued he. "There is a shot due to me, and I have come to discharge my pistol. Are you ready?"

'His pistol protruded from a side pocket. I measured twelve paces and took my stand there in that corner, begging him to fire quickly, before my wife arrived. He hesitated, and asked for a light. Candles were brought in. I closed the doors, gave orders that nobody was to enter, and again begged him to fire. He drew out his pistol and took aim... I counted the seconds... I thought of her... A terrible minute passed! Silvio lowered his hand.

"'I regret,' said he, "that the pistol is not loaded with cherry-stones...the bullet is heavy. It seems to me that this is not a duel, but a murder. I am not accustomed to taking aim at unarmed men. Let us begin all over again; we will cast lots as to who shall fire first."

'My head went round... I think I raised some objection... At last we loaded another pistol, and rolled up two pieces of paper. He placed these latter in his cap—the same through which I had once sent a bullet—and again I drew the first number.

"'You are devilish lucky, Count," said he, with a smile that I shall never forget.

'I don't know what was the matter with me, or how it was that he managed to make me do it...but I fired and hit that picture.'

The Count pointed with his finger to the perforated picture; his face glowed like fire; the Countess was whiter than her own handkerchief; and I could not restrain an exclamation.

'I fired,' continued the Count, 'and, thank Heaven, missed my aim. Then Silvio...at that moment he was really terrible... Silvio raised his hand to take aim at me. Suddenly the door opens, Masha rushes into the room, and with a loud shriek throws herself upon my neck. Her presence restored to me all my courage.

"'My dear," said I to her, "don't you see that we are joking? How frightened you are! Go and drink a glass of water and then come back to us; I will introduce you to an old friend and comrade."

'Masha still doubted.

'"Tell me, is my husband speaking the truth?" said she, turning to the terrible Silvio: "is it true that you are only joking?"

'"He is always joking, Countess," replied Silvio: "once he gave me a slap in the face in a joke; on another occasion he sent a bullet through my cap in a joke; and just now, when he fired at me and missed me, it was all in a joke. And now I feel inclined for a joke."

'With these words he raised his pistol to take aim at me—right before her! Masha threw herself at his feet.

'"Rise, Masha; are you not ashamed!" I cried in a rage: "and you, sir, will you cease to make fun of a poor woman? Will you fire or not?"

'"I will not," replied Silvio: "I am satisfied. I have seen your confusion, your alarm. I forced you to fire at me. That is sufficient. You will remember me. I leave you to your conscience."

'Then he turned to go, but pausing in the doorway, and looking at the picture that my shot had passed through, he fired at it almost without taking aim, and disappeared. My wife had fainted away; the servants did not venture to stop him, the mere look of him filled them with terror. He went out upon the steps, called his coachman, and drove off before I could recover myself.'

The Count was silent. In this way I learned the end of the story, whose beginning had once made such a deep impression upon me. The hero of it I never saw again. It is said that Silvio commanded a detachment of Hetairists during the revolt under Alexander Ipsilanti, and that he was killed in the battle of Skoulana.

10

EPIPHANY

Guy de Maupassant

I should say I did remember that Epiphany supper during the war! exclaimed Count de Garens, an army captain.

I was quartermaster of cavalry at the time, and for a fortnight had been scouting in front of the German advance guard. The evening before we had cut down a few Uhlans and had lost three men, one of whom was that poor little Raudeville. You remember Joseph de Raudeville, of course.

Well, on that day my commanding officer ordered me to take six troopers and to go and occupy the village of Porterin, where there had been five skirmishes in three weeks, and to hold it all night. There were not twenty houses left standing, not a dozen houses in that wasps' nest. So I took ten troopers and set out about four o'clock, and at five o'clock, while it was still pitch dark, we reached the first houses of Porterin. I halted and ordered Marchas—you know Pierre de Marchas, who afterwards married little Martel-Auvelin, the daughter of the Marquis de Martel-Auvelin—to go alone into the village, and to report to me what he saw.

I had selected nothing but volunteers, all men of good family. It is pleasant when on duty not to be forced to be on intimate terms with unpleasant fellows. This Marchas was as smart as possible, cunning as a fox and supple as a serpent. He could scent the Prussians as a dog can scent a hare, could discover food where we should have died of hunger without him, and obtained information from everybody, and information which was always reliable, with incredible cleverness.

In ten minutes he returned. 'All right,' he said; 'there have been no Prussians here for three days. It is a sinister place, is this village. I have been talking to a Sister of Mercy, who is caring for four or five wounded men in an abandoned convent.'

I ordered them to ride on, and we entered the principal street. On the right and left we could vaguely see roofless walls, which were hardly visible in the profound darkness. Here and there a light was burning in a room; some family had remained to keep its house standing as well as they were able; a family of brave or of poor people. The rain began to fall, a fine, icy cold rain, which froze as it fell on our cloaks. The horses stumbled against stones, against beams, against furniture. Marchas guided us, going before us on foot, and leading his horse by the bridle.

'Where are you taking us to?' I asked him. And he replied: 'I have a place for us to lodge in, and a rare good one.' And we presently stopped before a small house, evidently belonging to some proprietor of the middle class. It stood on the street, was quite inclosed, and had a garden in the rear.

Marchas forced open the lock by means of a big stone which he picked up near the garden gate; then he mounted the steps, smashed in the front door with his feet and shoulders, lit a bit of wax candle, which he was never without, and went before us into the comfortable apartments of some rich private individual, guiding us with admirable assurance, as if he lived in this house which he now saw for the first time.

Two troopers remained outside to take care of our horses, and Marchas said to stout Ponderel, who followed him: 'The stables must be on the left; I saw that as we came in; go and put the animals up there, for we do not need them'; and then, turning to me, he said: 'Give your orders, confound it all!'

This fellow always astonished me, and I replied with a laugh:

'I will post my sentinels at the country approaches and will return to you here.'

'How many men are you going to take?'

'Five. The others will relieve them at five o'clock in the evening.'

'Very well. Leave me four to look after provisions, to do the cooking and to set the table. I will go and find out where the wine is hidden.'

I went off, to reconnoitre the deserted streets until they ended in the open country, so as to post my sentries there.

Half an hour later I was back, and found Marchas lounging in a great easy-chair, the covering of which he had taken off, from love of luxury, as he said. He was warming his feet at the fire and smoking an excellent cigar, whose perfume filled the room. He was alone, his elbows resting on the arms of the chair, his head sunk between his shoulders, his cheeks flushed, his eyes bright, and looking delighted.

I heard the noise of plates and dishes in the next room, and Marchas said to me, smiling in a contented manner: 'This is famous; I found the champagne under the flight of steps outside, the brandy—fifty bottles of the very finest in the kitchen garden under a pear tree, which did not seem to me to be quite straight when I looked at it by the light of my lantern. As for solids, we have two fowls, a goose, a duck, and three pigeons. They are being cooked at this moment. It is a delightful district.'

I sat down opposite him, and the fire in the grate was burning my nose and cheeks. 'Where did you find this wood?' I asked. 'Splendid wood,' he replied. 'The owner's carriage. It is the paint which is causing all this flame, an essence of punch and varnish. A capital house!'

I laughed, for I saw the creature was funny, and he went on: 'Fancy this being the Epiphany! I have had a bean put into the goose dressing; but there is no queen; it is really very annoying!'

And I repeated like an echo: 'It is annoying, but what do you want me to do in the matter?' 'To find some, of course.' 'Some women. Women?—you must be mad?' 'I managed to find the brandy under the pear tree, and the champagne under the steps; and yet there was nothing to guide me, while as for you, a petticoat is a sure bait. Go and look, old fellow.'

He looked so grave, so convinced, that I could not tell whether he was joking or not, and so I replied: 'Look here, Marchas, are you having a joke with me?' 'I never joke on duty.' 'But where the devil do you expect me to find any women?' 'Where you like; there must be two or three remaining in the neighbourhood, so ferret them out and bring them here.'

I got up, for it was too hot in front of the fire, and Marchas went off:

'Do you want an idea?' 'Yes.' 'Go and see the priest.' 'The priest? What for?' 'Ask him to supper, and beg him to bring a woman with him.' 'The priest! A woman! Ha! ha! ha!'

But Marchas continued with extraordinary gravity: 'I am not laughing; go and find the priest and tell him how we are situated, and, as he must be horribly dull, he will come. But tell him that we want one woman at least, a lady, of course, since we, are all men of the world. He is sure to know his female parishioners on the tips of his fingers, and if there is one to suit us, and you manage it well, he will suggest her to you.'

'Come, come, Marchas, what are you thinking of?' 'My dear Garens, you can do this quite well. It will even be very funny. We are well bred, by Jove! and we will put on our most distinguished manners and our grandest style. Tell the abbe who we are, make him laugh, soften his heart, coax him and persuade him!' 'No, it is impossible.'

He drew his chair close to mine, and as he knew my special weakness, the scamp continued: 'Just think what a swaggering thing it will be to do and how amusing to tell about; the whole army will talk about it, and it will give you a famous reputation.'

I hesitated, for the adventure rather tempted me, and he persisted: 'Come, my little Garens. You are the head of this detachment, and you alone can go and call on the head of the church in this neighbourhood. I beg of you to go, and I promise you that after the war I will relate the whole affair in verse in the Revue de Deux Mondes. You owe this much to your men, for you have made them march enough during the last month.'

I got up at last and asked: 'Where is the priest's house?' 'Take the second turning at the end of the street, you will see an avenue, and at the end of the avenue you will find the church. The parsonage is beside it.' As I went out, he called out: 'Tell him the bill of fare, to make him hungry!'

I discovered the ecclesiastic's little house without any difficulty; it was by the side of a large, ugly brick church. I knocked at the door with my fist, as there was neither bell nor knocker, and a loud voice from inside asked: 'Who is there?' To which I replied: 'A quartermaster of hussars.'

I heard the noise of bolts and of a key being turned, and found myself face to face with a tall priest with a large stomach, the chest of a prizefighter, formidable hands projecting from turned-up sleeves, a red face, and the look of a kind man. I gave him a military salute and said: 'Good-day, Monsieur le Cure.'

He had feared a surprise, some marauders' ambush, and he smiled as he replied: 'Good-day, my friend; come in.' I followed him into a small room with a red tiled floor, in which a small fire was burning, very different to Marchas' furnace, and he gave me a chair and said: 'What can I do for you?' 'Monsieur, allow me first of all to introduce myself'; and I gave him my card, which he took and read half aloud: 'Le Comte de Garens.'

I continued: 'There are eleven of us here, Monsieur l'Abbe, five on picket duty, and six installed at the house of an unknown inhabitant. The names of the six are: Garens, myself; Pierre de

Marchas, Ludovic de Ponderel, Baron d'Streillis, Karl Massouligny, the painter's son, and Joseph Herbon, a young musician. I have come to ask you, in their name and my own, to do us the honour of supping with us. It is an Epiphany supper, Monsieur le Cure, and we should like to make it a little cheerful.'

The priest smiled and murmured: 'It seems to me to be hardly a suitable occasion for amusing one's self.' And I replied: 'We are fighting during the day, monsieur. Fourteen of our comrades have been killed in a month, and three fell as late as yesterday. It is war time. We stake our life at every moment; have we not, therefore, the right to amuse ourselves freely? We are Frenchmen, we like to laugh, and we can laugh everywhere. Our fathers laughed on the scaffold! This evening we should like to cheer ourselves up a little, like gentlemen, and not like soldiers; you understand me, I hope. Are we wrong?'

He replied quickly: 'You are quite right, my friend, and I accept your invitation with great pleasure.' Then he called out: 'Hermance!'

An old bent, wrinkled, horrible peasant woman appeared and said: 'What do you want?' 'I shall not dine at home, my daughter.' 'Where are you going to dine then?' 'With some gentlemen, the hussars.'

I felt inclined to say: 'Bring your servant with you,' just to see Marchas' face, but I did not venture, and continued: 'Do you know any one among your parishioners, male or female, whom I could invite as well?' He hesitated, reflected, and then said: 'No, I do not know anybody!'

I persisted: 'Nobody! Come, monsieur, think; it would be very nice to have some ladies, I mean to say, some married couples! I know nothing about your parishioners. The baker and his wife, the grocer, the—the—the—watchmaker—the—shoemaker—the—the druggist with Mrs Druggist. We have a good spread and plenty of wine, and we should be enchanted to leave pleasant recollections of ourselves with the people here.'

The priest thought again for a long time, and then said resolutely: 'No, there is nobody.' I began to laugh. 'By Jove, Monsieur le Cure, it is very annoying not to have an Epiphany queen, for we have the bean. Come, think. Is there not a married mayor, or a married deputy mayor, or a married municipal councillor or a schoolmaster?' 'No, all the ladies have gone away.' 'What, is there not in the whole place some good tradesman's wife with her good tradesman, to whom we might give this pleasure, for it would be a pleasure to them, a great pleasure under present circumstances?'

But, suddenly, the cure began to laugh, and laughed so violently that he fairly shook, and presently exclaimed: 'Ha! ha! ha! I have got what you want, yes. I have got what you want! Ha! ha! ha! We will laugh and enjoy ourselves, my children; we will have some fun. How pleased the ladies will be, I say, how delighted they will be! Ha! ha! Where are you staying?'

I described the house, and he understood where it was. 'Very good,' he said. 'It belongs to Monsieur Bertin-Lavaille. I will be there in half an hour, with four ladies! Ha! ha! ha! four ladies!'

He went out with me, still laughing, and left me, repeating: 'That is capital; in half an hour at Bertin-Lavaille's house.'

I returned quickly, very much astonished and very much puzzled. 'Covers for how many?' Marchas asked, as soon as he saw me. 'Eleven. There are six of us hussars, besides the priest and four ladies.' He was thunderstruck, and I was triumphant. He repeated: 'Four ladies! Did you say, four ladies?' 'I said four women.' 'Real women?' 'Real women.' 'Well, accept my compliments!' 'I will, for I deserve them.'

He got out of his armchair, opened the door, and I saw a beautiful white tablecloth on a long table, round which three hussars in blue aprons were setting out the plates and glasses. 'There are some women coming!' Marchas cried. And the three men began to dance and to cheer with all their might.

Everything was ready, and we were waiting. We waited for nearly an hour, while a delicious smell of roast poultry pervaded the whole house. At last, however, a knock against the shutters made us all jump up at the same moment. Stout Ponderel ran to open the door, and in less than a minute a little Sister of Mercy appeared in the doorway. She was thin, wrinkled and timid, and successively greeted the four bewildered hussars who saw her enter. Behind her, the noise of sticks sounded on the tiled floor in the vestibule, and as soon as she had come into the drawing-room, I saw three old heads in white caps, following each other one by one, who came in, swaying with different movements, one inclining to the right, while the other inclined to the left. And three worthy women appeared, limping, dragging their legs behind them, crippled by illness and deformed through old age, three infirm old women, past service, the only three pensioners who were able to walk in the home presided over by Sister Saint-Benedict.

She had turned round to her invalids, full of anxiety for them, and then, seeing my quartermaster's stripes, she said to me: 'I am much obliged to you for thinking of these poor women. They have very little pleasure in life, and you are at the same time giving them a great treat and doing them a great honour.'

I saw the priest, who had remained in the dark hallway, and was laughing heartily, and I began to laugh in my turn, especially when I saw Marchas' face. Then, motioning the nun to the seats, I said:

'Sit down, sister; we are very proud and very happy that you have accepted our unpretentious invitation.'

She took three chairs which stood against the wall, set them before the fire, led her three old women to them, settled them on them, took their sticks and shawls, which she put into a corner, and then, pointing to the first, a thin woman with an enormous stomach, who was evidently suffering from the dropsy, she said: 'This is Mother Paumelle; whose husband was killed by falling from a roof, and whose son died in Africa; she is sixty years old.' Then she pointed to another, a tall woman, whose head trembled unceasingly: 'This is Mother Jean-Jean, who is sixty-seven. She is nearly blind, for her face was terribly singed in a fire, and her right leg was half burned off.'

Then she pointed to the third, a sort of dwarf, with protruding, round, stupid eyes, which she rolled incessantly in all directions, 'This is La Putois, an idiot. She is only forty-four.'

I bowed to the three women as if I were being presented to some royal highnesses, and turning to the priest, I said: 'You are an excellent man, Monsieur l'Abbe, to whom all of us here owe a debt of gratitude.'

Everybody was laughing, in fact, except Marchas, who seemed furious, and just then Karl Massouligny cried: 'Sister Saint-Benedict, supper is on the table!'

I made her go first with the priest, then I helped up Mother Paumelle, whose arm I took and dragged her into the next room, which was no easy task, for she seemed heavier than a lump of iron.

Stout Ponderel gave his arm to Mother Jean-Jean, who bemoaned her crutch, and little Joseph Herbon took the idiot, La Putois, to the dining-room, which was filled with the odour of the viands.

As soon as we were opposite our plates, the sister clapped her hands three times, and, with the precision of soldiers presenting arms, the women made a rapid sign of the cross, and then the priest slowly repeated the Benedictus in Latin. Then we sat down, and the two fowls appeared, brought in by Marchas, who chose to wait at table, rather than to sit down as a guest to this ridiculous repast.

But I cried: 'Bring the champagne at once!' and a cork flew out with the noise of a pistol, and in spite of the resistance of the priest and of the kind sister, the three hussars, sitting by the side of the three invalids, emptied their three full glasses down their throats by force.

Massouligny, who possessed the faculty of making himself at home, and of being on good terms with every one, wherever he was, made love to Mother Paumelle in the drollest manner. The dropsical woman, who had retained her cheerfulness in spite of her misfortunes, answered him banteringly in a high falsetto voice which appeared as if it were put on, and she laughed so heartily at her neighbour's jokes that it was quite alarming. Little Herbon had seriously undertaken the task of making the idiot drunk, and Baron d'Streillis, whose wits were not always particularly sharp, was questioning old Jean-Jean about the life, the habits, and the rules of the hospital.

The nun said to Massouligny in consternation:

'Oh! oh! you will make her ill; pray do not make her laugh like that, monsieur. Oh! monsieur—' Then she got up and rushed at Herbon to take from him a full glass which he was hastily emptying down La Putois' throat, while the priest shook with laughter, and said to the sister: 'Never mind; just this once, it will not hurt them. Do leave them alone.'

After the two fowls they ate the duck, which was flanked by the three pigeons and the blackbird, and then the goose appeared, smoking, golden-brown, and diffusing a warm odour of hot, browned roast meat. La Paumelle, who was getting lively, clapped her hands; La Jean-Jean left off answering the baron's numerous questions, and La Putois uttered grunts of pleasure, half cries and half sighs, as little children do when one shows them candy. 'Allow me to take charge of this animal,' the cure said. 'I understand these sort of operations better than most people.' 'Certainly, Monsieur l'Abbe,' and the sister said: 'How would it be to open the window a little? They are too warm, and I am afraid they will be ill.'

I turned to Marchas: 'Open the window for a minute.' He did so; the cold outer air as it came in made the candles flare, and the steam from the goose, which the cure was scientifically carving, with a table napkin round his neck, whirl about. We watched him doing it, without speaking now, for we were interested in his attractive handiwork, and seized with renewed appetite at the sight of that enormous golden-brown bird, whose limbs fell one after another into the brown gravy at the bottom of the dish. At that moment, in the midst of that greedy silence which kept us all attentive, the distant report of a shot came in at the open window.

I started to my feet so quickly that my chair fell down behind me, and I shouted: 'To saddle, all of you! You, Marchas, take two men and go and see what it is. I shall expect you back here in five minutes.' And while the three riders went off at full gallop through the night, I got into the saddle with my three remaining hussars, in front of the steps of the villa, while the cure, the sister and the three old women showed their frightened faces at the window.

We heard nothing more, except the barking of a dog in the distance. The rain had ceased, and it was cold, very cold, and soon I heard the gallop of a horse, of a single horse, coming back. It was Marchas, and I called out to him: 'Well?' 'It is nothing; Francois has wounded an old peasant who refused to answer his challenge: 'Who goes there?' and who continued to advance in spite of the order to keep off; but they are bringing him here, and we shall see what is the matter.'

I gave orders for the horses to be put back in the stable, and I sent my two soldiers to meet the others, and returned to the house. Then the cure, Marchas, and I took a mattress into the room to lay the wounded man on; the sister tore up a table napkin in order to make lint, while the three frightened women remained huddled up in a corner.

Soon I heard the rattle of sabres on the road, and I took a candle to show a light to the men who were returning; and they soon appeared, carrying that inert, soft, long, sinister object which a human body becomes when life no longer sustains it.

They put the wounded man on the mattress that had been prepared for him, and I saw at the first glance that he was dying. He had the death rattle and was spitting up blood, which ran out of the corners of his mouth at every gasp. The man was covered with blood! His cheeks, his beard, his hair, his neck and his clothes seemed to have been soaked, to have been dipped in a red tub; and that blood stuck to him, and had become a dull colourwhich was horrible to look at.

The wounded man, wrapped up in a large shepherd's cloak, occasionally opened his dull, vacant eyes, which seemed stupid with astonishment, like those of animals wounded by a sportsman, which fall at his feet, more than half dead already, stupefied with terror and surprise.

The cure exclaimed: 'Ah, it is old Placide, the shepherd from Les Moulins. He is deaf, poor man, and heard nothing. Ah! Oh, God! they have killed the unhappy man!' The sister had opened his blouse and shirt, and was looking at a little blue hole in his chest, which was not bleeding any more. 'There is nothing to be done,' she said.

The shepherd was gasping terribly and bringing up blood with every last breath, and in his throat, to the very depth of his lungs, they could hear an ominous and continued gurgling. The cure, standing in front of him, raised his right hand, made the sign of the cross, and in a slow and solemn voice pronounced the Latin words which purify men's souls, but before they were finished, the old man's body trembled violently, as if something had given way inside him, and he ceased to breathe. He was dead.

When I turned round, I saw a sight which was even more horrible than the death struggle of this unfortunate man; the three old women were standing up huddled close together, hideous, and grimacing with fear and horror. I went up to them, and they began to utter shrill screams, while La Jean-Jean, whose burned leg could no longer support her, fell to the ground at full length.

Sister Saint-Benedict left the dead man, ran up to her infirm old women, and without a word or a look for me, wrapped their shawls round them, gave them their crutches, pushed them to the door, made them go out, and disappeared with them into the dark night.

I saw that I could not even let a hussar accompany them, for the mere rattle of a sword would have sent them mad with fear.

The cure was still looking at the dead man; but at last he turned round to me and said:

'Oh! What a horrible thing!'

11

THE STORY OF YOSHITSUNE

Yei Theodora Ozaki

In old Japan more than seven hundred years ago a fierce war was raging between the two great clans, the Taira and the Minamoto, also called the Heike and the Genji. These two famous clans were always contesting together for political power and military supremacy, and the country was torn in two with the many bitter battles that were fought. Indeed it may be said that the history of Japan for many years was the history of these two mighty martial families; sometimes the Minamoto and sometimes the Taira gaining the victory, or being beaten, as the case might be; but their swords knew no rest for a period of many years. At last a strong and valiant general arose in the House of Minamoto. His name was Yoshitomo. At this time there were two aspirants for the Imperial throne and civil war was raging in the capital. One Imperial candidate was supported by the Taira, the other by the Minamoto. Yoshitomo, though a Minamoto, sided at first with the Taira against the reigning Emperor; but when he saw how cruel and relentless their chief, Kiyomori, was, he turned against him and called all his followers to rally round the Minamoto standard and fight to put down the Taira.

But fate was against the gallant and doughty warrior Yoshitomo, and he suffered a crushing defeat at the hands of the Taira. He and his men, while fleeing from the vigilance of their enemies, were overtaken within the city gates, and ruthlessly slaughtered by Kiyomori and his soldiers.

Yoshitomo left behind him his beautiful young wife, Tokiwa

Gozen, and eight children, to mourn his untimely death. Five of the elder children were by a first wife. The third of these became Yoritomo, the great first Shogun of Japan, while the eighth and youngest child was Ushiwaka, about whom this story is written. Ushiwaka and the hero Yoshitsune were one and the same person. Ushiwaka (Young Ox—he was so called because of his wonderful strength) was his name as a boy, and Yoshitsune was the name he took when he became of age.

At the time of his father's death, Ushiwaka was a babe in the arms of his mother, Tokiwa Gozen, but his tender age would not have saved his life had he been found by his father's enemies.

After the defeat they had inflicted on the rival clan, the Taira were all-powerful for a time. The Minamoto clan were in dire straits and in danger of being exterminated now, for so fierce was Kiyomori's hatred against his enemies that when a Minamoto fell into his cruel hands he immediately put the captive to death.

Realizing the great peril of the situation, Tokiwa Gozen, the widow of Yoshitomo, full of fear and anxiety for the safety of her little ones, quietly hid herself in the country, taking with her Ushiwaka and her two other children. So successful was Tokiwa Gozen in concealing her hiding-place that, though the Taira clan either killed or banished to a far-away island all the elder sons, relations, and partisans of the Minamoto chief, they could not discover the whereabouts of the mother and her children, notwithstanding the strict search Kiyomori had made.

Determined to have his will, and angry at being thwarted by a woman, Kiyomori at last hit on a plan which he felt sure would not fail to draw the wife of Yoshitomo from her hiding-place. He gave orders that Sekiya, the mother of the fair Tokiwa, should be seized and brought before him. He told her sternly that if she would reveal her daughter's hiding-place she should be well treated, but if she refused to do as she was told she would be tortured and put to death. When the old lady declared that she did not know where Tokiwa was, as in truth she did not, Kiyomori thrust her into prison and had her treated cruelly day after day.

Now the reason why Kiyomori was so set on finding Tokiwa and her sons was that while Yoshitomo's heirs lived he and his family could know no safety, for the strongest moral law in every Japanese heart was the old command, 'A man may not live under the same heaven with the murderer of his father,' and the Japanese warrior recked nothing of life or death, of home or love in obeying this—as he deemed—supreme commandment. Women too burned with the same zeal in avenging the wrongs of their fathers and husbands.

Tokiwa Gozen, though hiding in the country, heard of what had befallen her mother, and great was her sorrow and distress. She sat down on the mats and moaned aloud: 'It is wrong of me to let my poor innocent mother suffer to save myself and my children, but if I give myself up, Kiyomori will surely take my lord's sons and kill them.—What shall I do? Oh! what shall I do?'

Poor Tokiwa! Her heart was torn between her love for her mother and her love for her children. Her anxiety and distraction were pitiful to see. Finally she decided that it was impossible for her to remain still and silent under the circumstances; she could not endure the thought that her mother was suffering persecution while she had the power of preventing it, so holding the infant Ushiwaka in her bosom under her kimono, she took his two elder brothers (one seven and the other five years of age) by the hand and started for the capital.

There were no trains in those days and all travelling by ordinary people had to be done on foot. *Daimios* and great and important personages were carried in palanquins, and they only could travel in comfort and in state. Tokiwa could not hope to meet with kindness or hospitality on the way, for she was a Minamoto, and the Taira being all-powerful it was death to any one to harbour a Minamoto fugitive. So the obstacles that beset Tokiwa were great; but she was a *samurai* woman, and she quailed not at duty, however hard or stern that duty was. The greater the difficulties, the higher her courage rose to meet them. At last she set out on her momentous and celebrated journey.

It was winter-time and snow lay on the ground, and the wind blew piercingly cold and the roads were bad. What Tokiwa, a delicately nurtured woman, suffered from cold and fatigue, from loneliness and fear, from anxiety for her little children, from dread lest she should reach the capital too late to save her old mother, who might die under the cruel treatment to which she was being subjected, or be put to death by Kiyomori, in his wrath, or finally lest she herself should be seized by the Taira, and her filial plan be frustrated before she could reach the capital—all this must have been greater than any words can tell.

Sometimes poor distressed Tokiwa sat down by the wayside to hush the wailing babe she carried in her bosom, or to rest the two little boys, who, tired and faint and famished, clung to her robes, crying for their usual rice. On and on she went, soothing and consoling them as best she could, till at last she reached Kyoto, weary, footsore, and almost heartbroken. But though she was well-nigh overcome with physical exhaustion, yet her purpose never flagged. She went at once to the enemy's camp and asked to be admitted to the presence of General Kiyomori.

When she was shown into the dread man's presence, she prostrated herself at his feet and said that she had come to give herself up and to release her mother.

'I am Tokiwa—the widow of Yoshitomo. I have come with my three children to beseech you to spare my mother's life and to set her free. My poor old mother has done nothing wrong. I am guilty of hiding myself and the little ones, yet I pray humbly for your august forgiveness.'

She pleaded in such an agonizing way that Kiyomori, the

Taira chieftain, was struck with admiration for her filial piety, a virtue more highly esteemed than any other in Japan. He felt sincerely sorry for Tokiwa in her woe, and her beauty and her tears melted his hard heart, and he promised her that if she would become his wife he would spare not only her mother's life, but her three children also.

For the sake of saving her children's lives the sad-hearted woman consented to Kiyomori's proposal. It must have been terrible to her to wed with her lord's enemy, the very man who had caused his death; but the thought that by so doing she saved the lives of his sons, who would one day surely arise to avenge their father's cruel death, must have been her consolation and her recompense for the sacrifice.

Kiyomori showed himself kinder to Tokiwa than he had ever shown himself to any one, for he allowed her to keep the babe Ushiwaka by her side. The two elder boys he sent to a temple to be trained as acolytes under the tutelage of priests.

By placing them out of the world in the seclusion of priesthood, Kiyomori felt that he would have little to fear from them when they attained manhood. How terribly and bitterly he was mistaken we learn from history, for two of Yoshitomo's sons, banished though they had been for years and years, arose like a rushing, mighty whirlwind from the obscurity of the monastery to avenge their father, and they wiped the Taira from off the face of the earth.

Time passed by, and when the little babe Ushiwaka at last reached the age of seven, Kiyomori likewise took him from his mother and sent him to the priests. The sorrow of Tokiwa, bereft of the last child of her beloved lord Yoshitomo, can better be imagined than described. But in her golden captivity even Kiyomori had not been able to deprive her of one iota of the incomparable power of motherhood, that of influencing the life of her child to the end of his days. As the little fellow had lain in her arms night and day, as she crooned him to sleep and taught him to walk, she forever whispered the name of Minamoto Yoshitomo in his ear.

At last one day her patience was rewarded and Ushiwaka lisped his father's name correctly. Then Tokiwa clasped him proudly to her breast, and wept tears of thankfulness and joy and of sorrowing remembrance, for she could never even for a day banish Yoshitomo from her mind. As Ushiwaka grew older and could understand better what she said, Tokiwa would daily whisper, 'Remember thy father, Minamoto Yoshitomo! Grow strong and avenge his death, for he died at the hands of the Taira!' And day by day she told him stories of his great and good father—of his martial prowess in battle, and of his great strength and wonderful wielding of the sword, and she bade her little son remember and be like his father. And the mother's words and tears, sown in long years of patience and bitter endurance, bore fruit beyond all she had ever hoped or dreamed.

So Ushiwaka was taken from his mother at the age of seven, and was sent to the Tokobo Monastery, at Kuramayama, to be trained as a monk.

Even at that early age he showed great intelligence, read the Sacred Books with avidity, and surprised the priests by his diligence and quickness of memory. He was naturally a very high-spirited youth, and could brook no control and hated to yield to others in anything whatsoever. As the years passed by and he grew older, he came to hear from his teachers and school friends of how his father Yoshitomo and his clan the Minamoto had been overthrown by the Taira, and this filled him with such intense sorrow and bitterness that sleeping or waking he could never banish the subject from his mind. As he listened daily to these things the words of his mother, which she had whispered in his ear as a child, now came throbbing back to his mind, and he understood their full meaning for the first time. In the lonely nights he felt again her hot tears falling on his face, and heard her repeat as clearly as a bell in the silence of the darkness: 'Remember thy father, Minamoto Yoshitomo! Avenge his death, for he died at the hands of the Taira!'

At last one night the lad dreamed that his mother, beautiful and sad as he remembered her in the days of his childhood, came to his bedside and said to him, while the tears streamed down her face: 'Avenge thy father, Yoshitomo! Unless thou remember my last words, I cannot rest in my grave. I am dying, Ushiwaka, remember!'

And Ushiwaka awoke as he cried aloud in his agony: 'I will! Honourable mother, I will!' From that night his heart burned within him and the fire and love of clan-race stirred his soul. Continual brooding over the wrongs of his clan generated in his heart a fierce desire for revenge, and he finally resolved to abandon the priesthood, become a great general like his father, and punish the Taira. And as his ambition was fired and exalted and his mind thrilled back to the days when his poor unhappy mother Tokiwa prayed and wept over him, daily whispering in his ear the name of his father, his will grew to purpose strong. Tokiwa had not suffered in vain. From this time on, Ushiwaka bided his time every night till all in the temple were fast asleep. When he heard the priests snoring, and knew himself safe from observation, he would steal out from the temple, and, making his way down the hillside into the valley, he would draw his wooden sword and practise fencing by himself, and, striking the trees and the stones imagine that they were his Taira foes. As he worked in this way night after night, he felt his muscles grow strong, and this practice taught him how to wield his sword with skill.

One night as usual Ushiwaka had gone out to the valley and was diligently brandishing about his wooden sword. His mind fully bent upon his self-taught lesson, he was marching up and down, chanting snatches of war-songs and striking the trees and the rocks, when suddenly a great cloud spread over the heavens, the rain fell, the thunder roared, and the lightning flashed, and a great noise went through the valley, as if all the trees were being torn up by the roots and their trunks were splitting.

While Ushiwaka wondered what this could mean, a great giant over ten feet in height stood before him. He had large round glaring eyes that glinted like metal mirrors; his nose was bright red, and it must have been about a foot long; his hands were like the claws of a bird, and to each there were only two fingers. The feathers of long wings at each side peeped from under the creature's robes, and he looked like a gigantic goblin. Fearful indeed was this apparition. But Ushiwaka was a brave and spirited youth and the son of a soldier, and he was not to be daunted by anything. Without moving a muscle of his face he gripped his sword more tightly and simply asked: 'Who are you, sirrah?'

The goblin laughed aloud and said: 'I am the King of the Tengu, the elves of the mountains, and I have made this valley my home for many a long year. I have admired your perseverance in coming to this place night after night for the purpose of practising fencing all by yourself, and I have come to meet you, with the intention of teaching you all I know of the art of the sword.'

Ushiwaka was delighted when he heard this, for the Tengu have supernatural powers, and fortunate indeed are those whom they favour. He thanked the giant elf and expressed his readiness to begin at once. He then whirled up his sword and began to attack the Tengu, but the elf shifted his position with the quickness of lightning, and taking from his belt a fan made of seven feathers parried the showering blows right and left so cleverly that the young knight's interest became thoroughly aroused. Every night he came out for the lesson. He never missed once, summer or winter, and in this way he learned all the secrets of the art which the Tengu could teach him.

The Tengu was a great master and Ushiwaka an apt pupil. He became so proficient in fencing that he could overcome ten or twenty small Tengu in the twinkling of an eye, and he acquired extraordinary skill and dexterity in the use of the sword; and the Tengu also imparted to him the wonderful adroitness and agility which made him so famous in after-life.

Now Ushiwaka was about fifteen years old, a comely youth, and tall for his age. At this time there lived on Mount Hiei, just outside the capital, a wild bonze named Musashi Bo Benkei, who was such a lawless and turbulent fellow that he had become notorious for his deeds of violence. The city rang with the stories of his misdeeds, and so well known had he become that people could not hear his name without fear and trembling.

Benkei suddenly made up his mind that it would be good sport to steal a thousand swords from various knights.

No sooner did the wild idea enter his head than he began to put it into practice. Every night he sauntered forth to the Gojo Bridge of Kyoto, and when a knight or any man carrying a sword passed by, Benkei would snatch the weapon from his girdle. If the owners yielded up their blades quietly, Benkei allowed them to pass unhurt, but if not, he would strike them dead with a single blow of the huge halberd he carried. So great was Benkei's strength that he always overcame his victim,—resistance was useless,—and night by night one and sometimes two men met death at his hands on the Gojo Bridge. In this way Benkei gained such a terrible reputation that everybody far and near feared to meet him, and after dark no one dared to pass near the bridge he was known to haunt, so fearful were the tales told of the dreaded robber of swords.

At last this story reached the ears of Ushiwaka, and he said to himself: 'What an interesting man this must be! If it is true that he is a bonze, he must be a strange one indeed; but as he only robs people of their swords, he cannot be a common highwayman. If I could make such a strong man a retainer of mine, he would be of great assistance to me when I punish my enemies, the Taira clan. Good! To-night I will go to the Gojo Bridge and try the mettle of this Benkei!'

Ushiwaka, being a youth of great courage, had no sooner made up his mind to meet Benkei than he proceeded to put his plan into execution. He started out that same evening. It was a beautiful moonlight night, and taking with him his favourite flute he strolled forth through the streets of the sleeping city till he came to the Gojo Bridge. Then from the opposite direction came a tall figure which appeared to touch the clouds, so gigantic was its stature. The stranger was clad in a suit of coal-black armour and carried an immense halberd.

'This must be the sword-robber! He is indeed strong!' said Ushiwaka to himself, but he was not in the least daunted, and went on playing his flute quite calmly.

Presently the armed giant halted and gazed at Ushiwaka, but evidently thought him a mere youth, and decided to let him go unmolested, for he was about to pass him by without lifting a hand. This indifference on the part of Benkei not only disappointed but angered Ushiwaka. Having waited in vain for the stranger to offer violence, our hero approached Benkei, and, with the intention of picking a quarrel, suddenly kicked the latter's halberd out of his hand.

Benkei, who had first thought to spare Ushiwaka on account of his youth, became very angry when he found himself insulted by a lad to whom he had been intentionally kind. In a fury he exclaimed, 'Miserable stripling!' and raising his halberd struck sideways at Ushiwaka, thinking to slice him in two at the waist and to see his body fall asunder. But the young knight nimbly avoided the blow which would have killed him, and springing back a few paces he flung his fan at Benkei's head and uttered a loud cry of defiance. The fan struck Benkei on the forehead right between the eyes, making him mad with pain. In a transport of rage Benkei aimed a fearful blow at Ushiwaka, as if he were splitting a log of wood with an axe. This time Ushiwaka sprang up to the parapet of the bridge, clapped his hands, and laughed in derision, saying:

'Here I am! Don't you see? Here I am!' and Benkei was again thwarted thus.

Benkei, who had never known his strokes miss before, had now failed twice in catching this nimble opponent. Frantic with chagrin and baffled rage, he now rushed furiously to the attack, whirling his great halberd round in all directions till it looked like a water-wheel in motion, striking wildly and blindly at Ushiwaka. But the young knight had been taught tricks innumerable by the giant Tengu of Kuramayama, and he had profited so well by his lessons that the King Tengu had at last said that even he could teach him nothing more, and now, as it may well be imagined, he was too quick for the heavy Benkei. When Benkei struck in front, Ushiwaka was behind, and when Benkei aimed a blow behind, Ushiwaka darted in front. Nimble as a monkey and swift as a swallow, Ushiwaka avoided all the blows aimed at him, and, finding himself outmatched, even the redoubtable Benkei grew tired.

Ushiwaka saw that Benkei was played out. He kept up the game a little longer and then changed his tactics. Seizing his opportunity, he knocked Benkei's halberd out of his hand. When the giant stooped to pick his weapon up, Ushiwaka ran behind him and with a quick movement tripped him up. There lay the big man on all fours, while Ushiwaka nimbly strode across his back and pressing him down asked him how he liked this kind of play.

All this time Benkei had wondered at the courage of the youth in attacking and challenging a man so much larger than himself, but now he was filled with amazement at Ushiwaka's wonderful strength and adroitness.

'I am indeed astonished at what you have done,' said Benkei. 'Who in the world can you be? I have fought with many men on this bridge, but you are the first of my antagonists who has displayed such strength. Are you a god or a *tengu*? You certainly cannot be an ordinary human being!'

Ushiwaka laughed and said: 'Are you afraid for the first time, then?'

'I am,' answered Benkei.

'Will you from henceforth be my retainer?' demanded Ushiwaka.

'I will in very truth be your retainer, but may I know who you are?' asked Benkei meekly.

Ushiwaka now felt sure that Benkei was in earnest. He therefore allowed him to get up from the ground, and then said: 'I have nothing to hide from you. I am the youngest son of Minamoto Yoshitomo and my name is Ushiwaka.'

Benkei started with surprise when he heard these words and said: 'What is this I hear? Are you in truth a son of the Lord Yoshitomo of the Minamoto clan? That is the reason I felt from the first moment of our encounter that your deeds were not those of a common person. No wonder that I thought this! I am only too happy to become the retainer of such a distinguished and spirited young knight. I will follow you as my lord and master from this very moment, if you will allow me. I can wish for no greater honour.'

So there and then, on the Gojo Bridge in the silver moonlight, the bonze Benkei vowed to be the true and faithful vassal of the young knight Ushiwaka and to serve him loyally till death, and thus was the compact between lord and vassal made. From that time on, Benkei gave up his wild and lawless ways and devoted his life to the service of Ushiwaka, who was highly pleased at having won such a strong liegeman to his side.

Although Ushiwaka had now secured Benkei, it was impossible

for only two men, however strong, to think of fighting the Taira clan, so they both decided that the cherished plan must wait till the Minamoto were stronger. While thus waiting they heard a report to the effect that a descendant of Tawara Toda Hidesato named Hidehira was now a famous general in Kaiwai of the Ashu Province, and that he was so powerful that no one dared oppose him. Hearing this, Ushiwaka thought that it would be a good plan to pay the general a visit and try to interest him, if possible, in the fortunes of the House of Minamoto. He consulted with Benkei, who encouraged the young knight in his scheme of enlisting the General Hidehira as a partisan, and the two therefore left Kyoto secretly and journeyed as quickly as possible to Oshu on this errand.

On the way there, Ushiwaka and Benkei came to the Temple of Atsuta, and as they considered it important that the young knight should look older now, Ushiwaka performed the ceremony of Gembuku at the shrine. This was a rite performed in olden times when youths reached the age of manhood, They then had to shave off the front part of their hair and to change their names as a sign that they had left childhood behind. Ushiwaka now took the name of Yoshitsune. As he was the eighth son, it would have been more correct for him to have assumed the name of Hachiro, but as his uncle Tametomo the Archer, of whom you have already read, was named Hachiro, he purposely did not take this name. From this time forth our hero is known as Yoshitsune, and this name he has glorified forever by his wonderful bravery and many heroic exploits. In Japanese history he is the knight without fear and without reproach, the darling of the people, to them almost an incarnation of Hachiman, the popular God of War. And as for Benkei, never can you find in all history a vassal who was more true or loyal to his master than Benkei. He was Yoshitsune's right hand in everything, and his strength and wisdom carried them successfully through many a dire emergency.

From Kyoto to Oshu is a long journey of about three hundred miles, but at length Yoshitsune (as we must now call him) and Benkei reached their destination and craved the General Hidehira's assistance. They found that Hidehira was a warm adherent of the Minamoto cause, and under the late Lord Yoshitomo he and his family had enjoyed great favour. When the general learned, therefore, that Yoshitsune was the son of the illustrious Minamoto chief, his joy knew no bounds, and he made Yoshitsune and Benkei heartily welcome and treated them both as guests of honour and importance.

Just at this time Yoshitsune's eldest brother, Yoritomo, who had been banished to an island in Idzu, collected a great army and raised his standard against the Taira. When the news about Yoritomo reached Yoshitsune, he rejoiced, for he felt that the hour had at last come when the Minamoto would be revenged on the Taira for all the wrongs they had suffered at the hands of the latter.

With the help of Hidehira and the faithful Benkei, he collected a small army of warriors and at once marched over to his brother's camp in Idzu. He sent a messenger ahead to inform Yoritomo that his youngest brother, now named Yoshitsune, was coming to aid him in his fight against the Taira.

Yoritomo was exceedingly glad at this unexpected good news, for all that helped to swell his forces now brought nearer the day when he would be able to strike his long-planned blow at the power of the hated Taira. As soon as Yoshitsune reached Idzu, Yoritomo arranged for an immediate meeting. Although the two men were brothers, it must be remembered that their father had been killed, and the family utterly scattered, when they were mere children, Yoshitsune being at that time but an infant in his mother's arms. As this was therefore the first time they had met Yoritomo knew nothing of his young brother's character.

One of Yoshitsune's elder brothers had come with him, and

Yoritomo being a shrewd general wished to test them both to see of what mettle they were made. He ordered his retainers to bring a brass basin full of boiling water. When it was brought, Yoritomo ordered Noriyori, the elder of the two, to carry it to him first. Now brass being a good conductor of heat, the basin was very hot and Noriyori stupidly let it fall. Yoritomo ordered it to be filled again and bade Yoshitsune bring it to him. Without moving a muscle of his handsome face Yoshitsune took hold of the almost unbearably hot vessel and carried it with due ceremony slowly across the room. This exhibition of nerve and endurance filled Yoritomo with admiration and he was favourably struck with Yoshitsune's character. As for Noriyori, who had been unable to hold a hot basin for a few moments, he had no use for him at all, except as a common soldier.

Yoritomo begged Yoshitsune to become his right-hand man and zealously to espouse his cause. Yoshitsune declared that this had been his lifelong ambition ever since he could remember,—as they both were sons of the same father, so was their cause and destiny one. Yoritomo made Yoshitsune a general of part of his army and ordered him in the name of his father Yoshitomo to chastise the Taira.

Delighted beyond all words at the wonderfully auspicious turn events were taking, Yoshitsune hastened his preparations for the march. The longed-for hour had come to which through his whole childhood and youth he had looked forward, and for which his whole being had thirsted for many years. He could now fulfil the last words of his unhappy mother, and punish the Taira for all the evil they had wrought against the Minamoto. All the wild restlessness of his youth, which had driven him forth to wield his wooden sword against the rocks in the Kuramayama Valley and to try his strength against Benkei on the Gojo Bridge, now found vent in action most dear to a born warrior's heart. With several thousands of troops under him, Yoshitsune marched up to Kyoto and waged war against the Taira, and defeated them in a series of brilliant engagements.

The stricken Taira multitudes fled before the avenger like autumn leaves before the blast, and Yoshitsune pursued them to the sea. At Dan-no-Ura the Taira made a last stand, but all in vain. Their lion leader, Kiyomori, was dead, and there was no great chieftain to rally them in the disordered retreat that now ensued. Yoshitsune came sweeping down upon them, and they and their fleet and their infant Emperor likewise, with their women and children, sank beneath the waves. Only a scattered few lived to tell the tale of the terrible destruction that overtook them on the sea.

12

THE GLORY OF WAR

M.B. Levick

He was an orderly in the hospital and had got the job through a friend in his Grand Army Post. The work was not for a fastidious man, but John was not fastidious. In his duties he affected the bluff manner of a veteran, and, peering at the internes with a wise squint, would say, 'Oh, this ain't nothin'; an old soldier is used to such things. If y' want t' see the real thing, jus' go to war.' And he would laugh at them and they would laugh at him.

He wore his G.A.R. emblem conspicuously on all occasions. At the slightest chance he became a bore with long tales of fighting, of how he had chased Johnny Reb and how *those* were the days. The students, still near enough to the classroom to hold a lingering repugnance for the text-books' overemphasis on the Civil War, would guy him, but John never suspected.

On Decoration Day he marched and attended as many exercises as he could squeeze into the too short hours. He wore a committee ribbon like a decoration for valour. Once he carried a flag in a parade, and for weeks talked about Old Glory, the Stars and Stripes, and regimental colours that had changed hands in distant frays.

And he had fought only to save his country, he would assert. He didn't have no eye on Uncle Sam's purse, not he; he could take care of himself, and if not, why, there was them as would. When the youths accused him of sinking his pension, he turned hotly to remind them of their lack of beard.

He was ever so ready to defend himself with an ancient vigour that the students and the nurses were sorry when he fell ill. Perhaps his campaigning had taken from his vitality, they surmised. The house surgeon told them he would never get up. After that—and the afterwards was not long—John told his tales to more sober auditors.

He had been in bed a week and had begun to suspect the state of affairs when he called to him one evening the youth who of all had shown him the most deference.

'Sit down,' he said, without looking the youngster in the eye; and for a time there were heard only the noises of the day-weary ward. Presently John spoke, in an apprehensive tone of confidences.

'I've been a soldier now for forty-five years,' he said, 'an' for once I want to be just myself... I kind o' like you, an' there ain't nobody else I can talk to, for I ain't got any one...

'In '61 I was on my father's farm in Pennsylvani'. I was on'y a kid then—fifteen—but when the war come I wanted the worst way to go. But my mother, she cried an' begged me not to, an' my daddy said he'd lick me, so I tried t' forget it.

'But I couldn't. Lots o' other boys was goin' away t' enlist an' they was all treated like heroes. Ye'd 'a' thought they'd won the war already by themselves the way folks carried on when they left—the girls cryin' about 'em an' the teacher an' the minister an' the circuit judge speakin' to 'em an' all the stay-at-homes mad because they wasn't goin', too.

'It kept gettin' harder an' harder to work on the farm, an' finally I said, 'Well, I'll go anyway.' I knew pa an' ma wouldn't change their mind, so I didn't say nothin' to them. But I went to all the other boys an' told *them*. 'I'm goin' away t' enlist,' I'd say, an' when they'd laugh an' say, 'Why, y'r ma won't let ye,' I'd look wise an' tell 'em to watch me, an' I'd strut aroun' an' wink sly-like.

'They got to talkin' about it so much I was scairt my dad would find out, but he didn't, an' I held back as long as I could, because all the other boys was lookin' up to me. I was a man, all right, then. None o' 'em that went away was the mogul I was. The girls got wind of it, too, an' I could see 'em out o' the tail o' my eye watchin' me an' whisperin' an' sayin', girl-like, all the things the boys was tryin' not to say. That on'y made the boys talk more, too.

'So after a few days I ran away. The first night I hung roun' near the town an' after dark sneaked back to hear 'em talkin'. 'He'll be back soon,' one feller said. Another, just to show he knew more, spoke up, 'No, he won' come back 'less in blue or in a coffin.' An' the others laughed.

'I thought that was fine—in blue or a coffin. 'You bet I won't; I'm the man f'r that,' says I to myself.

'It took me three days to walk to the city. When I told the recruitin' sergeant I wanted to be high corporal he laughed an' pounded me an' put me through my paces. Then he said I couldn't be a soldier. My eyes wasn't good enough.

'I cried at that; on'y a kid, y' know—the' was lots of 'em younger than me fightin'. But I remembered the feller what said, 'He won't come back 'cept in blue or a coffin,' so I went where the soldiers was an' bummed an' hobnobbed with 'em till they let me help at peelin' vegetables and pot-wrastlin' an' such things. Then I got to be a sort o' water boy. My, I was proud!... But that on'y lasted a month, an' I had to get out.

'I jus' couldn't go home without the blue, an' it seemed too soon to get a coffin yet, so I went to New York an' stayed all through the war. Nearly starved, too.

'After it was over I went back home. They didn't suspicion, o' course, an' the first thing I knew I'd told 'em I'd been in the army. Hadn't planned to, but some way it just popped out.

'Right away it was hail-fellow-well-met with them that had

been at the front, an' we were goin' roun' givin' oursel's airs an' the girls seemed to think we was better than all the rest... Well, sometimes I...

'I was jus' a young fellow, y' know, an' kep' gettin' in deeper an' deeper an' never thought it'd mean anything. When a man says, 'John, you remember that clump o' trees the Fifty-eighth lay under at Antietam?' why, you say, 'Yes.' An' the next time y'r tellin' about Antietam you jus' throw in them trees without thinkin'. That's the way it was with me. An' I read books to get my facks straight an' no one never caught me nappin'. I used t' correct *them*... At last I got to believe it all myself...

'Then the G.A.R. Post was organized in our town... An' so it went.

'Well, it's been a long time. If I'd 'a' known in the first place maybe it'd 'a' been different... But it was my right, anyway, wasn't it, now? Say, don't you think it was comin' to me? It wasn't my fault. By God, I wanted to fight! Jus' one chance an' so help me—

'They cheated me out o' it an' I got even. That's all it was. I never took no pension. I've had the glory, like 'em... I've paid for it... I on'y took my own.

'And the Post will bury me.'

13

THE COUP DE GRÂCE

Ambrose Bierce

The fighting had been hard and continuous; that was attested by all the senses. The very taste of battle was in the air. All was now over; it remained only to succor the wounded and bury the dead—to 'tidy up a bit,' as the humourist of a burial squad put it. A good deal of 'tidying up' was required. As far as one could see through the forests, among the splintered trees, lay wrecks of men and horses. Among them moved the stretcher-bearers, gathering and carrying away the few who showed signs of life. Most of the wounded had died of neglect while the right to minister to their wants was in dispute. It is an army regulation that the wounded must wait; the best way to care for them is to win the battle. It must be confessed that victory is a distinct advantage to a man requiring attention, but many do not live to avail themselves of it.

The dead were collected in groups of a dozen or a score and laid side by side in rows while the trenches were dug to receive them.

Some, found at too great a distance from these rallying points, were buried where they lay. There was little attempt at identification, though in most cases, the burial parties being detailed to glean the same ground which they had assisted to reap, the names of the victorious dead were known and listed. The enemy's fallen had to be content with counting. But of that they got enough: many of them were counted several times, and the total, as given afterwards in the official report of the victorious commander, denoted rather a hope than a result.

At some little distance from the spot where one of the burial parties had established its 'bivouac of the dead,' a man in the uniform of a Federal officer stood leaning against a tree. From his feet upwards to his neck his attitude was that of weariness reposing; but he turned his head uneasily from side to side; his mind was apparently not at rest. He was perhaps uncertain in which direction to go; he was not likely to remain long where he was, for already the level rays of the setting sun straggled redly through the open spaces of the wood and the weary soldiers were quitting their task for the day. He would hardly make a night of it alone there among the dead.

Nine men in ten whom you meet after a battle inquire the way to some fraction of the army—as if any one could know. Doubtless this officer was lost. After resting himself a moment he would presumably follow one of the retiring burial squads.

When all were gone he walked straight away into the forest towards the red west, its light staining his face like blood. The air of confidence with which he now strode along showed that he was on familiar ground; he had recovered his bearings. The dead on his right and on his left were unregarded as he passed. An occasional low moan from some sorely-stricken wretch whom the relief-parties had not reached, and who would have to pass a comfortless night beneath the stars with his thirst to keep him company, was equally unheeded. What, indeed, could the officer have done, being no surgeon and having no water?

At the head of a shallow ravine, a mere depression of the ground, lay a small group of bodies. He saw, and swerving suddenly from his course walked rapidly towards them. Scanning each one sharply as he passed, he stopped at last above one which lay at a slight remove from the others, near a clump of small trees. He looked at it narrowly. It seemed to stir. He stooped and laid his hand upon its face. It screamed.

The officer was Captain Downing Madwell, of a Massachusetts regiment of infantry, a daring and intelligent soldier, an honourable man.

In the regiment were two brothers named Halcrow—Caffal and Creede Halcrow. Caffal Halcrow was a sergeant in Captain Madwell's company, and these two men, the sergeant and the captain, were devoted friends. In so far as disparity of rank, difference in duties and considerations of military discipline would permit they were commonly together. They had, indeed, grown up together from childhood. A habit of the heart is not easily broken off. Caffal Halcrow had nothing military in his taste nor disposition, but the thought of separation from his friend was disagreeable; he enlisted in the company in which Madwell was second-lieutenant. Each had taken two steps upwards in rank, but between the highest non-commissioned and the lowest commissioned officer the gulf is deep and wide and the old relation was maintained with difficulty and a difference.

Creede Halcrow, the brother of Caffal, was the major of the regiment—a cynical, saturnine man, between whom and Captain Madwell there was a natural antipathy which circumstances had nourished and strengthened to an active animosity. But for the restraining influence of their mutual relation to Caffal these two patriots would doubtless have endeavoured to deprive their country of each other's services.

At the opening of the battle that morning the regiment was performing outpost duty a mile away from the main army. It was attacked and nearly surrounded in the forest, but stubbornly held its ground. During a lull in the fighting, Major Halcrow came to Captain Madwell. The two exchanged formal salutes, and the major said: 'Captain, the colonel directs that you push your company to the head of this ravine and hold your place there until recalled. I need hardly apprise you of the dangerous character of the movement, but if you wish, you can, I suppose, turn over the command to your first-lieutenant. I was not, however, directed to authorize the substitution; it is merely a suggestion of my own, unofficially made.'

To this deadly insult Captain Madwell coolly replied:

'Sir, I invite you to accompany the movement. A mounted officer would be a conspicuous mark, and I have long held the opinion that it would be better if you were dead.'

The art of repartee was cultivated in military circles as early as 1862.

A half-hour later Captain Madwell's company was driven from its position at the head of the ravine, with a loss of one-third its number. Among the fallen was Sergeant Halcrow. The regiment was soon afterwards forced back to the main line, and at the close of the battle was miles away. The captain was now standing at the side of his subordinate and friend.

Sergeant Halcrow was mortally hurt. His clothing was deranged; it seemed to have been violently torn apart, exposing the abdomen. Some of the buttons of his jacket had been pulled off and lay on the ground beside him and fragments of his other garments were strewn about. His leather belt was parted and had apparently been dragged from beneath him as he lay. There had been no great effusion of blood. The only visible wound was a wide, ragged opening in the abdomen.

It was defiled with earth and dead leaves. Protruding from it was a loop of small intestine. In all his experience Captain Madwell had not seen a wound like this. He could neither conjecture how it was made nor explain the attendant circumstances—the strangely torn clothing, the parted belt, the besmirching of the white skin. He knelt and made a closer examination. When he rose to his feet, he turned his eyes in different directions as if looking for an enemy. Fifty yards away, on the crest of a low, thinly wooded hill, he saw several dark objects moving about among the fallen men—a herd of swine. One stood with its back to him, its shoulders sharply elevated. Its forefeet were upon a human body, its head was depressed and invisible. The bristly ridge of its chine showed black against the red west. Captain Madwell drew away his eyes and fixed them again upon the thing which had been his friend.

The man who had suffered these monstrous mutilations was alive. At intervals he moved his limbs; he moaned at every breath. He stared blankly into the face of his friend and if touched screamed. In his giant agony he had torn up the ground on which he lay; his clenched hands were full of leaves and twigs and earth. Articulate speech was beyond his power; it was impossible to know if he were sensible to anything but pain. The expression of his face was an appeal; his eyes were full of prayer. For what?

There was no misreading that look; the captain had too frequently seen it in eyes of those whose lips had still the power to formulate it by an entreaty for death. Consciously or unconsciously, this writhing fragment of humanity, this type and example of acute sensation, this handiwork of man and beast, this humble, unheroic Prometheus, was imploring everything, all, the whole non-ego, for the boon of oblivion. To the earth and the sky alike, to the trees, to the man, to whatever took form in sense or consciousness, this incarnate suffering addressed that silent plea.

For what, indeed? For that which we accord to even the meanest creature without sense to demand it, denying it only to the wretched of our own race: for the blessed release, the rite of uttermost compassion, the *coup de grâce*.

Captain Madwell spoke the name of his friend. He repeated it over and over without effect until emotion choked his utterance.

His tears plashed upon the livid face beneath his own and blinded himself. He saw nothing but a blurred and moving object, but the moans were more distinct than ever, interrupted at briefer intervals by sharper shrieks. He turned away, struck his hand upon his forehead, and strode from the spot. The swine, catching sight of him, threw up their crimson muzzles, regarding him suspiciously a second, and then with a gruff, concerted grunt, raced away out of sight. A horse, its foreleg splintered by a cannon-shot, lifted its head sidewise from the ground and neighed piteously. Madwell stepped forward, drew his revolver and shot the poor beast between the eyes, narrowly observing its death-struggle, which, contrary to his expectation, was violent and long; but at last it lay still. The tense muscles of its lips, which had uncovered the teeth in a horrible grin, relaxed; the sharp, clean-cut profile took on a look of profound peace and rest.

Along the distant, thinly wooded crest to westwards the fringe of sunset fire had now nearly burned itself out. The light upon the trunks of the trees had faded to a tender grey; shadows were in their tops, like great dark birds aperch. Night was coming and there were miles of haunted forest between Captain Madwell and camp. Yet he stood there at the side of the dead animal, apparently lost to all sense of his surroundings. His eyes were bent upon the earth at his feet; his left hand hung loosely at his side, his right still held the pistol. Presently he lifted his face, turned it towards his dying friend and walked rapidly back to his side. He knelt upon one knee, cocked the weapon, placed the muzzle against the man's forehead, and turning away his eyes pulled the trigger. There was no report. He had used his last cartridge for the horse.

The sufferer moaned and his lips moved convulsively. The froth that ran from them had a tinge of blood.

Captain Madwell rose to his feet and drew his sword from the scabbard. He passed the fingers of his left hand along the edge from hilt to point. He held it out straight before him, as if to test his nerves. There was no visible tremor of the blade; the ray of bleak skylight that it reflected was steady and true. He stooped and with his left hand tore away the dying man's shirt, rose and placed the point of the sword just over the heart. This time he did not withdraw his eyes. Grasping the hilt with both hands, he thrust downwards with all his strength and weight. The blade sank into the man's body—through his body into the earth; Captain Madwell came near falling forward upon his work. The dying man drew up his knees and at the same time threw his right arm across his breast and grasped the steel so tightly that the knuckles of the hand visibly whitened. By a violent but vain effort to withdraw the blade the wound was enlarged; a rill of blood escaped, running sinuously down into the deranged clothing. At that moment three men stepped silently forward from behind the clump of young trees which had concealed their approach. Two were hospital attendants and carried a stretcher.

The third was Major Creede Halcrow.

14

THE FORCED MARCH

Hornell Hart

Intermittently, when the snow ceased falling for a moment, Wojak could see the regiments ahead, black against the white fields, crawling interminably over the hilltop under the dull sky. Wojak was a burly, bearded fellow. These winter days pleased him. He liked the tingle that came with marching in the cold air. He liked the dull, rhythmic 'scruff' of the hundreds of feet as the regiment swung along, welded by its months of marching into a living unity.

This was his own country they were marching through. His homestead lay not twenty miles away, near this very road. As he trudged along thoughts of Sophy and little Stephan kept slipping into his mind.

At the crest of the hill the regiment came to a halt. Back from the road, half hidden in trees that were cut sharp and black against the snow and the sky, stood the ruin of a house.

'Just so stands my house,' thought Wojak. 'Behind, among the trees, should be the pigsty to the left, the stable to the right.'

He turned and waded through the newly fallen snow towards the dwelling. Charred beams at one end showed where a fire had been checked by the snowfall. In the yard beneath the fluffy new snow the old layer had evidently been tramped. Behind the house he found the pigsty and the stable.

'But the stable is bigger than mine,' he murmured.

He looked in. A pile of hay was in the corner, and on it lay some rags. The stable was so dark that Wojak thought he saw a child lying there. He went over to the corner. On the hay was a yellow head, the round cheeks streaked with tears. The child was sleeping, but its breath came in little sobs. With clumsy gentleness the soldier picked the baby up.

'Stephan had curls like that,' he whispered.

As he stepped out into the light the child awoke. A chubby arm slipped about the burly neck, and the blue eyes looked at him with the beginning of a smile. But in a moment the fact that this was not father, but a strange man, came over the baby, and he began to sob, not angrily, but with a worn anguish that gripped Wojak's heart.

The company was falling in after the halt when he came to the road. The curly head lay close to his bearded face, and a great clumsy hand protected the little body.

'Where did you get that, Wojak?' growled the lieutenant, staring blankly at the sorrowful little bundle. 'Leave the kid and fall in,' he commanded. 'There's no time for nonsense on this march.'

Wojak started to protest, but the habit of obedience was too strong. Sullenly he stood the baby in the snow and took his place in the ranks. The child's sobs turned to a heartbroken wail.

'Forward, march!' commanded the officer, and the company moved away down the road. Wojak looked back and saw the tiny arms stretched out after him while snowflakes settled on the yellow head. Long after the hilltop was hidden in swirling snow he seemed to see them and to hear the wail of the orphaned baby.

The sun was setting when the army bivouacked four miles from Wojak's farm. The orders were that no leaves of absence should be granted; but he knew the sentinel on guard, and home was too near to be left unseen for another four months.

The stars were glittering from an all but clear sky when he slipped silently through the lines and started down the familiar roads towards Sophy and Stephan. Four months was a terrible length of time. The passage of armies had marked the country. The great tree by the cottage of Ivanovicz had been shattered by a shell and had crashed through the roof. Jablonowski's barns had been burned. The windows of the church at the corners were shattered and a great hole had been shot in the steeple. Wojak walked faster, and a twinge of anxiety came over him as he entered the lane that led up to his barnyard. His heart stopped: the thatch of the stable had been burned and only the walls were standing. His eyes strained for a glimpse of the house. It was not there. A few charred beams marked the place where his home had stood.

He ran nearer. Snow had covered everything. Beside the place where the door had been was a white mound with a stick standing in the earth at its head. To the stick was nailed a little shoe. Wojak seized it with shaking hands.

'Stephan!' he choked. 'My little Stephan!'

After a while he looked up. Looming above him was a man on horseback who had ridden up unheard through the muffling snow.

'You are under arrest,' said the voice of the lieutenant.

15

THE BLACK DOOR

Gordon Seagrove

'Lieutenant Townley,' said Captain Von Dee sharply, 'as a spy you will be executed in two hours. Pursuant to my custom you will be given a choice in the matter. Either you may elect to be shot in the customary manner, or you may pass through the Black Door which you see behind me. State your choice when the hour comes.'

Von Dee—'Von Dee the whimsical' they called him in the trenches—turned to his reports while Lieutenant Townley was led back to the cell. A great hopelessness fell upon the latter. So this was the end then? All his hopes, his plans with regard to marriage to Cecile were to be swept away. It was difficult to realize that in another hour he would be separated by an unfathomable void from the woman whom he loved like life itself and trusted like no man had ever trusted woman before.

'Shot...or the Black Door...' Von Dee's words came back to him. What horrible fate—which legend held was worse than death—met those who passed beyond the Black Door? He knew that not one of death prisoners had dared to pass beyond it. Each had chosen death at the hands of the firing squad.

A half hour passed. Then, suddenly, a scrap of paper fluttered into his hands. He opened it and read:

'Choose the Black Door. I know.' It was signed Cecile.

Now the hour for the execution could not come soon enough. Cecile had remembered! Cecile had saved him. Perhaps behind the Black Door he would only be maimed or crippled and could go back to Cecile. As the guards led him into Von Dee's quarters his heart pounded gladly. In the gloom of the room he could see Von Dee and a stranger talking. In another moment he would tell Captain Von Dee that he, Lieutenant Townley, elected to pass through the Black Door.

He waited. Apparently his presence was not noted. He could hear scraps of conversation: 'I've always maintained,' Von Dee was saying, 'that, no matter how brave a man, he will choose a known form of death rather than an unknown...'

There was a lull, and then the other voice said: 'And you are the only one who knows what lies beyond the Black Door?'

'No,' Von Dee answered his brother. 'A woman knows.' Then he added with a light laugh: 'She was a former mistress of mine!'

Lieutenant Townley heard, trembled, turned white, then stiffened. Von Dee was before him, talking. 'Well, Lieutenant,' he said, 'do you elect the Black Door?'

'I do not!' the prisoner answered. Von Dee nodded to the guards who led Lieutenant Townley away. A moment later came the report of the firing squad on the drill grounds.

'What did I tell you!' cried Von Dee to his brother. 'Lieutenant Townley, one of the bravest, couldn't face the unknown. He went the usual way.' For several moments he puffed his cigar silently, then: 'Birwitz,' he asked suddenly, 'do you know what lies beyond the Black Door?'

The younger Von Dee shook his head.

'Freedom,' said Captain Von Dee. 'And I've never met a man brave enough to take it!'

16

THE OLD MAN AT THE BRIDGE

Ernest Hemingway

An old man with steel rimmed spectacles and very dusty clothes sat by the side of the road. There was a pontoon bridge across the river and carts, trucks, and men, women and children were crossing it. The mule-drawn carts staggered up the steep bank from the bridge with soldiers helping push against the spokes of the wheels. The trucks ground up and away heading out of it all and the peasants plodded along in the ankle deep dust. But the old man sat there without moving. He was too tired to go any farther.

It was my business to cross the bridge, explore the bridgehead beyond and find out to what point the enemy had advanced. I did this and returned over the bridge. There were not so many carts now and very few people on foot, but the old man was still there.

'Where do you come from?' I asked him.

'From San Carlos,' he said, and smiled.

That was his native town and so it gave him pleasure to mention it and he smiled.

'I was taking care of animals,' he explained.

'Oh,' I said, not quite understanding.

'Yes,' he said, 'I stayed, you see, taking care of animals. I was the last one to leave the town of San Carlos.'

He did not look like a shepherd nor a herdsman and I looked at his black dusty clothes and his grey dusty face and his steel rimmed spectacles and said, 'What animals were they?'

'Various animals,' he said, and shook his head. 'I had to leave them.'

I was watching the bridge and the African looking country of the Ebro Delta and wondering how long now it would be before we would see the enemy, and listening all the while for the first noises that would signal that ever mysterious event called contact, and the old man still sat there.

'What animals were they?' I asked.

'There were three animals altogether,' he explained. 'There were two goats and a cat and then there were four pairs of pigeons.'

'And you had to leave them?' I asked.

'Yes. Because of the artillery. The captain told me to go because of the artillery.'

'And you have no family?' I asked, watching the far end of the bridge where a few last carts were hurrying down the slope of the bank.

'No,' he said, 'only the animals I stated. The cat, of course, will be all right. A cat can look out for itself, but I cannot think what will become of the others.'

'What politics have you?' I asked.

'I am without politics,' he said. 'I am seventy-six years old. I have come twelve kilometres now and I think now I can go no further.'

'This is not a good place to stop,' I said. 'If you can make it, there are trucks up the road where it forks for Tortosa.'

'I will wait a while,' he said, ' and then I will go. Where do the trucks go?'

'Towards Barcelona,' I told him.

'I know no one in that direction,' he said, 'but thank you very much. Thank you again very much.'

He looked at me very blankly and tiredly, and then said, having to share his worry with someone, 'The cat will be all right,

I am sure. There is no need to be unquiet about the cat. But the others. Now what do you think about the others?'

'Why they'll probably come through it all right.'

'You think so?'

'Why not,' I said, watching the far bank where now there were no carts.

'But what will they do under the artillery when I was told to leave because of the artillery?'

'Did you leave the dove cage unlocked?' I asked.

'Yes.'

'Then they'll fly.'

'Yes, certainly they'll fly. But the others. It's better not to think about the others,' he said.

'If you are rested I would go,' I urged. 'Get up and try to walk now.'

'Thank you,' he said and got to his feet, swayed from side to side and then sat down backwards in the dust.

'I was taking care of animals,' he said dully, but no longer to me. 'I was only taking care of animals.'

There was nothing to do about him. It was Easter Sunday and the Fascists were advancing towards the Ebro. It was a grey overcast day with a low ceiling so their planes were not up. That and the fact that cats know how to look after themselves was all the good luck that old man would ever have.

17

THE LONE CHARGE OF WILLIAM B. PERKINS

Stephen Crane

He could not distinguish between a five-inch quick-firing gun and a nickle-plated ice-pick, and so, naturally, he had been elected to fill the position of war-correspondent. The responsible party was the editor of the 'Minnesota Herald.' Perkins had no information of war, and no particular rapidity of mind for acquiring it, but he had that rank and fibrous quality of courage which springs from the thick soil of Western America.

It was morning in Guantanamo Bay. If the marines encamped on the hill had had time to turn their gaze seawards, they might have seen a small newspaper despatch-boat wending its way towards the entrance of the harbour over the blue, sunlit waters of the Caribbean. In the stern of this tug Perkins was seated upon some coal bags, while the breeze gently ruffled his greasy pajamas. He was staring at a brown line of entrenchments surmounted by a flag, which was Camp McCalla. In the harbour were anchored two or three grim, grey cruisers and a transport. As the tug steamed up the radiant channel, Perkins could see men moving on shore near the charred ruins of a village. Perkins was deeply moved; here already was more war than he had ever known in Minnesota. Presently he, clothed in the essential garments of a war-correspondent, was rowed to the sandy beach. Marines in yellow linen were handling an ammunition supply. They paid no attention to the visitor, being morose from the inconveniences of two days and nights of fighting. Perkins toiled up the zigzag path to the top of the hill, and looked with eager eyes at the trenches, the field-pieces, the funny little Colts, the flag, the grim marines lying wearily on their arms. And still more, he looked through the clear air over 1,000 yards of mysterious woods from which emanated at inopportune times repeated flocks of Mauser bullets.

Perkins was delighted. He was filled with admiration for these jaded and smoky men who lay so quietly in the trenches waiting for a resumption of guerilla enterprise. But he wished they would heed him. He wanted to talk about it. Save for sharp inquiring glances, no one acknowledged his existence.

Finally he approached two young lieutenants, and in his innocent Western way he asked them if they would like a drink. The effect on the two young lieutenants was immediate and astonishing. With one voice they answered, 'Yes, we would.' Perkins almost wept with joy at this amiable response, and he exclaimed that he would immediately board the tug and bring off a bottle of Scotch. This attracted the officers, and in a burst of confidence one explained that there had not been a drop in camp. Perkins lunged down the hill, and fled to his boat, where in his exuberance he engaged in a preliminary altercation with some whisky. Consequently he toiled again up the hill in the blasting sun with his enthusiasm in no ways abated. The parched officers were very gracious, and such was the state of mind of Perkins that he did not note properly how serious and solemn was his engagement with the whisky. And because of this fact, and because of his antecedents, there happened the lone charge of William B. Perkins.

Now, as Perkins went down the hill, something happened. A private in those high trenches found that a cartridge was clogged in his rifle. It then becomes necessary with most kinds of rifles to explode the cartridge. The private took the rifle to his captain, and explained the case. But it would not do in that camp to fire a rifle for mechanical purposes and without warning, because the eloquent sound would bring six hundred tired marines to tension and high expectancy. So the captain turned, and in a loud voice announced to the camp that he found it necessary to shoot into the air. The communication rang sharply from voice to voice. Then the captain raised the weapon and fired. Whereupon—and whereupon—a large line of guerillas lying in the bushes decided swiftly that their presence and position were discovered, and swiftly they volleyed.

In a moment the woods and the hills were alive with the crack and sputter of rifles. Men on the warships in the harbour heard the old familiar flut-flut-fluttery-fluttery-flut-flut-flut from the entrenchments. Incidentally the launch of the 'Marblehead,' commanded by one of our headlong American ensigns, streaked for the strategic woods like a galloping marine dragoon, peppering away with its blunderbuss in the bow.

Perkins had arrived at the foot of the hill, where began the arrangement of 150 marines that protected the short line of communication between the main body and the beach. These men had all swarmed into line behind fortifications improvised from the boxes of provisions. And to them were gathering naked men who had been bathing, naked men who arrayed themselves speedily in cartridge belts and rifles. The woods and the hills went flut-flut-flut-fluttery-fluttery-flut-flllluttery-flut. Under the boughs of a beautiful tree lay five wounded men thinking vividly.

And now it befell Perkins to discover a Spaniard in the bush. The distance was some five hundred yards. In a loud voice he announced his perception. He also declared hoarsely, that if he only had a rifle, he would go and possess himself of this particular enemy. Immediately an amiable lad shot in the arm said: 'Well, take mine.' Perkins thus acquired a rifle and a clip of five cartridges.

'Come on!' he shouted. This part of the battalion was lying

very tight, not yet being engaged, but not knowing when the business would swirl around to them.

To Perkins they replied with a roar. 'Come back here, you—fool. Do you want to get shot by your own crowd? Come back,—!' As a detail, it might be mentioned that the fire from a part of the hill swept the journey upon which Perkins had started.

Now behold the solitary Perkins adrift in the storm of fighting, even as a champagne jacket of straw is lost in a great surf. He found it out quickly. Four seconds elapsed before he discovered that he was an almshouse idiot plunging through hot, crackling thickets on a June morning in Cuba. Sss-s-swing-singing-pop went the lightning-swift metal grasshoppers over him and beside him. The beauties of rural Minnesota illuminated his conscience with the gold of lazy corn, with the sleeping green of meadows, with the cathedral gloom of pine forests. Sshsh-swing-pop! Perkins decided that if he cared to extract himself from a tangle of imbecility he must shoot. The entire situation was that he must shoot. It was necessary that he should shoot. Nothing would save him but shooting. It is a law that men thus decide when the waters of battle close over their minds. So with a prayer that the Americans would not hit him in the back nor the left side, and that the Spaniards would not hit him in the front, he knelt like a supplicant alone in the desert of chaparral, and emptied his magazine at his Spaniard before he discovered that his Spaniard was a bit of dried palm branch.

Then Perkins flurried like a fish. His reason for being was a Spaniard in the bush. When the Spaniard turned into a dried palm branch, he could no longer furnish himself with one adequate reason.

Then did he dream frantically of some anthracite hiding-place, some profound dungeon of peace where blind mules live placidly chewing the far-gathered hay.

'Sss-swing-win-pop! Prut-prut-prrrut!' Then a field-gun spoke.

'*Boom*-ra-swow-ow-ow-ow-*pum*.' Then a Colt automatic began to bark. 'Crack-crk-crk-crk-crk-crk' endlessly. Raked, enfiladed, flanked, surrounded, and overwhelmed, what hope was there for William B. Perkins of the 'Minnesota Herald?'

But war is a spirit. War provides for those that it loves. It provides sometimes death and sometimes a singular and incredible safety. There were few ways in which it was possible to preserve Perkins. One way was by means of a steam-boiler.

Perkins espied near him an old, rusty steam-boiler lying in the bushes. War only knows how it was there, but there it was, a temple shining resplendent with safety. With a moan of haste, Perkins flung himself through that hole which expressed the absence of the steam-pipe.

Then ensconced in his boiler, Perkins comfortably listened to the ring of a fight which seemed to be in the air above him. Sometimes bullets struck their strong, swift blow against the boiler's sides, but none entered to interfere with Perkins's rest.

Time passed. The fight, short anyhow, dwindled to prut… prut…prut-prut…prut. And when the silence came, Perkins might have been seen cautiously protruding from the boiler. Presently he strolled back towards the marine lines with his hat not able to fit his head for the new bumps of wisdom that were on it.

The marines, with an annoyed air, were settling down again when an apparitional figure came from the bushes. There was great excitement.

'It's that crazy man,' they shouted, and as he drew near they gathered tumultuously about him and demanded to know how he had accomplished it.

Perkins made a gesture, the gesture of a man escaping from an unintentional mud-bath, the gesture of a man coming out of battle, and then he told them.

The incredulity was immediate and general. 'Yes, you did!

What? In an old boiler? An old boiler? Out in that brush? Well, we guess not.' They did not believe him until two days later, when a patrol happened to find the rusty boiler, relic of some curious transaction in the ruin of the Cuban sugar industry. The patrol then marvelled at the truthfulness of war-correspondents until they were almost blind.

Soon after his adventure Perkins boarded the tug, wearing a countenance of poignant thoughtfulness.

18

EDITHA

William D. Howells

The air was thick with the war feeling, like the electricity of a storm which had not yet burst. Editha sat looking out into the hot spring afternoon, with her lips parted, and panting with the intensity of the question whether she could let him go. She had decided that she could not let him stay, when she saw him at the end of the still leafless avenue, making slowly up towards the house, with his head down and his figure relaxed. She ran impatiently out on the veranda, to the edge of the steps, and imperatively demanded greater haste of him with her will before she called him aloud to him: 'George!'

He had quickened his pace in mystical response to her mystical urgence, before he could have heard her; now he looked up and answered, 'Well?'

'Oh, how united we are!' she exulted, and then she swooped down the steps to him, 'What is it?' she cried.

'It's war,' he said and he pulled her up to him and kissed her.

She kissed him back intensely, but irrelevantly, as to their passion, and uttered from deep in her throat. 'How glorious!'

'It's war,' he repeated, without consenting to her sense of it; and she did not know just what to think at first. She never knew what to think of him; that made his mystery, his charm. All through their courtship, which was contemporaneous with the growth of the war feeling, she had been puzzled by his want of seriousness about it. He seemed to despise it even more than he abhorred it. She could have understood his abhorring any sort of bloodshed; that would have been a survival of his old life when he thought he would be a minister, and before he changed and took up the law. But making light of a cause so high and noble seemed to show a want of earnestness at the core of his being. Not but that she felt herself able to cope with a congenital defect of that sort, and make his love for her save him from himself. Now perhaps the miracle was already wrought in him. In the presence of the tremendous fact that he announced, all triviality seemed to have gone out of him; she began to feel that. He sank down on the top step, and wiped his forehead with his handkerchief, while she poured out upon him her question of the origin and authenticity of his news.

All the while, in her duplex-emotioning, she was aware that now at the very beginning she must put a guard upon herself against urging him, by any word or act, to take the part that her whole soul willed him to take, for the completion of her ideal of him. He was very nearly perfect as he was, and he must be allowed to perfect himself. But he was peculiar, and he might very well be reasoned out of his peculiarity. Before her reasoning went her emotioning: her nature pulling upon his nature, her womanhood upon his manhood, without her knowing the means she was using to the end she was willing. She had always supposed that the man who won her would have done something to win her; she did not know what, but something. George Gearson had simply asked her for her love, on the way home from a concert, and she gave her love to him, without, as it were, thinking. But now, it flashed upon her, if he could do something worthy to *have* won her—be a hero, *her* hero—it would be even better than if he had done it before asking her; it would be grander. Besides, she had believed in the war from the beginning.

'But don't you see, dearest,' she said, 'that it wouldn't have come to this if it hadn't been in the order of Providence? And I call any war glorious that is for the liberation of people who have been struggling for years against the cruelest oppression. Don't you think so, too?'

'I suppose so,' he returned, languidly. 'But war! Is it glorious to break the peace of the world?'

'That ignoble peace! It was no peace at all, with that crime and shame at our very gates.' She was conscious of parroting the current phrases of the newspapers, but it was no time to pick and choose her words. She must sacrifice anything to the high ideal she had for him, and after a good deal of rapid argument she ended with the climax: 'But now it doesn't matter about the how or why. Since the war has come, all that is gone. There are no two sides any more. There is nothing now but our country.'

He sat with his eyes closed and his head leant back against the veranda, and he remarked, with a vague smile, as if musing aloud, 'Our country—right or wrong.'

'Yes, right or wrong!' she returned, fervidly. 'I'll go and get you some lemonade.' She rose rustling, and whisked away; when she came back with two tall glasses of clouded liquid on a tray, and the ice clucking in them, he still sat as she had left him, and she said, as if there had been no interruption: 'But there is no question of wrong in this case. I call it a sacred war. A war for liberty and humanity, if ever there was one. And I know you will see it just as I do, yet.'

He took half the lemonade at a gulp, and he answered as he set the glass down: 'I know you always have the highest ideal. When I differ from you I ought to doubt myself.'

A generous sob rose in Editha's throat for the humility of a man, so very nearly perfect, who was willing to put himself below her.

Besides, she felt, more subliminally, that he was never so near slipping through her fingers as when he took that meek way.

'You shall not say that! Only, for once I happen to be right.' She seized his hand in her two hands, and poured her soul from her eyes into his. 'Don't you think so?' she entreated him.

He released his hand and drank the rest of his lemonade, and she added, 'Have mine, too,' but he shook his head in answering, 'I've no business to think so, unless I act so, too.'

Her heart stopped a beat before it pulsed on with leaps that she felt in her neck. She had noticed that strange thing in men: they seemed to feel bound to do what they believed, and not think a thing was finished when they said it, as girls did. She knew what was in his mind, but she pretended not, and she said, 'Oh, I am not sure,' and then faltered.

He went on as if to himself, without apparently heeding her: 'There's only one way of proving one's faith in a thing like this.'

She could not say that she understood, but she did understand.

He went on again. 'If I believed—if I felt as you do about this war— Do you wish me to feel as you do?'

Now she was really not sure; so she said: 'George, I don't know what you mean.'

He seemed to muse away from her as before. 'There is a sort of fascination in it. I suppose that at the bottom of his heart every man would like at times to have his courage tested, to see how he would act.'

'How can you talk in that ghastly way?'

'It *is* rather morbid. Still, that's what it comes to, unless you're swept away by ambition or driven by conviction. I haven't the conviction or the ambition, and the other thing is what it comes to with me. I ought to have been a preacher, after all; then I couldn't have asked it of myself, as I must, now I'm a lawyer. And you believe it's a holy war, Editha?' he suddenly addressed her. 'Oh, I know you do! But you wish me to believe so, too?'

She hardly knew whether he was mocking or not, in the ironical way he always had with her plainer mind. But the only thing was to be outspoken with him.

'George, I wish you to believe whatever you think is true,

at any and every cost. If I've tried to talk you into anything, I take it all back.'

'Oh, I know that, Editha. I know how sincere you are, and how—I wish I had your undoubting spirit! I'll think it over; I'd like to believe as you do. But I don't, now; I don't, indeed. It isn't this war alone; though this seems peculiarly wanton and needless; but it's every war—so stupid; it makes me sick. Why shouldn't this thing have been settled reasonably?'

'Because,' she said, very throatily again, 'God meant it to be war.'

'You think it was God? Yes, I suppose that is what people will say.'

'Do you suppose it would have been war if God hadn't meant it?'

'I don't know. Sometimes it seems as if God had put this world into men's keeping to work it as they pleased.'

'Now, George, that is blasphemy.'

'Well, I won't blaspheme. I'll try to believe in your pocket Providence,' he said, and then he rose to go.

'Why don't you stay to dinner?' Dinner at Balcom's Works was at one o'clock.

'I'll come back to supper, if you'll let me. Perhaps I shall bring you a convert.'

'Well, you may come back, on that condition.'

'All right. If I don't come, you'll understand.'

He went away without kissing her, and she felt it a suspension of their engagement. It all interested her intensely; she was undergoing a tremendous experience, and she was being equal to it. While she stood looking after him, her mother came out through one of the long windows onto the veranda, with a catlike softness and vagueness.

'Why didn't he stay to dinner?'

'Because—because—war has been declared,' Editha

pronounced, without turning.

Her mother said, 'Oh, my!' and then said nothing more until she had sat down in one of the large Shaker chairs and rocked herself for some time. Then she closed whatever tacit passage of thought there had been in her mind with the spoken words: 'Well, I hope *he* won't go.'

'And *I* hope he *will*,' the girl said, and confronted her mother with a stormy exaltation that would have frightened any creature less unimpressionable than a cat.

Her mother rocked herself again for an interval of cogitation. What she arrived at in speech was: 'Well, I guess you've done a wicked thing, Editha Balcom.'

The girl said, as she passed indoors through the same window her mother had come out by: 'I haven't done anything—yet.'

In her room, she put together all her letters and gifts from Gearson, down to the withered petals of the first flower he had offered, with that timidity of his veiled in that irony of his. In the heart of the packet she enshrined her engagement ring which she had restored to the pretty box he had brought it her in. Then she sat down, if not calmly yet strongly, and wrote:

'George:—I understood when you left me. But I think we had better emphasize your meaning that if we cannot be one in everything we had better be one in nothing. So I am sending these things for your keeping till you have made up your mind.

'I shall always love you, and therefore I shall never marry any one else. But the man I marry must love his country first of all, and be able to say to me,

'I could not love thee, dear, so much,
Loved I not honour more.'

'There is no honour above America with me. In this great hour there is no other honour.

'Your heart will make my words clear to you. I had never

expected to say so much, but it has come upon me that I must say the utmost. Editha.'

She thought she had worded her letter well, worded it in a way that could not be bettered; all had been implied and nothing expressed.

She had it ready to send with the packet she had tied with red, white, and blue ribbon, when it occurred to her that she was not just to him, that she was not giving him a fair chance. He had said he would go and think it over, and she was not waiting. She was pushing, threatening, compelling. That was not a woman's part. She must leave him free, free, free. She could not accept for her country or herself a forced sacrifice.

In writing her letter she had satisfied the impulse from which it sprang; she could well afford to wait till he had thought it over. She put the packet and the letter by, and rested serene in the consciousness of having done what was laid upon her by her love itself to do, and yet used patience, mercy, justice.

She had her reward. Gearson did not come to tea, but she had given him till morning, when, late at night there came up from the village the sound of a fife and drum, with a tumult of voices, in shouting, singing, and laughing. The noise drew nearer and nearer; it reached the street end of the avenue; there it silenced itself, and one voice, the voice she knew best, rose over the silence. It fell; the air was filled with cheers; the fife and drum struck up, with the shouting, singing, and laughing again, but now retreating; and a single figure came hurrying up the avenue.

She ran down to meet her lover and clung to him. He was very gay, and he put his arm round her with a boisterous laugh. 'Well, you must call me Captain now; or Cap, if you prefer; that's what the boys call me. Yes, we've had a meeting at the town-hall, and everybody has volunteered; and they selected me for captain, and I'm going to the war, the big war, the glorious war, the holy war ordained by the pocket Providence that blesses butchery.

Come along; let's tell the whole family about it. Call them from their downy beds, father, mother, Aunt Hitty, and all the folks!'

But when they mounted the veranda steps he did not wait for a larger audience; he poured the story out upon Editha alone.

'There was a lot of speaking, and then some of the fools set up a shout for me. It was all going one way, and I thought it would be a good joke to sprinkle a little cold water on them. But you can't do that with a crowd that adores you. The first thing I knew I was sprinkling hell-fire on them. 'Cry havoc, and let slip the dogs of war.' That was the style. Now that it had come to the fight, there were no two parties; there was one country, and the thing was to fight to a finish as quick as possible. I suggested volunteering then and there, and I wrote my name first of all on the roster. Then they elected me—that's all. I wish I had some ice-water.'

She left him walking up and down the veranda, while she ran for the ice-pitcher and a goblet, and when she came back he was still walking up and down, shouting the story he had told her to her father and mother, who had come out more sketchily dressed than they commonly were by day. He drank goblet after goblet of the ice-water without noticing who was giving it, and kept on talking, and laughing through his talk wildly. 'It's astonishing,' he said, 'how well the worse reason looks when you try to make it appear the better. Why, I believe I was the first convert to the war in that crowd to-night! I never thought I should like to kill a man; but now I shouldn't care; and the smokeless powder lets you see the man drop that you kill. It's all for the country! What a thing it is to have a country that *can't* be wrong, but if it is, is right, anyway!'

Editha had a great, vital thought, an inspiration. She set down the ice-pitcher on the veranda floor, and ran up-stairs and got the letter she had written him. When at last he noisily bade her father and mother, 'Well, good-night. I forgot I woke you up; I sha'n't want any sleep myself,' she followed him down the avenue to the gate. There, after the whirling words that seemed to fly away from her thoughts and refuse to serve them, she made a last effort to solemnize the moment that seemed so crazy, and pressed the letter she had written upon him.

'What's this?' he said. 'Want me to mail it?'

'No, no. It's for you. I wrote it after you went this morning. Keep it—keep it—and read it sometime—' She thought, and then her inspiration came: 'Read it if ever you doubt what you've done, or fear that I regret your having done it. Read it after you've started.'

They strained each other in embraces that seemed as ineffective as their words, and he kissed her face with quick, hot breaths that were so unlike him, that made her feel as if she had lost her old lover and found a stranger in his place. The stranger said: 'What a gorgeous flower you are, with your red hair, and your blue eyes that look black now, and your face with the colourpainted out by the white moonshine! Let me hold you under the chin, to see whether I love blood, you tiger-lily!' Then he laughed Gearson's laugh, and released her, scared and giddy. Within her wilfulness she had been frightened by a sense of subtler force in him, and mystically mastered as she had never been before.

She ran all the way back to the house, and mounted the steps panting. Her mother and father were talking of the great affair. Her mother said: 'Wa'n't Mr Gearson in rather of an excited state of mind? Didn't you think he acted curious?'

'Well, not for a man who'd just been elected captain and had set 'em up for the whole of Company A,' her father chuckled back.

'What in the world do you mean, Mr Balcom? Oh! There's Editha!' She offered to follow the girl indoors.

'Don't come, mother!' Editha called, vanishing.

Mrs Balcom remained to reproach her husband. 'I don't see

much of anything to laugh at.'

'Well, it's catching. Caught it from Gearson. I guess it won't be much of a war, and I guess Gearson don't think so either. The other fellows will back down as soon as they see we mean it. I wouldn't lose any sleep over it. I'm going back to bed, myself.'

Gearson came again next afternoon, looking pale and rather sick, but quite himself, even to his languid irony. 'I guess I'd better tell you, Editha, that I consecrated myself to your god of battles last night by pouring too many libations to him down my own throat. But I'm all right now. One has to carry off the excitement, somehow.'

'Promise me,' she commanded, 'that you'll never touch it again!'

'What! Not let the cannikin clink? Not let the soldier drink? Well, I promise.'

'You don't belong to yourself now; you don't even belong to *me*. You belong to your country, and you have a sacred charge to keep yourself strong and well for your country's sake. I have been thinking, thinking all night and all day long.'

'You look as if you had been crying a little, too,' he said, with his queer smile.

'That's all past. I've been thinking, and worshipping *you*. Don't you suppose I know all that you've been through, to come to this? I've followed you every step from your old theories and opinions.'

'Well, you've had a long row to hoe.'

'And I know you've done this from the highest motives—'

'Oh, there won't be much pettifogging to do till this cruel war is—'

'And you haven't simply done it for my sake. I couldn't respect you if you had.'

'Well, then we'll say I haven't. A man that hasn't got his own respect intact wants the respect of all the other people he can corner. But we won't go into that. I'm in for the thing now, and we've got to face our future. My idea is that this isn't going to be a very protracted struggle; we shall just scare the enemy to death before it comes to a fight at all. But we must provide for contingencies, Editha. If anything happens to me—'

'Oh, George!' She clung to him, sobbing.

'I don't want you to feel foolishly bound to my memory. I should hate that, wherever I happened to be.'

'I am yours, for time and eternity—time and eternity.' She liked the words; they satisfied her famine for phrases.

'Well, say eternity; that's all right; but time's another thing; and I'm talking about time. But there is something! My mother! If anything happens—'

She winced, and he laughed. 'You're not the bold soldier-girl of yesterday!' Then he sobered. 'If anything happens, I want you to help my mother out. She won't like my doing this thing. She brought me up to think war a fool thing as well as a bad thing. My father was in the Civil War; all through it; lost his arm in it.' She thrilled with the sense of the arm round her; what if that should be lost? He laughed as if divining her: 'Oh, it doesn't run in the family, as far as I know!' Then he added gravely: 'He came home with misgivings about war, and they grew on him. I guess he and mother agreed between them that I was to be brought up in his final mind about it; but that was before my time. I only knew him from my mother's report of him and his opinions; I don't know whether they were hers first; but they were hers last. This will be a blow to her. I shall have to write and tell her—'

He stopped, and she asked: 'Would you like me to write, too, George?'

'I don't believe that would do. No, I'll do the writing. She'll understand a little if I say that I thought the way to minimize it was to make war on the largest possible scale at once—that I felt I must have been helping on the war somehow if I hadn't helped keep it from coming, and I knew I hadn't; when it came, I had no right to stay out of it.'

Whether his sophistries satisfied him or not, they satisfied her. She clung to his breast, and whispered, with closed eyes and quivering lips: 'Yes, yes, yes!'

'But if anything should happen, you might go to her and see what you could do for her. You know? It's rather far off; she can't leave her chair—'

'Oh, I'll go, if it's the ends of the earth! But nothing will happen! Nothing *can!* I—'

She felt her lifted with his rising, and Gearson was saying, with his arm still round her, to her father: 'Well, we're off at once, Mr Balcom. We're to be formally accepted at the capital, and then bunched up with the rest somehow, and sent into camp somewhere, and got to the front as soon as possible. We all want to be in the van, of course; we're the first company to report to the Governor. I came to tell Editha, but I hadn't got round to it.'

She saw him again for a moment at the capital, in the station, just before the train started southwards with his regiment. He looked well, in his uniform, and very soldierly, but somehow girlish, too, with his clean-shaven face and slim figure. The manly eyes and the strong voice satisfied her, and his preoccupation with some unexpected details of duty flattered her. Other girls were weeping and bemoaning themselves, but she felt a sort of noble distinction in the abstraction, the almost unconsciousness, with which they parted. Only at the last moment he said: 'Don't forget my mother. It mayn't be such a walk-over as I supposed,' and he laughed at the notion.

He waved his hand to her as the train moved off—she knew it among a score of hands that were waved to other girls from the platform of the car, for it held a letter which she knew was hers. Then he went inside the car to read it, doubtless, and she did not see him again. But she felt safe for him through the strength of what she called her love. What she called her God, always speaking the name in a deep voice and with the implication of a mutual understanding, would watch over him and keep him and bring him back to her. If with an empty sleeve, then he should have three arms instead of two, for both of hers should be his for life. She did not see, though, why she should always be thinking of the arm his father had lost.

There were not many letters from him, but they were such as she could have wished, and she put her whole strength into making hers such as she imagined he could have wished, glorifying and supporting him. She wrote to his mother glorifying him as their hero, but the brief answer she got was merely to the effect that Mrs Gearson was not well enough to write herself, and thanking her for her letter by the hand of someone who called herself 'Yrs truly, Mrs W.J. Andrews.'

Editha determined not to be hurt, but to write again quite as if the answer had been all she expected. Before it seemed as if she could have written, there came news of the first skirmish, and in the list of the killed, which was telegraphed as a trifling loss on our side, was Gearson's name. There was a frantic time of trying to make out that it might be, must be, some other Gearson; but the name and the company and the regiment and the State were too definitely given.

Then there was a lapse into depths out of which it seemed as if she never could rise again; then a lift into clouds far above all grief, black clouds, that blotted out the sun, but where she soared with him, with George—George! She had the fever that she expected of herself, but she did not die in it; she was not even delirious, and it did not last long. When she was well enough to leave her bed, her one thought was of George's mother, of his strangely worded wish that she should go to her and see what she could do for her. In the exaltation of the duty laid upon her—it buoyed her up instead of burdening her—she rapidly recovered.

Her father went with her on the long railroad journey from northern New York to western Iowa; he had business out at Davenport, and he said he could just as well go then as any other time; and he went with her to the little country town where George's mother lived in a little house on the edge of the illimitable cornfields, under trees pushed to a top of the rolling prairie. George's father had settled there after the Civil War, as so many other old soldiers had done; but they were Eastern people, and Editha fancied touches of the East in the June rose overhanging the front door, and the garden with early summer flowers stretching from the gate of the paling fence.

It was very low inside the house, and so dim, with the closed blinds, that they could scarcely see one another: Editha tall and black in her crapes which filled the air with the smell of their dyes; her father standing decorously apart with his hat on his forearm, as at funerals; a woman rested in a deep arm-chair, and the woman who had let the strangers in stood behind the chair.

The seated woman turned her head round and up, and asked the woman behind her chair: '*Who* did you say?'

Editha, if she had done what she expected of herself, would have gone down on her knees at the feet of the seated figure and said, 'I am George's Editha,' for answer.

But instead of her own voice she heard that other woman's voice, saying: 'Well, I don't know as I *did* get the name just right. I guess I'll have to make a little more light in here,' and she went and pushed two of the shutters ajar.

Then Editha's father said, in his public will-now-address-a-few-remarks tone: 'My name is Balcom, ma'am—Junius H. Balcom, of Balcom's Works, New York; my daughter—'

'Oh!' the seated woman broke in, with a powerful voice, the voice that always surprised Editha from Gearson's slender frame. 'Let me see you. Stand round where the light can strike on your face,' and Editha dumbly obeyed. 'So, you're Editha Balcom,' she sighed.

'Yes,' Editha said, more like a culprit than a comforter.

'What did you come for?' Mrs Gearson asked.

Editha's face quivered and her knees shook. 'I came—because—because George—' She could go no further.

'Yes,' the mother said, 'he told me he had asked you to come if he got killed. You didn't expect that, I suppose, when you sent him.'

'I would rather have died myself than done it!' Editha said, with more truth in her deep voice than she ordinarily found in it. 'I tried to leave him free—'

'Yes, that letter of yours, that came back with his other things, left him free.'

Editha saw now where George's irony came from.

'It was not to be read before—unless—until— I told him so,' she faltered.

'Of course, he wouldn't read a letter of yours, under the circumstances, till he thought you wanted him to. Been sick?' the woman abruptly demanded.

'Very sick,' Editha said, with self-pity.

'Daughter's life,' her father interposed, 'was almost despaired of, at one time.'

Mrs Gearson gave him no heed. 'I suppose you would have been glad to die, such a brave person as you! I don't believe *he* was glad to die. He was always a timid boy, that way; he was afraid of a good many things; but if he was afraid he did what he made up his mind to. I suppose he made up his mind to go, but I knew what it cost him by what it cost me when I heard of it. I had been through *one* war before. When you sent him you didn't expect he would get killed.'

The voice seemed to compassionate Editha, and it was time. 'No,' she huskily murmured.

'No, girls don't; women don't, when they give their men up to their country. They think they'll come marching back, somehow, just as gay as they went, or if it's an empty sleeve, or even an empty pantaloon, it's all the more glory, and they're so much the prouder of them, poor things!'

The tears began to run down Editha's face; she had not wept till then; but it was now such a relief to be understood that the tears came.

'No, you didn't expect him to get killed,' Mrs Gearson repeated, in a voice which was startlingly like George's again. 'You just expected him to kill some one else, some of those foreigners, that weren't there because they had any say about it, but because they had to be there, poor wretches—conscripts, or whatever they call 'em. You thought it would be all right for my George, *your* George, to kill the sons of those miserable mothers and the husbands of those girls that you would never see the faces of.' The woman lifted her powerful voice in a psalmlike note. 'I thank my God he didn't live to do it! I thank my God they killed him first, and that he ain't livin' with their blood on his hands!' She dropped her eyes, which she had raised with her voice, and glared at Editha. 'What you got that black on for?' She lifted herself by her powerful arms so high that her helpless body seemed to hang limp its full length. 'Take it off, take it off, before I tear it from your back!'

The lady who was passing the summer near Balcom's Works was sketching Editha's beauty, which lent itself wonderfully to the effects of a colourist. It had come to that confidence which is rather apt to grow between artist and sitter, and Editha had told her everything.

'To think of your having such a tragedy in your life!' the lady said. She added: 'I suppose there are people who feel that way about war. But when you consider the good this war has done—how much it has done for the country! I can't understand such people, for my part. And when you had come all the way out there to console her—got up out of a sick-bed! Well!'

'I think,' Editha said, magnanimously, 'she wasn't quite in her right mind; and so did papa.'

'Yes,' the lady said, looking at Editha's lips in nature and then at her lips in art, and giving an empirical touch to them in the picture. 'But how dreadful of her! How perfectly—excuse me—how *vulgar!*'

A light broke upon Editha in the darkness which she felt had been without a gleam of brightness for weeks and months. The mystery that had bewildered her was solved by the word; and from that moment she rose from grovelling in shame and self-pity, and began to live again in the ideal.

19

WAR

Luigi Pirandello

The passengers who had left Rome by the night express had had to stop until dawn at the small station of Fabriano in order to continue their journey by the small old-fashioned local joining the main line with Sulmona.

At dawn, in a stuffy and smoky second-class carriage in which five people had already spent the night, a bulky woman in deep mourning was hosted in—almost like a shapeless bundle. Behind her—puffing and moaning, followed her husband—a tiny man; thin and weakly, his face death-white, his eyes small and bright and looking shy and uneasy.

Having at last taken a seat he politely thanked the passengers who had helped his wife and who had made room for her; then he turned round to the woman trying to pull down the collar of her coat and politely inquired:

'Are you all right, dear?'

The wife, instead of answering, pulled up her collar again to her eyes, so as to hide her face.

'Nasty world,' muttered the husband with a sad smile.

And he felt it his duty to explain to his travelling companions that the poor woman was to be pitied for the war was taking away from her her only son, a boy of twenty to whom both had devoted their entire life, even breaking up their home at Sulmona to follow him to Rome, where he had to go as a student, then allowing him to volunteer for war with an assurance, however, that at least six months he would not be sent to the front and now, all of a sudden, receiving a wire saying that he was due to leave in three days' time and asking them to go and see him off.

The woman under the big coat was twisting and wriggling, at times growling like a wild animal, feeling certain that all those explanations would not have aroused even a shadow of sympathy from those people who—most likely—were in the same plight as herself. One of them, who had been listening with particular attention, said:

'You should thank God that your son is only leaving now for the front. Mine has been sent there the first day of the war. He has already come back twice wounded and been sent back again to the front.'

'What about me? I have two sons and three nephews at the front,' said another passenger.

'Maybe, but in our case it is our only son,' ventured the husband.

'What difference can it make? You may spoil your only son by excessive attentions, but you cannot love him more than you would all your other children if you had any. Parental love is not like bread that can be broken to pieces and split amongst the children in equal shares. A father gives all his love to each one of his children without discrimination, whether it be one or ten, and if I am suffering now for my two sons, I am not suffering half for each of them but double...'

'True...true...' sighed the embarrassed husband, 'but suppose (of course we all hope it will never be your case) a father has two sons at the front and he loses one of them, there is still one left to console him...while...'

'Yes,' answered the other, getting cross, 'a son left to console him but also a son left for whom he must survive, while in the case of the father of an only son if the son dies the father can die too and put an end to his distress. Which of the two positions is worse? Don't you see how my case would be worse than yours?'

'Nonsense,' interrupted another traveller, a fat, red-faced man with bloodshot eyes of the palest grey.

He was panting. From his bulging eyes seemed to spurt inner violence of an uncontrolled vitality which his weakened body could hardly contain.

'Nonsense,' he repeated, trying to cover his mouth with his hand so as to hide the two missing front teeth. 'Nonsense. Do we give life to our own children for our own benefit?'

The other travellers stared at him in distress. The one who had had his son at the front since the first day of the war sighed: 'You are right. Our children do not belong to us, they belong to the country...'

'Bosh,' retorted the fat traveller. 'Do we think of the country when we give life to our children? Our sons are born because... well, because they must be born and when they come to life they take our own life with them. This is the truth. We belong to them but they never belong to us. And when they reach twenty they are exactly what we were at their age. We too had a father and mother, but there were so many other things as well...girls, cigarettes, illusions, new ties...and the Country, of course, whose call we would have answered—when we were twenty—even if father and mother had said no. Now, at our age, the love of our Country is still great, of course, but stronger than it is the love of our children. Is there any one of us here who wouldn't gladly take his son's place at the front if he could?'

There was a silence all round, everybody nodding as to approve.

'Why then,' continued the fat man, 'should we consider the feelings of our children when they are twenty? Isn't it natural that at their age they should consider the love for their Country (I am speaking of decent boys, of course) even greater than the love for us? Isn't it natural that it should be so, as after all they must look upon us as upon old boys who cannot move any more and must sit at home? If Country is a natural necessity like bread of which each of us must eat in order not to die of hunger, somebody must go to defend it. And our sons go, when they are twenty, and they don't want tears, because if they die, they die inflamed and happy (I am speaking, of course, of decent boys). Now, if one dies young and happy, without having the ugly sides of life, the boredom of it, the pettiness, the bitterness of disillusion...what more can we ask for him? Everyone should stop crying; everyone should laugh, as I do...or at least thank God—as I do—because my son, before dying, sent me a message saying that he was dying satisfied at having ended his life in the best way he could have wished. That is why, as you see, I do not even wear mourning...'

He shook his light fawn coat as to show it; his livid lip over his missing teeth was trembling, his eyes were watery and motionless, and soon after he ended with a shrill laugh which might well have been a sob.

'Quite so...quite so...' agreed the others.

The woman who, bundled in a corner under her coat, had been sitting and listening had—for the last three months—tried to find in the words of her husband and her friends something to console her in her deep sorrow, something that might show her how a mother should resign herself to send her son not even to death but to a probable danger of life. Yet not a word had she found amongst the many that had been said...and her grief had been greater in seeing that nobody—as she thought—could share her feelings.

But now the words of the traveller amazed and almost stunned her. She suddenly realized that it wasn't the others who were wrong and could not understand her but herself who could not rise up to the same height of those fathers and mothers willing to resign themselves, without crying, not only to the departure of their sons but even to their death.

She lifted her head, she bent over from her corner trying to listen with great attention to the details which the fat man was giving to his companions about the way his son had fallen as a hero, for his King and his Country, happy and without regrets. It seemed to her that she had stumbled into a world she had never dreamt of, a world so far unknown to her, and she was so pleased to hear everyone joining in congratulating that brave father who could so stoically speak of his child's death.

Then suddenly, just as if she had heard nothing of what had been said and almost as if waking up from a dream, she turned to the old man, asking him:

'Then...is your son really dead?'

Everyone stared at her. The old man, too, turned to look at her, fixing his great, bulging, horribly watery light grey eyes, deep in her face. For some time he tried to answer, but words failed him. He looked and looked at her, almost as if only then—at that silly, incongruous question—he had suddenly realized at last that his son was really dead—gone for ever—for ever. His face contracted, became horribly distorted, then he snatched in haste a handkerchief from his pocket and, to the amazement of everyone, broke into harrowing, heart-breaking, uncontrollable sobs.

20

WHY THE TRENCH WAS LOST

Charles F. Pietsch

Not two miles away lay his home. Metre by metre, Joffre's 'nibbling' had forced the Boches back over the death-sown fields of the Argonne. And now as he sat in his cunningly hidden nest aloft in a treetop, observer for a battery of 75's, his telescope, wandering from the German trenches, brought home so close that he seemed almost to be standing in his own garden.

It was so close, he thought—just over there. And it was so good to be able to watch little Marie playing at the door, and to peep inside into the kitchen where Jeanne was working—or to follow her from room to room as her slim figure flitted past the windows.

He had worried so when 'Papa' Joffre's masterly retreat had left her there alone. But this was the fourth day now that he had kept watch over her, and soon, he said to himself with a smile—soon that little home was sure to lie back of the French lines in safety.

The day was quiet. Only intermittently a cannon barked or a rifle spat across the wire entanglements. And all the morning he had sat watching Marie's flaxen tresses bobbing among the rose bushes—and dreaming of when the war ended.

And suddenly the picture changed.

Marie has dropped her dolls and is racing into the kitchen. The door slams. He almost hears the bolt shot to, he thinks. And a squad of Uhlans rides into the yard.

For months past he had driven that picture from his mind.

It couldn't be—oh! it couldn't be. And now in sight of home it came in grim reality. So close—and yet as well be at the ends of the earth with that German line between them.

He steadied the telescope in time to see a gun butt smash in the door and the officer stride in. The German batteries opened with a crash. A charge was coming. But he had no eyes for the enemy. He felt, rather than saw, a grey-green wave with a crest of steel flow up from the German trenches and over the 'dead man's land.' And instinctively he shot orders into the transmitter at his lips.

'Two hundred metres.'

'One hundred and seventy-five metres—left.'

And as the little puffs of shrapnel began to blossom over the grey-green wave, his gaze swung back to the little cottage.

And then he forgot the Germans—forgot his comrades in the endangered trench—forgot war—everything. For a figure—a woman's figure—struggling—fell past a window in the arms of a uniformed figure.

He thought a scream came to his ears. For one insane second he started down from his station: he must go; he was so close. She needed him. And then as his eyes fell on the struggle below he realized how far it was—how helpless he was. And—

But there was a way. And he began to snap orders into the transmitter.

'One thousand five hundred metres—eight degrees left.'

A puff rose on the highway running past his home.

'One thousand six hundred metres.'

And a shell exploded at the little stable.

'One thousand six hundred and fifty metres'—he shot another order over the wire—and another—and another—and then:

'Battery, fire!' And with a cry, fell headlong from the treetop as the little home and its tragedy vanished in a whirl of smoke and wreckage.

21

THE QUEST OF THE V.C.

A. Byers Fletcher

There was tumultuous cheering in the ranks of the Irish Guards somewhere in France. Sergeant O'Reilly, V.C., had returned to the trenches. Two months before, Private O'Reilly had, with a scorching-hot machine-gun, held, single-handed, an important trench after all his comrades had fallen. Incidentally, he had also saved the life of an officer, who lay wounded and exposed on the parapet of the trench. His was but one of many such brave deeds which occurred almost daily along that terrible front, but O'Reilly's deed had the advantage of being conspicuous. Hence his two-months' leave, his journey to London, and his reception at Buckingham Palace, where the King himself pinned the little bronze cross to his khaki jacket. Hence, his public reception in his native village of Tullameelan, where they hung garlands of flowers about his neck, and his old mother wept tears of joyful pride. Hence, too, his return with the sergeant's stripes. The story of the honours heaped upon him had been duly chronicled and illustrated in the press, and had preceded his return to the trenches. Hence, his joyful reception by the regiment.

Private Finnessy and Private Moloney had been among the first to grasp the hero's hand, and had joined heartily in the vociferous cheering, but now that affairs had again resumed their normal round, these two companions sat at the bottom of the trench, smoking thoughtfully.

'O'Reilly's a brave man,' said Finnessy, then added, after a pause, 'the lucky devil!'

'I believe ye,' replied Moloney.

'And he only five feet sivin,' continued Finnessy.

'With one punch,' said Moloney, contemplating his hairy fist, 'I could lift him into the inemy's trenches!'

'Do ye mind how all the girls in Tullameelan kissed him?' said Finnessy.

'I know one girl there that didn't!' said Moloney hotly.

'And I know another!' as hotly replied Finnessy.

'The papers are nothin' but lyin' rags,' said Moloney.

'I believe ye,' said Finnessy.

Viciously whistled the bullets across the top of the trench, and a shell or two whined overhead, unheeded by the comrades, long accustomed to the sound.

'But I'm not denyin',' said Finnessy, after a pause, 'that the little brown cross is a great timptation to anny girl.'

'It is that!' agreed Moloney.

'At five o'clock!' the whisper ran along the trench. Since three o'clock the guns massed on the hills behind them had been sending a shrieking death-storm into the enemy's trenches in front of the Irish Guards. At five, promptly, the storm of shell would cease. At a given signal the men would clamber out over the parapet, make their way through the openings in the wire entanglements, and rush the trenches before them. There was no outward excitement. The aspect of the men remained unchanged, but one could feel the nervous tension. A young subaltern, near Finnessy and Moloney, glanced occasionally at his wrist watch and smoked his cigarette more rapidly than usual.

'If he falls,' whispered Finnessy to Moloney, ''tis mesilf that will bring him in.'

'You will not,' said Moloney, 'I've had me eye on him f'r wakes!'

'Ye can have the Major,' said Finnessy.

'I'll not!' said Moloney, ''twud take a horse to carry him in!'

The batteries ceased firing. A low whistle sounded. The men grasped their rifles with bayonets fixed. Cold steel alone must do the work now. Another whistle. With a hoarse cheer the men climbed out over the front of the trench and the charge was on.

Side by side raced Finnessy and Moloney, with eyes fixed on the young subaltern, who, carrying a rifle, was sprinting on before them. For a few moments it seemed that the batteries had effectually silenced the trenches of the enemy immediately in front. A hundred yards farther and they would be reached. Now, however, from that line of piled earth and barbed wire came the crackling roar of machine-guns. For a moment the men wavered and many fell, but, with a growl, the others rushed on. Fifty yards farther, and then the ground seemed to heave up and hit Finnessy and Moloney. Side by side they lay, with their faces partly rooted in the trampled ground. To their ears came dully the sound of the fierce hand-to-hand fighting beyond them. Slowly they scraped the dirt from their faces and looked at each other.

'Where did they get ye, Finnessy?' asked Moloney.

'In the leg,' groaned Finnessy.

'The same f'r me,' moaned Moloney.

The bullets of the machine-guns still sang over them, and both men began to dig into the soft earth and pile it into a mound in front of their heads.

Now back across the torn ground came the remnant of the charge, for the trenches had not been taken. Some ran, others walked or crawled or were carried, but always over them and among them whirled the leaden death. Soon Moloney and Finnessy were left alone in their little self-made trenches, for none of their retreating comrades had noticed them.

Twilight was fading, when a brilliant idea flashed across the mind of Finnessy. The intensity of the illumination almost dazed him for a moment.

'Moloney,' said Finnessy, "tis not very sthrong ye're feelin', I'm thinkin'.'

'Ye'er think-tank is overflowin', shut it off!' growled Moloney.

'Sure, Moloney, ye'er voice is very wake! Ye'll be faintin' in a minute!' said Finnessy soothingly.

'I'll not!' cried Moloney. 'What's eatin' ye?'

'Poor old boy!' purred Finnessy, 'ye're in a disperate state. Ye must be rescued. I'm goin' to take ye in!'

'How?' asked Moloney.

'I'm goin' to take ye on me back and crawl in with ye. It's me duty to do it, and England expicts every Irishman to do his duty! Me only reward will be ye'er gratitood!' said Finnessy.

Slowly the brilliant idea spread to the mind of Moloney.

'Sure, Finnessy,' said Moloney, "tis brave and kind of ye, but I can't accipt ye'er sacrifice. 'Tis ye'ersilf that must be saved. I can hear the trimble in ye'er speech. No one can say that a Moloney iver diserted a friend! I'll take ye in if I die f'r it!'

'Don't be a fool, Moloney, ye know ye're waker than I am!'

'I'm not!' cried Moloney. 'I'm as sthrong as a horse, and I am goin' to save ye or perish in the attempt!'

'Ye silfish baste!' howled Finnessy. 'Ye'd spoil me chance for the V.C., would ye!'

'Silfish baste ye'ersilf!' roared Moloney. "Tis me own chance! And in ye'll go on me back, dead or alive!'

Moloney and Finnessy reached for each other.

Back in the trenches of the Irish Guards the young subaltern, peering through a loop-hole, saw dimly through the growing dusk the struggles of Moloney and Finnessy.

'Poor devils,' he muttered, 'must be in agony. Didn't know any were left alive out there.'

Even as he spoke a wiry figure beside him sprang to the top of the parapet and started towards the struggling men.

Now the enemy's trench awoke again, but presently, through

the zone of death, the subaltern and all who could secure loop-holes saw that wiry figure slowly crawling, crawling back towards their trench, dragging behind him two reluctant but exhausted men.

As the limp bodies of Finnessy and Moloney slid down into the trench a cheer broke forth from the men which drowned the noise of the firing.

Slowly Finnessy and Moloney opened their eyes. The subaltern was speaking:

'Sergeant O'Reilly,' he said, 'if such a thing were possible, you deserve and should have another Victoria Cross!'

Again the cheers broke forth.

Finnessy looked at Moloney.

'For the love of Mike!' said Finnessy.

'I believe ye,' said Moloney.

22

SOMEWHERE IN BELGIUM

Percy Godfrey Savage

The crude little cottage had been surrounded and two stalwart peasant boys routed out, but only one gun had been found. Each lad stoutly swore that he was responsible for the sniping. The old mother stood near them.

'Choose one or we will shoot both!' the German officer again ordered the old woman.

Her shrunken, toil-worn frame seemed to suffer pain of death. She wound her rough hands in her apron. Terror, hatred, love, devotion, helplessness filled her eyes.

Alphonse, the tall, light-haired boy, was urging the smaller and more delicate Petro by gestures and eager, low words to yield the punishment to him.

With equal intensity the little fellow pleaded to take the blame because Alphonse would be better able to care for their mother.

The imperturbable German, not asking for more than one life, set the decision before the mother herself. Apparently it would be necessary to shoot both of them.

The soldiers stood waiting for their part in the procedure.

The old woman turned aside. 'Take Alphonse,' she groaned.

Surprised, but satisfied, they took the boy to the side of the house and fired upon him.

Perhaps a thought of another youth, perhaps the wonder of why the old woman had chosen, perhaps a burden of conscience delayed the officer as he followed his men from the yard.

'Quick, Petro,' whispered the mother, and the boy who had been standing rigid, with the horror of his brother's death gripping his heart, came to life. Like a shadow he disappeared. The next instant there was a shot and the German officer fell in the road.

A pack of wild beasts rushed towards the house. Two of them fell.

Somewhere inside the dwelling Petro was killed, but there was neither shot nor cry.

They found the old peasant kneeling beside the doorway.

'I said, "take Alphonse!" oh, God,' she moaned, 'but,' she shrieked with fierce satisfaction as her enemies appeared, 'because Petro could aim better with his gun!'

Three graves on the right of the cottage held the peasants, but three graves on the left held their toll.

23

SOLDIER'S HOME

Ernest Hemingway

Krebs went to the war from a Methodist college in Kansas. There is a picture which shows him among his fraternity brothers, all of them wearing exactly the same height and style collar. He enlisted in the Marines in 1917 and did not return to the United States until the second division returned from the Rhine in the summer of 1919.

There is a picture which shows him on the Rhine with two German girls and another corporal. Krebs and the corporal look too big for their uniforms. The German girls are not beautiful. The Rhine does not show in the picture.

By the time Krebs returned to his home town in Oklahoma the greeting of heroes was over. He came back much too late. The men from the town who had been drafted had all been welcomed elaborately on their return. There had been a great deal of hysteria. Now the reaction had set in. People seemed to think it was rather ridiculous for Krebs to be getting back so late, years after the war was over.

At first Krebs, who had been at Belleau Wood, Soissons, the Champagne, St Mihiel and in the Argonne did not want to talk about the war at all. Later he felt the need to talk but no one wanted to hear about it. His town had heard too many atrocity stories to be thrilled by actualities. Krebs found that to be listened to at all he had to lie and after he had done this twice he, too, had a reaction against the war and against talking about it. A distaste for everything that had happened to him in the war set in because of the lies he had told. All of the times that had been able to make him feel cool and clear inside himself when he thought of them; the times so long back when he had done the one thing, the only thing for a man to do, easily and naturally, when he might have done something else, now lost their cool, valuable quality and then were lost themselves.

His lies were quite unimportant lies and consisted in attributing to himself things other men had seen, done or heard of, and stating as facts certain apocryphal incidents familiar to all soldiers. Even his lies were not sensational at the pool room. His acquaintances, who had heard detailed accounts of German women found chained to machine guns in the Argonne and who could not comprehend, or were barred by their patriotism from interest in, any German machine gunners who were not chained, were not thrilled by his stories.

Krebs acquired the nausea in regard to experience that is the result of untruth or exaggeration, and when he occasionally met another man who had really been a soldier and they talked a few minutes in the dressing room at a dance he fell into the easy pose of the old soldier among other soldiers: that he had been badly, sickeningly frightened all the time. In this way he lost everything.

During this time, it was late summer, he was sleeping late in bed, getting up to walk down town to the library to get a book, eating lunch at home, reading on the front porch until he became bored and then walking down through the town to spend the hottest hours of the day in the cool dark of the pool room. He loved to play pool.

In the evening he practised on his clarinet, strolled down town, read and went to bed. He was still a hero to his two young sisters. His mother would have given him breakfast in bed if he had wanted it. She often came in when he was in bed and asked him to tell her about the war, but her attention always wandered. His father was non-committal.

Before Krebs went away to the war he had never been allowed to drive the family motor car. His father was in the real estate business and always wanted the car to be at his command when he required it to take clients out into the country to show them a piece of farm property. The car always stood outside the First National Bank building where his father had an office on the second floor. Now, after the war, it was still the same car.

Nothing was changed in the town except that the young girls had grown up. But they lived in such a complicated world of already defined alliances and shifting feuds that Krebs did not feel the energy or the courage to break into it. He liked to look at them, though. There were so many good-looking young girls. Most of them had their hair cut short. When he went away only little girls wore their hair like that or girls that were fast. They all wore sweaters and shirt waists with round Dutch collars. It was a pattern. He liked to look at them from the front porch as they walked on the other side of the street. He liked to watch them walking under the shade of the trees. He liked the round Dutch collars above their sweaters. He liked their silk stockings and flat shoes. He liked their bobbed hair and the way they walked.

When he was in town their appeal to him was not very strong. He did not like them when he saw them in the Greek's ice cream parlor. He did not want them themselves really. They were too complicated. There was something else.

Vaguely he wanted a girl but he did not want to have to work to get her. He would have liked to have a girl but he did not want to have to spend a long time getting her. He did not want to get into the intrigue and the politics. He did not want to have to do any courting. He did not want to tell any more lies. It wasn't worth it.

He did not want any consequences. He did not want any consequences ever again.

He wanted to live along without consequences. Besides he did not really need a girl. The army had taught him that. It was all right to pose as though you had to have a girl. Nearly everybody did that. But it wasn't true. You did not need a girl.

That was the funny thing. First a fellow boasted how girls mean nothing to him, that he never thought of them, that they could not touch him. Then a fellow boasted that he could not get along without girls, that he had to have them all the time, that he could not go to sleep without them.

That was all a lie. It was all a lie both ways. You did not need a girl unless you thought about them. He learned that in the army. Then sooner or later you always got one. When you were really ripe for a girl you always got one. You did not have to think about it. Sooner or later it could come. He had learned that in the army.

Now he would have liked a girl if she had come to him and not wanted to talk.

But here at home it was all too complicated. He knew he could never get through it all again. It was not worth the trouble. That was the thing about French girls and German girls. There was not all this talking. You couldn't talk much and you did not need to talk. It was simple and you were friends. He thought about France and then he began to think about Germany. On the whole he had liked Germany better. He did not want to leave Germany. He did not want to come home. Still, he had come home. He sat on the front porch.

He liked the girls that were walking along the other side of the street. He liked the look of them much better than the French girls or the German girls. But the world they were in was not the world he was in. He would like to have one of them. But it was not worth it. They were such a nice pattern. He liked the pattern. It was exciting. But he would not go through all the talking. He did not want one badly enough. He liked to look at them all, though. It was not worth it. Not now when things were getting good again.

He sat there on the porch reading a book on the war. It was a history and he was reading about all the engagements he had been in. It was the most interesting reading he had ever done. He wished there were more maps. He looked forward with a good feeling to reading all the really good histories when they would come out with good detail maps. Now he was really learning about the war. He had been a good soldier. That made a difference.

One morning after he had been home about a month his mother came into his bedroom and sat on the bed. She smoothed her apron.

'I had a talk with your father last night, Harold,' she said, 'and he is willing for you to take the car out in the evenings.'

'Yeah?' said Krebs, who was not fully awake. 'Take the car out? Yeah?'

'Yes. Your father has felt for some time that you should be able to take the car out in the evenings whenever you wished but we only talked it over last night.'

'I'll bet you made him,' Krebs said.

'No. It was your father's suggestion that we talk the matter over.'

'Yeah. I'll bet you made him,' Krebs sat up in bed.

'Will you come down to breakfast, Harold?' his mother said.

'As soon as I get my clothes on,' Krebs said.

His mother went out of the room and he could hear her frying something downstairs while he washed, shaved and dressed to go down into the dining-room for breakfast. While he was eating breakfast, his sister brought in the mail.

'Well, Hare,' she said. 'You old sleepy-head. What do you ever get up for?'

Krebs looked at her. He liked her. She was his best sister.

'Have you got the paper?' he asked.

She handed him *The Kansas City Star* and he shucked off its brown wrapper and opened it to the sporting page. He folded *The Star* open and propped it against the water pitcher with his cereal dish to steady it, so he could read while he ate.

'Harold,' his mother stood in the kitchen doorway, 'Harold, please don't muss up the paper. Your father can't read his Star if its been mussed.'

'I won't muss it,' Krebs said.

His sister sat down at the table and watched him while he read.

'We're playing indoor over at school this afternoon,' she said. 'I'm going to pitch.'

'Good,' said Krebs. 'How's the old wing?'

'I can pitch better than lots of the boys. I tell them all you taught me. The other girls aren't much good.'

'Yeah?' said Krebs.

'I tell them all you're my beau. Aren't you my beau, Hare?'

'You bet.'

'Couldn't your brother really be your beau just because he's your brother?'

'I don't know.'

'Sure you know. Couldn't you be my beau, Hare, if I was old enough and if you wanted to?'

'Sure. You're my girl now.'

'Am I really your girl?'

'Sure.'

'Do you love me?'

'Uh, huh.'

'Do you love me always?'

'Sure.'

'Will you come over and watch me play indoor?'

'Maybe.'

'Aw, Hare, you don't love me. If you loved me, you'd want to come over and watch me play indoor.'

Krebs's mother came into the dining-room from the kitchen. She carried a plate with two fried eggs and some crisp bacon on it and a plate of buckwheat cakes.

'You run along, Helen,' she said. 'I want to talk to Harold.'

She put the eggs and bacon down in front of him and brought in a jug of maple syrup for the buckwheat cakes. Then she sat down across the table from Krebs.

'I wish you'd put down the paper a minute, Harold,' she said.

Krebs took down the paper and folded it.

'Have you decided what you are going to do yet, Harold?' his mother said, taking off her glasses.

'No,' said Krebs.

'Don't you think it's about time?' His mother did not say this in a mean way. She seemed worried.

'I hadn't thought about it,' Krebs said.

'God has some work for every one to do,' his mother said. 'There can be no idle hands in His Kingdom.'

'I'm not in His Kingdom,' Krebs said.

'We are all of us in His Kingdom.'

Krebs felt embarrassed and resentful as always.

'I've worried about you too much, Harold,' his mother went on. 'I know the temptations you must have been exposed to. I know how weak men are. I know what your own dear grandfather, my own father, told us about the Civil War and I have prayed for you. I pray for you all day long, Harold.'

Krebs looked at the bacon fat hardening on his plate.

'Your father is worried, too,' his mother went on. 'He thinks you have lost your ambition, that you haven't got a definite aim in life. Charley Simmons, who is just your age, has a good job and is going to be married. The boys are all settling down; they're all determined to get somewhere; you can see that boys like

Charley Simmons are on their way to being really a credit to the community.'

Krebs said nothing.

'Don't look that way, Harold,' his mother said. 'You know we love you and I want to tell you for your own good how matters stand. Your father does not want to hamper your freedom. He thinks you should be allowed to drive the car. If you want to take some of the nice girls out riding with you, we are only too pleased.

We want you to enjoy yourself. But you are going to have to settle down to work, Harold. Your father doesn't care what you start in at. All work is honourable as he says. But you've got to make a start at something. He asked me to speak to you this morning and then you can stop in and see him at his office.'

'Is that all?' Krebs said.

'Yes. Don't you love your mother dear boy?'

'No,' Krebs said.

His mother looked at him across the table. Her eyes were shiny. She started crying.

'I don't love anybody,' Krebs said.

It wasn't any good. He couldn't tell her, he couldn't make her see it. It was silly to have said it. He had only hurt her. He went over and took hold of her arm. She was crying with her head in her hands.

'I didn't mean it,' he said. 'I was just angry at something. I didn't mean I didn't love you.'

His mother went on crying. Krebs put his arm on her shoulder.

'Can't you believe me, mother?'

His mother shook her head.

'Please, please, mother. Please believe me.'

'All right,' his mother said chokily. She looked up at him. 'I believe you, Harold.'

Krebs kissed her hair. She put her face up to him.

'I'm your mother,' she said. 'I held you next to my heart when you were a tiny baby.'

Krebs felt sick and vaguely nauseated.

'I know, Mummy,' he said. 'I'll try and be a good boy for you.'

'Would you kneel and pray with me, Harold?' his mother asked.

They knelt down beside the dining-room table and Krebs's mother prayed.

'Now, you pray, Harold,' she said.

'I can't,' Krebs said.

'Try, Harold.'

'I can't.'

'Do you want me to pray for you?'

'Yes.'

So his mother prayed for him and then they stood up and Krebs kissed his mother and went out of the house. He had tried so to keep his life from being complicated. Still, none of it had touched him. He had felt sorry for his mother and she had made him lie. He would go to Kansas City and get a job and she would feel all right about it. There would be one more scene maybe before he got away. He would not go down to his father's office. He would miss that one. He wanted his life to go smoothly. It had just gotten going that way. Well, that was all over now, anyway. He would go over to the schoolyard and watch Helen play indoor baseball.

24

THE SOUL OF A REGIMENT

Talbot Mundy

I

So long as its colours remain, and there is one man left to carry them, a regiment can never die; they can recruit it again around that one man, and the regiment will continue on its road to future glory with the same old traditions behind it and the same atmosphere surrounding it that made brave men of its forbears. So although the colours are not exactly the soul of a regiment, they are the concrete embodiment of it, and are even more sacred than the person of a reigning sovereign.

The First Egyptian Foot had colours—and has them still, thanks to Billy Grogram; so the First Egyptian Foot is still a regiment. It was the very first of all the regiments raised in Egypt, and the colours were lovely crimson things on a brand new polished pole, cased in the regulation jacket of black waterproof and housed with all pomp and ceremony in the mess-room at the barracks. There were people who said it was bad policy to present colours to a native regiment; that they were nothing more than a symbol of a decadent and waning monarchism in any case, and that the respect which would be due them might lead dangerously near to fetish-worship. As a matter of cold fact, though, the raw recruits of the regiment failed utterly to understand them, and it was part of Billy Grogram's business to instill in them a wholesome respect for the sacred symbol of regimental honour.

He was Sergeant-Instructor William Stanford Grogram, V.C.,

D.S.M., to give him his full name and title, late a sergeant-major of the True and Tried, time expired, and retired from service on a pension. His pension would have been enough for him to live on, for he was unmarried, his habits were exemplary, and his wants were few; but an elder brother had been a ne'er-do-well, and Grogram, who was the type that will die rather than let any one of his depend on charity, left the army with a sister-in-law and a small tribe of children dependent on him. Work, of course, was the only thing left for it, and he applied promptly for the only kind of work that he knew how to do.

The British are always making new regiments out of native material in some part of the world; they come cheaper than white troops, and, with a sprinkling of white troops among them, they do wonderfully good service in time of war—thanks to the sergeant instructors. The officers get the credit for it, but it is the ex-noncommissioned officers of the Line who do the work, as Grogram was destined to discover. They sent him out to Instruct the First Egyptian Foot, and it turned out to be the toughest proposition that any one lonely, determined, homesick fighting-man ever ran up against.

He was not looking for a life of idleness and ease, so the discomfort of his new quarters did not trouble him over much, though they would have disgusted another man at the very beginning. They gave him a little, white-washed, mud-walled hut, with two bare rooms in it, and a lovely view on three sides of aching desert sand; on the fourth a blind wall.

It was as hot inside as a baker's oven, but it had the one great advantage of being easily kept clean, and Grogram, whose fetish was cleanliness, bore that in mind, and forbore to grumble at the absence of a sergeant's mess and the various creature comforts that his position had entitled him to for years.

What did disgust him, though, was the unfairness of saddling the task that lay in front of him on the shoulders of one lone man; his officers made it quite clear that they had no intention of helping him in the least; from the Colonel downwards they were ashamed of the regiment, and they expected Grogram to work it into something like shape before they even began to take an interest in it. The Colonel went even further than that; he put in an appearance at Orderly Room every morning and once a week attended a parade out on the desert where nobody could see the awful evolutions of his raw command, but he, actually threw cold water on Grogram's efforts at enthusiasm.

'You can't make a silk purse out of a sow's ear,' he told him a few mornings after Grogram joined, 'or well-drilled soldiers out of Gyppies. Heaven only knows what the Home Government means by trying to raise a regiment out here; at the very best we'll only be teaching the enemy to fight us! But you'll find they won't learn. However, until the Government finds out what a ghastly mistake's being made, there's nothing for it but to obey orders and drill Gyppies. Go ahead, Grogram; I give you a free hand. Try anything you like on them, but don't ask me to believe there'll be any result from it. Candidly I don't.'

But Grogram happened to be a different type of man from his new Colonel. After a conversation such as that, he could have let things go hang had he chosen to, drawing his pay, doing his six hours' work a day along the line of least resistance, and blaming the inevitable consequences on the Colonel. But to him a duty was something to be done; an impossibility was something to set his clean-shaven, stubborn jaw at and to overcome; and a regiment was a regiment, to be kneaded and pummeled and damned and coaxed and drilled, till it began to look as the True and Tried used to look in the days when he was sergeant-major. So he twisted his little brown moustache and drew himself up to the full height of his five feet eight inches, spread his well-knit shoulders, straightened his ramrod of a back and got busy on the job, while his Colonel and the other officers did the social rounds in Cairo and cursed their luck.

The material that Grogram had to work with were fellaheen—good, honest coal-black negroes, giants in stature, the embodiment of good-humoured incompetence, children of the soil weaned on raw-hide whips under the blight of Turkish misrule and Arab cruelty. They had no idea that they were even men till Grogram taught them; and he had to learn Arabic first before he could teach them even that.

They began by fearing him, as their ancestors had feared every new breed of task-master for centuries; gradually they learned to look for instant and amazing justice at his hands, and from then on they respected him. He caned them instead of getting them fined by the Colonel or punished with pack-drill for failing things they did not understand; they were thoroughly accustomed to the lash, and his light swagger-cane laid on their huge shoulders was a joke that served merely to point his arguments and fix his lessons in their memories; they would not have understood the Colonel's wrath had he known that the men of his regiment were being beaten by a non-commissioned officer.

They began to love him when he harked back to the days when he was a recruit himself, and remembered the steps of a double-shuffle that he had learned in the barrack-room; when he danced a buck and wing dance for them they recognized him as a man and a brother, and from that time on, instead of giving him all the trouble they could and laughing at his lectures when his back was turned, they genuinely tried to please him.

So he studied out more steps, and danced his way into their hearts, growing daily stricter on parade, daily more exacting of pipe-clay and punctuality, and slowly, but surely as the march of time, molding them into something like a regiment.

Even he could not teach them to shoot, though he sweated over them on the dazzling range until the sun dried every drop of sweat out of him. And for a long time he could not even teach them how to march; they would keep step for a hundred yards or so, and then lapse into the listless shrinking stride that was the birthright of centuries.

He pestered the Colonel for a band of sorts until the Colonel told him angrily to go to blazes; then he wrote home and purchased six fifes with his own money, bought a native drum in the bazaar, and started a band on his own account.

Had he been able to read music himself he would have been no better off, because of course the fellaheen he had to teach could not have read it either, though possibly he might have slightly increased the number of tunes in their repertoire.

As it was, he knew only two tunes himself—'The Campbells Are Coming,' and the National Anthem.

He picked the six most intelligent men he could find and whistled those two tunes to them until his lips were dry and his cheeks ached and his very soul revolted at the sound of them. But the six men picked them up; and, of course, any negro in the world can beat a drum. One golden morning before the sun had heated up the desert air the regiment marched past in really good formation, all in step, and tramping to the tune of 'God Save the Queen.'

The Colonel nearly had a fit, but the regiment tramped on and the band played them back to barracks with a swing and a rhythm that was new not only to the First Egyptian Foot; it was new to Egypt! The tune was half a tone flat maybe, and the drum was a sheepskin business bought in the bazaar, but a new regiment marched behind it. And behind the regiment—two paces right flank, as the regulations specify—marched a sergeant-instructor with a new light in his eyes—the grey eyes that had looked out so wearily from beneath the shaggy eyebrows, and that shone now with the pride of a deed well done.

Of course the Colonel was still scornful. But Billy Grogram, who had handled men when the Colonel was cutting his teeth at

Sandhurst, and who knew men from the bottom up, knew that the mob of unambitious countrymen, who had grinned at him in uncomfortable silence when he first arrived, was beginning to forget its mobdom. He, who spent his hard-earned leisure talking to them and answering their childish questions in hard-won Arabic, knew that they were slowly grasping the theory of the thing—that a soul was forming in the regiment—an indefinable, unexplainable, but obvious change, perhaps not unlike the change from infancy to manhood.

And Billy Grogram, who above all was a man of clean ideals, began to feel content. He still described them in his letters home as 'blooming mummies made of Nile mud, roasted black for their sins, and good for nothing but the ash-heap.' He still damned them on parade, whipped them when the Colonel wasn't looking, and worked at them until he was much too tired to sleep; but he began to love them. And to a big, black, grinning man of them, they loved him. To encourage that wondrous band of his, he set them to playing their two tunes on guest nights outside the officers' mess; and the officers endured it until the Colonel returned from furlough. He sent for Grogram and offered to pay him back all he had spent on instruments, provided the band should keep away in future.

Grogram refused the money and took the hint, inventing weird and hitherto unheard-of reasons why it should be unrighteous for the band to play outside the mess, and preaching respect for officers in spite of it. Like all great men he knew when he had made a mistake, and how to minimize it.

His hardest task was teaching the Gyppies what their colours meant. The men were Mohammedans; they believed in Allah; they had been taught from the time when they were old enough to speak that idols and the outward symbols of religion are the signs of heresy; and Grogram's lectures, delivered in stammering and uncertain Arabic, seemed to them like the ground-plan of a new religion. But Grogram stuck to it. He made opportunities for saluting the colours—took them down each morning and uncased them, and treated them with an ostentatious respect that would have been laughed at among his own people.

When his day's work was done and he was too tired to dance for them, he would tell them long tales, done into halting Arabic, of how regiments had died rallying round their colours; of a brand new paradise, invented by himself and suitable to all religions, where soldiers went who honoured their colours as they ought to do; of the honour that befell a man who died fighting for them, and of the tenfold honour of the man whose privilege it was to carry them into action. And in the end, although they did not understand him, they respected the colours because he told them to.

II

When England hovered on the brink of indecision and sent her greatest general to hold Khartoum with only a handful of native troops to help him, the First Egyptian Foot refused to leave their gaudy crimson behind them. They marched with colours flying down to the steamer that was to take them on the first long stage of their journey up the Nile, and there were six fifes and a drum in front of them that told whoever cared to listen that 'The Campbells are coming—hurrah! hurrah!'

They marched with the measured tramp of a real regiment; they carried their chins high; their tarbooshes were cocked at a knowing angle and they swung from the hips like grown men. At the head of the regiment rode a Colonel whom the regiment scarcely knew, and beside it marched a dozen officers in a like predicament; but behind it, his sword strapped to his side and his little swagger-cane tucked under his left arm-pit, inconspicuous, smiling and content, marched Sergeant-Instructor Grogram, whom the regiment knew and loved, and who had made and knew the regiment.

The whole civilized world knows—and England knows to her enduring shame—what befell General Gordon and his handful of men when they reached Khartoum. Gordon surely guessed what was in store for him even before he started, his subordinates may have done so, and the native soldiers knew. But Sergeant-Instructor Grogram neither knew nor cared.

He looked no further than his duty, which was to nurse the big black babies of his regiment and to keep them good tempered, grinning and efficient; he did that as no other living man could have done it, and kept on doing it until the bitter end.

And his task can have been no sinecure. The Mahdi—the ruthless terror of the Upper Nile who ruled by systematized and savage cruelty and lived by plunder—was as much a bogy to peaceful Egypt as Napoleon used to be in Europe, and with far more reason. Mothers frightened their children into prompt obedience by the mere mention of his name, and the coal-black natives of the Nile-mouth country are never more than grown-up children.

It must have been as easy to take that regiment to Khartoum as to take a horse into a burning building, but when they reached there not a man was missing; they marched in with colours flying and their six-fife band playing, and behind them—two paces right flank rear—marched Billy Grogram, his little swagger-cane under his left arm-pit, neat, respectful and very wide awake. For a little while Cairo kept in touch with them, and then communication ceased. Nobody ever learned all the details of the tragedy that followed; there was a curtain drawn—of mystery and silence such as has always veiled the heart of darkest Africa.

Lord Wolseley took his expedition up the Nile, whipped the Dervishes at El Teb and Tel-el-Kebir, and reached Khartoum, to learn of Gordon's death, but not the details of it. Then he came back again; and the Mahdi followed him, closing up the route behind him, wiping all trace of civilization off the map and placing what he imagined was an insuperable barrier between him and the British—a thousand miles of plundered, ravished, depopulated wilderness.

So a clerk in a musty office drew a line below the record of the First Egyptian Foot; widows were duly notified; a pension or two was granted; and the regiment that Billy Grogram had worked so hard to build was relegated to the past, like Billy Grogram.

Rumours had come back along with Wolseley's men that Grogram had gone down fighting with his regiment; there was a story that the band had been taken alive and turned over to the Mahdi's private service, and one prisoner, taken near Khartoum, swore that he had seen Grogram speared as he lay wounded before the Residency. There was a battalion of the True and Tried with Wolseley; and the men used methods that may have been not strictly ethical in seeking tidings of their old sergeant-major; but even they could get no further details; he had gone down fighting with his regiment, and that was all about him.

Then men forgot him. The long steady preparation soon began for the new campaign that was to wipe the Mahdi off the map, restore peace to Upper Egypt, regain Khartoum and incidentally avenge Gordon. Regiments were slowly drafted out from home as barracks could be built for them; new regiments of native troops were raised and drilled by ex-sergeants of the Line who never heard of Grogram; new men took charge; and the Sirdar superintended everything and laid his reputation brick by brick, of bricks which he made himself, and men were too busy under him to think of anything except the work in hand.

But rumours kept coming in, as they always do in Egypt, filtering in from nowhere over the illimitable desert, borne by stray camel-drivers, carried by Dervish spies, tossed from tongue to tongue through the fishmarket, and carried up back stairs to Clubs and Department Offices. There were tales of a drummer and three men who played the fife and a wonderful mad feringhee who danced as no man surely ever danced before. The tales varied, but there were always four musicians and a feringhee.

When one Dervish spy was caught and questioned he swore by the beard of the prophet that he had seen the men himself. He was told promptly that he was a liar; how came it that a feringhee—a pork-fed, infidel Englishman—should be allowed to live anywhere the Mahdi's long arm reached?

'Whom God hath touched—' the Dervish quoted; and men remembered that madness is the surest passport throughout the whole of Northern Africa. But nobody connected Grogram with the feringhee who danced.

But another man was captured who told a similar tale; and then a Greek trader, turned Mohammedan to save his skin, who had made good his escape from the Mahdi's camp. He swore to having seen this man as he put in one evening at a Nile-bank village in a native dhow. He was dressed in an ancient khaki tunic and a loin-cloth; he was bare-legged, shoeless, and his hair was long over his shoulders and plastered thick with mud. No, he did not look in the least like a British soldier, though he danced as soldiers sometimes did beside the camp-fires.

Three natives who were with him played fifes while the feringhee danced, and one man beat a drum. Yes, the tunes were English tunes, though very badly played; he had heard them before, and recognized them. No, he could not hum them; he knew no music. Why had he not spoken to the man who danced? He had not dared. The man appeared to be a prisoner and so were the natives with him; the man had danced that evening until he could dance no longer, and then the Dervishes had beaten him with a kurbash for encouragement: the musicians had tried to interfere, and they had all been beaten and left lying there for dead. He was not certain, but he was almost certain they were dead before he came away.

Then, more than three years after Gordon died, there came another rumour, this time from closer at hand—somewhere in the neutral desert zone that lay between the Dervish outpost and the part of Lower Egypt that England held. This time the dancer was reported to be dying, but the musicians were still with him. They got the name of the dancer this time; it was reported to be Goglam, and though that was not at all a bad native guess for Grogram, nobody apparently noted the coincidence.

Men were too busy with their work; the rumour was only one of a thousand that filtered across the desert every month, and nobody remembered the non-commissioned officer who had left for Khartoum with the First Egyptian Foot; they could have recalled the names of all the officers almost without an effort, but not Grogram's.

III

Egypt was busy with the hum of building—empire-building under a man who knew his job. Almost the only game the Sirdar countenanced was polo, and that only because it kept officers and civilians fit. He gave them all the polo, though, that they wanted, and the men grew keen on it, spent money on it, and needless to say, grew extraordinarily proficient.

And with the proficiency of course came competition— matches between regiments for the regimental cup and finally the biggest event of the Cairo season, the match between the Civil Service and the Army of Occupation, or, as it was more usually termed, 'The Army vs The Rest.' That was the one society event that the Sirdar made a point of presiding over in person.

He attended it in mufti always, but sat in the seat of honour, just outside the touch-line, half-way down the field; and behind him, held back by ropes, clustered the whole of Cairene society, on foot, on horseback and in dog-carts, buggies, gigs and every kind of carriage imaginable. Opposite and at either end, the garrison lined up—all the British and native troops rammed in together; and the native population crowded in between them and wherever they could find standing-room.

It was the one event of the year for which all Egypt, Christian and Mohammedan, took a holiday. Regimental bands were there to play before the game and between the chukkers, and nothing was left undone that could in any way tend to make the event spectacular.

Two games had been played since the cup had been first presented by the Khedive, and honours lay even—one match for the Army and one for the Civil Service. So on the third anniversary feeling ran fairly high. It ran higher still when half time was called and honours still lay even at one goal all; to judge by the excitement of the crowd, a stranger might have guessed that polo was the most important thing in Egypt. The players rode off the pavilion for the half-time interval, and the infantry band that came out onto the field was hard put to drown the noise of conversation and laughter and argument. At that minute there was surely nothing in the world to talk about but polo.

But suddenly the band stopped playing, as suddenly as though the music were a concrete thing and had been severed with an ax. The Sirdar turned his head suddenly and gazed at one corner of the field, and the noise of talking ceased—not so suddenly as the music had done, for not everybody could see what was happening at first—but dying down gradually and fading away to nothing as the amazing thing came into view.

It was a detachment of five men—a drummer and three fifes, and one other man who marched behind them—though he scarcely resembled a man. He marched, though, like a British soldier.

He was ragged—they all were—dirty and unkempt. He seemed very nearly starved, for his bare legs were thinner than a mummy's; round his loins was a native loin-cloth, and his hair was plastered down with mud like a religious fanatic's. His only other garment was a tattered khaki tunic that might once have been a soldier's, and he wore no shoes or sandals of any kind.

He marched though, with a straight back and his chin up, and anybody who was half observant might have noticed that he was marching two paces right flank rear; it is probable, though, that in the general amazement, nobody did notice it.

As the five debouched upon the polo ground, four of them abreast and one behind, the four men raised their arms, the man behind issued a sharp command, the right hand man thumped his drum, and a wail proceeded from the fifes. They swung into a regimental quickstep now, and the wail grew louder, rising and falling fitfully and distinctly keeping time with the drum.

Then the tune grew recognizable. The crowd listened now in awe-struck silence. The five approaching figures were grotesque enough to raise a laugh and the tune was grotesquer, and more pitiable still; but there was something electric in the atmosphere that told of tragedy, and not even the natives made a sound as the five marched straight across the field to where the Sirdar sat beneath the Egyptian flag.

Louder and louder grew the tune as the fifes warmed up to it; louder thumped the drum. It was flat, and notes were missing here and there. False notes appeared at unexpected intervals, but the tune was unmistakable. 'The Campbells are coming! Hurrah! Hurrah!' wailed the three fifes, and the five men marched to it as no undrilled natives ever did.

'Halt!' ordered the man behind when the strange cortege had reached the Sirdar; and his 'Halt!' rang out in good clean military English.

'Front!' he ordered, and they 'fronted' like a regiment. 'Right

Dress!' They were in line already, but they went through the formality of shuffling their feet. 'Eyes Front!' The five men faced the Sirdar, and no one breathed. 'General salute—pre-sent arms!'

They had no arms. The band stood still at attention. The fifth man he of the bare legs and plastered hair—whipped his right hand to his forehead in the regulation military salute—held it there for the regulation six seconds, swaying as he did so and tottering from the knees, then whipped it to his side again, and stood at rigid attention. He seemed able to stand better that way, for his knees left off shaking.

'Who are you?' asked the Sirdar then.

'First Egyptian Foot, sir.'

The crowd behind was leaning forward, listening; those that had been near enough to hear that gasped. The Sirdar's face changed suddenly to the look of cold indifference behind which a certain type of Englishman hides his emotion.

Then came the time-honoured question, prompt as the ax of a guillotine—inevitable as Fate itself:

'Where are your colours?'

The fifth man—he who had issued the commands fumbled with his tunic. The buttons were missing, and the front of it was fastened up with a string; his fingers seemed to have grown feeble; he plucked at it, but it would not come undone.

'Where are—'

The answer to that question should be like an echo, and nobody should need to ask it twice. But the string burst suddenly, and the first time of asking sufficed. The ragged, unkempt long-haired mummy undid his tunic and pulled it open.

'Here, sir!' he answered.

The colours, blood-soaked, torn—unrecognizable almost—were round his body! As the ragged tunic fell apart, the colours fell with it; Grogram caught them, and stood facing the Sirdar with them in his hand. His bare chest was seared with half-healed wounds and criss-crossed with the marks of floggings, and his skin seemed to be drawn tight as a mummy's across his ribs. He was a living skeleton!

The Sirdar sprang to his feet and raised his hat; for the colours of a regiment are second, in holiness, to the Symbols of the Church. The watching, listening crowd followed suit; there was a sudden rustling as a sea of hats and helmets rose and descended. The band of four, that had stood in stolid silence while all this was happening, realized that the moment was auspicious to play their other tune.

They had only one other, and they had played 'The Campbells are coming' across the polo field; so up went the fifes, 'Bang!' went the drum, and, 'God Save Our Gracious Queen' wailed the three in concert, while strong men hid their faces and women sobbed.

Grogram whipped his hand up to the answering salute, faced the crowd in front of him for six palpitating seconds, and fell dead at the Sirdar's feet.

And so they buried him; his shroud was the flag that had flown above the Sirdar at that ever-memorable match, and his soul went into the regiment.

They began recruiting it again next day round the blood-soaked colours he had carried with him, and the First Egyptian Foot did famously at the Atbara and Omdurman. They buried him in a hollow square formed by massed brigades, European and native regiments alternating, and saw him on his way with twenty-one parting volleys, instead of the regulation five. His tombstone is a monolith of rough-hewn granite, tucked away in a quiet corner of the European graveyard at Cairo—quiet and inconspicuous as Grogram always was—but the truth is graven on it in letters two inches deep:

HERE LIES A MAN

25

A CURIOUS EXPERIENCE

Mark Twain

This is the story which the Major told me, as nearly as I can recall it:—

In the winter of 1862-3, I was commandant of Fort Trumbull, at New London, Conn. Maybe our life there was not so brisk as life at 'the front'; still it was brisk enough, in its way—one's brains didn't cake together there for lack of something to keep them stirring. For one thing, all the Northern atmosphere at that time was thick with mysterious rumours—rumours to the effect that rebel spies were flitting everywhere, and getting ready to blow up our Northern forts, burn our hotels, send infected clothing into our towns, and all that sort of thing. You remember it. All this had a tendency to keep us awake, and knock the traditional dulness out of garrison life. Besides, ours was a recruiting station—which is the same as saying we hadn't any time to waste in dozing, or dreaming, or fooling around. Why, with all our watchfulness, fifty per cent of a day's recruits would leak out of our hands and give us the slip the same night. The bounties were so prodigious that a recruit could pay a sentinel three or four hundred dollars to let him escape, and still have enough of his bounty-money left to constitute a fortune for a poor man. Yes, as I said before, our life was not drowsy.

Well, one day I was in my quarters alone, doing some writing, when a pale and ragged lad of fourteen or fifteen entered, made a neat bow, and said,—

'I believe recruits are received here?'

'Yes.'

'Will you please enlist me, sir?'

'Dear me, no! You are too young, my boy, and too small.'

A disappointed look came into his face, and quickly deepened into an expression of despondency. He turned slowly away, as if to go; hesitated, then faced me again, and said, in a tone which went to my heart,—

'I have no home, and not a friend in the world. If you could only enlist me!'

But of course the thing was out of the question, and I said so as gently as I could. Then I told him to sit down by the stove and warm himself, and added,—

'You shall have something to eat, presently. You are hungry?'

He did not answer; he did not need to; the gratitude in his big soft eyes was more eloquent than any words could have been. He sat down by the stove, and I went on writing. Occasionally I took a furtive glance at him. I noticed that his clothes and shoes, although soiled and damaged, were of good style and material. This fact was suggestive. To it I added the facts that his voice was low and musical; his eyes deep and melancholy; his carriage and address gentlemanly; evidently the poor chap was in trouble. As a result, I was interested.

However, I became absorbed in my work, by and by, and forgot all about the boy. I don't know how long this lasted; but, at length, I happened to look up. The boy's back was towards me, but his face was turned in such a way that I could see one of his cheeks—and down that cheek a rill of noiseless tears was flowing.

'God bless my soul!' I said to myself; 'I forgot the poor rat was starving.' Then I made amends for my brutality by saying to him, 'Come along, my lad; you shall dine with me; I am alone to-day.'

He gave me another of those grateful looks, and a happy light broke in his face. At the table he stood with his hand on his chair-back until I was seated, then seated himself. I took up my knife and fork and—well, I simply held them, and kept still; for the boy had inclined his head and was saying a silent grace. A thousand hallowed memories of home and my childhood poured in upon me, and I sighed to think how far I had drifted from religion and its balm for hurt minds, its comfort and solace and support.

As our meal progressed, I observed that young Wicklow—Robert Wicklow was his full name—knew what to do with his napkin; and well, in a word, I observed that he was a boy of good breeding; never mind the details. He had a simple frankness, too, which won upon me. We talked mainly about himself, and I had no difficulty in getting his history out of him. When he spoke of his having been born and reared in Louisiana, I warmed to him decidedly, for I had spent some time down there. I knew all the 'coast' region of the Mississippi, and loved it, and had not been long enough away from it for my interest in it to begin to pale. The very names that fell from his lips sounded good to me,—so good that I steered the talk in directions that would bring them out. Baton Rouge, Plaquemine, Donaldsonville, Sixty-mile Point, Bonnet-Carre, the Stock-Landing, Carrollton, the Steamship Landing, the Steamboat Landing, New Orleans, Tchoupitoulas Street, the Esplanade, the Rue des Bons Enfants, the St Charles Hotel, the Tivoli Circle, the Shell Road, Lake Pontchartrain; and it was particularly delightful to me to hear once more of the 'R.E. Lee,' the 'Natchez,' the 'Eclipse,' the 'General Quitman,' the 'Duncan F. Kenner,' and other old familiar steamboats. It was almost as good as being back there, these names so vividly reproduced in my mind the look of the things they stood for. Briefly, this was little Wicklow's history:—

When the war broke out, he and his invalid aunt and his father were living near Baton Rouge, on a great and rich plantation which had been in the family for fifty years. The father was a Union man. He was persecuted in all sorts of ways, but clung to his principles. At last, one night, masked men burned his mansion down, and the family had to fly for their lives. They were hunted from place to place, and learned all there was to know about poverty, hunger, and distress. The invalid aunt found relief at last: misery and exposure killed her; she died in an open field, like a tramp, the rain beating upon her and the thunder booming overhead. Not long afterwards, the father was captured by an armed band; and while the son begged and pleaded, the victim was strung up before his face. (At this point a baleful light shone in the youth's eyes, and he said, with the manner of one who talks to himself: 'If I cannot be enlisted, no matter—I shall find a way—I shall find a way.') As soon as the father was pronounced dead, the son was told that if he was not out of that region within twenty-four hours, it would go hard with him. That night he crept to the riverside and hid himself near a plantation landing. By and by the 'Duncan F. Kenner,' stopped there, and he swam out and concealed himself in the yawl that was dragging at her stern. Before daylight the boat reached the Stock-Landing, and he slipped ashore. He walked the three miles which lay between that point and the house of an uncle of his in Good-Children Street, in New Orleans, and then his troubles were over for the time being. But this uncle was a Union man, too, and before very long he concluded that he had better leave the South. So he and young Wicklow slipped out of the country on board a sailing vessel, and in due time reached New York. They put up at the Astor House. Young Wicklow had a good time of it for a while, strolling up and down Broadway, and observing the strange Northern sights; but in the end a change came,—and not for the better. The uncle had been cheerful at first, but now he began to look troubled and despondent; moreover, he became moody and irritable; talked of money giving out, and no way to get more,—'not enough left for one, let alone two.' Then, one morning, he was missing—did not come to breakfast. The boy inquired at the office, and was told that the uncle had paid his bill the night before and gone away—to Boston, the clerk believed, but was not certain.

The lad was alone and friendless. He did not know what to do, but concluded he had better try to follow and find his uncle. He went down to the steamboat landing; learned that the trifle of money in his pocket would not carry him to Boston; however, it would carry him to New London; so he took passage for that port, resolving to trust to Providence to furnish him means to travel the rest of the way. He had now been wandering about the streets of New London three days and nights, getting a bite and a nap here and there for charity's sake. But he had given up at last; courage and hope were both gone. If he could enlist, nobody could be more thankful; if he could not get in as a soldier, couldn't he be a drummer-boy? Ah, he would work so hard to please, and would be so grateful!

Well, there's the history of young Wicklow, just as he told it to me, barring details. I said,—

'My boy, you are among friends, now,—don't you be troubled any more.' How his eyes glistened! I called in Sergeant John Rayburn,—he was from Hartford; lives in Hartford yet; maybe you know him,—and said, 'Rayburn, quarter this boy with the musicians. I am going to enrol him as a drummer-boy, and I want you to look after him and see that he is well treated.'

Well, of course, intercourse between the commandant of the post and the drummer-boy came to an end, now; but the poor little friendless chap lay heavy on my heart, just the same. I kept on the lookout, hoping to see him brighten up and begin to be cheery and gay; but no, the days went by, and there was no change. He associated with nobody; he was always absent-minded, always thinking; his face was always sad. One morning Rayburn asked leave to speak to me privately. Said he,—

'I hope I don't offend, sir; but the truth is, the musicians are in such a sweat it seems as if somebody's got to speak.'

'Why, what is the trouble?'

'It's the Wicklow boy, sir. The musicians are down on him to an extent you can't imagine.'

'Well, go on, go on. What has he been doing?'

'Prayin', sir.'

'Praying!'

'Yes, sir; the musicians haven't any peace of their life for that boy's prayin'. First thing in the morning he's at it; noons he's at it; and nights—well, nights he just lays into 'em like all possessed! Sleep? Bless you, they can't sleep: he's got the floor, as the sayin' is, and then when he once gets his supplication-mill agoin', there just simply ain't any let-up to him. He starts in with the bandmaster, and he prays for him; next he takes the head bugler, and he prays for him; next the bass drum, and he scoops him in; and so on, right straight through the band, givin' them all a show, and takin' that amount of interest in it which would make you think he thought he warn't but a little while for this world, and believed he couldn't be happy in heaven without he had a brass band along, and wanted to pick 'em out for himself, so he could depend on 'em to do up the national tunes in a style suitin' to the place. Well, sir, heavin' boots at him don't have no effect; it's dark in there; and, besides, he don't pray fair, anyway, but kneels down behind the big drum; so it don't make no difference if they rain boots at him, he don't give a dern—warbles right along, same as if it was applause. They sing out, 'Oh, dry up!' 'Give us a rest!' 'Shoot him!' 'Oh, take a walk!' and all sorts of such things. But what of it? It don't phaze him. He don't mind it.' After a pause: 'Kind of a good little fool, too; gits up in the mornin' and carts all that stock of boots back, and sorts 'em out and sets each man's pair where they belong. And they've been thronged at him so much now, that he knows every boot in the band,—can sort 'em out with his eyes shut.'

After another pause, which I forebore to interrupt,—

'But the roughest thing about it is, that when he's done prayin',—when he ever does get done,—he pipes up and begins to sing. Well, you know what a honey kind of a voice he's got when he talks; you know how it would persuade a cast-iron dog to come down off of a doorstep and lick his hand. Now if you'll take my word for it, sir, it ain't a circumstance to his singin'! Flute music is harsh to that boy's singin'. Oh, he just gurgles it out so soft and sweet and low, there in the dark, that it makes you think you are in heaven.'

'What is there "rough" about that?'

'Ah, that's just it, sir. You hear him sing—

"Just as I am—poor, wretched, blind,"

'—just you hear him sing that, once, and see if you don't melt all up and the water come into your eyes! I don't care what he sings, it goes plum straight home to you—it goes deep down to where you live—and it fetches you every time! Just you hear him sing:—

"Child of sin and sorrow, filled with dismay,
Wait not till to-morrow, yield thee to-day;
Grieve not that love
Which, from above"

'—and so on. It makes a body feel like the wickedest, ungratefulest brute that walks. And when he sings them songs of his about home, and mother, and childhood, and old memories, and things that's vanished, and old friends dead and gone, it fetches everything before your face that you've ever loved and lost in all your life—and it's just beautiful, it's just divine to listen to, sir—but, Lord, Lord, the heart-break of it! The band—well, they all cry—every rascal of them blubbers, and don't try to hide it, either; and first you know, that very gang that's been slammin' boots at that boy will skip out of their bunks all of a sudden, and rush over in the dark and hug him! Yes, they do—and slobber all over him, and call him pet names, and beg him to forgive them. And just at that time, if a regiment was to offer to hurt a hair of that cub's head, they'd go for that regiment, if it was a whole army corps!'

Another pause.

'Is that all?' said I.

'Yes, sir.'

'Well, dear me, what is the complaint? What do they want done?'

'Done? Why, bless you, sir, they want you to stop him from singin'.'

'What an idea! You said his music was divine.'

'That's just it. It's too divine. Mortal man can't stand it. It stirs a body up so; it turns a body inside out; it racks his feelin's all to rags; it makes him feel bad and wicked, and not fit for any place but perdition. It keeps a body in such an everlastin' state of repentin', that nothin' don't taste good and there ain't no comfort in life. And then the cryin', you see—every mornin' they are ashamed to look one another in the face.'

'Well, this is an odd case, and a singular complaint. So they really want the singing stopped?'

'Yes, sir, that is the idea. They don't wish to ask too much; they would like powerful well to have the prayin' shut down on, or leastways trimmed off around the edges; but the main thing's the singin'. If they can only get the singin' choked off, they think they can stand the prayin', rough as it is to be bully-ragged so much that way.'

I told the sergeant I would take the matter under consideration. That night I crept into the musicians' quarters and listened. The sergeant had not overstated the case. I heard the praying voice pleading in the dark; I heard the execrations of the harassed men; I heard the rain of boots whiz through the air, and bang and thump around the big drum. The thing touched me, but it amused me, too. By and by, after an impressive silence, came the singing. Lord, the pathos of it, the enchantment of it! Nothing in the world was ever so sweet, so gracious, so tender, so holy, so moving. I made my stay very brief; I was beginning to experience emotions of a sort not proper to the commandant of a fortress.

Next day I issued orders which stopped the praying and singing. Then followed three or four days which were so full of bounty-jumping excitements and irritations that I never once thought of my drummer-boy. But now comes Sergeant Rayburn, one morning, and says,—

'That new boy acts mighty strange, sir.'

'How?'

'Well, sir, he's all the time writing.'

'Writing? What does he write—letters?'

'I don't know, sir; but whenever he's off duty, he is always poking and nosing around the fort, all by himself,—blest if I think there's a hole or corner in it he hasn't been into,—and every little while he outs with pencil and paper and scribbles something down.'

This gave me a most unpleasant sensation. I wanted to scoff at it, but it was not a time to scoff at anything that had the least suspicious tinge about it. Things were happening all around us, in the North, then, that warned us to be always on the alert, and always suspecting. I recalled to mind the suggestive fact that this boy was from the South,—the extreme South, Louisiana,—and the thought was not of a reassuring nature, under the circumstances. Nevertheless, it cost me a pang to give the orders which I now gave to Rayburn. I felt like a father who plots to expose his own child to shame and injury. I told Rayburn to keep quiet, bide his time, and get me some of those writings whenever he could manage it without the boy's finding it out. And I charged him not to do anything which might let the boy discover that he was being watched. I also ordered that he allow the lad his usual liberties, but that he be followed at a distance when he went out into the town.

During the next two days, Rayburn reported to me several times. No success. The boy was still writing, but he always pocketed his paper with a careless air whenever Rayburn appeared in his vicinity. He had gone twice to an old deserted stable in the town, remained a minute or two, and come out again. One could not pooh-pooh these things—they had an evil look. I was obliged to confess to myself that I was getting uneasy. I went into my private quarters and sent for my second in command—an officer of intelligence and judgement, son of General James Watson Webb. He was surprised and troubled. We had a long talk over the matter, and came to the conclusion that it would be worth while to institute a secret search. I determined to take charge of that myself. So I had myself called at two in the morning; and, pretty soon after, I was in the musicians' quarters, crawling along the floor on my stomach among the snorers. I reached my slumbering waif's bunk at last, without disturbing anybody, captured his clothes and kit, and crawled stealthily back again. When I got to my own quarters, I found Webb there, waiting and eager to know the result. We made search immediately. The clothes were a disappointment. In the pockets we found blank paper and a pencil; nothing else, except a jackknife and such queer odds and ends and useless trifles as boys hoard and value. We turned to the kit hopefully. Nothing there but a rebuke for us!—a little Bible with this written on the fly-leaf: 'Stranger, be kind to my boy, for his mother's sake.'

I looked at Webb—he dropped his eyes; he looked at me—I dropped mine. Neither spoke. I put the book reverently back in its place. Presently Webb got up and went away, without remark.

After a little I nerved myself up to my unpalatable job, and took the plunder back to where it belonged, crawling on my stomach as before. It seemed the peculiarly appropriate attitude for the business I was in.

I was most honestly glad when it was over and done with.

About noon next day Rayburn came, as usual, to report. I cut him short. I said,—

'Let this nonsense be dropped. We are making a bugaboo out of a poor little cub who has got no more harm in him than a hymn-book.'

The sergeant looked surprised, and said,—

'Well, you know it was your orders, sir, and I've got some of the writing.'

'And what does it amount to? How did you get it?'

'I peeped through the key-hole, and see him writing. So when I judged he was about done, I made a sort of a little cough, and I see him crumple it up and throw it in the fire, and look all around to see if anybody was coming. Then he settled back as comfortable and careless as anything. Then I comes in, and passes the time of day pleasantly, and sends him of an errand. He never looked uneasy, but went right along. It was a coal-fire and new-built; the writing had gone over behind a chunk, out of sight; but I got it out; there it is; it ain't hardly scorched, you see.'

I glanced at the paper and took in a sentence or two. Then I dismissed the sergeant and told him to send Webb to me. Here is the paper in full:—

'FORT TRUMBULL, the 8th.

'COLONEL,—I was mistaken as to the calibre of the three guns I ended my list with. They are 18-pounders; all the rest of the armament is as I stated. The garrison remains as before reported, except that the two light infantry companies that were to be detached for service at the front are to stay here for the present—can't find out for how long, just now, but will soon.

We are satisfied that, all things considered, matters had better be postponed un—'

There it broke off—there is where Rayburn coughed and interrupted the writer. All my affection for the boy, all my respect for him and charity for his forlorn condition, withered in a moment under the blight of this revelation of cold-blooded baseness.

But never mind about that. Here was business,— business that required profound and immediate attention, too. Webb and I turned the subject over and over, and examined it all around. Webb said,—

'What a pity he was interrupted! Something is going to be postponed until—when? And what is the something? Possibly he would have mentioned it, the pious little reptile!'

'Yes,' I said, 'we have missed a trick. And who is "we," in the letter? Is it conspirators inside the fort or outside?'

That 'we' was uncomfortably suggestive. However, it was not worth while to be guessing around that, so we proceeded to matters more practical. In the first place, we decided to double the sentries and keep the strictest possible watch. Next, we thought of calling Wicklow in and making him divulge everything; but that did not seem wisest until other methods should fail. We must have some more of the writings; so we began to plan to that end. And now we had an idea: Wicklow never went to the post-office,—perhaps the deserted stable was his post-office. We sent for my confidential clerk—a young German named Sterne, who was a sort of natural detective—and told him all about the case and ordered him to go to work on it. Within the hour we got word that Wicklow was writing again. Shortly afterwards, word came that he had asked leave to go out into the town. He was detained awhile, and meantime Sterne hurried off and concealed himself in the stable. By and by he saw Wicklow saunter in, look about him, then hide something under some rubbish in a corner, and take leisurely leave again. Sterne pounced upon the hidden article—a letter—and brought it to us. It had no superscription and no signature. It repeated what we had already read, and then went on to say:—

'We think it best to postpone till the two companies are gone. I mean the four inside think so; have not communicated with the others—afraid of attracting attention. I say four because we have lost two; they had hardly enlisted and got inside when they were shipped off to the front. It will be absolutely necessary to have two in their places. The two that went were the brothers from Thirty-mile Point. I have something of the greatest importance to reveal, but must not trust it to this method of communication; will try the other.'

'The little scoundrel!' said Webb; 'who could have supposed he was a spy? However, never mind about that; let us add up our particulars, such as they are, and see how the case stands to date. First, we've got a rebel spy in our midst, whom we know; secondly, we've got three more in our midst whom we don't know; thirdly, these spies have been introduced among us through the simple and easy process of enlisting as soldiers in the Union army—and evidently two of them have got sold at it, and been shipped off to the front; fourthly, there are assistant spies "outside"—number indefinite; fifthly, Wicklow has very important matter which he is afraid to communicate by the "present method"—will "try the other." That is the case, as it now stands. Shall we collar Wicklow and make him confess? Or shall we catch the person who removes the letters from the stable and make him tell? Or shall we keep still and find out more?'

We decided upon the last course. We judged that we did not need to proceed to summary measures now, since it was evident that the conspirators were likely to wait till those two light infantry companies were out of the way. We fortified Sterne with pretty ample powers, and told him to use his best endeavours to find out Wicklow's 'other method' of communication. We meant to play a bold game; and to this end we proposed to keep the spies in an unsuspecting state as long as possible. So we ordered Sterne to return to the stable immediately, and, if he found the coast clear, to conceal Wicklow's letter where it was before, and leave it there for the conspirators to get.

The night closed down without further event. It was cold and dark and sleety, with a raw wind blowing; still I turned out of my warm bed several times during the night, and went the rounds in person, to see that all was right and that every sentry was on the alert. I always found them wide awake and watchful; evidently whispers of mysterious dangers had been floating about, and the doubling of the guards had been a kind of indorsement of those rumours. Once, towards morning, I encountered Webb, breasting his way against the bitter wind, and learned then that he, also, had been the rounds several times to see that all was going right.

Next day's events hurried things up somewhat. Wicklow wrote another letter; Sterne preceded him to the stable and saw him deposit it; captured it as soon as Wicklow was out of the way, then slipped out and followed the little spy at a distance, with a detective in plain clothes at his own heels, for we thought it judicious to have the law's assistance handy in case of need. Wicklow went to the railway station, and waited around till the train from New York came in, then stood scanning the faces of the crowd as they poured out of the cars. Presently an aged gentleman, with green goggles and a cane, came limping along, stopped in Wicklow's neighbourhood, and began to look about him expectantly. In an instant Wicklow darted forward, thrust an envelope into his hand, then glided away and disappeared in the throng. The next instant Sterne had snatched the letter; and as he hurried past the detective, he said: 'Follow the old gentleman—don't lose sight of him.' Then Sterne skurried out with the crowd, and came straight to the fort.

We sat with closed doors, and instructed the guard outside to allow no interruption.

First we opened the letter captured at the stable. It read as follows:—

'HOLY ALLIANCE,—Found, in the usual gun, commands from the Master, left there last night, which set aside the instructions heretofore received from the subordinate quarter. Have left in the gun the usual indication that the commands reached the proper hand—'

Webb, interrupting: 'Isn't the boy under constant surveillance now?'

I said yes; he had been under strict surveillance ever since the capturing of his former letter.

'Then how could he put anything into a gun, or take anything out of it, and not get caught?'

'Well,' I said, 'I don't like the look of that very well.'

'I don't, either,' said Webb. 'It simply means that there are conspirators among the very sentinels. Without their connivance in some way or other, the thing couldn't have been done.'

I sent for Rayburn, and ordered him to examine the batteries and see what he could find. The reading of the letter was then resumed:—

'The new commands are peremptory, and require that the MMMM shall be FFFFF at 3 o'clock to-morrow morning. Two hundred will arrive, in small parties, by train and otherwise, from various directions, and will be at appointed place at right time. I will distribute the sign to-day. Success is apparently sure, though something must have got out, for the sentries have been doubled, and the chiefs went the rounds last night several times. W.W. comes from southerly to-day and will receive secret orders—by the other method. All six of you must be in 166 at sharp 2.00 a.m. You will find B.B. there, who will give you detailed instructions. Password same as last time, only reversed—put first syllable last and last syllable first. REMEMBER XXXX. Do not forget. Be of good heart; before the next sun rises you will be heroes; your fame will be permanent; you will have added a deathless page to history. Amen.'

'Thunder and Mars,' said Webb, 'but we are getting into mighty hot quarters, as I look at it!'

I said there was no question but that things were beginning to wear a most serious aspect. Said I,—

'A desperate enterprise is on foot, that is plain enough. Tonight is the time set for it,—that, also, is plain. The exact nature of the enterprise—I mean the manner of it—is hidden away under those blind bunches of M's and F's, but the end and aim, I judge, is the surprise and capture of the post. We must move quick and sharp now. I think nothing can be gained by continuing our clandestine policy as regards Wicklow. We must know, and as soon as possible, too, where "166" is located, so that we can make a descent upon the gang there at 2.00 a.m.; and doubtless the quickest way to get that information will be to force it out of that boy. But first of all, and before we make any important move, I must lay the facts before the War Department, and ask for plenary powers.'

The despatch was prepared in cipher to go over the wires; I read it, approved it, and sent it along.

We presently finished discussing the letter which was under consideration, and then opened the one which had been snatched from the lame gentleman. It contained nothing but a couple of perfectly blank sheets of notepaper! It was a chilly check to our hot eagerness and expectancy. We felt as blank as the paper, for a moment, and twice as foolish. But it was for a moment only; for, of course, we immediately afterwards thought of 'sympathetic ink.' We held the paper close to the fire and watched for the characters to come out, under the influence of the heat; but nothing appeared but some faint tracings, which we could make nothing of. We then called in the surgeon, and sent him off with orders to apply every test he was acquainted with till he got the right one, and report the contents of the letter to me the instant he brought them to the surface. This check was a confounded annoyance, and we naturally chafed under the delay; for we had fully expected to get out of that letter some of the most important secrets of the plot.

Now appeared Sergeant Rayburn, and drew from his pocket a piece of twine string about a foot long, with three knots tied in it, and held it up.

'I got it out of a gun on the water-front,' said he. 'I took the tompions out of all the guns and examined close; this string was the only thing that was in any gun.'

So this bit of string was Wicklow's 'sign' to signify that the 'Master's' commands had not miscarried. I ordered that every sentinel who had served near that gun during the past twenty-four hours be put in confinement at once and separately, and not allowed to communicate with any one without my privity and consent.

A telegram now came from the Secretary of War. It read as follows:—

'Suspend habeas corpus. Put town under martial law. Make necessary arrests. Act with vigour and promptness. Keep the Department informed.'

We were now in shape to go to work. I sent out and had the lame gentleman quietly arrested and as quietly brought into the fort; I placed him under guard, and forbade speech to him or from him. He was inclined to bluster at first, but he soon dropped that.

Next came word that Wicklow had been seen to give something to a couple of our new recruits; and that, as soon as his back was turned, these had been seized and confined. Upon each was found a small bit of paper, bearing these words and signs in pencil:—

'EAGLE'S THIRD FLIGHT. REMEMBER XXXX. 166.

In accordance with instructions, I telegraphed to the Department, in cipher, the progress made, and also described the above ticket. We seemed to be in a strong enough position now to venture to throw off the mask as regarded Wicklow; so I sent for him. I also sent for and received back the letter written in sympathetic ink, the surgeon accompanying it with the information that thus far it had resisted his tests, but that there were others he could apply when I should be ready for him to do so.

Presently Wicklow entered. He had a somewhat worn and anxious look, but he was composed and easy, and if he suspected anything it did not appear in his face or manner. I allowed him to stand there a moment or two, then I said pleasantly,—

'My boy, why do you go to that old stable so much?'

He answered, with simple demeanour and without embarrassment,—

'Well, I hardly know, sir; there isn't any particular reason, except that I like to be alone, and I amuse myself there.'

'You amuse yourself there, do you?'

'Yes, sir,' he replied, as innocently and simply as before.

'Is that all you do there?'

'Yes, sir,' he said, looking up with childlike wonderment in his big soft eyes.

'You are sure?'

'Yes, sir, sure.'

After a pause, I said,—

'Wicklow, why do you write so much?'

'I? I do not write much, sir.'

'You don't?'

'No, sir. Oh, if you mean scribbling, I do scribble some, for amusement.'

'What do you do with your scribblings?'

'Nothing, sir—throw them away.'

'Never send them to anybody?'

'No, sir.'

I suddenly thrust before him the letter to the 'Colonel.' He started slightly, but immediately composed himself. A slight tinge spread itself over his cheek.

'How came you to send this piece of scribbling, then?'

'I nev—never meant any harm, sir.'

'Never meant any harm! You betray the armament and condition of the post, and mean no harm by it?'

He hung his head and was silent.

'Come, speak up, and stop lying. Whom was this letter intended for?'

He showed signs of distress, now; but quickly collected himself, and replied, in a tone of deep earnestness,—

'I will tell you the truth, sir—the whole truth. The letter was never intended for anybody at all. I wrote it only to amuse myself. I see the error and foolishness of it, now,—but it is the only offence, sir, upon my honour.'

'Ah, I am glad of that. It is dangerous to be writing such letters. I hope you are sure this is the only one you wrote?'

'Yes, sir, perfectly sure.'

His hardihood was stupefying. He told that lie with as sincere a countenance as any creature ever wore. I waited a moment to soothe down my rising temper, and then said,—

'Wicklow, jog your memory now, and see if you can help me with two or three little matters which I wish to inquire about.'

'I will do my very best, sir.'

'Then, to begin with—who is 'the Master'?'

It betrayed him into darting a startled glance at our faces, but that was all. He was serene again in a moment, and tranquilly answered,—

'I do not know, sir.'

'You do not know?'

'I do not know.'

'You are sure you do not know?'

He tried hard to keep his eyes on mine, but the strain was too great; his chin sunk slowly towards his breast and he was silent; he stood there nervously fumbling with a button, an object to command one's pity, in spite of his base acts. Presently I broke the stillness with the question,—

'Who are the "Holy Alliance"?'

His body shook visibly, and he made a slight random gesture with his hands, which to me was like the appeal of a despairing creature for compassion. But he made no sound. He continued to stand with his face bent towards the ground. As we sat gazing at him, waiting for him to speak, we saw the big tears begin to roll down his cheeks. But he remained silent. After a little, I said,—

'You must answer me, my boy, and you must tell me the truth. Who are the Holy Alliance?'

He wept on in silence. Presently I said, somewhat sharply,

'Answer the question!'

He struggled to get command of his voice; and then, looking up appealingly, forced the words out between his sobs,—

'Oh, have pity on me, sir! I cannot answer it, for I do not know.'

'What!'

'Indeed, sir, I am telling the truth. I never have heard of the Holy Alliance till this moment. On my honour, sir, this is so.'

'Good heavens! Look at this second letter of yours; there, do you see those words, 'Holy Alliance?' What do you say now?'

He gazed up into my face with the hurt look of one upon whom a great wrong had been wrought, then said, feelingly,—

'This is some cruel joke, sir; and how could they play it upon me, who have tried all I could to do right, and have never done harm to anybody? Some one has counterfeited my hand; I never wrote a line of this; I have never seen this letter before!'

'Oh, you unspeakable liar! Here, what do you say to this?'— and I snatched the sympathetic-ink letter from my pocket and thrust it before his eyes.

His face turned white!—as white as a dead person's. He wavered slightly in his tracks, and put his hand against the wall to steady himself. After a moment he asked, in so faint a voice that it was hardly audible,—

'Have you—read it?'

Our faces must have answered the truth before my lips could get out a false 'yes,' for I distinctly saw the courage come back into that boy's eyes. I waited for him to say something, but he kept silent. So at last I said,—

'Well, what have you to say as to the revelations in this letter?'

He answered, with perfect composure,—

'Nothing, except that they are entirely harmless and innocent; they can hurt nobody.'

I was in something of a corner now, as I couldn't disprove his assertion. I did not know exactly how to proceed. However, an idea came to my relief, and I said,—

'You are sure you know nothing about the Master and the Holy Alliance, and did not write the letter which you say is a forgery?'

'Yes, sir—sure.'

I slowly drew out the knotted twine string and held it up without speaking. He gazed at it indifferently, then looked at me inquiringly. My patience was sorely taxed. However, I kept my temper down, and said in my usual voice,—

'Wicklow, do you see this?'

'Yes, sir.'

'What is it?'

'It seems to be a piece of string.'

'Seems? It is a piece of string. Do you recognize it?'

'No, sir,' he replied, as calmly as the words could be uttered.

His coolness was perfectly wonderful! I paused now for several seconds, in order that the silence might add impressiveness to what I was about to say; then I rose and laid my hand on his shoulder, and said gravely,—

'It will do you no good, poor boy, none in the world. This sign to the "Master," this knotted string, found in one of the guns on the water-front—'

'Found in the gun! Oh, no, no, no! do not say in the gun, but in a crack in the tompion!—it must have been in the crack!' and down he went on his knees and clasped his hands and lifted up a face that was pitiful to see, so ashy it was, and wild with terror.

'No, it was in the gun.'

'Oh, something has gone wrong! My God, I am lost!' and he sprang up and darted this way and that, dodging the hands that were put out to catch him, and doing his best to escape from the place. But of course escape was impossible. Then he flung himself on his knees again, crying with all his might, and clasped me around the legs; and so he clung to me and begged and pleaded, saying, 'Oh, have pity on me! Oh, be merciful to me! Do not betray me; they would not spare my life a moment! Protect me, save me. I will confess everything!'

It took us some time to quiet him down and modify his fright, and get him into something like a rational frame of mind. Then I began to question him, he answering humbly, with downcast eyes, and from time to time swabbing away his constantly flowing tears.

'So you are at heart a rebel?'

'Yes, sir.'

'And a spy?'

'Yes, sir.'

'And have been acting under distinct orders from outside?'
'Yes, sir.'
'Willingly?'
'Yes, sir.'
'Gladly, perhaps?'
'Yes, sir; it would do no good to deny it. The South is my country; my heart is Southern, and it is all in her cause.'

'Then the tale you told me of your wrongs and the persecution of your family was made up for the occasion?'

'They—they told me to say it, sir.'

'And you would betray and destroy those who pitied and sheltered you. Do you comprehend how base you are, you poor misguided thing?'

He replied with sobs only.

'Well, let that pass. To business. Who is the "Colonel," and where is he?'

He began to cry hard, and tried to beg off from answering. He said he would be killed if he told. I threatened to put him in the dark cell and lock him up if he did not come out with the information. At the same time I promised to protect him from all harm if he made a clean breast. For all answer, he closed his mouth firmly and put on a stubborn air which I could not bring him out of. At last I started with him; but a single glance into the dark cell converted him. He broke into a passion of weeping and supplicating, and declared he would tell everything.

So I brought him back, and he named the 'Colonel,' and described him particularly. Said he would be found at the principal hotel in the town, in citizen's dress. I had to threaten him again, before he would describe and name the 'Master.' Said the Master would be found at No. 15 Bond Street, New York, passing under the name of R. F. Gaylord. I telegraphed name and description to the chief of police of the metropolis, and asked that Gaylord be arrested and held till I could send for him.

'Now,' said I, 'it seems that there are several of the conspirators "outside," presumably in New London. Name and describe them.'

He named and described three men and two women,—all stopping at the principal hotel. I sent out quietly, and had them and the "Colonel" arrested and confined in the fort.

'Next, I want to know all about your three fellow-conspirators who are here in the fort.'

He was about to dodge me with a falsehood, I thought; but I produced the mysterious bits of paper which had been found upon two of them, and this had a salutary effect upon him. I said we had possession of two of the men, and he must point out the third. This frightened him badly, and he cried out,—

'Oh, please don't make me; he would kill me on the spot!'

I said that that was all nonsense; I would have somebody near by to protect him, and, besides, the men should be assembled without arms. I ordered all the raw recruits to be mustered, and then the poor trembling little wretch went out and stepped along down the line, trying to look as indifferent as possible. Finally he spoke a single word to one of the men, and before he had gone five steps the man was under arrest.

As soon as Wicklow was with us again, I had those three men brought in. I made one of them stand forward, and said,—

'Now, Wicklow, mind, not a shade's divergence from the exact truth. Who is this man, and what do you know about him?

Being 'in for it,' he cast consequences aside, fastened his eyes on the man's face, and spoke straight along without hesitation,— to the following effect.

'His real name is George Bristow. He is from New Orleans; was second mate of the coast-packet "Capitol," two years ago; is a desperate character, and has served two terms for manslaughter,— one for killing a deck-hand named Hyde with a capstan-bar, and one for killing a roustabout for refusing to heave the lead, which is no part of a roustabout's business. He is a spy, and was sent here by the Colonel, to act in that capacity. He was third mate of the "St Nicholas," when she blew up in the neighbourhood of Memphis, in '58, and came near being lynched for robbing the dead and wounded while they were being taken ashore in an empty wood-boat.'

And so forth and so on—he gave the man's biography in full. When he had finished, I said to the man,—

'What have you to say to this?'

'Barring your presence, sir, it is the infernalest lie that ever was spoke!'

I sent him back into confinement, and called the others forward in turn. Same result. The boy gave a detailed history of each, without ever hesitating for a word or a fact; but all I could get out of either rascal was the indignant assertion that it was all a lie. They would confess nothing. I returned them to captivity, and brought out the rest of my prisoners, one by one. Wicklow told all about them—what towns in the South they were from, and every detail of their connection with the conspiracy.

But they all denied his facts, and not one of them confessed a thing. The men raged, the women cried. According to their stories, they were all innocent people from out West, and loved the Union above all things in this world. I locked the gang up, in disgust, and fell to catechising Wicklow once more.

'Where is No. 166, and who is B.B.?'

But there he was determined to draw the line. Neither coaxing nor threats had any effect upon him. Time was flying—it was necessary to institute sharp measures. So I tied him up a-tiptoe by the thumbs. As the pain increased, it wrung screams from him which were almost more than I could bear. But I held my ground, and pretty soon he shrieked out,—

'Oh, please let me down, and I will tell!'

'No—you'll tell before I let you down.'

Every instant was agony to him, now, so out it came,—

'No. 166, Eagle Hotel!'—naming a wretched tavern down by the water, a resort of common labourers, 'longshoremen, and less reputable folk.

So I released him, and then demanded to know the object of the conspiracy.

'To take the fort to-night,' said he, doggedly and sobbing.

'Have I got all the chiefs of the conspiracy?'

'No. You've got all except those that are to meet at 166.'

'What does "Remember XXXX" mean?'

No reply.

'What is the password to No. 166?'

No reply.

'What do those bunches of letters mean,—"FFFFF" and "MMMM"? Answer! or you will catch it again.'

'I never will answer! I will die first. Now do what you please.'

'Think what you are saying, Wicklow. Is it final?'

He answered steadily, and without a quiver in his voice,—

'It is final. As sure as I love my wronged country and hate everything this Northern sun shines on, I will die before I will reveal those things.'

I triced him up by the thumbs again. When the agony was full upon him, it was heartbreaking to hear the poor thing's shrieks, but we got nothing else out of him. To every question he screamed the same reply: 'I can die, and I will die; but I will never tell.'

Well, we had to give it up. We were convinced that he certainly would die rather than confess. So we took him down and imprisoned him, under strict guard.

Then for some hours we busied ourselves with sending telegrams to the War Department, and with making preparations for a descent upon No. 166.

It was stirring times, that black and bitter night. Things had leaked out, and the whole garrison was on the alert. The sentinels were trebled, and nobody could move, outside or in, without being brought to a stand with a musket levelled at his head. However, Webb and I were less concerned now than we had previously been, because of the fact that the conspiracy must necessarily be in a pretty crippled condition, since so many of its principals were in our clutches.

I determined to be at No. 166 in good season, capture and gag B.B., and be on hand for the rest when they arrived. At about a quarter past one in the morning I crept out of the fortress with half a dozen stalwart and gamy U.S. regulars at my heels—and the boy Wicklow, with his hands tied behind him. I told him we were going to No. 166, and that if I found he had lied again and was misleading us, he would have to show us the right place or suffer the consequences.

We approached the tavern stealthily and reconnoitred. A light was burning in the small bar-room, the rest of the house was dark. I tried the front door; it yielded, and we softly entered, closing the door behind us. Then we removed our shoes, and I led the way to the bar-room. The German landlord sat there, asleep in his chair. I woke him gently, and told him to take off his boots and precede us; warning him at the same time to utter no sound. He obeyed without a murmur, but evidently he was badly frightened. I ordered him to lead the way to 166. We ascended two or three flights of stairs as softly as a file of cats; and then, having arrived near the farther end of a long hall, we came to a door through the glazed transom of which we could discern the glow of a dim light from within. The landlord felt for me in the dark and whispered me that that was 166. I tried the door—it was locked on the inside. I whispered an order to one of my biggest soldiers; we set our ample shoulders to the door and with one heave we burst it from its hinges. I caught a half-glimpse of a figure in a bed—saw its head dart towards the candle; out went the light, and we were in pitch darkness. With one big bound I lit on that bed and pinned its occupant down with my knees. My prisoner struggled fiercely, but I got a grip on his throat with my left hand, and that was a good assistance to my knees in holding him down. Then straightway I snatched out my revolver, cocked it, and laid the cold barrel warningly against his cheek.

'Now somebody strike a light!' said I. 'I've got him safe.'

It was done. The flame of the match burst up. I looked at my captive, and, by George, it was a young woman!

I let go and got off the bed, feeling pretty sheepish. Everybody stared stupidly at his neighbour. Nobody had any wit or sense left, so sudden and overwhelming had been the surprise. The young woman began to cry, and covered her face with the sheet. The landlord said, meekly,—

'My daughter, she has been doing something that is not right, nicht wahr?'

'Your daughter? Is she your daughter?'

'Oh, yes, she is my daughter. She is just to-night come home from Cincinnati a little bit sick.'

'Confound it, that boy has lied again. This is not the right 166; this is not B.B. Now, Wicklow, you will find the correct 166 for us, or—hello! where is that boy?'

Gone, as sure as guns! And, what is more, we failed to find a trace of him. Here was an awkward predicament. I cursed my stupidity in not tying him to one of the men; but it was of no use to bother about that now. What should I do in the present circumstances?—that was the question. That girl might be B.B., after all. I did not believe it, but still it would not answer to take unbelief for proof. So I finally put my men in a vacant room across the hall from 166, and told them to capture anybody and everybody that approached the girl's room, and to keep the landlord with them, and under strict watch, until further orders. Then I hurried back to the fort to see if all was right there yet.

Yes, all was right. And all remained right. I stayed up all night to make sure of that. Nothing happened. I was unspeakably glad to see the dawn come again, and be able to telegraph the Department that the Stars and Stripes still floated over Fort Trumbull.

An immense pressure was lifted from my breast. Still I did not relax vigilance, of course, nor effort either; the case was too grave for that. I had up my prisoners, one by one, and harried them by the hour, trying to get them to confess, but it was a failure. They only gnashed their teeth and tore their hair, and revealed nothing.

About noon came tidings of my missing boy. He had been seen on the road, tramping westwards, some eight miles out, at six in the morning. I started a cavalry lieutenant and a private on his track at once. They came in sight of him twenty miles out. He had climbed a fence and was wearily dragging himself across a slushy field towards a large old-fashioned mansion in the edge of a village. They rode through a bit of woods, made a detour, and closed up on the house from the opposite side; then dismounted and skurried into the kitchen. Nobody there. They slipped into the next room, which was also unoccupied; the door from that room into the front or sitting room was open. They were about to step through it when they heard a low voice; it was somebody praying. So they halted reverently, and the lieutenant put his head in and saw an old man and an old woman kneeling in a corner of that sitting-room. It was the old man that was praying, and just as he was finishing his prayer, the Wicklow boy opened the front door and stepped in. Both of those old people sprang at him and smothered him with embraces, shouting,—

'Our boy! our darling! God be praised. The lost is found! He that was dead is alive again!'

Well, sir, what do you think! That young imp was born and reared on that homestead, and had never been five miles away from it in all his life, till the fortnight before he loafed into my quarters and gulfed me with that maudlin yarn of his! It's as true as gospel. That old man was his father—a learned old retired clergyman; and that old lady was his mother.

Let me throw in a word or two of explanation concerning that boy and his performances. It turned out that he was a ravenous devourer of dime novels and sensation-story papers—therefore, dark mysteries and gaudy heroisms were just in his line. Then he had read newspaper reports of the stealthy goings and comings of rebel spies in our midst, and of their lurid purposes and their two or three startling achievements, till his imagination was all aflame on that subject. His constant comrade for some months had been a Yankee youth of much tongue and lively fancy, who had served for a couple of years as 'mud clerk' (that is, subordinate purser) on certain of the packet-boats plying between New Orleans and points two or three hundred miles up the Mississippi—hence his easy facility in handling the names and other details pertaining to that region. Now I had spent two or three months in that part of the country before the war; and I knew just enough about it to be easily taken in by that boy, whereas a born Louisianian would probably have caught him tripping before he had talked fifteen minutes. Do you know the reason he said he would rather die than explain certain of his treasonable enigmas? Simply because he couldn't explain them!—they had no meaning; he had fired them out of his imagination without forethought or afterthought; and so, upon sudden call, he wasn't able to invent an explanation of them. For instance, he couldn't reveal what was hidden in the 'sympathetic ink' letter, for the ample reason that there wasn't anything hidden in it; it was blank paper only. He hadn't put anything into a gun, and had never intended to—for his letters were all written to imaginary persons, and when he hid one in the stable he always removed the one he had put there the day before; so he was not acquainted with that knotted string, since he was seeing it for the first time when I showed it to him; but as soon as I had let him find out where it came from, he straightway adopted it, in his romantic fashion, and got some fine effects out of it. He invented Mr 'Gaylord'; there wasn't any 15 Bond Street, just then—it had been pulled down three months before. He invented the 'Colonel'; he invented the glib histories of those unfortunates whom I captured and confronted with him; he invented 'B.B.'; he even invented No. 166, one may say, for he didn't know there was such a number in the Eagle Hotel until we went there. He stood ready to invent anybody or anything whenever it was wanted. If I called for 'outside' spies, he promptly described strangers whom he had seen at the hotel, and whose names he had happened to hear. Ah, he lived in a gorgeous, mysterious, romantic world during those few stirring days, and I think it was real to him, and that he enjoyed it clear down to the bottom of his heart.

But he made trouble enough for us, and just no end of humiliation. You see, on account of him we had fifteen or twenty people under arrest and confinement in the fort, with sentinels before their doors. A lot of the captives were soldiers and such, and to them I didn't have to apologize; but the rest were first-class citizens, from all over the country, and no amount of apologies was sufficient to satisfy them. They just fumed and raged and made no end of trouble! And those two ladies,—one was an Ohio Congressman's wife, the other a Western bishop's sister,—well, the scorn and ridicule and angry tears they poured out on me made up a keepsake that was likely to make me remember them for a considerable time,—and I shall. That old lame gentleman with the goggles was a college president from Philadelphia, who had come up to attend his nephew's funeral. He had never seen young Wicklow before, of course. Well, he not only missed the funeral, and got jailed as a rebel spy, but Wicklow had stood up there in my quarters and coldly described him as a counterfeiter, rigger-trader, horse-thief, and fire-bug from the most notorious rascal-nest in Galveston; and this was a thing which that poor old gentleman couldn't seem to get over at all.

And the War Department! But, O my soul, let's draw the curtain over that part!

26

ROGER MALVIN'S BURIAL

Nathaniel Hawthorne

One of the few incidents of Indian warfare naturally susceptible of the moonlight of romance was that expedition undertaken for the defence of the frontiers in the year 1725, which resulted in the well-remembered 'Lovell's Fight.' Imagination, by casting certain circumstances judicially into the shade, may see much to admire in the heroism of a little band who gave battle to twice their number in the heart of the enemy's country. The open bravery displayed by both parties was in accordance with civilized ideas of valour; and chivalry itself might not blush to record the deeds of one or two individuals. The battle, though so fatal to those who fought, was not unfortunate in its consequences to the country; for it broke the strength of a tribe and conduced to the peace which subsisted during several ensuing years. History and tradition are unusually minute in their memorials of their affair; and the captain of a scouting party of frontier men has acquired as actual a military renown as many a victorious leader of thousands. Some of the incidents contained in the following pages will be recognized, notwithstanding the substitution of fictitious names, by such as have heard, from old men's lips, the fate of the few combatants who were in a condition to retreat after 'Lovell's Fight.'

The early sunbeams hovered cheerfully upon the tree-tops, beneath which two weary and wounded men had stretched their limbs the night before. Their bed of withered oak leaves was strewn upon the small level space, at the foot of a rock, situated near the summit of one of the gentle swells by which the face of the country is there diversified. The mass of granite, rearing its smooth, flat surface fifteen or twenty feet above their heads, was not unlike a gigantic gravestone, upon which the veins seemed to form an inscription in forgotten characters. On a tract of several acres around this rock, oaks and other hard-wood trees had supplied the place of the pines, which were the usual growth of the land; and a young and vigorous sapling stood close beside the travellers.

The severe wound of the elder man had probably deprived him of sleep; for, so soon as the first ray of sunshine rested on the top of the highest tree, he reared himself painfully from his recumbent posture and sat erect. The deep lines of his countenance and the scattered grey of his hair marked him as past the middle age; but his muscular frame would, but for the effect of his wound, have been as capable of sustaining fatigue as in the early vigor of life. Languor and exhaustion now sat upon his haggard features; and the despairing glance which he sent forward through the depths of the forest proved his own conviction that his pilgrimage was at an end. He next turned his eyes to the companion who reclined by his side. The youth—for he had scarcely attained the years of manhood—lay, with his head upon his arm, in the embrace of an unquiet sleep, which a thrill of pain from his wounds seemed each moment on the point of breaking. His right hand grasped a musket; and, to judge from the violent action of his features, his slumbers were bringing back a vision of the conflict of which he was one of the few survivors. A shout deep and loud in his dreaming fancy—found its way in an imperfect murmur to his lips; and, starting even at the slight sound of his own voice, he suddenly awoke. The first act of reviving recollection was to make anxious inquiries respecting the condition of his wounded fellow-traveller. The latter shook his head.

'Reuben, my boy,' said he, 'this rock beneath which we sit will serve for an old hunter's gravestone. There is many and many a long mile of howling wilderness before us yet; nor would it avail me anything if the smoke of my own chimney were but on the other side of that swell of land. The Indian bullet was deadlier than I thought.'

'You are weary with our three days' travel,' replied the youth, 'and a little longer rest will recruit you. Sit you here while I search the woods for the herbs and roots that must be our sustenance; and, having eaten, you shall lean on me, and we will turn our faces homewards. I doubt not that, with my help, you can attain to some one of the frontier garrisons.'

'There is not two days' life in me, Reuben,' said the other, calmly, 'and I will no longer burden you with my useless body, when you can scarcely support your own. Your wounds are deep and your strength is failing fast; yet, if you hasten onwards alone, you may be preserved. For me there is no hope, and I will await death here.'

'If it must be so, I will remain and watch by you,' said Reuben, resolutely.

'No, my son, no,' rejoined his companion. 'Let the wish of a dying man have weight with you; give me one grasp of your hand, and get you hence. Think you that my last moments will be eased by the thought that I leave you to die a more lingering death? I have loved you like a father, Reuben; and at a time like this I should have something of a father's authority. I charge you to be gone that I may die in peace.'

'And because you have been a father to me, should I therefore leave you to perish and to lie unburied in the wilderness?' exclaimed the youth. 'No; if your end be in truth approaching, I will watch by you and receive your parting words. I will dig a grave here by the rock, in which, if my weakness overcome me, we will rest together; or, if Heaven gives me strength, I will seek my way home.'

'In the cities and wherever men dwell,' replied the other, 'they bury their dead in the earth; they hide them from the sight of the living; but here, where no step may pass perhaps for a hundred years, wherefore should I not rest beneath the open sky, covered only by the oak leaves when the autumn winds shall strew them? And for a monument, here is this grey rock, on which my dying hand shall carve the name of Roger Malvin, and the traveller in days to come will know that here sleeps a hunter and a warrior. Tarry not, then, for a folly like this, but hasten away, if not for your own sake, for hers who will else be desolate.'

Malvin spoke the last few words in a faltering voice, and their effect upon his companion was strongly visible. They reminded him that there were other and less questionable duties than that of sharing the fate of a man whom his death could not benefit. Nor can it be affirmed that no selfish feeling strove to enter Reuben's heart, though the consciousness made him more earnestly resist his companion's entreaties.

'How terrible to wait the slow approach of death in this solitude!' exclaimed he. 'A brave man does not shrink in the battle; and, when friends stand round the bed, even women may die composedly; but here—'

'I shall not shrink even here, Reuben Bourne,' interrupted Malvin. 'I am a man of no weak heart, and, if I were, there is a surer support than that of earthly friends. You are young, and life is dear to you. Your last moments will need comfort far more than mine; and when you have laid me in the earth, and are alone, and night is settling on the forest, you will feel all the bitterness of the death that may now be escaped. But I will urge no selfish motive to your generous nature. Leave me for my sake, that, having said a prayer for your safety, I may have space to settle my account undisturbed by worldly sorrows.'

'And your daughter,—how shall I dare to meet her eye?' exclaimed Reuben. 'She will ask the fate of her father, whose life I vowed to defend with my own. Must I tell her that he travelled three days' march with me from the field of battle and that then I left him to perish in the wilderness? Were it not better to lie down and die by your side than to return safe and say this to Dorcas?'

'Tell my daughter,' said Roger Malvin, 'that, though yourself sore wounded, and weak, and weary, you led my tottering footsteps many a mile, and left me only at my earnest entreaty, because I would not have your blood upon my soul. Tell her that through pain and danger you were faithful, and that, if your lifeblood could have saved me, it would have flowed to its last drop; and tell her that you will be something dearer than a father, and that my blessing is with you both, and that my dying eyes can see a long and pleasant path in which you will journey together.'

As Malvin spoke he almost raised himself from the ground, and the energy of his concluding words seemed to fill the wild and lonely forest with a vision of happiness; but, when he sank exhausted upon his bed of oak leaves, the light which had kindled in Reuben's eye was quenched. He felt as if it were both sin and folly to think of happiness at such a moment. His companion watched his changing countenance, and sought with generous art to wile him to his own good.

'Perhaps I deceive myself in regard to the time I have to live,' he resumed. 'It may be that, with speedy assistance, I might recover of my wound. The foremost fugitives must, ere this, have carried tidings of our fatal battle to the frontiers, and parties will be out to succor those in like condition with ourselves. Should you meet one of these and guide them hither, who can tell but that I may sit by my own fireside again?'

A mournful smile strayed across the features of the dying man as he insinuated that unfounded hope,—which, however, was not without its effect on Reuben. No merely selfish motive, nor even the desolate condition of Dorcas, could have induced him to desert his companion at such a moment—but his wishes seized on the thought that Malvin's life might be preserved, and his sanguine nature heightened almost to certainty the remote possibility of procuring human aid.

'Surely there is reason, weighty reason, to hope that friends are not far distant,' he said, half aloud. 'There fled one coward, unwounded, in the beginning of the fight, and most probably he made good speed. Every true man on the frontier would shoulder his musket at the news; and, though no party may range so far into the woods as this, I shall perhaps encounter them in one day's march. Counsel me faithfully,' he added, turning to Malvin, in distrust of his own motives. 'Were your situation mine, would you desert me while life remained?'

'It is now twenty years,' replied Roger Malvin,—sighing, however, as he secretly acknowledged the wide dissimilarity between the two cases,— 'it is now twenty years since I escaped with one dear friend from Indian captivity near Montreal. We journeyed many days through the woods, till at length overcome with hunger and weariness, my friend lay down and besought me to leave him; for he knew that, if I remained, we both must perish; and, with but little hope of obtaining succor, I heaped a pillow of dry leaves beneath his head and hastened on.'

'And did you return in time to save him?' asked Reuben, hanging on Malvin's words as if they were to be prophetic of his own success.

'I did,' answered the other. 'I came upon the camp of a hunting party before sunset of the same day. I guided them to the spot where my comrade was expecting death; and he is now a hale and hearty man upon his own farm, far within the frontiers, while I lie wounded here in the depths of the wilderness.'

This example, powerful in affecting Reuben's decision, was aided, unconsciously to himself, by the hidden strength of many another motive. Roger Malvin perceived that the victory was nearly won.

'Now, go, my son, and Heaven prosper you!' he said. 'Turn not back with your friends when you meet them, lest your wounds and weariness overcome you; but send hitherward two or three, that may be spared, to search for me; and believe me, Reuben, my heart will be lighter with every step you take towards home.' Yet there was, perhaps, a change both in his countenance and voice as he spoke thus; for, after all, it was a ghastly fate to be left expiring in the wilderness.

Reuben Bourne, but half convinced that he was acting rightly, at length raised himself from the ground and prepared himself for his departure. And first, though contrary to Malvin's wishes, he collected a stock of roots and herbs, which had been their only food during the last two days. This useless supply he placed within reach of the dying man, for whom, also, he swept together a bed of dry oak leaves. Then climbing to the summit of the rock, which on one side was rough and broken, he bent the oak sapling downwards, and bound his handkerchief to the topmost branch. This precaution was not unnecessary to direct any who might come in search of Malvin; for every part of the rock, except its broad, smooth front, was concealed at a little distance by the dense undergrowth of the forest. The handkerchief had been the bandage of a wound upon Reuben's arm; and, as he bound it to the tree, he vowed by the blood that stained it that he would return, either to save his companion's life or to lay his body in the grave. He then descended, and stood, with downcast eyes, to receive Roger Malvin's parting words.

The experience of the latter suggested much and minute advice respecting the youth's journey through the trackless forest. Upon this subject he spoke with calm earnestness, as if he were sending Reuben to the battle or the chase while he himself remained secure at home, and not as if the human countenance that was about to leave him were the last he would ever behold. But his firmness was shaken before he concluded.

'Carry my blessing to Dorcas, and say that my last prayer shall be for her and you. Bid her to have no hard thoughts because you left me here,'—Reuben's heart smote him,— 'for that your life would not have weighed with you if its sacrifice could have done me good. She will marry you after she has mourned a little while for her father; and Heaven grant you long and happy days, and may your children's children stand round your death bed! And, Reuben,' added he, as the weakness of mortality made its way at last, 'return, when your wounds are healed and your weariness refreshed,—return to this wild rock, and lay my bones in the grave, and say a prayer over them.'

An almost superstitious regard, arising perhaps from the customs of the Indians, whose war was with the dead as well as the living, was paid by the frontier inhabitants to the rites of sepulture; and there are many instances of the sacrifice of life in the attempt to bury those who had fallen by the 'sword of the wilderness.' Reuben, therefore, felt the full importance of the promise which he most solemnly made to return and perform Roger Malvin's obsequies. It was remarkable that the latter, speaking his whole heart in his parting words, no longer endeavoured to persuade the youth that even the speediest succor might avail to the preservation of his life. Reuben was internally convinced that he should see Malvin's living face no more. His generous nature would fain have delayed him, at whatever risk, till the dying scene were past; but the desire of existence and the hope of happiness had strengthened in his heart, and he was unable to resist them.

'It is enough,' said Roger Malvin, having listened to Reuben's promise. 'Go, and God speed you!'

The youth pressed his hand in silence, turned, and was departing. His slow and faltering steps, however, had borne him but a little way before Malvin's voice recalled him.

'Reuben, Reuben,' said he, faintly; and Reuben returned and knelt down by the dying man.

'Raise me, and let me lean against the rock,' was his last request. 'My face will be turned towards home, and I shall see you a moment longer as you pass among the trees.'

Reuben, having made the desired alteration in his companion's posture, again began his solitary pilgrimage. He walked more hastily at first than was consistent with his strength; for a sort of guilty feeling, which sometimes torments men in their most justifiable acts, caused him to seek concealment from Malvin's eyes; but after he had trodden far upon the rustling forest leaves he crept back, impelled by a wild and painful curiosity, and, sheltered by the earthy roots of an uptorn tree, gazed earnestly at the desolate man. The morning sun was unclouded, and the trees and shrubs imbibed the sweet air of the month of May; yet there seemed a gloom on Nature's face, as if she sympathized with mortal pain and sorrow. Roger Malvin's hands were uplifted in a fervent prayer, some of the words of which stole through the stillness of the woods and entered Reuben's heart, torturing it with an unutterable pang. They were the broken accents of a petition for his own happiness and that of Dorcas; and, as the youth listened, conscience, or something in its similitude, pleaded strongly with him to return and lie down again by the rock. He felt how hard was the doom of the kind and generous being whom he had deserted in his extremity. Death would come like the slow approach of a corpse, stealing gradually towards him through the forest, and showing its ghastly and motionless features from behind a nearer and yet a nearer tree. But such must have been Reuben's own fate had he tarried another sunset; and who shall impute blame to him if he shrink from so useless a sacrifice? As he gave a parting look, a breeze waved the little banner upon the sapling oak and reminded Reuben of his vow.

Many circumstances combined to retard the wounded traveller in his way to the frontiers. On the second day the clouds, gathering densely over the sky, precluded the possibility of regulating his course by the position of the sun; and he knew not but that every effort of his almost exhausted strength was removing him farther from the home he sought. His scanty sustenance was supplied by the berries and other spontaneous products of the forest. Herds of deer, it is true, sometimes bounded past him, and partridges frequently whirred up before his footsteps; but his ammunition had been expended in the fight, and he had no means of slaying them. His wounds, irritated by the constant exertion in which lay the only hope of life, wore away his strength and at intervals confused his reason. But, even in the wanderings of intellect, Reuben's young heart clung strongly to existence; and it was only through absolute incapacity of motion that he at last sank down beneath a tree, compelled there to await death.

In this situation he was discovered by a party who, upon the first intelligence of the fight, had been despatched to the relief of the survivors. They conveyed him to the nearest settlement, which chanced to be that of his own residence.

Dorcas, in the simplicity of the olden time, watched by the bedside of her wounded lover, and administered all those comforts that are in the sole gift of woman's heart and hand. During several days Reuben's recollection strayed drowsily among the perils and hardships through which he had passed, and he was incapable of returning definite answers to the inquiries with which many were eager to harass him. No authentic particulars of the battle had yet been circulated; nor could mothers, wives, and children tell whether their loved ones were detained by captivity or by the stronger chain of death. Dorcas nourished her apprehensions in silence till one afternoon when Reuben awoke from an unquiet sleep, and seemed to recognize her more perfectly than at any previous time. She saw that his intellect had become composed, and she could no longer restrain her filial anxiety.

'My father, Reuben?' she began; but the change in her lover's countenance made her pause.

The youth shrank as if with a bitter pain, and the blood gushed vividly into his wan and hollow cheeks. His first impulse was to cover his face; but, apparently with a desperate effort, he half raised himself and spoke vehemently, defending himself against an imaginary accusation.

'Your father was sore wounded in the battle, Dorcas; and he bade me not burden myself with him, but only to lead him to the lakeside, that he might quench his thirst and die. But I would not desert the old man in his extremity, and, though bleeding myself, I supported him; I gave him half my strength, and led him away with me. For three days we journeyed on together, and your father was sustained beyond my hopes, but, awaking at sunrise on the fourth day, I found him faint and exhausted; he was unable to proceed; his life had ebbed away fast; and—'

'He died!' exclaimed Dorcas, faintly.

Reuben felt it impossible to acknowledge that his selfish love of life had hurried him away before her father's fate was decided. He spoke not; he only bowed his head; and, between shame and exhaustion, sank back and hid his face in the pillow. Dorcas wept when her fears were thus confirmed; but the shock, as it had been long anticipated, was on that account the less violent.

'You dug a grave for my poor father in the wilderness, Reuben?' was the question by which her filial piety manifested itself.

'My hands were weak; but I did what I could,' replied the youth in a smothered tone. 'There stands a noble tombstone above his head; and I would to Heaven I slept as soundly as he!'

Dorcas, perceiving the wildness of his latter words, inquired no further at the time; but her heart found ease in the thought that Roger Malvin had not lacked such funeral rites as it was possible to bestow. The tale of Reuben's courage and fidelity lost nothing when she communicated it to her friends; and the poor youth, tottering from his sick chamber to breathe the sunny air, experienced from every tongue the miserable and humiliating torture of unmerited praise. All acknowledged that he might worthily demand the hand of the fair maiden to whose father he had been 'faithful unto death;' and, as my tale is not of love, it shall suffice to say that in the space of a few months Reuben became the husband of Dorcas Malvin. During the marriage ceremony the bride was covered with blushes, but the bridegroom's face was pale.

There was now in the breast of Reuben Bourne an incommunicable thought—something which he was to conceal most heedfully from her whom he most loved and trusted. He regretted, deeply and bitterly, the moral cowardice that had restrained his words when he was about to disclose the truth to Dorcas; but pride, the fear of losing her affection, the dread of universal scorn, forbade him to rectify this falsehood. He felt that for leaving Roger Malvin he deserved no censure. His presence, the gratuitous sacrifice of his own life, would have added only another and a needless agony to the last moments of the dying man; but concealment had imparted to a justifiable act much of the secret effect of guilt; and Reuben, while reason told him that he had done right, experienced in no small degree the mental horrors which punish the perpetrator of undiscovered crime. By a certain association of ideas, he at times almost imagined himself a murderer. For years, also, a thought would occasionally recur, which, though he perceived all its folly and extravagance, he had not power to banish from his mind. It was a haunting and torturing fancy that his father-in-law was yet sitting at the foot of the rock, on the withered forest leaves, alive, and awaiting his pledged assistance. These mental deceptions, however, came and went, nor did he ever mistake them for realities: but in the calmest and clearest moods of his mind he was conscious that he had a deep vow unredeemed, and that an unburied corpse was calling to him out of the wilderness. Yet such was the consequence of his prevarication that he could not obey the call. It was now too late to require the assistance of Roger Malvin's friends in performing his long-deferred sepulture; and superstitious fears, of which none were more susceptible than the people of the outward settlements, forbade Reuben to go alone. Neither did he know where in the pathless and illimitable forest to seek that smooth and lettered rock at the base of which the body lay: his remembrance of every portion of his travel thence was indistinct, and the latter part had left no impression upon his mind. There was, however, a continual impulse, a voice audible only to himself, commanding him to go forth and redeem his vow; and he had a strange impression that, were he to make the trial, he would be led straight to Malvin's bones. But year after year that summons, unheard but felt, was disobeyed. His one secret thought became like a chain binding down his spirit and like a serpent gnawing into his heart; and he was transformed into a sad and downcast yet irritable man.

In the course of a few years after their marriage changes began to be visible in the external prosperity of Reuben and Dorcas. The only riches of the former had been his stout heart and strong arm; but the latter, her father's sole heiress, had made her husband master of a farm, under older cultivation, larger, and better stocked than most of the frontier establishments. Reuben Bourne, however, was a neglectful husbandman; and, while the lands of the other settlers became annually more fruitful, his deteriorated in the same proportion. The discouragements to agriculture were greatly lessened by the cessation of Indian war, during which men held the plough in one hand and the musket in the other, and were fortunate if the products of their dangerous labour were not destroyed, either in the field or in the barn, by the savage enemy. But Reuben did not profit by the altered condition of the country; nor can it be denied that his intervals of industrious attention to his affairs were but scantily rewarded with success. The irritability by which he had recently become distinguished was another cause of his declining prosperity, as it occasioned frequent quarrels in his unavoidable intercourse with the neighbouring settlers. The results of these were innumerable lawsuits; for the people of New England, in the earliest stages and wildest circumstances of the country, adopted, whenever attainable, the legal mode of deciding their differences. To be brief, the world did not go well with Reuben Bourne; and, though not till many years after his marriage, he was finally a ruined man, with but one remaining expedient against the evil fate that had pursued him. He was to throw sunlight into some deep recess of the forest, and seek subsistence from the virgin bosom of the wilderness.

The only child of Reuben and Dorcas was a son, now arrived at the age of fifteen years, beautiful in youth, and giving promise of a glorious manhood. He was peculiarly qualified for, and already began to excel in, the wild accomplishments of frontier life. His foot was fleet, his aim true, his apprehension quick, his heart glad and high; and all who anticipated the return of Indian war spoke of Cyrus Bourne as a future leader in the land. The boy was loved by his father with a deep and silent strength, as if whatever was good and happy in his own nature had been transferred to his child, carrying his affections with it. Even Dorcas, though loving and beloved, was far less dear to him; for Reuben's secret thoughts and insulated emotions had gradually made him a selfish man, and he could no longer love deeply except where he saw or imagined some reflection or likeness of his own mind. In Cyrus he recognized what he had himself been in other days; and at intervals he seemed to partake of the boy's spirit, and to be revived with a fresh and happy life. Reuben was accompanied by his son in the expedition, for the purpose of selecting a tract of land and felling and burning the timber, which necessarily preceded the removal of the household gods. Two months of autumn were thus occupied, after which Reuben Bourne and his young hunter returned to spend their last winter in the settlements.

It was early in the month of May that the little family snapped asunder whatever tendrils of affections had clung to inanimate objects, and bade farewell to the few who, in the blight of fortune, called themselves their friends. The sadness of the parting moment had, to each of the pilgrims, its peculiar alleviations. Reuben, a moody man, and misanthropic because unhappy, strode onwards with his usual stern brow and downcast eye, feeling few regrets and disdaining to acknowledge any. Dorcas, while she wept abundantly over the broken ties by which her simple and affectionate nature had bound itself to everything, felt that the inhabitants of her inmost heart moved on with her, and that all else would be supplied wherever she might go. And the boy dashed one tear-drop from his eye, and thought of the adventurous pleasures of the untrodden forest.

Oh, who, in the enthusiasm of a daydream, has not wished that he were a wanderer in a world of summer wilderness, with one fair and gentle being hanging lightly on his arm? In youth his free and exulting step would know no barrier but the rolling ocean or the snow-topped mountains; calmer manhood would choose a home where Nature had strewn a double wealth in the vale of some transparent stream; and when hoary age, after long, long years of that pure life, stole on and found him there, it would find him the father of a race, the patriarch of a people, the founder of a mighty nation yet to be. When death, like the sweet sleep which we welcome after a day of happiness, came over him, his far descendants would mourn over the venerated dust. Enveloped by tradition in mysterious attributes, the men of future generations would call him godlike; and remote posterity would see him standing, dimly glorious, far up the valley of a hundred centuries.

The tangled and gloomy forest through which the personages of my tale were wandering differed widely from the dreamer's land of fantasy; yet there was something in their way of life that Nature asserted as her own, and the gnawing cares which went with them from the world were all that now obstructed their happiness. One stout and shaggy steed, the bearer of all their wealth, did not shrink from the added weight of Dorcas; although her hardy breeding sustained her, during the latter part of each day's journey, by her husband's side. Reuben and his son, their muskets on their shoulders and their axes slung behind them, kept an unwearied pace, each watching with a hunter's eye for the game that supplied their food. When hunger bade, they halted and prepared their meal on the bank of some unpolluted forest brook, which, as they knelt down with thirsty lips to drink, murmured a sweet unwillingness, like a maiden at love's first kiss. They slept beneath a hut of branches, and awoke at peep of light refreshed for the toils of another day. Dorcas and the boy went on joyously, and even Reuben's spirit shone at intervals with an outward gladness; but inwardly there was a cold cold sorrow, which he compared to the snowdrifts lying deep in the glens and hollows of the rivulets while the leaves were brightly green above.

Cyrus Bourne was sufficiently skilled in the travel of the woods to observe that his father did not adhere to the course they had pursued in their expedition of the preceding autumn. They were now keeping farther to the north, striking out more directly from the settlements, and into a region of which savage beasts and savage men were as yet the sole possessors. The boy sometimes hinted his opinions upon the subject, and Reuben listened attentively, and once or twice altered the direction of their march in accordance with his son's counsel; but, having so done, he seemed ill at ease. His quick and wandering glances were sent forward apparently in search of enemies lurking behind the tree trunks, and, seeing nothing there, he would cast his eyes backwards as if in fear of some pursuer. Cyrus, perceiving that his father gradually resumed the old direction, forbore to interfere; nor, though something began to weigh upon his heart, did his adventurous nature permit him to regret the increased length and the mystery of their way.

On the afternoon of the fifth day they halted, and made their simple encampment nearly an hour before sunset. The face of the country, for the last few miles, had been diversified by swells of land resembling huge waves of a petrified sea; and in one of the corresponding hollows, a wild and romantic spot, had the family reared their hut and kindled their fire. There is something chilling, and yet heart-warming, in the thought of these three, united by strong bands of love and insulated from all that breathe beside. The dark and gloomy pines looked down upon them, and, as the wind swept through their tops, a pitying sound was heard in the forest; or did those old trees groan in fear that men were come to lay the axe to their roots at last? Reuben and his son, while Dorcas made ready their meal, proposed to wander out in search of game, of which that day's march had afforded no supply. The boy, promising not to quit the vicinity of the encampment, bounded off with a step as light and elastic as that of the deer he hoped to slay; while his father, feeling a transient happiness as he gazed after him, was about to pursue an opposite direction. Dorcas in the meanwhile, had seated herself near their fire of fallen branches upon the mossgrown and mouldering trunk of a tree uprooted years before. Her employment, diversified by an occasional glance at the pot, now beginning to simmer over the blaze, was the perusal of the current year's Massachusetts Almanac, which, with the exception of an old black-letter Bible, comprised all the literary wealth of the family. None pay a greater regard to arbitrary divisions of time than those who are excluded from society; and Dorcas mentioned, as if the information were of importance, that it was now the twelfth of May. Her husband started.

'The twelfth of May! I should remember it well,' muttered he, while many thoughts occasioned a momentary confusion in his mind. 'Where am I? Whither am I wandering? Where did I leave him?'

Dorcas, too well accustomed to her husband's wayward moods to note any peculiarity of demeanour, now laid aside the almanac and addressed him in that mournful tone which the tender hearted appropriate to griefs long cold and dead.

'It was near this time of the month, eighteen years ago, that my poor father left this world for a better. He had a kind arm to hold his head and a kind voice to cheer him, Reuben, in his last moments; and the thought of the faithful care you took of him has comforted me many a time since. Oh, death would have been awful to a solitary man in a wild place like this!'

'Pray Heaven, Dorcas,' said Reuben, in a broken voice,—'pray Heaven that neither of us three dies solitary and lies unburied in this howling wilderness!' And he hastened away, leaving her to watch the fire beneath the gloomy pines.

Reuben Bourne's rapid pace gradually slackened as the pang, unintentionally inflicted by the words of Dorcas, became less acute. Many strange reflections, however, thronged upon him; and, straying onwards rather like a sleep walker than a hunter, it was attributable to no care of his own that his devious course kept him in the vicinity of the encampment. His steps were imperceptibly led almost in a circle; nor did he observe that he was on the verge of a tract of land heavily timbered, but not with pine-trees. The place of the latter was here supplied by oaks and other of the harder woods; and around their roots clustered a dense and bushy under-growth, leaving, however, barren spaces between the trees, thick strewn with withered leaves. Whenever the rustling of the branches or the creaking of the trunks made a sound, as if the forest were waking from slumber, Reuben instinctively raised the musket that rested on his arm, and cast a quick, sharp glance on every side; but, convinced by a partial observation that no animal was near, he would again give himself up to his thoughts. He was musing on the strange influence that had led him away from his premeditated course, and so far into the depths of the wilderness. Unable to penetrate to the secret place of his soul where his motives lay hidden, he believed that a supernatural voice had called him onwards, and that a supernatural power had obstructed his retreat. He trusted that it was Heaven's intent to afford him an opportunity of expiating his sin; he hoped that he might find the bones so long unburied; and that, having laid the earth over them, peace would throw its sunlight into the sepulchre of his heart. From these thoughts he was aroused by a rustling in the forest at some distance from the spot to which he had wandered. Perceiving the motion of some object behind a thick veil of undergrowth, he fired, with the instinct of a hunter and the aim of a practised marksman. A low moan, which told his success, and by which even animals cars express their dying agony, was unheeded by Reuben Bourne. What were the recollections now breaking upon him?

The thicket into which Reuben had fired was near the summit of a swell of land, and was clustered around the base of a rock, which, in the shape and smoothness of one of its surfaces, was not unlike a gigantic gravestone. As if reflected in a mirror, its likeness was in Reuben's memory. He even recognized the veins which seemed to form an inscription in forgotten characters: everything remained the same, except that a thick covert of bushes shrouded the lowerpart of the rock, and would have hidden Roger Malvin had he still been sitting there. Yet in the next moment Reuben's eye was caught by another change that time had effected since he last stood where he was now standing again behind the earthy roots of the uptorn tree. The sapling to which he had bound the bloodstained symbol of his vow had increased and strengthened into an oak, far indeed from its maturity, but with no mean spread of shadowy branches. There was one singularity observable in this tree which made Reuben tremble. The middle and lower branches were in luxuriant life, and an excess of vegetation had fringed the trunk almost to the ground; but a blight had apparently stricken the upper part of the oak, and the very topmost bough was withered, sapless, and utterly dead. Reuben remembered how the little banner had fluttered on that topmost bough, when it was green and lovely, eighteen years before. Whose guilt had blasted it?

Dorcas, after the departure of the two hunters, continued her preparations for their evening repast. Her sylvan table was the moss-covered trunk of a large fallen tree, on the broadest part of which she had spread a snow-white cloth and arranged what were left of the bright pewter vessels that had been her pride in the settlements. It had a strange aspect that one little spot of homely comfort in the desolate heart of Nature. The sunshine yet lingered upon the higher branches of the trees that grew on rising ground; but the shadows of evening had deepened into the hollow where the encampment was made, and the firelight began to redden as it gleamed up the tall trunks of the pines or hovered on the dense and obscure mass of foliage that circled round the spot. The heart of Dorcas was not sad; for she felt that it was better to journey in the wilderness with two whom she loved than to be a lonely woman in a crowd that cared not for her. As she busied herself in arranging seats of mouldering wood, covered with leaves, for Reuben and her son, her voice danced through the gloomy forest in the measure of a song that she had learned in youth.

The rude melody, the production of a bard who won no name, was descriptive of a winter evening in a frontier cottage, when, secured from savage inroad by the high-piled snow-drifts, the family rejoiced by their own fireside. The whole song possessed the nameless charm peculiar to unborrowed thought, but four continually-recurring lines shone out from the rest like the blaze of the hearth whose joys they celebrated. Into them, working magic with a few simple words, the poet had instilled the very essence of domestic love and household happiness, and they were poetry and picture joined in one. As Dorcas sang, the walls of her forsaken home seemed to encircle her; she no longer saw the gloomy pines, nor heard the wind which still, as she began each verse, sent a heavy breath through the branches, and died away in a hollow moan from the burden of the song. She was aroused by the report of a gun in the vicinity of the encampment; and either the sudden sound, or her loneliness by the glowing fire, caused her to tremble violently. The next moment she laughed in the pride of a mother's heart.

'My beautiful young hunter! My boy has slain a deer!' she exclaimed, recollecting that in the direction whence the shot proceeded Cyrus had gone to the chase.

She waited a reasonable time to hear her son's light step bounding over the rustling leaves to tell of his success. But he did not immediately appear; and she sent her cheerful voice among the trees in search of him.

'Cyrus! Cyrus!'

His coming was still delayed; and she determined, as the report had apparently been very near, to seek for him in person. Her assistance, also, might be necessary in bringing home the venison which she flattered herself he had obtained. She therefore set forward, directing her steps by the long-past sound, and singing as she went, in order that the boy might be aware of her approach and run to meet her. From behind the trunk of every tree, and from every hiding-place in the thick foliage of the undergrowth, she hoped to discover the countenance of her son, laughing with the sportive mischief that is born of affection. The sun was now beneath the horizon, and the light that came down among the leaves was sufficiently dim to create many illusions in her expecting fancy. Several times she seemed indistinctly to see his face gazing out from among the leaves; and once she imagined that he stood beckoning to her at the base of a craggy rock. Keeping her eyes on this object, however, it proved to be no more than the trunk of an oak fringed to the very ground with little branches, one of which, thrust out farther than the rest, was shaken by the breeze. Making her way round the foot of the rock, she suddenly found herself close to her husband, who had approached in another direction. Leaning upon the butt of his gun, the muzzle of which rested upon the withered leaves, he was apparently absorbed in the contemplation of some object at his feet.

'How is this, Reuben? Have you slain the deer and fallen asleep over him?' exclaimed Dorcas, laughing cheerfully, on her first slight observation of his posture and appearance.

He stirred not, neither did he turn his eyes towards her; and a cold, shuddering fear, indefinite in its source and object, began to creep into her blood. She now perceived that her husband's face was ghastly pale, and his features were rigid, as if incapable of assuming any other expression than the strong despair which had hardened upon them. He gave not the slightest evidence that he was aware of her approach.

'For the love of Heaven, Reuben, speak to me!' cried Dorcas; and the strange sound of her own voice affrighted her even more than the dead silence.

Her husband started, stared into her face, drew her to the front of the rock, and pointed with his finger.

Oh, there lay the boy, asleep, but dreamless, upon the fallen forest leaves! His cheek rested upon his arm—his curled locks were thrown back from his brow—his limbs were slightly relaxed. Had a sudden weariness overcome the youthful hunter? Would his mother's voice arouse him? She knew that it was death.

'This broad rock is the gravestone of your near kindred, Dorcas,' said her husband. 'Your tears will fall at once over your father and your son.'

She heard him not. With one wild shriek, that seemed to force its way from the sufferer's inmost soul, she sank insensible by the side of her dead boy. At that moment the withered topmost bough of the oak loosened itself in the stilly air, and fell in soft, light fragments upon the rock, upon the leaves, upon Reuben, upon his wife and child, and upon Roger Malvin's bones. Then Reuben's heart was stricken, and the tears gushed out like water from a rock. The vow that the wounded youth had made the blighted man had come to redeem. His sin was expiated,—the curse was gone from him; and in the hour when he had shed blood dearer to him than his own, a prayer, the first for years, went up to Heaven from the lips of Reuben Bourne.

27

ONE OFFICER, ONE MAN

Ambrose Bierce

Captain Graffenreid stood at the head of his company. The regiment was not engaged. It formed a part of the front line-of-battle, which stretched away to the right with a visible length of nearly two miles through the open ground. The left flank was veiled by woods; to the right also the line was lost to sight, but it extended many miles. A hundred yards in rear was a second line; behind this, the reserve brigades and divisions in column. Batteries of artillery occupied the spaces between and crowned the low hills. Groups of horsemen—generals with their staffs and escorts, and field officers of regiments behind the colours—broke the regularity of the lines and columns. Numbers of these figures of interest had field-glasses at their eyes and sat motionless, stolidly scanning the country in front; others came and went at a slow canter, bearing orders. There were squads of stretcher-bearers, ambulances, wagon-trains with ammunition, and officers' servants in rear of all—of all that was visible—for still in rear of these, along the roads, extended for many miles all that vast multitude of non-combatants who with their various *impedimenta* are assigned to the inglorious but important duty of supplying the fighters' many needs.

An army in line-of-battle awaiting attack, or prepared to deliver it, presents strange contrasts. At the front are precision, formality, fixity, and silence. Towards the rear these characteristics are less and less conspicuous, and finally, in point of space, are lost altogether in confusion, motion and noise. The homogeneous becomes heterogeneous. Definition is lacking; repose is replaced by an apparently purposeless activity; harmony vanishes in hubbub, form in disorder. Commotion everywhere and ceaseless unrest. The men who do not fight are never ready.

From his position at the right of his company in the front rank, Captain Graffenreid had an unobstructed outlook towards the enemy. A half-mile of open and nearly level ground lay before him, and beyond it an irregular wood, covering a slight acclivity; not a human being anywhere visible. He could imagine nothing more peaceful than the appearance of that pleasant landscape with its long stretches of brown fields over which the atmosphere was beginning to quiver in the heat of the morning sun. Not a sound came from forest or field—not even the barking of a dog or the crowing of a cock at the half-seen plantation house on the crest among the trees. Yet every man in those miles of men knew that he and death were face to face.

Captain Graffenreid had never in his life seen an armed enemy, and the war in which his regiment was one of the first to take the field was two years old. He had had the rare advantage of a military education, and when his comrades had marched to the front he had been detached for administrative service at the capital of his State, where it was thought that he could be most useful. Like a bad soldier he protested, and like a good one obeyed. In close official and personal relations with the governor of his State, and enjoying his confidence and favour, he had firmly refused promotion and seen his juniors elevated above him. Death had been busy in his distant regiment; vacancies among the field officers had occurred again and again; but from a chivalrous feeling that war's rewards belonged of right to those who bore the storm and stress of battle he had held his humble rank and generously advanced the fortunes of others. His silent devotion to principle had conquered at last: he had been relieved of his hateful duties and ordered to the front, and now, untried by fire, stood in the van of battle in command of a company of hardy veterans, to whom he had been only a name, and that name a by-word. By none—not even by those of his brother officers in whose favour he had waived his rights—was his devotion to duty understood. They were too busy to be just; he was looked upon as one who had shirked his duty, until forced unwillingly into the field. Too proud to explain, yet not too insensible to feel, he could only endure and hope.

Of all the Federal Army on that summer morning none had accepted battle more joyously than Anderton Graffenreid. His spirit was buoyant, his faculties were riotous. He was in a state of mental exaltation and scarcely could endure the enemy's tardiness in advancing to the attack. To him this was opportunity—for the result he cared nothing. Victory or defeat, as God might will; in one or in the other he should prove himself a soldier and a hero; he should vindicate his right to the respect of his men and the companionship of his brother officers—to the consideration of his superiors. How his heart leaped in his breast as the bugle sounded the stirring notes of the 'assembly'! With what a light tread, scarcely conscious of the earth beneath his feet, he strode forward at the head of his company, and how exultingly he noted the tactical dispositions which placed his regiment in the front line! And if perchance some memory came to him of a pair of dark eyes that might take on a tenderer light in reading the account of that day's doings, who shall blame him for the unmartial thought or count it a debasement of soldierly ardor?

Suddenly, from the forest a half-mile in front—apparently from among the upper branches of the trees, but really from the ridge beyond—rose a tall column of white smoke. A moment later came a deep, jarring explosion, followed—almost attended—by a hideous rushing sound that seemed to leap forward across the intervening space with inconceivable rapidity, rising from whisper to roar with too quick a gradation for attention to note the successive stages of its horrible progression! A visible tremor ran along the lines of men; all were startled into motion. Captain Graffenreid dodged and threw up his hands to one side of his head, palms outwards.

As he did so he heard a keen, ringing report, and saw on a hillside behind the line a fierce roll of smoke and dust—the shell's explosion. It had passed a hundred feet to his left! He heard, or fancied he heard, a low, mocking laugh and turning in the direction whence it came saw the eyes of his first lieutenant fixed upon him with an unmistakable look of amusement. He looked along the line of faces in the front ranks. The men were laughing. At him? The thought restored the colour to his bloodless face—restored too much of it. His cheeks burned with a fever of shame.

The enemy's shot was not answered: the officer in command at that exposed part of the line had evidently no desire to provoke a cannonade. For the forbearance Captain Graffenreid was conscious of a sense of gratitude. He had not known that the flight of a projectile was a phenomenon of so appalling character. His conception of war had already undergone a profound change, and he was conscious that his new feeling was manifesting itself in visible perturbation. His blood was boiling in his veins; he had a choking sensation and felt that if he had a command to give it would be inaudible, or at least unintelligible. The hand in which he held his sword trembled; the other moved automatically, clutching at various parts of his clothing. He found a difficulty in standing still and fancied that his men observed it. Was it fear? He feared it was.

From somewhere away to the right came, as the wind served, a low, intermittent murmur like that of ocean in a storm—like that of a distant railway train—like that of wind among the pines—three sounds so nearly alike that the ear, unaided by the judgement, cannot distinguish them one from another. The eyes of the troops were drawn in that direction; the mounted officers turned their field-glasses that way. Mingled with the sound was an irregular throbbing. He thought it, at first, the beating of his fevered blood in his ears; next, the distant tapping of a bass drum.

'The ball is opened on the right flank,' said an officer.

Captain Graffenreid understood: the sounds were musketry and artillery. He nodded and tried to smile. There was apparently nothing infectious in the smile.

Presently a light line of blue smoke-puffs broke out along the edge of the wood in front, succeeded by a crackle of rifles. There were keen, sharp hissings in the air, terminating abruptly with a thump near by. The man at Captain Graffenreid's side dropped his rifle; his knees gave way and he pitched awkwardly forward, falling upon his face. Somebody shouted 'Lie down!' and the dead man was hardly distinguishable from the living. It looked as if those few rifle-shots had slain ten thousand men. Only the field officers remained erect; their concession to the emergency consisted in dismounting and sending their horses to the shelter of the low hills immediately in rear.

Captain Graffenreid lay alongside the dead man, from beneath whose breast flowed a little rill of blood. It had a faint, sweetish odour that sickened him. The face was crushed into the earth and flattened. It looked yellow already, and was repulsive. Nothing suggested the glory of a soldier's death nor mitigated the loathsomeness of the incident. He could not turn his back upon the body without facing away from his company.

He fixed his eyes upon the forest, where all again was silent. He tried to imagine what was going on there—the lines of troops forming to attack, the guns being pushed forward by hand to the edge of the open. He fancied he could see their black muzzles protruding from the undergrowth, ready to deliver their storm of missiles—such missiles as the one whose shriek had so unsettled his nerves. The distension of his eyes became painful; a mist seemed to gather before them; he could no longer see across the field, yet would not withdraw his gaze lest he see the dead man at his side.

The fire of battle was not now burning very brightly in this warrior's soul. From inaction had come introspection. He sought rather to analyze his feelings than distinguish himself by courage and devotion. The result was profoundly disappointing. He covered his face with his hands and groaned aloud.

The hoarse murmur of battle grew more and more distinct upon the right; the murmur had, indeed, become a roar, the throbbing, a thunder. The sounds had worked round obliquely to the front; evidently the enemy's left was being driven back, and the propitious moment to move against the salient angle of his line would soon arrive. The silence and mystery in front were ominous; all felt that they boded evil to the assailants.

Behind the prostrate lines sounded the hoofbeats of galloping horses; the men turned to look. A dozen staff officers were riding to the various brigade and regimental commanders, who had remounted. A moment more and there was a chorus of voices, all uttering out of time the same words—'Attention, battalion!' The men sprang to their feet and were aligned by the company commanders. They awaited the word 'forward'—awaited, too, with beating hearts and set teeth the gusts of lead and iron that were to smite them at their first movement in obedience to that word. The word was not given; the tempest did not break out. The delay was hideous, maddening! It unnerved like a respite at the guillotine.

Captain Graffenreid stood at the head of his company, the dead man at his feet. He heard the battle on the right—rattle and crash of musketry, ceaseless thunder of cannon, desultory cheers of invisible combatants. He marked ascending clouds of smoke from distant forests. He noted the sinister silence of the forest in front. These contrasting extremes affected the whole range of his sensibilities. The strain upon his nervous organization was insupportable. He grew hot and cold by turns. He panted like a dog, and then forgot to breathe until reminded by vertigo.

Suddenly he grew calm. Glancing downwards, his eyes had fallen upon his naked sword, as he held it, point to earth. Foreshortened to his view, it resembled somewhat, he thought, the short heavy blade of the ancient Roman. The fancy was full of suggestion, malign, fateful, heroic!

The sergeant in the rear rank, immediately behind Captain Graffenreid, now observed a strange sight. His attention drawn by an uncommon movement made by the captain—a sudden reaching forward of the hands and their energetic withdrawal, throwing the elbows out, as in pulling an oar—he saw spring from between the officer's shoulders a bright point of metal which prolonged itself outwards, nearly a half-arm's length—a blade! It was faintly streaked with crimson, and its point approached so near to the sergeant's breast, and with so quick a movement, that he shrank backwards in alarm. That moment Captain Graffenreid pitched heavily forward upon the dead man and died.

A week later the major-general commanding the left corps of the Federal Army submitted the following official report:

'SIR: I have the honour to report, with regard to the action of the 19th inst, that owing to the enemy's withdrawal from my front to reinforce his beaten left, my command was not seriously engaged. My loss was as follows: Killed, one officer, one man.'

28

TWO LITTLE SOLDIERS

Guy de Maupassant

Every Sunday, as soon as they were free, the little soldiers would go for a walk. They turned to the right on leaving the barracks, crossed Courbevoie with rapid strides, as though on a forced march; then, as the houses grew scarcer, they slowed down and followed the dusty road which leads to Bezons.

They were small and thin, lost in their ill-fitting capes, too large and too long, whose sleeves covered their hands; their ample red trousers fell in folds around their ankles. Under the high, stiff shako one could just barely perceive two thin, hollow-cheeked Breton faces, with their calm, naive blue eyes. They never spoke during their journey, going straight before them, the same idea in each one's mind taking the place of conversation. For at the entrance of the little forest of Champioux they had found a spot which reminded them of home, and they did not feel happy anywhere else.

At the crossing of the Colombes and Chatou roads, when they arrived under the trees, they would take off their heavy, oppressive headgear and wipe their foreheads.

They always stopped for a while on the bridge at Bezons, and looked at the Seine. They stood there several minutes, bending over the railing, watching the white sails, which perhaps reminded them of their home, and of the fishing smacks leaving for the open.

As soon as they had crossed the Seine, they would purchase provisions at the delicatessen, the baker's, and the wine merchant's.

A piece of bologna, four cents' worth of bread, and a quart of wine, made up the luncheon which they carried away, wrapped up in their handkerchiefs. But as soon as they were out of the village their gait would slacken and they would begin to talk.

Before them was a plain with a few clumps of trees, which led to the woods, a little forest which seemed to remind them of that other forest at Kermarivan. The wheat and oat fields bordered on the narrow path, and Jean Kerderen said each time to Luc Le Ganidec:

'It's just like home, just like Plounivon.'

'Yes, it's just like home.'

And they went on, side by side, their minds full of dim memories of home. They saw the fields, the hedges, the forests, and beaches.

Each time they stopped near a large stone on the edge of the private estate, because it reminded them of the dolmen of Locneuven.

As soon as they reached the first clump of trees, Luc Le Ganidec would cut off a small stick, and, whittling it slowly, would walk on, thinking of the folks at home.

Jean Kerderen carried the provisions.

From time to time Luc would mention a name, or allude to some boyish prank which would give them food for plenty of thought. And the home country, so dear and so distant, would little by little gain possession of their minds, sending them back through space, to the well-known forms and noises, to the familiar scenery, with the fragrance of its green fields and sea air. They no longer noticed the smells of the city. And in their dreams they saw their friends leaving, perhaps forever, for the dangerous fishing grounds.

They were walking slowly, Luc Le Ganidec and Jean Kerderen, contented and sad, haunted by a sweet sorrow, the slow and penetrating sorrow of a captive animal which remembers the days of its freedom.

And when Luc had finished whittling his stick, they came to a little nook, where every Sunday they took their meal. They found the two bricks, which they had hidden in a hedge, and they made a little fire of dry branches and roasted their sausages on the ends of their knives.

When their last crumb of bread had been eaten and the last drop of wine had been drunk, they stretched themselves out on the grass side by side, without speaking, their half-closed eyes looking away in the distance, their hands clasped as in prayer, their red-trousered legs mingling with the bright colours of the wild flowers.

Towards noon they glanced, from time to time, towards the village of Bezons, for the dairy maid would soon be coming. Every Sunday she would pass in front of them on the way to milk her cow, the only cow in the neighbourhood which was sent out to pasture.

Soon they would see the girl, coming through the fields, and it pleased them to watch the sparkling sunbeams reflected from her shining pail. They never spoke of her. They were just glad to see her, without understanding why.

She was a tall, strapping girl, freckled and tanned by the open air—a girl typical of the Parisian suburbs.

Once, on noticing that they were always sitting in the same place, she said to them:

'Do you always come here?'

Luc Le Ganidec, more daring than his friend, stammered:

'Yes, we come here for our rest.'

That was all. But the following Sunday, on seeing them, she smiled with the kindly smile of a woman who understood their shyness, and she asked:

'What are you doing here? Are you watching the grass grow?'

Luc, cheered up, smiled: 'P'raps.'

She continued: 'It's not growing fast, is it?'

He answered, still laughing: 'Not exactly.'

She went on. But when she came back with her pail full of milk, she stopped before them and said:

'Want some? It will remind you of home.'

She had, perhaps instinctively, guessed and touched the right spot.

Both were moved. Then not without difficulty, she poured some milk into the bottle in which they had brought their wine. Luc started to drink, carefully watching lest he should take more than his share. Then he passed the bottle to Jean. She stood before them, her hands on her hips, her pail at her feet, enjoying the pleasure that she was giving them. Then she went on, saying: 'Well, bye-bye until next Sunday!'

For a long time they watched her tall form as it receded in the distance, blending with the background, and finally disappeared.

The following week as they left the barracks, Jean said to Luc:

'Don't you think we ought to buy her something good?'

They were sorely perplexed by the problem of choosing something to bring to the dairy maid. Luc was in favour of bringing her some chitterlings; but Jean, who had a sweet tooth, thought that candy would be the best thing. He won, and so they went to a grocery to buy two sous' worth, of red and white candies.

This time they ate more quickly than usual, excited by anticipation.

Jean was the first one to notice her. 'There she is,' he said; and Luc answered: 'Yes, there she is.'

She smiled when she saw them, and cried:

'Well, how are you to-day?'

They both answered together:

'All right! How's everything with you?'

Then she started to talk of simple things which might interest them; of the weather, of the crops, of her masters.

They didn't dare to offer their candies, which were slowly melting in Jean's pocket. Finally Luc, growing bolder, murmured:

'We have brought you something.'

She asked: 'Let's see it.'

Then Jean, blushing to the tips of his ears, reached in his pocket, and drawing out the little paper bag, handed it to her.

She began to eat the little sweet dainties. The two soldiers sat in front of her, moved and delighted.

At last she went to do her milking, and when she came back she again gave them some milk.

They thought of her all through the week and often spoke of her. The following Sunday she sat beside them for a longer time.

The three of them sat there, side by side, their eyes looking far away in the distance, their hands clasped over their knees, and they told each other little incidents and little details of the villages where they were born, while the cow, waiting to be milked, stretched her heavy head towards the girl and mooed.

Soon the girl consented to eat with them and to take a sip of wine. Often she brought them plums pocket for plums were now ripe. Her presence enlivened the little Breton soldiers, who chattered away like two birds.

One Tuesday something unusual happened to Luc Le Ganidec; he asked for leave and did not return until ten o'clock at night.

Jean, worried and racked his brain to account for his friend's having obtained leave.

The following Friday, Luc borrowed ten sons from one of his friends, and once more asked and obtained leave for several hours.

When he started out with Jean on Sunday he seemed queer, disturbed, changed. Kerderen did not understand; he vaguely suspected something, but he could not guess what it might be.

They went straight to the usual place, and lunched slowly.

Neither was hungry.

Soon the girl appeared. They watched her approach as they always did. When she was near, Luc arose and went towards her. She placed her pail on the ground and kissed him. She kissed him passionately, throwing her arms around his neck, without paying attention to Jean, without even noticing that he was there.

Poor Jean was dazed, so dazed that he could not understand. His mind was upset and his heart broken, without his even realizing why.

Then the girl sat down beside Luc, and they started to chat.

Jean was not looking at them. He understood now why his friend had gone out twice during the week. He felt the pain and the sting which treachery and deceit leave in their wake.

Luc and the girl went together to attend to the cow.

Jean followed them with his eyes. He saw them disappear side by side, the red trousers of his friend making a scarlet spot against the white road. It was Luc who sank the stake to which the cow was tethered. The girl stooped down to milk the cow, while he absent-mindedly stroked the animal's glossy neck. Then they left the pail in the grass and disappeared in the woods.

Jean could no longer see anything but the wall of leaves through which they had passed. He was unmanned so that he did not have strength to stand. He stayed there, motionless, bewildered and grieving—simple, passionate grief. He wanted to weep, to run away, to hide somewhere, never to see anyone again.

Then he saw them coming back again. They were walking slowly, hand in hand, as village lovers do. Luc was carrying the pail.

After kissing him again, the girl went on, nodding carelessly to Jean. She did not offer him any milk that day.

The two little soldiers sat side by side, motionless as always, silent and quiet, their calm faces in no way betraying the trouble in their hearts. The sun shone down on them. From time to time they could hear the plaintive lowing of the cow. At the usual time they arose to return.

Luc was whittling a stick. Jean carried the empty bottle. He left it at the wine merchant's in Bezons. Then they stopped on the bridge, as they did every Sunday, and watched the water flowing by.

Jean leaned over the railing, farther and farther, as though he had seen something in the stream which hypnotized him. Luc said to him:

'What's the matter? Do you want a drink?'

He had hardly said the last word when Jean's head carried away the rest of his body, and the little blue and red soldier fell like a shot and disappeared in the water.

Luc, paralyzed with horror, tried vainly to shout for help. In the distance he saw something move; then his friend's head bobbed up out of the water only to disappear again.

Farther down he again noticed a hand, just one hand, which appeared and again went out of sight. That was all.

The boatmen who had rushed to the scene found the body that day.

Luc ran back to the barracks, crazed, and with eyes and voice full of tears, he related the accident: 'He leaned—he—he was leaning—so far over—that his head carried him away—and—he—fell—he fell—'

Emotion choked him so that he could say no more. If he had only known.

29

LUCK

Mark Twain

It was at a banquet in London in honour of one of the two or three conspicuously illustrious English military names of this generation. For reasons which will presently appear, I will withhold his real name and titles, and call him Lieutenant General Lord Arthur Scoresby, VC, KCB, etc., etc., etc. What a fascination there is in a renowned name! There sat the man, in actual flesh, whom I had heard of so many thousands of times since that day, thirty years before, when his name shot suddenly to the zenith from a Crimean battlefield, to remain forever celebrated. It was food and drink to me to look, and look, and look at that demigod; scanning, searching, noting: the quietness, the reserve, the noble gravity of his countenance; the simple honesty that expressed itself all over him; the sweet unconsciousness of his greatness—unconsciousness of the hundreds of admiring eyes fastened upon him, unconsciousness of the deep, loving, sincere worship welling out of the breasts of those people and flowing towards him.

The clergyman at my left was an old acquaintance of mine—clergyman now, but had spent the first half of his life in the camp and field, and as an instructor in the military school at Woolwich. Just at the moment I have been talking about, a veiled and singular light glimmered in his eyes, and he leaned down and muttered confidentially to me—indicating the hero of the banquet with a gesture:

'Privately—he's an absolute fool.'

This verdict was a great surprise to me. If its subject had been Napoleon, or Socrates, or Solomon, my astonishment could not have been greater. Two things I was well aware of: that the Reverend was a man of strict veracity, and that his judgement of men was good. Therefore I knew, beyond doubt or question, that the world was mistaken about this hero: he was a fool. So I meant to find out, at a convenient moment, how the Reverend, all solitary and alone, had discovered the secret.

Some days later the opportunity came, and this is what the Reverend told me.

About forty years ago I was an instructor in the military academy at Woolwich. I was present in one of the sections when young Scoresby underwent his preliminary examination. I was touched to the quick with pity; for the rest of the class answered up brightly and handsomely, while he—why, dear me, he didn't know anything, so to speak. He was evidently good, and sweet, and lovable, and guileless; and so it was exceedingly painful to see him stand there, as serene as a graven image, and deliver himself of answers which were veritably miraculous for stupidity and ignorance. All the compassion in me was aroused in his behalf. I said to myself, when he comes to be examined again, he will be flung over, of course; so it will be simply a harmless act of charity to ease his fall as much as I can. I took him aside, and found that he knew a little of Cæsar's history; and as he didn't know anything else, I went to work and drilled him like a galley slave on a certain line of stock questions concerning Cæsar which I knew would be used. If you'll believe me, he went through with flying colours on examination day! He went through on that purely superficial 'cram,' and got compliments too, while others, who knew a thousand times more than he, got plucked. By some strangely lucky accident—an accident not likely to happen twice in a century—he was asked no question outside of the narrow limits of his drill.

It was stupefying. Well, all through his course I stood by him, with something of the sentiment which a mother feels for a crippled child; and he always saved himself—just by miracle, apparently.

Now of course the thing that would expose him and kill him at last was mathematics. I resolved to make his death as easy as I could; so I drilled him and crammed him, and crammed him and drilled him, just on the line of questions which the examiners would be most likely to use, and then launching him on his fate. Well, sir, try to conceive of the result: to my consternation, he took the first prize! And with it he got a perfect ovation in the way of compliments.

Sleep? There was no more sleep for me for a week. My conscience tortured me day and night. What I had done I had done purely through charity, and only to ease the poor youth's fall—I never had dreamed of any such preposterous result as the thing that had happened. I felt as guilty and miserable as the creator of Frankenstein. Here was a woodenhead whom I had put in the way of glittering promotions and prodigious responsibilities, and but one thing could happen: he and his responsibilities would all go to ruin together at the first opportunity.

The Crimean war had just broken out. Of course there had to be a war, I said to myself: we couldn't have peace and give this donkey a chance to die before he is found out. I waited for the earthquake. It came. And it made me reel when it did come. He was actually gazetted to a captaincy in a marching regiment! Better men grow old and grey in the service before they climb to a sublimity like that. And who could ever have foreseen that they would go and put such a load of responsibility on such green and inadequate shoulders? I could just barely have stood it if they had made him a cornet; but a captain—think of it! I thought my hair would turn white.

Consider what I did—I who so loved repose and inaction. I said to myself, I am responsible to the country for this, and I must go along with him and protect the country against him as far as I can. So I took my poor little capital that I had saved up through years of work and grinding economy, and went with a sigh and bought a cornetcy in his regiment, and away we went to the field.

And there—oh dear, it was awful. Blunders? Why, he never did anything but blunder. But, you see, nobody was in the fellow's secret—everybody had him focused wrong, and necessarily misinterpreted his performance every time—consequently they took his idiotic blunders for inspirations of genius; they did, honestly! His mildest blunders were enough to make a man in his right mind cry; and they did make me cry—and rage and rave too, privately. And the thing that kept me always in a sweat of apprehension was the fact that every fresh blunder he made increased the lustre of his reputation! I kept saying to myself, he'll get so high, that when discovery does finally come, it will be like the sun falling out of the sky.

He went right along up, from grade to grade, over the dead bodies of his superiors, until at last, in the hottest moment of the battle of—down went our colonel, and my heart jumped into my mouth, for Scoresby was next in rank! Now for it, said I; we'll all land in Sheol in ten minutes, sure.

The battle was awfully hot; the allies were steadily giving way all over the field. Our regiment occupied a position that was vital; a blunder now must be destruction. At this crucial moment, what does this immortal fool do but detach the regiment from its place and order a charge over a neighbouring hill where there wasn't a suggestion of an enemy! 'There you go!' I said to myself; 'this is the end at last.'

And away we did go, and were over the shoulder of the hill before the insane movement could be discovered and stopped.

And what did we find? An entire and unsuspected Russian army in reserve! And what happened? We were eaten up? That is necessarily what would have happened in ninety-nine cases out of a hundred. But no, those Russians argued that no single regiment would come browsing around there at such a time. It must be the entire English army, and that the sly Russian game was detected and blocked; so they turned tail, and away they went, pell-mell, over the hill and down into the field, in wild confusion, and we after them; they themselves broke the solid Russian centre in the field, and tore through, and in no time there was the most tremendous rout you ever saw, and the defeat of the allies was turned into a sweeping and splendid victory! Marshal Canrobert looked on, dizzy with astonishment, admiration, and delight; and sent right off for Scoresby, and hugged him, and decorated him on the field, in presence of all the armies!

And what was Scoresby's blunder that time? Merely the mistaking his right hand for his left—that was all. An order had come to him to fall back and support our right; and instead, he fell forward and went over the hill to the left. But the name he won that day as a marvelous military genius filled the world with his glory, and that glory will never fade while history books last.

He is just as good and sweet and lovable and unpretending as a man can be, but he doesn't know enough to come in when it rains. Now that is absolutely true. He is the supremest ass in the universe; and until half an hour ago nobody knew it but himself and me. He has been pursued, day by day and year by year, by a most phenomenal and astonishing luckiness. He has been a shining soldier in all our wars for a generation; he has littered his whole military life with blunders, and yet has never committed one that didn't make him a knight or a baronet or a lord or something. Look at his breast; why, he is just clothed in domestic and foreign decorations. Well, sir, every one of them is the record of some shouting stupidity or other; and taken together, they are proof that the very best thing in all this world that can befall a man is to be born lucky. I say again, as I said at the banquet, Scoresby's an absolute fool.

30

THE DOG OF TITHWAL

Saadat Hasan Manto

The soldiers had been entrenched in their positions for several weeks, but there was little, if any, fighting, except for the dozen rounds they ritually exchanged every day.

The weather was extremely pleasant. The air was heavy with the scent of wild flowers and nature seemed to be following its course, quite oblivious to the soldiers hiding behind rocks and camouflaged by mountain shrubbery. The birds sang as they always had and the flowers were in bloom. Bees buzzed about lazily.

Only when a shot rang out, the birds got startled and took flight, as if a musician had struck a jarring note on his instrument. It was almost the end of September, neither hot nor cold. It seemed as if summer and winter had made their peace. In the blue skies, cotton clouds floated all day like barges on a lake.

The soldiers seemed to be getting tired of this indecisive war where nothing much ever happened. Their positions were quite impregnable. The two hills on which they were placed faced each other and were about the same height, so no one side had an advantage. Down below in the valley, a stream zigzagged furiously on its stony bed like a snake.

The air force was not involved in the combat and neither of the adversaries had heavy guns or mortars. At night, they would light huge fires and hear each other's voices echoing through the hills.

The last round of tea had just been taken. The fire had gone cold. The sky was clear and there was a chill in the air and a sharp, though not unpleasant, smell of pine cones. Most of the soldiers were already asleep, except Jamadar Harnam Singh, who was on night watch. At two o'clock, he woke up Ganda Singh to take over. Then he lay down, but sleep was as far away from his eyes as the stars in the sky. He began to hum a Punjabi folk song:

> 'Bring me a pair of star-spangled shoes
> yes, star-spangled
> Harnam Singh, O darlin'
> should it cost you your buffalo.'

On all sides, Harnam Singh could see star-spangled shoes, scattered over the sky and twinkling softly.

> 'Them star-spangled shoes I'll bring you
> yes, star-spangled
> Harnam Kaur, O darlin'
> should it cost me my buffalo.'

He smiled, and knowing that sleep now would not come, he woke the others. The thought of a woman had excited his mind; he wanted to make foolish conversation; conversation in which he might re-live his feeling for Harnam Kaur.

Talk did begin, but it was abrupt and disjointed. Banta Singh, who was the youngest among them, and had the best voice, sat to one side as the others chatted, yawning now and then. After a while, Banta Singh, in his mournful voice, began to sing 'Hir':

> 'Hir said, "the yogi lied; no one pacifies an aggrieved lover
> I searched and searched, but found no one
> who could call back the departed.
> A hawk lost a crane to the crow;
> look, does he lament or not?
> Give not to those who suffer fond tales."'

Then a moment later, he sang Ranjha's reply to Hir's words:

> "'That hawk that lost the crane to the crow is thankfully annihilated
> He is like the fakir that gave up all his possessions, and was ruined
> Be contented, feel less and God becomes your witness
> Quit the world, wear the sackcloth
> and ashes and Sayyed Waris becomes Waris Shah.'"

A deep sadness fell over them. Even the grey hills seemed to have been affected by the melancholy of the songs.

Some moments later, Corporal Harnam Singh, after hurling filthy abuse at an invisible object, lay down.

This mood was shattered by the barking of a dog. Jamadar Harnam Singh said, 'Where has this son of a bitch materialized from?' The dog barked again. He sounded closer. There was a rustle in the bushes. Banta Singh got up to investigate and came back with an ordinary mongrel in tow. He was wagging his tail. 'I found him behind the bushes and he told me his name was Jhun Jhun,' Banta Singh announced. Everybody burst out laughing.

The dog went to Harnam Singh, who produced a cracker from his kitbag and threw it on the ground. The dog sniffed at it and was about to eat it, when Harnam Singh snatched it away…'Wait, you could be a Pakistani dog.'

They laughed. Banta Singh patted the animal and said to Harnam Singh, 'Jamadar sahib, Jhun Jhun is an Indian dog.'

'Prove your identity,' Harnam Singh ordered the dog, who began to wag his tail.

'This is no proof of identity. All dogs can wag their tails,' Harnam Singh said.

'He is only a poor refugee,' Banta Singh said, playing with his tail.

Harnam Singh threw the dog a cracker, which he caught in mid-air. 'Even dogs will now have to decide if they are Indian or Pakistani,' one of the soldiers observed.

Harnam Singh produced another cracker from his kitbag. 'And all Pakistanis, including dogs, will be shot.'

A soldier shouted, 'India Zindabad! Long live India!'

The dog, who was about to munch his cracker, stopped dead in his tracks, put his tail between his legs and looked scared. Harnam Singh laughed. 'Why are you afraid of your own country? Here, Jhun Jhun, have another cracker.'

The morning broke very suddenly, as if someone had switched on a light in a dark room. It spread across the hills and valleys of Tithwal, which is what the area was called.

The war had been going on for months but nobody could be quite sure who was winning it.

Jamadar Harnam Singh surveyed the area with his binoculars. He could see smoke rising from the opposite hill, which meant that, like them, the enemy was busy preparing breakfast.

Subedar Himmat Khan of the Pakistan army gave his huge moustache a twirl and began to study the map of the Tithwal sector. Next to him sat his wireless operator, who was trying to establish contact with the platoon commander to obtain instructions. A few feet away, the soldier Bashir sat on the ground, his back against a rock and his rifle in front of him. He was humming:

'Where did you spend the night, my love, my moon?
Where did you spend the night?'

Enjoying himself, he began to sing more loudly, savouring the words. Suddenly he heard Subedar Himmat Khan scream, 'Where did you spend the night?'

But this was not addressed to Bashir. It was a dog he was shouting at. He had come to them from nowhere a few days ago, stayed in the camp quite happily and then suddenly disappeared last night. However, he had now returned like a bad coin.

Bashir smiled and began to sing to the dog. 'Where did you spend the night, where did you spend the night?' But he only wagged his tail. Subedar Himmat Khan threw a pebble at him. 'All he can do is wag his tail, the idiot.'

'What has he got around his neck?' Bashir asked.

One of the soldiers grabbed the dog and undid his makeshift rope collar. There was a small piece of cardboard tied to it. 'What does it say?' the soldier, who could not read, asked.

Bashir stepped forward and with some difficulty was able to decipher the writing. 'It says Jhun Jhun.'

Subedar Himmat Khan gave his famous moustache another mighty twirl and said, 'Perhaps it is a code. Does it say anything else, Bashirey?'

'Yes sir, it says it is an Indian dog.'

'What does that mean?' Subedar Himmat Khan asked.

'Perhaps it is a secret,' Bashir answered seriously.

'If there is a secret, it is in the word Jhun Jhun,' another soldier ventured in a wise guess.

'You may have something there,' Subedar Himmat Khan observed.

Dutifully, Bashir read the whole thing again. 'Jhun Jhun. This is an Indian dog.'

Subedar Himmat Khan picked up the wireless set and spoke to his platoon commander, providing him with a detailed account of the dog's sudden appearance in their position, his equally sudden disappearance the night before and his return that morning. 'What are you talking about?' the platoon commander asked.

Subedar Himmat Khan studied the map again. Then he tore up a packet of cigarettes, cut a small piece from it and gave it to Bashir. 'Now write on it in Gurmukhi, the language of those Sikhs…'

'What should I write?'

'Well…'

Bashir had an inspiration. 'Shun Shun, yes, that's right. We counter Jhun Jhun with Shun Shun.'

'Good,' Subedar Himmat Khan said approvingly. 'And add: this is a Pakistani dog.'

Subedar Himmat Khan personally threaded the piece of paper through the dog's collar and said, 'Now go join your family.'

He gave him something to eat and then said, 'Look here, my friend, no treachery. The punishment for treachery is death.'

The dog kept eating his food and wagging his tail. Then Subedar Himmat Khan turned him round to face the Indian position and said, 'Go and take this message to the enemy, but come back. These are the orders of your commander.'

The dog wagged his tail and moved down the winding hilly track that led into the valley dividing the two hills. Subedar Himmat Khan picked up his rifle and fired in the air.

The Indians were a bit puzzled, as it was somewhat early in the day for that sort of thing. Jamadar Harnam Singh, who in any case was feeling bored, shouted, 'Let's give it to them.'

The two sides exchanged fire for half an hour, which of course was a complete waste of time. Finally, Jamadar Harnam Singh ordered that enough was enough. He combed his long hair, looked at himself in the mirror and asked Banta Singh, 'Where has that dog Jhun Jhun gone?'

'Dogs can never digest butter, goes the famous saying,' Banta Singh observed philosophically.

Suddenly the soldier on lookout duty shouted, 'There he comes.'

'Who?' Jamadar Harnam Singh asked.

'What was his name? Jhun Jhun,' the soldier answered.

'What is he doing?' Harnam Singh asked.

'Just coming our way,' the soldier replied, peering through his binoculars.

Subedar Harnam Singh snatched them from him. 'That's him all right and there's something around his neck. But, wait, that's the Pakistani hill he's coming from, the motherfucker.'

He picked up his rifle, aimed and fired. The bullet hit some rocks close to where the dog was. He stopped.

Subedar Himmat Khan heard the report and looked through his binoculars. The dog had turned round and was running back. 'The brave never run away from battle. Go forward and complete your mission,' he shouted at the dog. To scare him, he fired at the same time. The bullet passed within inches of the dog, who leapt in the air, flapping his ears. Subedar Himmat Khan fired again, hitting some stones.

It soon became a game between the two soldiers, with the dog running round in circles in a state of great terror. Both Himmat Khan and Harnam Singh were laughing boisterously. The dog began to run towards Harnam Singh, who abused him loudly and fired. The bullet caught him in the leg. He yelped, turned around and began to run towards Himmat Khan, only to meet more fire, which was only meant to scare him. 'Be a brave boy. If you are injured, don't let that stand between you and your duty. Go, go, go,' the Pakistani shouted.

The dog turned. One of his legs was now quite useless. He began to drag himself towards Harnam Singh, who picked up his rifle, aimed carefully and shot him dead.

Subedar Himmat Khan sighed, 'The poor bugger has been martyred.'

Jamadar Harnam Singh ran his hand over the still-hot barrel of his rifle and muttered, 'He died a dog's death.'

31

MARINES SIGNALLING UNDER FIRE AT GUANTANAMO

Stephen Crane

They were four Guantanamo marines, officially known for the time as signalmen, and it was their duty to lie in the trenches of Camp McCalla, that faced the water, and, by day, signal the *Marblehead* with a flag and, by night, signal the *Marblehead* with lanterns. It was my good fortune—at that time I considered it my bad fortune, indeed—to be with them on two of the nights when a wild storm of fighting was pealing about the hill; and, of all the actions of the war, none were so hard on the nerves, none strained courage so near the panic point, as those swift nights in Camp McCalla. With a thousand rifles rattling; with the field-guns booming in your ears; with the diabolic Colt automatics clacking; with the roar of the *Marblehead* coming from the bay, and, last, with Mauser bullets sneering always in the air a few inches over one's head, and with this enduring from dusk to dawn, it is extremely doubtful if any one who was there will be able to forget it easily. The noise; the impenetrable darkness; the knowledge from the sound of the bullets that the enemy was on three sides of the camp; the infrequent bloody stumbling and death of some man with whom, perhaps, one had messed two hours previous; the weariness of the body, and the more terrible weariness of the mind, at the endlessness of the thing, made it wonderful that at least some of the men did not come out of it with their nerves hopelessly in shreds.

But, as this interesting ceremony proceeded in the darkness, it was necessary for the signal squad to coolly take and send messages. Captain McCalla always participated in the defence of the camp by raking the woods on two of its sides with the guns of the *Marblehead*. Moreover, he was the senior officer present, and he wanted to know what was happening. All night long the crews of the ships in the bay would stare sleeplessly into the blackness towards the roaring hill.

The signal squad had an old cracker-box placed on top of the trench. When not signalling they hid the lanterns in this box; but as soon as an order to send a message was received, it became necessary for one of the men to stand up and expose the lights. And then—oh, my eye—how the guerillas hidden in the gulf of night would turn loose at those yellow gleams!

Signalling in this way is done by letting one lantern remain stationary—on top of the cracker-box, in this case—and moving the other over to the left and right and so on in the regular gestures of the wig-wagging code. It is a very simple system of night communication, but one can see that it presents rare possibilities when used in front of an enemy who, a few hundred yards away, is overjoyed at sighting so definite a mark.

How, in the name of wonders, those four men at Camp McCalla were not riddled from head to foot and sent home more as repositories of Spanish ammunition than as marines is beyond all comprehension. To make a confession—when one of these men stood up to wave his lantern, I, lying in the trench, invariably rolled a little to the right or left, in order that, when he was shot, he would not fall on me. But the squad came off scathless, despite the best efforts of the most formidable corps in the Spanish army—the Escuadra de Guantanamo. That it was the most formidable corps in the Spanish army of occupation has been told me by many Spanish officers and also by General Menocal and other insurgent officers. General Menocal was Garcia's chief-of-staff when the latter was operating busily in Santiago province. The regiment was composed solely of *practicos*, or guides, who knew every shrub and tree on the ground over which they moved.

Whenever the adjutant, Lieutenant Draper, came plunging along through the darkness with an order—such as: 'Ask the *Marblehead* to please shell the woods to the left'—my heart would come into my mouth, for I knew then that one of my pals was going to stand up behind the lanterns and have all Spain shoot at him.

The answer was always upon the instant:

'Yes, sir.' Then the bullets began to snap, snap, snap, at his head while all the woods began to crackle like burning straw. I could lie near and watch the face of the signalman, illumed as it was by the yellow shine of lantern light, and the absence of excitement, fright, or any emotion at all on his countenance, was something to astonish all theories out of one's mind. The face was in every instance merely that of a man intent upon his business, the business of wig-wagging into the gulf of night where a light on the *Marblehead* was seen to move slowly.

These times on the hill resembled, in some days, those terrible scenes on the stage—scenes of intense gloom, blinding lightning, with a cloaked devil or assassin or other appropriate character muttering deeply amid the awful roll of the thunder-drums. It was theatric beyond words: one felt like a leaf in this booming chaos, this prolonged tragedy of the night. Amid it all one could see from time to time the yellow light on the face of a preoccupied signalman.

Possibly no man who was there ever before understood the true eloquence of the breaking of the day. We would lie staring into the east, fairly ravenous for the dawn. Utterly worn to rags, with our nerves standing on end like so many bristles, we lay and watched the east—the unspeakably obdurate and slow east. It was a wonder that the eyes of some of us did not turn to glass balls from the fixity of our gaze.

Then there would come into the sky a patch of faint blue light. It was like a piece of moonshine. Some would say it was the beginning of daybreak; others would declare it was nothing of the kind. Men would get very disgusted with each other in these low-toned arguments held in the trenches. For my part, this development in the eastern sky destroyed many of my ideas and theories concerning the dawning of the day; but then I had never before had occasion to give it such solemn attention.

This patch widened and whitened in about the speed of a man's accomplishment if he should be in the way of painting Madison Square Garden with a camel's hair brush. The guerillas always set out to whoop it up about this time, because they knew the occasion was approaching when it would be expedient for them to elope. I, at least, always grew furious with this wretched sunrise. I thought I could have walked around the world in the time required for the old thing to get up above the horizon.

One midnight, when an important message was to be sent to the *Marblehead*, Colonel Huntington came himself to the signal place with Adjutant Draper and Captain McCauley, the quartermaster. When the man stood up to signal, the colonel stood beside him. At sight of the lights, the Spaniards performed as usual. They drove enough bullets into that immediate vicinity to kill all the marines in the corps.

Lieutenant Draper was agitated for his chief. 'Colonel, won't you step down, sir?'

'Why, I guess not,' said the grey old veteran in his slow, sad, always-gentle way. 'I am in no more danger than the man.'

'But, sir—' began the adjutant.

'Oh, it's all right, Draper.'

So the colonel and the private stood side to side and took the heavy fire without either moving a muscle.

Day was always obliged to come at last, punctuated by a

final exchange of scattering shots. And the light shone on the marines, the dumb guns, the flag. Grimy yellow face looked into grimy yellow face, and grinned with weary satisfaction. Coffee!

Usually it was impossible for many of the men to sleep at once. It always took me, for instance, some hours to get my nerves combed down. But then it was great joy to lie in the trench with the four signalmen, and understand thoroughly that that night was fully over at last, and that, although the future might have in store other bad nights, that one could never escape from the prison-house which we call the past.

At the wild little fight at Cusco there were some splendid exhibitions of wig-wagging under fire. Action began when an advanced detachment of marines under Lieutenant Lucas with the Cuban guides had reached the summit of a ridge overlooking a small valley where there was a house, a well, and a thicket of some kind of shrub with great broad, oily leaves. This thicket, which was perhaps an acre in extent, contained the guerillas. The valley was open to the sea. The distance from the top of the ridge to the thicket was barely two hundred yards.

The *Dolphin* had sailed up the coast in line with the marine advance, ready with her guns to assist in any action. Captain Elliott, who commanded the two hundred marines in this fight, suddenly called out for a signalman. He wanted a man to tell the *Dolphin* to open fire on the house and the thicket. It was a blazing, bitter hot day on top of the ridge with its shrivelled chaparral and its straight, tall cactus plants. The sky was bare and blue, and hurt like brass. In two minutes the prostrate marines were red and sweating like so many hull-buried stokers in the tropics.

Captain Elliott called out:

'Where's a signalman? Who's a signalman here?'

A red-headed 'mick'—I think his name was Clancy—at any

rate, it will do to call him Clancy—twisted his head from where he lay on his stomach pumping his Lee, and, saluting, said that he was a signalman.

There was no regulation flag with the expedition, so Clancy was obliged to tie his blue polka-dot neckerchief on the end of his rifle. It did not make a very good flag. At first Clancy moved a ways down the safe side of the ridge and wigwagged there very busily. But what with the flag being so poor for the purpose, and the background of ridge being so dark, those on the *Dolphin* did not see it. So Clancy had to return to the top of the ridge and outline himself and his flag against the sky.

The usual thing happened. As soon as the Spaniards caught sight of this silhouette, they let go like mad at it. To make things more comfortable for Clancy, the situation demanded that he face the sea and turn his back to the Spanish bullets. This was a hard game, mark you—to stand with the small of your back to volley firing. Clancy thought so. Everybody thought so. We all cleared out of his neighbourhood. If he wanted sole possession of any particular spot on that hill, he could have it for all we would interfere with him.

It cannot be denied that Clancy was in a hurry. I watched him. He was so occupied with the bullets that snarled close to his ears that he was obliged to repeat the letters of his message softly to himself. It seemed an intolerable time before the *Dolphin* answered the little signal. Meanwhile, we gazed at him, marvelling every second that he had not yet pitched headlong. He swore at times.

Finally the *Dolphin* replied to his frantic gesticulation, and he delivered his message. As his part of the transaction was quite finished—whoop!—he dropped like a brick into the firing line and began to shoot; began to get 'hunky' with all those people who had been plugging at him. The blue polka-dot neckerchief still fluttered from the barrel of his rifle. I am quite certain that he let it remain there until the end of the fight.

The shells of the *Dolphin* began to plough up the thicket, kicking the bushes, stones, and soil into the air as if somebody was blasting there.

Meanwhile, this force of two hundred marines and fifty Cubans and the force of—probably—six companies of Spanish guerillas were making such an awful din that the distant Camp McCalla was all alive with excitement. Colonel Huntington sent out strong parties to critical points on the road to facilitate, if necessary, a safe retreat, and also sent forty men under Lieutenant Magill to come up on the left flank of the two companies in action under Captain Elliott. Lieutenant Magill and his men had crowned a hill which covered entirely the flank of the fighting companies, but when the *Dolphin* opened fire, it happened that Magill was in the line of the shots. It became necessary to stop the *Dolphin* at once. Captain Elliott was not near Clancy at this time, and he called hurriedly for another signalman.

Sergeant Quick arose, and announced that he was a signalman. He produced from somewhere a blue polka-dot neckerchief as large as a quilt. He tied it on a long, crooked stick. Then he went to the top of the ridge, and turning his back to the Spanish fire, began to signal to the *Dolphin*. Again we gave a man sole possession of a particular part of the ridge. We didn't want it. He could have it and welcome. If the young sergeant had had the smallpox, the cholera, and the yellow fever, we could not have slid out with more celerity.

As men have said often, it seemed as if there was in this war a God of Battles who held His mighty hand before the Americans. As I looked at Sergeant Quick wig-wagging there against the sky, I would not have given a tin tobacco-tag for his life. Escape for him seemed impossible. It seemed absurd to hope that he would not be hit; I only hoped that he would be hit just a little, in the arm, the shoulder, or the leg.

I watched his face, and it was as grave and serene as that of a man writing in his own library. He was the very embodiment of tranquillity in occupation. He stood there amid the animal-like babble of the Cubans, the crack of rifles, and the whistling snarl of the bullets, and wig-wagged whatever he had to wig-wag without heeding anything but his business. There was not a single trace of nervousness or haste.

To say the least, a fight at close range is absorbing as a spectacle. No man wants to take his eyes from it until that time comes when he makes up his mind to run away. To deliberately stand up and turn your back to a battle is in itself hard work. To deliberately stand up and turn your back to a battle and hear immediate evidences of the boundless enthusiasm with which a large company of the enemy shoot at you from an adjacent thicket is, to my mind at least, a very great feat. One need not dwell upon the detail of keeping the mind carefully upon a slow spelling of an important code message.

I saw Quick betray only one sign of emotion. As he swung his clumsy flag to and fro, an end of it once caught on a cactus pillar, and he looked sharply over his shoulder to see what had it. He gave the flag an impatient jerk. He looked annoyed.

32

GUESTS OF THE NATION

Frank O'Connor

I

At dusk the big Englishman, Belcher, would shift his long legs out of the ashes and say 'Well, chums, what about it?' and Noble and myself would say 'All right, chum' (for we had picked up some of their curious expressions), and the little Englishman, Hawkins, would light the lamp and bring out the cards. Sometimes Jeremiah Donovan would come up and supervise the game, and get excited over Hawkins' cards, which he always played badly, and shout at him as if he was one of our own, 'Ah, you divil, why didn't you play the tray?'

But ordinarily Jeremiah was a sober and contented poor devil like the big Englishman, Belcher, and was looked up to only because he was a fair hand at documents, though he was slow even with them. He wore a small cloth hat and big gaiters over his long pants, and you seldom saw him with his hands out of his pockets. He reddened when you talked to him, tilting from toe to heel and back, and looking down all the time at his big farmer's feet. Noble and myself used to make fun of his broad accent, because we were both from the town.

I could not at the time see the point of myself and Noble guarding Belcher and Hawkins at all, for it was my belief that you could have planted that pair down anywhere from this to Claregalway and they'd have taken root there like a native weed. I never in my short experience saw two men take to the country as they did. They were passed on to us by the Second Battalion when the search for them became too hot, and Noble and myself, being young, took them over with a natural feeling of responsibility, but Hawkins made us look like fools when he showed that he knew the country better than we did.

'You're the bloke they call Bonaparte,' he says to me. 'Mary Brigid O'Connell told me to ask what you'd done with the pair of her brother's socks you borrowed.'

For it seemed, as they explained it, that the Second had little evenings, and some of the girls of the neighbourhood turned up, and, seeing they were such decent chaps, our fellows could not leave the two Englishmen out. Hawkins learned to dance 'The Walls of Limerick,' 'The Siege of Ennis' and 'The Waves of Tory' as well as any of them, though he could not return the compliment, because our lads at that time did not dance foreign dances on principle.

So whatever privileges Belcher and Hawkins had with the Second they just took naturally with us, and after the first couple of days we gave up all pretence of keeping an eye on them. Not that they could have got far, because they had accents you could cut with a knife, and wore khaki tunics and overcoats with civilian pants and boots, but I believe myself they never had any idea of escaping and were quite content to be where they were.

It was a treat to see how Belcher got off with the old woman in the house where we were staying. She was a great warrant to scold, and cranky even with us, but before ever she had a chance of giving our guests, as I may call them, a lick of her tongue, Belcher had made her his friend for life. She was breaking sticks, and Belcher, who had not been more than ten minutes in the house, jumped up and went over to her.

'Allow me, madam,' he said, smiling his queer little smile. 'Please allow me,' and he took the hatchet from her. She was too surprised to speak, and after that, Belcher would be at her heels, carrying a bucket, a basket or a load of turf. As Noble said, he got into looking before she leapt, and hot water, or any little thing she wanted, Belcher would have ready for her. For such a huge man (and though I am five foot ten myself I had to look up at him) he had an uncommon lack of speech. It took us a little while to get used to him, walking in and out like a ghost, without speaking. Especially because Hawkins talked enough for a platoon, it was strange to hear Belcher with his toes in the ashes come out with a solitary 'Excuse me, chum,' or 'That's right, chum.' His one and only passion was cards, and he was a remarkably good card player. He could have skinned myself and Noble, but whatever we lost to him, Hawkins lost to us, and Hawkins only played with the money Belcher gave him.

Hawkins lost to us because he had too much old gab, and we probably lost to Belcher for the same reason. Hawkins and Noble argued about religion into the early hours of the morning, and Hawkins worried the life out of Noble, who had a brother a priest, with a string of questions that would puzzle a cardinal. Even in treating of holy subjects, Hawkins had a deplorable tongue. I never met a man who could mix such a variety of cursing and bad language into any argument. He was a terrible man, and a fright to argue. He never did a stroke of work, and when he had no one else to argue with, he got stuck in the old woman.

He met his match in her, for when he tried to get her to complain profanely of the drought she gave him a great comedown by blaming it entirely on Jupiter Pluvius (a deity neither Hawkins nor I had ever heard of, though Noble said that among the pagans it was believed that he had something to do with the rain). Another day he was swearing at the capitalists for starting the German war when the old lady laid down her iron, puckered up her little crab's mouth and said:

'Mr Hawkins, you can say what you like about the war,

and think you'll deceive me because I'm only a simple poor countrywoman, but I know what started the war. It was the Italian Count that stole the heathen divinity out of the temple of Japan. Believe me, Mr Hawkins, nothing but sorrow and want can follow people who disturb the hidden powers.'

A queer old girl, all right.

II

One evening we had our tea and Hawkins lit the lamp and we all sat into cards. Jeremiah Donovan came in too, and sat and watched us for a while, and it suddenly struck me that he had no great love for the two Englishmen. It came as a surprise to me because I had noticed nothing of it before.

Late in the evening a really terrible argument blew up between Hawkins and Noble about capitalists and priests and love of country.

'The capitalists pay the priests to tell you about the next world so that you won't notice what the bastards are up to in this,' said Hawkins.

'Nonsense, man!' said Noble, losing his temper. 'Before ever a capitalist was thought of people believed in the next world.'

Hawkins stood up as though he was preaching. 'Oh, they did, did they?' he said with a sneer. 'They believed all the things you believe—isn't that what you mean? And you believe God created Adam, and Adam created Shem, and Shem created Jehoshophat. You believe all that silly old fairytale about Eve and Eden and the apple. Well listen to me, chum! If you're entitled to a silly belief like that, I'm entitled to my own silly belief—which is that the first thing your God created was a bleeding capitalist, with morality and Rolls-Royce complete. Am I right, chum?' he says to Belcher.

'You're right, chum,' says Belcher with a smile, and he got

up from the table to stretch his long legs into the fire and stroke his moustache. So, seeing that Jeremiah Donovan was going, and that there was no knowing when the argument about religion would be over, I went out with him. We strolled down to the village together, and then he stopped, blushing and mumbling, and said I should be behind, keeping guard. I didn't like the tone he took with me, and anyway I was bored with life in the cottage, so I replied by asking what the hell we wanted to guard them for at all.

He looked at me in surprise and said: 'I thought you knew we were keeping them as hostages.'

'Hostages?' I said.

'The enemy have prisoners belonging to us, and now they're talking of shooting them,' he said. 'If they shoot our prisoners, we'll shoot theirs.'

'Shoot Belcher and Hawkins?' I said.

'What else did you think we were keeping them for?' he said.

'Wasn't it very unforeseen of you not to warn Noble and myself of that in the beginning?' I said.

'How was it?' he said. 'You might have known that much.'

'We could not know it, Jeremiah Donovan,' I said. 'How could we when they were on our hands so long?'

'The enemy have our prisoners as long and longer,' he said.

'That's not the same thing at all,' said I.

'What difference is there?' said he.

I couldn't tell him, because I knew he wouldn't understand. If it was only an old dog that you had to take to the vet's, you'd try and not get too fond of him, but Jeremiah Donovan was not a man who would ever be in danger of that.

'And when is this to be decided?' I said.

'We might hear tonight,' he said. 'Or tomorrow or the next day at latest. So if it's only hanging round that's a trouble to you, you'll be free soon enough.'

It was not the hanging round that was a trouble to me at all by this time. I had worse things to worry about. When I got back to the cottage the argument was still on. Hawkins was holding forth in his best style, maintaining that there was no next world, and Noble saying that there was; but I could see that Hawkins had had the best of it.

'Do you know what, chum?' he was saying with a saucy smile. 'I think you're just as big a bleeding unbeliever as I am. You say you believe in the next world, and you know just as much about the next world as I do, which is sweet damn-all. What's heaven? You don't know. Where's heaven? You don't know. You know sweet damn-all! I ask you again, do they wear wings? '

'Very well, then,' said Noble. 'They do. Is that enough for you? They do wear wings.'

'Where do they get them then? Who makes them? Have they a factory for wings? Have they a sort of store where you hand in your chit and take your bleeding wings?'

'You're an impossible man to argue with,' said Noble. 'Now, listen to me...' And they were off again.

It was long after midnight when we locked up and went to bed. As I blew out the candle I told Noble. He took it very quietly. When we'd been in bed about an hour he asked if I thought we should tell the Englishmen. I didn't, because I doubted if the English would shoot our men. Even if they did, the Brigade officers, who were always up and down to the Second Battalion and knew the Englishmen well, would hardly want to see them plugged.

'I think so too,' said Noble.' It would be great cruelty to put the wind up them now.'

'It was very unforeseen of Jeremiah Donovan, anyhow,' said I.

It was next morning that we found it so hard to face Belcher and Hawkins. We went about the house all day, scarcely saying a word. Belcher didn't seem to notice; he was stretched into the ashes as usual, with his usual look of waiting in quietness for something unforeseen to happen, but Hawkins noticed it and put it down to Noble's being beaten in the argument of the night before. 'Why can't you take the discussion in the proper spirit?' he said severely. 'You and your Adam and Eve! I'm a Communist, that's what I am. Communist or Anarchist, it all comes to much the same thing.' And he went round the house, muttering when the fit took him: 'Adam and Eve! Adam and Eve! Nothing better to do with their time than pick bleeding apples!'

III

I don't know how we got through that day, but I was very glad when it was over, the tea things were cleared away, and Belcher said in his peaceable way: 'Well, chums, what about it?'

We sat round the table and Hawkins took out the cards, and just then I heard Jeremiah Donovan's footsteps on the path and a dark presentiment crossed my mind. I rose from the table and caught him before he reached the door.

'What do you want?' I asked.

'I want those two soldier friends of yours,' he said, getting red.

'Is that the way, Jeremiah Donovan?' I asked.

'That's the way. There were four of our lads shot this morning, one of them a boy of sixteen.'

'That's bad,' I said.

At that moment Noble followed me out, and the three of us walked down the path together, talking in whispers. Feeney, the local intelligence officer, was standing by the gate.

'What are you going to do about it?' I asked Jeremiah Donovan.

'I want you and Noble to get them out; tell them they're being shifted again; that'll be the quietest way.'

'Leave me out of that,' said Noble, under his breath. Jeremiah Donovan looked at him hard.

'All right,' he says. 'You and Feeney get a few tools from the shed and dig a hole by the far end of the bog. Bonaparte and myself will be after you. Don't let anyone see you with the tools. I wouldn't like it to go beyond ourselves.'

We saw Feeney and Noble go round to the shed and went in ourselves. I left Jeremiah Donovan to do the explanations. He told them that he had orders to send them back to the Second Battalion. Hawkins let out a mouthful of curses, and you could see that though Belcher didn't say anything, he was a bit upset too. The old woman was for having them stay in spite of us, and she didn't stop advising them until Jeremiah Donovan lost his temper and turned on her. He had a nasty temper, I noticed. It was pitch-dark in the cottage by this time, but no one thought of lighting the lamp, and in the darkness the two Englishmen fetched their topcoats and said good-bye to the old woman.

'Just as a man makes a home of a bleeding place, some bastard at headquarters thinks you're too cushy and shunts you off,' said Hawkins shaking her hand.

'A thousand thanks, madam,' said Belcher, 'A thousand thanks for everything'—as though he'd made it up.

We went round to the back of the house and down towards the bog. It was only then that Jeremiah Donovan told them. He was shaking with excitement.

'There were four of our fellows shot in Cork this morning and now you're to be shot as a reprisal.'

'What are you talking about?' snaps Hawkins. 'It's bad enough being mucked about as we are without having to put up with your funny jokes.'

'It isn't a joke,' says Donovan. 'I'm sorry, Hawkins, but it's true,' and begins on the usual rigmarole about duty and how unpleasant it is. I never noticed that people who talk a lot about duty find it much of a trouble to them.

'Oh, cut it out!' said Hawkins.

'Ask Bonaparte,' said Donovan, seeing that Hawkins wasn't taking him seriously. 'Isn't it true, Bonaparte?'

'It is,' I said, and Hawkins stopped.

'Ah, for Christ's sake, chum!'

'I mean it, chum,' I said.

'You don't sound as if you meant it.'

'If he doesn't mean it, I do,' said Donovan, working himself up.

'What have you against me, Jeremiah Donovan?'

'I never said I had anything against you. But why did your people take out four of your prisoners and shoot them in cold blood?'

He took Hawkins by the arm and dragged him on, but it was impossible to make him understand that we were in earnest. I had the Smith and Wesson in my pocket and I kept fingering it and wondering what I'd do if they put up a fight for it or ran, and wishing to God they'd do one or the other. I knew if they did run for it, that I'd never fire on them. Hawkins wanted to know was Noble in it, and when we said yes, he asked us why Noble wanted to plug him. Why did any of us want to plug him? What had he done to us? Weren't we all chums? Didn't we understand him and didn't he understand us? Did we imagine for an instant that he'd shoot us for all the so-and-so officers in the so-and-so British Army?

By this time we'd reached the bog, and I was so sick I couldn't even answer him. We walked along the edge of it in the darkness, and every now and then Hawkins would call a halt and begin all over again, as if he was wound up, about our being chums, and I knew that nothing but the sight of the grave would convince him that we had to do it. And all the time I was hoping that something would happen; that they'd run for it or that Noble would take over the responsibility from me. I had the feeling that it was worse on Noble than on me.

IV

At last we saw the lantern in the distance and made towards it. Noble was carrying it, and Feeney was standing somewhere in the darkness behind him, and the picture of them so still and silent in the bogland brought it home to me that we were in earnest, and banished the last bit of hope I had.

Belcher, on recognising Noble, said: 'Hallo, chum,' in his quiet way, but Hawkins flew at him at once, and the argument began all over again, only this time Noble had nothing to say for himself and stood with his head down, holding the lantern between his legs. It was Jeremiah Donovan who did the answering. For the twentieth time, as though it was haunting his mind, Hawkins asked if anybody thought he'd shoot Noble.

'Yes, you would,' said Jeremiah Donovan.

'No, I wouldn't, damn you!'

'You would, because you'd know you'd be shot for not doing it.'

'I wouldn't, not if I was to be shot twenty times over. I wouldn't shoot a pal. And Belcher wouldn't—isn't that right, Belcher? '

'That's right, chum,' Belcher said, but more by way of answering the question than of joining in the argument. Belcher sounded as though whatever unforeseen thing he'd always been waiting for had come at last.

'Anyway, who says Noble would be shot if I wasn't? What do you think I'd do if I was in his place, out in the middle of a blasted bog?'

'What would you do?' asked Donovan.

'I'd go with him wherever he was going, of course. Share my

last bob with him and stick by him through thick and thin. No one can ever say of me that I let down a pal.'

'We had enough of this,' said Jeremiah Donovan, cocking his revolver. 'Is there any message you want to send?'

'No, there isn't.'

'Do you want to say your prayers?'

Hawkins came out with a cold-blooded remark that even shocked me and turned on Noble again.

'Listen to me, Noble,' he said. 'You and me are chums. You can't come over to my side, so I'll come over to your side. That show you I mean what I say? Give me a rifle and I'll go along with you and the other lads.'

Nobody answered him. We knew that was no way out.

'Hear what I'm saying?' he said. 'I'm through with it. I'm a deserter or anything else you like. I don't believe in your stuff, but it's no worse than mine. That satisfy you?'

Noble raised his head, but Donovan began to speak and he lowered it again without replying.

'For the last time, have you any messages to send?' said Donovan in a cold, excited sort of voice.

'Shut up, Donovan! You don't understand me, but these lads do. They're not the sort to make a pal and kill a pal. They're not the tools of any capitalist.'

I alone of the crowd saw Donovan raise his Webley to the back of Hawkins's neck, and as he did so I shut my eyes and tried to pray. Hawkins had begun to say something else when Donovan fired, and as I opened my eyes at the bang, I saw Hawkins stagger at the knees and lie out flat at Noble's feet, slowly and as quiet as a kid falling asleep, with the lantern-light on his lean legs and bright farmer's boots. We all stood very still, watching him settle out in the last agony.

Then Belcher took out a handkerchief and began to tie it about his own eyes (in our excitement we'd forgotten to do the same for Hawkins), and, seeing it wasn't big enough, turned and asked for the loan of mine. I gave it to him and he knotted the two together and pointed with his foot at Hawkins.

'He's not quite dead.' he said. 'Better give him another,' Sure enough, Hawkins's left knee was beginning to rise. I bent down and put my gun to his head; then, recollecting myself, I got up again. Belcher understood what was in my mind.

'Give him his first,' he said, 'I don't mind. Poor bastard, we don't know what's happening to him now.'

I knelt and fired. By this time I didn't seem to know what I was doing. Belcher, who was fumbling a bit awkwardly with the handkerchiefs, came out with a laugh as he heard the shot. It was the first time I had heard him laugh and it sent a shudder down my back; it sounded so unnatural.

'Poor bugger!' he said quietly. 'And last night he was so curious about it all. It's very queer, chums, I always think. Now he knows as much about it as they'll ever let him know, and last night he was all in the dark.'

Donovan helped him to tie the handkerchiefs about his eyes.

'Thanks, chum,' he said. Donovan asked if there were any messages he wanted sent.

'No, chum,' he said. 'Not for me. If any of you would like to write to Hawkins's mother, you'll find a letter from her in his pocket. He and his mother were great chums. But my missus left me eight years ago. Went away with another fellow and took the kid with her. I like the feeling of a home, as you may have noticed, but I couldn't start another again after that.'

It was an extraordinary thing, but in those few minutes Belcher said more than in all the weeks before. It was just as if the sound of the shot had started a flood of talk in him and he could go on the whole night like that, quite happily, talking about himself. We stood around like fools now that he couldn't see us any longer. Donovan looked at Noble, and Noble shook his head. Then Donovan raised his Webley, and at that moment Belcher gave his queer laugh again. He may have thought we were talking about him, or perhaps he noticed the same thing I'd noticed and couldn't understand it.

'Excuse me, chums,' he said. 'I feel I'm talking the hell of a lot, and so silly, about my being so handy about a house and things like that. But this thing came on me suddenly. You'll forgive me, I'm sure.'

'You don't want to say a prayer?' asked Donovan.

'No, chum,' he said. 'I don't think it would help. I'm ready, and you boys want to get it over.'

'You understand that we're only doing our duty?' said Donovan.

Belcher's head was raised like a blind man's, so that you could only see his chin and the top of his nose in the lantern-light. 'I never could make out what duty was myself,' he said. 'I think you're all good lads, if that's what you mean. I'm not complaining.'

Noble, just as if he couldn't bear any more of it, raised his fist at Donovan, and in a flash Donovan raised his gun and fired. The big man went over like a sack of meal, and this time there was no need of a second shot.

I don't remember much about the burying, but that it was worse than all the rest because we had to carry them to the grave. It was all mad lonely with nothing but a patch of lantern-light between ourselves and the dark, and birds hooting and screeching all round, disturbed by the guns. Noble went through Hawkins's belongings to find the letter from his mother, and then joined his hands together. He did the same with Belcher. Then, when we'd filled in the grave, we separated from Jeremiah Donovan and Feeney and took our tools back to the shed. All the way we didn't speak a word. The kitchen was dark and as we'd left it, and the old woman was sitting over the hearth, saying her beads.

We walked past her into the room, and Noble struck a match to light the lamp. She rose quietly and came to the doorway with all her cantankerousness gone.

'What did ye do with them?' she asked in a whisper, and Noble started so that the match went out in his hand.

'What's that?' he asked without turning round.

'I heard ye,' she said.

'What did you hear?' asked Noble.

'I heard ye. Do ye think I didn't hear ye, putting the spade back in the shed?'

Noble struck another match and this time the lamp lit for him.

'Was that what ye did to them?' she asked.

Then, by God, in the very doorway, she fell on her knees and began praying, and after looking at her for a minute or two Noble did the same by the fireplace. I pushed my way out past her and left them at it. I stood at the door, watching the stars and listening to the shrieking of the birds dying out over the bogs. It is so strange what you feel at times like that that you can't describe it. Noble says he saw everything ten times the size, as though there were nothing in the whole world but that little patch of bog with the two Englishmen stiffening into it, but with me it was as if the patch of bog where the Englishmen were was a million miles away, and even Noble and the old woman, mumbling behind me, and the birds and the bloody stars were all far away, and I was somehow very small and very lost and lonely like a child astray in the snow. And anything that happened to me afterwards, I never felt the same about again.

33

A LATE ENCOUNTER WITH THE ENEMY

Flannery O'Connor

General Sash was a hundred and four years old. He lived with his granddaughter, Sally Poker Sash, who was sixty-two years old and who prayed every night on her knees that he would live until her graduation from college. The General didn't give two slaps for her graduation but he never doubted he would live for it. Living had got to be such a habit with him that he couldn't conceive of any other condition. A graduation exercise was not exactly his idea of a good time, even if, as she said, he would be expected to sit on the stage in his uniform.

She said there would be a long procession of teachers and students in their robes but that there wouldn't be anything to equal him in his uniform. He knew this well enough without her telling him, and as for the damn procession, it could march to hell and back and not cause him a quiver. He liked parades with floats full of Miss Americas and Miss Daytona Beaches and Miss Queen Cotton Products. He didn't have any use for processions and a procession full of schoolteachers was about as deadly as the River Styx to his way of thinking. However, he was willing to sit on the stage in his uniform so that they could see him.

Sally Poker was not as sure as he was that he would live until her graduation. There had not been any perceptible change in him for the last five years, but she had the sense that she might be cheated out of her triumph because she so often was. She had been going to summer school every year for the past twenty because when she started teaching, there were no such things as degrees. In those times, she said, everything was normal but nothing had been normal since she was sixteen, and for the past twenty summers, when she should have been resting, she had had to take a trunk in the burning heat to the state teacher's college; and though when she returned in the fall, she always taught in the exact way she had been taught not to teach, this was a mild revenge that didn't satisfy her sense of justice.

She wanted the General at her graduation because she wanted to show what she stood for, or, as she said, 'what all was behind her,' and was not behind them. This them was not anybody in particular. It was just all the upstarts who had turned the world on its head and unsettled the ways of decent living. She meant to stand on that platform in August with the General sitting in his wheel chair on the stage behind her and she meant to hold her head very high as if she were saying, 'See him! See him! My kin, all you upstarts! Glorious upright old man standing for the old traditions! Dignity! Honour! Courage! See him!'

One night in her sleep she screamed, 'See him! See him!' and turned her head and found him sitting in his wheel chair behind her with a terrible expression on his face and with all his clothes off except the general's hat and she had waked up and had not dared to go back to sleep again that night.

For his part, the General would not have consented even to attend her graduation if she had not promised to see to it that he sit on the stage. He liked to sit on any stage. He considered that he was still a very handsome man. When he had been able to stand up, he had measured five feet four inches of pure game cock. He had white hair that reached to his shoulders behind and he would not wear teeth because he thought his profile was more striking without them. When he put on his full-dress general's uniform, he knew well enough that there was nothing to match him anywhere.

This was not the same uniform he had worn in the War

between the States. He had not actually been a general in that war. He had probably been a foot soldier; he didn't remember what he had been; in fact, he didn't remember that war at all.

It was like his feet, which hung down now shriveled at the very end of him, without feeling, covered with a blue-grey afghan that Sally Poker had crocheted when she was a little girl. He didn't remember the Spanish-American War in which he had lost a son; he didn't even remember the son. He didn't have any use for history because he never expected to meet it again. To his mind, history was connected with processions and life with parades and he liked parades. People were always asking him if he remembered this or that—a dreary black procession of questions about the past. There was only one event in the past that had any significance for him and that he cared to talk about: that was twelve years ago when he had received the general's uniform and had been in the premiere.

'I was in that preemy they had in Atlanta,' he would tell visitors sitting on his front porch. 'Surrounded by beautiful guls. It wasn't a thing local about it. It was nothing local about it. Listen here. It was a nashnul event and they had me in it—up onto the stage. There was no bob-tails at it. Every person at it had paid ten dollars to get in and had to wear his tuxseeder. I was in this uniform. A beautiful gul presented me with it that afternoon in a hotel room.'

'It was in a suite in the hotel and I was in it too, Papa,' Sally Poker would say, winking at the visitors. 'You weren't alone with any young lady in a hotel room.'

'Was, I'd a known what to do,' the old General would say with a sharp look and the visitors would scream with laughter. 'This was a Hollywood, California, gul,' he'd continue. 'She was from Hollywood, California, and didn't have any part in the pitcher. Out there they have so many beautiful guls that they don't need that they call them a extra and they don't use them for nothing but presenting people with things and having their pitchers taken. They took my pitcher with her. No, it was two of them. One on either side and me in the middle with my arms around each of them's waist and their waist ain't any bigger than a half a dollar.'

Sally Poker would interrupt again. 'It was Mr Govisky that gave you the uniform, Papa, and he gave me the most exquisite corsage. Really, I wish you could have seen it. It was made with gladiola petals taken off and painted gold and put back together to look like a rose. It was exquisite. I wish you could have seen it, it was…'

'It was as big as her head,' the General would snarl. 'I was tellin it. They gimme this uniform and they gimme this soward and they say, "Now General, we don't want you to start a war on us. All we want you to do is march right up on that stage when you're innerduced tonight and answer a few questions. Think you can do that?" "Think I can do it!" I say. "Listen here. I was doing things before you were born," and they hollered.'

'He was the hit of the show,' Sally Poker would say, but she didn't much like to remember the premiere on account of what had happened to her feet at it. She had bought a new dress for the occasion—a long black crepe dinner dress with a rhinestone buckle and a bolero—and a pair of silver slippers to wear with it, because she was supposed to go up on the stage with him to keep him from falling.

Everything was arranged for them. A real limousine came at ten minutes to eight and took them to the theatre. It drew up under the marquee at exactly the right time, after the big stars and the director and the author and the governor and the mayor and some less important stars. The police kept traffic from jamming and there were ropes to keep the people off who couldn't go. All the people who couldn't go watched them step out of the limousine into the lights. Then they walked down the red and gold foyer and an usherette in a Confederate cap and little short skirt conducted them to their special seats. The audience was already there and a group of UDC members began to clap when they saw the General in his uniform and that started everybody to clap. A few more celebrities came after them and then the doors closed and the lights went down.

A young man with blond wavy hair who said he represented the motion-picture industry came out and began to introduce everybody and each one who was introduced walked up on the stage and said how really happy he was to be here for this great event. The General and his granddaughter were introduced sixteenth on the program. He was introduced as General Tennessee Flintrock Sash of the Confederacy, though Sally Poker had told Mr Govisky that his name was George Poker Sash and that he had only been a major. She helped him up from his seat but her heart was beating so fast she didn't know whether she'd make it herself.

The old man walked up the aisle slowly with his fierce white head high and his hat held over his heart. The orchestra began to play the Confederate Battle Hymn very softly and the UDC members rose as a group and did not sit down again until the General was on the stage. When he reached the centre of the stage with Sally Poker just behind him guiding his elbow, the orchestra burst out in a loud rendition of the Battle Hymn and the old man, with real stage presence, gave a vigorous trembling salute and stood at attention until the last blast had died away. Two of the usherettes in Confederate caps and short skirts held a Confederate and a Union flag crossed behind them.

The General stood in the exact centre of the spotlight and it caught a weird moon-shaped slice of Sally Poker—the corsage, the rhinestone buckle and one hand clenched around a white glove and handkerchief. The young man with the blond wavy hair inserted himself into the circle of light and said he was really happy to have here tonight for this great event, one, he said, who had fought and bled in the battles they would soon see daringly reacted on the screen, and 'Tell me, General,' he asked, 'how old are you?'

'Niiiiiinnttty-two!' the General screamed.

The young man looked as if this were just about the most impressive thing that had been said all evening. 'Ladies and gentlemen,' he said, 'let's give the General the biggest hand we've got!' and there was applause immediately and the young man indicated to Sally Poker with a motion of his thumb that she could take the old man back to his seat now so that the next person could be introduced; but the General had not finished. He stood immovable in the exact centre of the spotlight, his neck thrust forward, his mouth slightly open, and his voracious grey eyes drinking in the glare and the applause. He elbowed his granddaughter roughly away. 'How I keep so young,' he screeched, 'I kiss all the pretty guls!'

This was met with a great din of spontaneous applause and it was at just that instant that Sally Poker looked down at her feet and discovered that in the excitement of getting ready she had forgotten to change her shoes: two brown Girl Scout oxfords protruded from the bottom of her dress. She gave the General a yank and almost ran with him off the stage. He was very angry that he had not got to say how glad he was to be here for this event and on the way back to his seat, he kept saying as loud as he could, 'I'm glad to be here at this preemy with all these beautiful guls!' but there was another celebrity going up the other aisle and nobody paid any attention to him. He slept through the picture, muttering fiercely every now and then in his sleep.

Since then, his life had not been very interesting. His feet were completely dead now, his knees worked like old hinges, his kidneys functioned when they would, but his heart persisted doggedly to beat. The past and the future were the same thing to him, one forgotten and the other not remembered; he had no more notion of dying than a cat. Every year on Confederate Memorial Day, he was bundled up and lent to the Capitol City Museum where he was displayed from one to four in a musty room full of old photographs, old uniforms, old artillery, and historic documents. All these were carefully preserved in glass cases so that children would not put their hands on them. He wore his general's uniform from the premiere and sat, with a fixed scowl, inside a small roped area. There was nothing about him to indicate that he was alive except an occasional movement in his milky grey eyes, but once when a bold child touched his sword, his arm shot forward and slapped the hand off in an instant. In the spring when the old homes were opened for pilgrimages, he was invited to wear his uniform and sit in some conspicuous spot and lend atmosphere to the scene. Some of these times he only snarled at the visitors but sometimes he told about the premiere and the beautiful girls.

If he had died before Sally Poker's graduation, she thought she would have died herself. At the beginning of the summer term, even before she knew if she would pass, she told the Dean that her grandfather, General Tennessee Flintrock Sash of the Confederacy, would attend her graduation and that he was a hundred and four years old and that his mind was still clear as a bell. Distinguished visitors were always welcome and could sit on the stage and be introduced. She made arrangements with her nephew, John Wesley Poker Sash, a Boy Scout, to come wheel the General's chair. She thought how sweet it would be to see the old man in his courageous grey and the young boy in his clean khaki—the old and the new, she thought appropriately—they would be behind her on the stage when she received her degree.

Everything went almost exactly as she had planned. In the summer while she was away at school, the General stayed with other relatives and they brought him and John Wesley, the Boy Scout, down to the graduation. A reporter came to the hotel where they stayed and took the General's picture with Sally Poker on one side of him and John Wesley on the other. The General, who had had his picture taken with beautiful girls, didn't think much of this. He had forgotten precisely what kind of event this was he was going to attend but he remembered that he was to wear his uniform and carry the sword.

On the morning of the graduation, Sally Poker had to line up in the academic procession with the B.S.'s in Elementary Education and she couldn't see to getting him on the stage herself—but John Wesley, a fat blond boy of ten with an executive expression, guaranteed to take care of everything. She came in her academic gown to the hotel and dressed the old man in his uniform. He was as frail as a dried spider. 'Aren't you just thrilled, Papa?' she asked. 'I'm just thrilled to death!'

'Put the soward acrost my lap, damm you,' the old man said, 'where it'll shine.'

She put it there and then stood back looking at him. 'You look just grand,' she said.

'God damm it,' the old man said in a slow monotonous certain tone as if he were saying it to the beating of his heart. 'Goddamm every goddam thing to hell.'

'Now, now,' she said and left happily to join the procession.

The graduates were lined up behind the Science building and she found her place just as the line started to move. She had not slept much the night before and when she had, she had dreamed of the exercises, murmuring, 'See him, see him?' in her sleep but waking up every time just before she turned her head to look at him behind her. The graduates had to walk three blocks in the hot sun in their black wool robes and as she plodded stolidly along she thought that if anyone considered this academic procession something impressive to behold, they need only wait until they saw that old General in his courageous grey and that clean young Boy Scout stoutly wheeling his chair across the stage with the sunlight catching the sword. She imagined that John Wesley had the old man ready now behind the stage.

The black procession wound its way up the two blocks and started on the main walk leading to the auditorium. The visitors stood on the grass, picking out their graduates. Men were pushing back their hats and wiping their foreheads and women were lifting their dresses slightly from the shoulders to keep them from sticking to their backs. The graduates in their heavy robes looked as if the last beads of ignorance were being sweated out of them. The sun blazed off the fenders of automobiles and beat from the columns of the buildings and pulled the eye from one spot of glare to another. It pulled Sally Poker's towards the big red Coca-Cola machine that had been set up by the side of the auditorium. Here she saw the General parked, scowling and hatless in his chair in the blazing sun while John Wesley, his blouse loose behind, his hip and cheek pressed to the red machine, was drinking a Coca-Cola. She broke from the line and galloped to them and snatched the bottle away. She shook the boy and thrust in his blouse and put the hat on the old man's head. 'Now get him in there!' she said, pointing one rigid finger to the side door of the building.

For his part the General felt as if there were a little hole beginning to widen in the top of his head. The boy wheeled him rapidly down a walk and up a ramp and into a building and bumped him over the stage entrance and into position where he had been told and the General glared in front of him at heads that all seemed to flow together and eyes that moved from one face to another. Several figures in black robes came and picked up his hand and shook it. A black procession was flowing up each aisle and forming to stately music in a pool in front of him. The music seemed to be entering his head through the little hole and he thought for a second that the procession would try to enter it too.

He didn't know what procession this was but there was something familiar about it. It must be familiar to him since it had come to meet him, but he didn't like a black procession. Any procession that came to meet him, he thought irritably, ought to have floats with beautiful guls on them like the floats before the preemy. It must be something connected with history like they were always having. He had no use for any of it. What happened then wasn't anything to a man living now and he was living now.

When all the procession had flowed into the black pool, a black figure began orating in front of it. The figure was telling something about history and the General made up his mind he wouldn't listen, but the words kept seeping in through the little hole in his head. He heard his own name mentioned and his chair was shuttled forward roughly and the Boy Scout took a big bow. They called his name and the fat brat bowed. Goddam you, the old man tried to say, get out of my way, I can stand up!—but he was jerked back again before he could get up and take the bow. He supposed the noise they made was for him. If he was over, he didn't intend to listen to any more of it. If it hadn't been for the little hole in the top of his head, none of the words would have got to him. He thought of putting his finger up there into the hole to block them but the hole was a little wider than his finger and it felt as if it were getting deeper.

Another black robe had taken the place of the first one and was talking now and he heard his name mentioned again but they were not talking about him, they were still talking about history. 'If we forget our past,' the speaker was saying, 'we won't remember our future and it will be as well for we won't have one.'

The General heard some of these words gradually. He had forgotten history and he didn't intend to remember it again. He had forgotten the name and face of his wife and the names and faces of his children or even if he had a wife and children, and he had forgotten the names of places and the places themselves and what had happened at them.

He was considerably irked by the hole in his head. He had not expected to have a hole in his head at this event. It was the slow black music that had put it there and though most of the music had stopped outside, there was still a little of it in the hole, going deeper and moving around in his thoughts, letting the words he heard into the dark places of his brain. He heard the words, Chickamauga, Shiloh, Johnston, Lee, and he knew he was inspiring all these words that meant nothing to him. He wondered if he had been a general at Chickamauga or at Lee. Then he tried to see himself and the horse mounted in the middle of a float full of beautiful girls, being driven slowly through downtown Atlanta. Instead, the old words began to stir in his head as if they were trying to wrench themselves out of place and come to life.

The speaker was through with that war and had gone on to the next one and now he was approaching another and all his words, like the black procession, were vaguely familiar and irritating. There was a long finger of music in the General's head, probing various spots that were words, letting in a little light on the words and helping them to live. The words began to come towards him and he said, Dammit! I ain't going to have it! and he started edging backwards to get out of the way. Then he saw the figure in the black robe sit down and there was a noise and the black pool in front of him began to rumble and to flow towards him from either side to the black slow music, and he said, Stop dammit! I can't do but one thing at a time! He couldn't protect himself from the words and attend to the procession too and the words were coming at him fast. He felt that he was running backwards and the words were coming at him like musket fire, just escaping him but getting nearer and nearer. He turned around and began to run as fast as he could but he found himself running towards the words. He was running into a regular volley of them and meeting them with quick curses. As the music swelled towards him, the entire past opened up on him out of nowhere and he felt his body riddled in a hundred places with sharp stabs of pain and he fell down, returning a curse for every hit. He saw his wife's narrow face looking at him critically through her round gold-rimmed glasses; he saw one of his squinting bald-headed sons; and his mother ran towards him with an anxious look; then a succession of places—Chickamauga, Shiloh, Marthasville—rushed at him as if the past were the only future now and he had to endure it. Then suddenly he saw that the black procession was almost on him. He recognized it, for it had been dogging all his days. He made such a desperate effort to see over it and find out what comes after the past that his hand clenched the sword until the blade touched bone.

The graduates were crossing the stage in a long file to receive their scrolls and shake the president's hand. As Sally Poker, who was near the end, crossed, she glanced at the General and saw him sitting fixed and fierce, his eyes wide open, and she turned her head forward again and held it a perceptible degree higher and received her scroll. Once it was all over and she was out of the auditorium in the sun again, she located her kin and they waited together on a bench in the shade for John Wesley to wheel the old man out. That crafty scout had bumped him out the back way and rolled him at high speed down a flagstone path and was waiting now, with the corpse, in the long line at the Coca-Cola machine.

34

WEE WILLIE WINKIE

Rudyard Kipling

His full name was Percival William Williams, but he picked up the other name in a nursery-book, and that was the end of the christened titles. His mother's *ayah* called him Willie-*Baba*, but as he never paid the faintest attention to anything that the *ayah* said, her wisdom did not help matters.

His father was the Colonel of the 195th, and as soon as Wee Willie Winkie was old enough to understand what Military Discipline meant, Colonel Williams put him under it. There was no other way of managing the child. When he was good for a week, he drew good-conduct pay; and when he was bad, he was deprived of his good-conduct stripe. Generally he was bad, for India offers many chances of going wrong to little six-year-olds.

Children resent familiarity from strangers, and Wee Willie Winkie was a very particular child. Once he accepted an acquaintance, he was graciously pleased to thaw. He accepted Brandis, a subaltern of the 195th, on sight. Brandis was having tea at the Colonel's, and Wee Willie Winkie entered strong in the possession of a good-conduct badge won for not chasing the hens round the compound. He regarded Brandis with gravity for at least ten minutes, and then delivered himself of his opinion.

'I like you,' said he slowly, getting off his chair and coming over to Brandis, 'I like you. I shall call you Coppy, because of your hair. Do you *mind* being called Coppy? It is because of ve hair, you know.'

Here was one of the most embarrassing of Wee Willie

Winkie's peculiarities. He would look at a stranger for some time, and then, without warning or explanation, would give him a name. And the name stuck. No regimental penalties could break Wee Willie Winkie of this habit. He lost his good-conduct badge for christening the Commissioner's wife 'Pobs'; but nothing that the Colonel could do made the Station forego the nickname, and Mrs Collen remained 'Pobs' till the end of her stay. So Brandis was christened 'Coppy,' and rose, therefore, in the estimation of the regiment.

If Wee Willie Winkie took an interest in any one, the fortunate man was envied alike by the mess and the rank and file. And in their envy lay no suspicion of self-interest. 'The Colonel's son' was idolized on his own merits entirely. Yet Wee Willie Winkie was not lovely. His face was permanently freckled, as his legs were permanently scratched, and in spite of his mother's almost tearful remonstrances he had insisted upon having his long yellow locks cut short in the military fashion. 'I want my hair like Sergeant Tummil's,' said Wee Willie Winkie, and, his father abetting, the sacrifice was accomplished.

Three weeks after the bestowal of his youthful affections on Lieutenant Brandis—henceforward to be called 'Coppy' for the sake of brevity—Wee Willie Winkie was destined to behold strange things and far beyond his comprehension.

Coppy returned his liking with interest. Coppy had let him wear for five rapturous minutes his own big sword—just as tall as Wee Willie Winkie. Coppy had promised him a terrier puppy; and Coppy had permitted him to witness the miraculous operation of shaving. Nay, more—Coppy had said that even he, Wee Willie Winkie, would rise in time to the ownership of a box of shiny knives, a silver soap-box, and a silver-handled 'sputter-brush,' as Wee Willie Winkie called it. Decidedly, there was no one except his father, who could give or take away good-conduct badges at pleasure, half so wise, strong, and valiant as Coppy with the

Afghan and Egyptian medals on his breast. Why, then, should Coppy be guilty of the unmanly weakness of kissing—vehemently kissing—a 'big girl,' Miss Allardyce to wit? In the course of a morning ride Wee Willie Winkie had seen Coppy so doing, and, like the gentleman he was, had promptly wheeled round and cantered back to his groom, lest the groom should also see.

Under ordinary circumstances he would have spoken to his father, but he felt instinctively that this was a matter on which Coppy ought first to be consulted.

'Coppy,' shouted Wee Willie Winkie, reining up outside that subaltern's bungalow early one morning—'I want to see you, Coppy!'

'Come in, young 'un,' returned Coppy, who was at early breakfast in the midst of his dogs. 'What mischief have you been getting into now?'

Wee Willie Winkie had done nothing notoriously bad for three days, and so stood on a pinnacle of virtue.

'*I've* been doing nothing bad,' said he, curling himself into a long chair with a studious affectation of the Colonel's languor after a hot parade. He buried his freckled nose in a tea-cup and, with eyes staring roundly over the rim, asked: 'I say, Coppy, is it pwoper to kiss big girls?'

'By Jove! You're beginning early. Who do you want to kiss?'

'No one. My muvver's always kissing me if I don't stop her. If it isn't pwoper, how was you kissing Major Allardyce's big girl last morning, by ve canal?'

Coppy's brow wrinkled. He and Miss Allardyce had with great craft managed to keep their engagement secret for a fortnight. There were urgent and imperative reasons why Major Allardyce should not know how matters stood for at least another month, and this small marplot had discovered a great deal too much.

'I saw you,' said Wee Willie Winkie calmly. 'But ve *sais* didn't see. I said, "*Hut jao!*"'

'Oh, you had that much sense, you young Rip,' groaned poor Coppy, half amused and half angry. 'And how many people may you have told about it?'

'Only me myself. You didn't tell when I twied to wide ve buffalo ven my pony was lame; and I fought you wouldn't like.'

'Winkie,' said Coppy enthusiastically, shaking the small hand, 'you're the best of good fellows. Look here, you can't understand all these things. One of these days—hang it, how can I make you see it!—I'm going to marry Miss Allardyce, and then she'll be Mrs Coppy, as you say. If your young mind is so scandalized at the idea of kissing big girls, go and tell your father.'

'What will happen?' said Wee Willie Winkie, who firmly believed that his father was omnipotent.

'I shall get into trouble,' said Coppy, playing his trump card with an appealing look at the holder of the ace.

'Ven I won't,' said Wee Willie Winkie briefly. 'But my faver says it's un-man-ly to be always kissing, and I didn't fink *you'd* do vat, Coppy.'

'I'm not always kissing, old chap. It's only now and then, and when you're bigger you'll do it too. Your father meant it's not good for little boys.'

'Ah!' said Wee Willie Winkie, now fully enlightened. 'It's like ve sputter-brush?'

'Exactly,' said Coppy gravely.

'But I don't fink I'll ever want to kiss big girls, nor no one, 'cept my muvver. And I *must* vat, you know.'

There was a long pause, broken by Wee Willie Winkie.

'Are you fond of vis big girl, Coppy?'

'Awfully!' said Coppy.

'Fonder van you are of Bell or ve Butcha—or me?'

'It's in a different way,' said Coppy. 'You see, one of these days Miss Allardyce will belong to me, but you'll grow up and command the Regiment and—all sorts of things. It's quite different, you see.'

'Very well,' said Wee Willie Winkie, rising. 'If you're fond of ve big girl I won't tell any one. I must go now.'

Coppy rose and escorted his small guest to the door, adding—'You're the best of little fellows, Winkie. I tell you what. In thirty days from now you can tell if you like—tell any one you like.'

Thus the secret of the Brandis-Allardyce engagement was dependent on a little child's word. Coppy, who knew Wee Willie Winkie's idea of truth, was at ease, for he felt that he would not break promises. Wee Willie Winkie betrayed a special and unusual interest in Miss Allardyce, and, slowly revolving round that embarrassed young lady, was used to regard her gravely with unwinking eye. He was trying to discover why Coppy should have kissed her. She was not half so nice as his own mother. On the other hand, she was Coppy's property, and would in time belong to him. Therefore it behoved him to treat her with as much respect as Coppy's big sword or shiny pistol.

The idea that he shared a great secret in common with Coppy kept Wee Willie Winkie unusually virtuous for three weeks. Then the Old Adam broke out, and he made what he called a 'campfire' at the bottom of the garden. How could he have foreseen that the flying sparks would have lighted the Colonel's little hay-rick and consumed a week's store for the horses? Sudden and swift was the punishment—deprivation of the good-conduct badge and, most sorrowful of all, two days' confinement to barracks—the house and veranda—coupled with the withdrawal of the light of his father's countenance.

He took the sentence like the man he strove to be, drew himself up with a quivering under-lip, saluted, and, once clear of the room, ran to weep bitterly in his nursery—called by him 'my quarters.' Coppy came in the afternoon and attempted to console the culprit.

'I'm under awwest,' said Wee Willie Winkie mournfully, 'and I didn't ought to speak to you.'

Very early the next morning he climbed on to the roof of the house—that was not forbidden—and beheld Miss Allardyce going for a ride.

'Where are you going?' cried Wee Willie Winkie.

'Across the river,' she answered, and trotted forward.

Now the cantonment in which the 195th lay was bounded on the north by a river—dry in the winter. From his earliest years, Wee Willie Winkie had been forbidden to go across the river, and had noted that even Coppy—the almost almighty Coppy—had never set foot beyond it. Wee Willie Winkie had once been read to, out of a big blue book, the history of the Princess and the Goblins—a most wonderful tale of a land where the Goblins were always warring with the children of men until they were defeated by one Curdie. Ever since that date it seemed to him that the bare black and purple hills across the river were inhabited by Goblins, and, in truth, every one had said that there lived the Bad Men. Even in his own house the lower halves of the windows were covered with green paper on account of the Bad Men who might, if allowed clear view, fire into peaceful drawing-rooms and comfortable bedrooms. Certainly, beyond the river, which was the end of all the Earth, lived the Bad Men. And here was Major Allardyce's big girl, Coppy's property, preparing to venture into their borders! What would Coppy say if anything happened to her? If the Goblins ran off with her as they did with Curdie's Princess? She must at all hazards be turned back.

The house was still. Wee Willie Winkie reflected for a moment on the very terrible wrath of his father; and then—broke his arrest! It was a crime unspeakable. The low sun threw his shadow, very large and very black, on the trim garden-paths, as he went down to the stables and ordered his pony. It seemed to him in the hush of the dawn that all the big world had been bidden to stand still and look at Wee Willie Winkie guilty of mutiny. The drowsy *sais* gave him his mount, and, since the one great sin made all others insignificant, Wee Willie Winkie said that he was going to ride over to Coppy Sahib, and went out at a foot-pace, stepping on the soft mould of the flower-borders.

The devastating track of the pony's feet was the last misdeed that cut him off from all sympathy of Humanity. He turned into the road, leaned forward, and rode as fast as the pony could put foot to the ground in the direction of the river.

But the liveliest of twelve-two ponies can do little against the long canter of a Waler. Miss Allardyce was far ahead, had passed through the crops, beyond the Police-posts, when all the guards were asleep, and her mount was scattering the pebbles of the river-bed as Wee Willie Winkie left the cantonment and British India behind him. Bowed forward and still flogging, Wee Willie Winkie shot into Afghan territory, and could just see Miss Allardyce, a black speck, flickering across the stony plain. The reason of her wandering was simple enough. Coppy, in a tone of too-hastily-assumed authority, had told her overnight that she must not ride out by the river. And she had gone to prove her own spirit and teach Coppy a lesson.

Almost at the foot of the inhospitable hills, Wee Willie Winkie saw the Waler blunder and come down heavily. Miss Allardyce struggled clear, but her ankle had been severely twisted, and she could not stand. Having fully shown her spirit, she wept, and was surprised by the apparition of a white, wide-eyed child in khaki, on a nearly spent pony.

'Are you badly, badly hurt?' shouted Wee Willie Winkie, as soon as he was within range. 'You didn't ought to be here,'

'I don't know,' said Miss Allardyce ruefully, ignoring the reproof. 'Good gracious, child, what are *you* doing here?'

'You said you was going acwoss ve wiver,' panted Wee Willie Winkie, throwing himself off his pony. 'And nobody—not even Coppy—must go acwoss ve wiver, and I came after you ever so hard, but you wouldn't stop, and now you've hurted yourself, and

Coppy will be angwy wiv me, and—I've bwoken my awwest! I've bwoken my awwest!'

The future Colonel of the 195th sat down and sobbed. In spite of the pain in her ankle the girl was moved.

'Have you ridden all the way from cantonments, little man? What for?'

'You belonged to Coppy. Coppy told me so!' wailed Wee Willie Winkie disconsolately. 'I saw him kissing you, and he said he was fonder of you van Bell or ve Butcha or me. And so I came. You must get up and come back. You didn't ought to be here. Vis is a bad place, and I've bwoken my awwest.'

'I can't move, Winkie,' said Miss Allardyce, with a groan. 'I've hurt my foot. What shall I do?'

She showed a readiness to weep anew, which steadied Wee Willie Winkie, who had been brought up to believe that tears were the depth of unmanliness. Still, when one is as great a sinner as Wee Willie Winkie, even a man may be permitted to break down.

'Winkie,' said Miss Allardyce, 'when you've rested a little, ride back and tell them to send out something to carry me back in. It hurts fearfully.'

The child sat still for a little time and Miss Allardyce closed her eyes; the pain was nearly making her faint. She was roused by Wee Willie Winkie tying up the reins on his pony's neck and setting it free with a vicious cut of his whip that made it whicker. The little animal headed towards the cantonments.

'Oh, Winkie, what are you doing?'

'Hush!' said Wee Willie Winkie. 'Vere's a man coming—one of ve Bad Men. I must stay wiv you. My faver says a man must *always* look after a girl. Jack will go home, and ven vey'll come and look for us. Vat's why I let him go.'

Not one man but two or three had appeared from behind the rocks of the hills, and the heart of Wee Willie Winkie sank within him, for just in this manner were the Goblins wont to steal out and vex Curdie's soul. Thus had they played in Curdie's garden—he had seen the picture—and thus had they frightened the Princess's nurse. He heard them talking to each other, and recognized with joy the bastard Pushto that he had picked up from one of his father's grooms lately dismissed. People who spoke that tongue could not be the Bad Men. They were only natives after all.

They came up to the boulders on which Miss Allardyce's horse had blundered.

Then rose from the rock Wee Willie Winkie, child of the Dominant Race, aged six and three-quarters, and said briefly and emphatically '*Jao!*' The pony had crossed the river-bed.

The men laughed, and laughter from natives was the one thing Wee Willie Winkie could not tolerate. He asked them what they wanted and why they did not depart. Other men with most evil faces and crooked-stocked guns crept out of the shadows of the hills, till, soon, Wee Willie Winkie was face to face with an audience some twenty strong. Miss Allardyce screamed.

'Who are you?' said one of the men.

'I am the Colonel Sahib's son, and my order is that you go at once. You black men are frightening the Miss Sahib. One of you must run into cantonments and take the news that the Miss Sahib has hurt herself, and that the Colonel's son is here with her.'

'Put our feet into the trap?' was the laughing reply. 'Hear this boy's speech!'

'Say that I sent you—I, the Colonel's son. They will give you money.'

'What is the use of this talk? Take up the child and the girl, and we can at least ask for the ransom. Ours are the villages on the heights,' said a voice in the background.

These *were* the Bad Men—worse than Goblins—and it needed all Wee Willie Winkie's training to prevent him from bursting into tears. But he felt that to cry before a native, excepting only his mother's *ayah*, would be an infamy greater than any mutiny. Moreover, he, as future Colonel of the 195th, had that grim regiment at his back.

'Are you going to carry us away?' said Wee Willie Winkie, very blanched and uncomfortable.

'Yes, my little *Sahib Bahadur*,' said the tallest of the men, 'and eat you afterwards.'

'That is child's talk,' said Wee Willie Winkie. 'Men do not eat men.'

A yell of laughter interrupted him, but he went on firmly—'And if you do carry us away, I tell you that all my regiment will come up in a day and kill you all without leaving one. Who will take my message to the Colonel Sahib?'

Speech in any vernacular—and Wee Willie Winkie had a colloquial acquaintance with three—was easy to the boy who could not yet manage his 'r's' and 'th's' aright.

Another man joined the conference, crying: 'O foolish men! What this babe says is true. He is the heart's heart of those white troops. For the sake of peace let them go both, for if he be taken, the regiment will break loose and gut the valley. *Our* villages are in the valley, and we shall not escape. That regiment are devils. They broke Khoda Yar's breastbone with kicks when he tried to take the rifles; and if we touch this child they will fire and rape and plunder for a month, till nothing remains. Better to send a man back to take the message and get a reward. I say that this child is their God, and that they will spare none of us, nor our women, if we harm him.'

It was Din Mahommed, the dismissed groom of the Colonel, who made the diversion, and an angry and heated discussion followed. Wee Willie Winkie, standing over Miss Allardyce, waited the upshot. Surely his 'wegiment,' his own 'wegiment,' would not desert him if they knew of his extremity.

The riderless pony brought the news to the 195th, though there had been consternation in the Colonel's household for an hour before. The little beast came in through the parade-ground in front of the main barracks, where the men were settling down to play Spoil-five till the afternoon. Devlin, the Colour-Sergeant of E Company, glanced at the empty saddle and tumbled through the barrack-rooms, kicking up each Room Corporal as he passed. 'Up, ye beggars! There's something happened to the Colonel's son,' he shouted.

'He couldn't fall off! S'elp me, 'e *couldn't* fall off,' blubbered a drummer-boy. 'Go an' hunt acrost the river. He's over there if he's anywhere, an' maybe those Pathans have got 'im. For the love o' Gawd don't look for 'im in the nullahs! Let's go over the river.'

'There's sense in Mott yet,' said Devlin. 'E Company, double out to the river—sharp!'

So E Company, in its shirt-sleeves mainly, doubled for the dear life, and in the rear toiled the perspiring Sergeant, adjuring it to double yet faster. The cantonment was alive with the men of the 195th hunting for Wee Willie Winkie, and the Colonel finally overtook E Company, far too exhausted to swear, struggling in the pebbles of the river-bed.

Up the hill under which Wee Willie Winkie's Bad Men were discussing the wisdom of carrying off the child and the girl, a look-out fired two shots.

'What have I said?' shouted Din Mahommed. 'There is the warning! The *pulton* are out already and are coming across the plain! Get away! Let us not be seen with the boy.'

The men waited for an instant, and then, as another shot was fired, withdrew into the hills, silently as they had appeared.

'The wegiment is coming,' said Wee Willie Winkie confidently to Miss Allardyce, 'and it's all wight. Don't cwy!'

He needed the advice himself, for ten minutes later, when

his father came up, he was weeping bitterly with his head in Miss Allardyce's lap.

And the men of the 195th carried him home with shouts and rejoicings; and Coppy, who had ridden a horse into a lather, met him, and, to his intense disgust, kissed him openly in the presence of the men.

But there was balm for his dignity. His father assured him that not only would the breaking of arrest be condoned, but that the good-conduct badge would be restored as soon as his mother could sew it on his blouse-sleeve. Miss Allardyce had told the Colonel a story that made him proud of his son.

'She belonged to you, Coppy,' said Wee Willie Winkie, indicating Miss Allardyce with a grimy forefinger. 'I *knew* she didn't ought to go acwoss ve wiver, and I knew ve wegiment would come to me if I sent Jack home.'

'You're a hero, Winkie,' said Coppy—'a *pukka* hero!'

'I don't know what vat means,' said Wee Willie Winkie, 'but you mustn't call me Winkie any no more. I'm Percival Will'am Will'ams.'

And in this manner did Wee Willie Winkie enter into his manhood.

35

WHAT THE WOUNDED SAY AND DO

Ira L. Reeves

No two men behave alike when hit in battle. There is just as much difference in their actions as there is in the behaviour of the members of a volunteer fire brigade at a country-town conflagration. The look of the mortally wounded is nearly always the same. There is always that deathly pallor that creeps over the face, and that fixed stare—horrible look of resignation—that tells so plainly that all is over with the unfortunate soldier. A few instances will serve to give a general idea of how the victims of the messengers of death receive them.

On the 1st of July, a company of regular infantry, in reserve, was lying flat on their stomachs in a sunken road, a few hundred yards from the stone block-house of El Caney, Cuba. The men were under a terrific fire, but were not allowed to reply to it, for ammunition was growing scarce. For hours they remained in this position. They began to get restless and to shift about. As long as they kept low, there was no danger from Spanish fire, for the bank of the road was sufficiently high to afford security. Curiosity occasionally got the better of a man, and he would poke his head above the embankment and peer in the direction from which the bullets were coming. In the company was a large, muscular German, who had early become restless and curious to see what was transpiring. He would occasionally break out and swear because he was not given a chance to fire at the hated Dons. Of a sudden he ripped out a choice lot of the best in his vocabulary, raised his head above the bank, and shook his huge fist at the line of sombreros to be seen just above the Spanish trenches to the right of the block-house. Ping! ping! thud! 'Wasn't that an awful sound?' a dozen soldiers chimed. There is no other sound produced that can be compared with it. It stands alone for all that is sickening and horrible. All knew that some one had been hit. A moment was passed in suspense. The German whispered, in the tones of death, to his comrade at his side: 'Wipe the blood off of my face!' It was his last words. He drew his knees to his chin in the agonies of death, turned over on one side, burrowing his face in the mud, and died without a groan. A Mauser had hit him squarely between the eyes.

A short time later a sergeant of one of the companies of the same regiment moved a few yards forward, trying to get a potshot at some Spanish sharpshooters who were snugly perched in the spreading tops of some royal palm trees, and were hitting some of our men. He sighted one and had his rifle to his shoulder, taking a fine bead, when all at once the rifle fell to the ground and his hands dropped helplessly by his side. He coolly faced about and walked towards the rear, his arms dangling like pendulums, not even so much as muttering a word. One of his company officers asked him what was the matter, to which he laconically replied, 'Hit,' and continued on his way to the dressing-station in the rear. He was shot through both shoulders—a serious wound, but he recovered.

About an hour after the German was killed the same company was ordered to take a position farther to the right. They walked along, goose-fashion, single file, moving by the right flank towards their new position. Next to the last man in the rear was a corporal, a new man, just a few months in the service. Biff! ping! bang! went the deadly missiles. One struck a man's rifle-barrel, cutting it almost in two. Another split the stock of a gun in a man's hand. Then one struck the recruit corporal's left arm, passing through the biceps. With an expression of great surprise he for a moment stood still, saying nothing. His eyes began to dilate, and then of a sudden he threw his fowling-piece high in the air, grasped his left arm with his right hand, and started for the rear at a disgraceful gait, yelling so as to be heard above the din of battle: 'I've got it! I've got it! I've got it!' The last that was seen of him that day he had 'it,' and was taking 'it' to the rear with him.

On San Juan Ridge, July 2nd, just as Chaffee's brigade had reached the crest, they were ordered to lie down and intrench, using the bayonet as a pick and the hands for shovels. A dashing young fellow of one of the companies on the right of the line was some distance in advance of his fellows when the halt was made. Instead of falling back on the line with the other men, he stopped where he was. One of the officers shouted at him several times to fall back, as he was in danger of his own men shooting him, but he did not hear. The officer then walked down to where he was, grabbed him by a leg, and started to drag him back to the line. He had but started when he felt the man's whole body quiver, and he flopped himself over on his back, saying as he did so, 'I'm done for.' Some of the men came to the soldier and assisted the officer to carry him to a place of security. With a bayonet one of the men cut off his clothing, when a Mauser hole was seen just above the heart, where the bullet entered, passing through his body and coming out between the shoulders, near the spine. The man said no more at the time. His wounds were bound by sympathetic hands. All except the wounded man returned to the firing-line. The Spanish fire was heavy, and kept up for four hours, occasionally a soldier dropping out, wounded or killed. When all was quiet, the officer and one of his soldiers returned to see if the young man were yet alive. They found him sitting against a small tree. His first words were: 'Bill, give me a cigarette.' The man is living to-day.

Just about the time this man was wounded a man in the next company on the right suddenly threw down his bayonet, jumped to his feet, paused for a second or two, looking in the direction of the Spanish trenches, then threw both hands to his breast, saying, 'I'm hit.' He turned about and walked into the dense thickets of cactus and Spanish bayonet, and was never seen nor heard of again. He undoubtedly crawled far back into the heavy tropical growth and died, where the vultures claimed him.

One of the coolest men who ever received a wound was an infantryman at San Fernando, in the Island of Luzon, on the 16th of June. The insurgents made a determined effort to retake the town early on the morning of that day. They opened up simultaneously from every quarter, and the kind and variety of missiles used would be beyond the wildest expectations of that sweet-throated midnight serenader, the Thomas-cat. Out of an old smooth-bore cannon they threw railroad spikes, horseshoes, old clocks, lemon-squeezers, and cobble-stones. From their Remingtons they shot large cubical and irregular-shaped lead slugs. One of these struck this cool man high in the right groin, deeply imbedding itself. The pain must have been excruciating, for the man was terribly lacerated. He hobbled to his company commander, saluted, and asked permission to fall out and lie down, as he had been hit. He was lying near a road where his comrades passed to and fro during the entire fight, but no one heard a word or a groan out of him unless he was spoken to.

During the same fight, in another company of the same regiment, a battalion sergeant-major was ordered to take two squads and proceed to a point about 400 yards down the Angeles Road, where there was a small trench, and defend it. When about half-way down, one of his men, a green 'rookie,' received a severe wound in the leg. The Sergeant endeavoured to start him to the rear, with a man to assist him along, but he protested. Nothing but to continue to the front with his squad would do. He loaded and fired with the other men till the fight was over. This man was recommended for a medal of honour by his captain.

36

THE WORST MAN IN THE TROOP

Charles King

Just why that young Irishman should have been so balefully branded was more than the first lieutenant of the troop could understand. To be sure, the lieutenant's opportunities for observation had been limited. He had spent some years on detached service in the East, and had joined his comrades in Arizona but a fortnight ago, and here he was already becoming rapidly initiated in the science of scouting through mountain-wilds against the wariest and most treacherous of foemen,—the Apaches of our Southwestern territory.

Coming, as he had done, direct from a station and duties where full-dress uniform, lavish expenditure for kid gloves, bouquets, and Lubin's extracts were matters of daily fact, it must be admitted that the sensations he experienced on seeing his detachment equipped for the scout were those of mild consternation. That much latitude as to individual dress and equipment was permitted he had previously been informed; that 'full dress,' and white shirts, collars, and the like would be left at home, he had sense enough to know; but that every officer and man in the command would be allowed to discard any and all portions of the regulation uniform and appear rigged out in just such motley guise as his poetic or practical fancy might suggest, had never been pointed out to him; and that he, commanding his troop while a captain commanded the little battalion, could by any military possibility take his place in front of his men without his sabre, had never for an instant occurred to him. As a consequence, when he bolted into the mess-room shortly after daybreak on a bright June morning with that imposing but at most times useless item of cavalry equipment clanking at his heels, the lieutenant gazed with some astonishment upon the attire of his brother-officers there assembled, but found himself the butt of much good-natured and not over-witty 'chaff,' directed partially at the extreme newness and neatness of his dark-blue flannel scouting-shirt and high-top boots, but more especially at the glittering sabre swinging from his waist-belt.

'Billings,' said Captain Buxton, with much solemnity, 'while you have probably learned through the columns of a horror-stricken Eastern press that we scalp, alive or dead, all unfortunates who fall into our clutches, I assure you that even for that purpose the cavalry sabre has, in Arizona at least, outlived its usefulness. It is too long and clumsy, you see. What you really want for the purpose is something like this,'—and he whipped out of its sheath a rusty but keen-bladed Mexican *cuchillo*,—'something you can wield with a deft turn of the wrist, you know. The sabre is apt to tear and mutilate the flesh, especially when you use both hands.' And Captain Buxton winked at the other subaltern and felt that he had said a good thing.

But Mr Billings was a man of considerable good nature and ready adaptability to the society or circumstances by which he might be surrounded. 'Chaff' was a very cheap order of wit, and the serenity of his disposition enabled him to shake off its effect as readily as water is scattered from the plumage of the duck.

'So you don't wear the sabre on a scout? So much the better. I have my revolvers and a Sharp's carbine, but am destitute of anything in the knife line.' And with that Mr Billings betook himself to the duty of despatching the breakfast that was already spread before him in an array tempting enough to a frontier appetite, but little designed to attract a *bon vivant* of civilization. Bacon, *frijoles*, and creamless coffee speedily become ambrosia and nectar under the influence of mountain-air and mountain-exercise; but Mr Billings had as yet done no climbing. A 'buck-board' ride had been his means of transportation to the garrison,—a lonely four-company post in a far-away valley in Northeastern Arizona,—and in the three or four days of intense heat that had succeeded his arrival exercise of any kind had been out of the question. It was with no especial regret, therefore, that he heard the summons of the captain, 'Hurry up, man; we must be off in ten minutes.' And in less than ten minutes the lieutenant was on his horse and superintending the formation of his troop.

If Mr Billings was astonished at the garb of his brother-officers at breakfast, he was simply aghast when he glanced along the line of Company 'A' (as his command was at that time officially designated) and the first sergeant rode out to report his men present or accounted for. The first sergeant himself was got up in an old grey-flannel shirt, open at and disclosing a broad, brown throat and neck; his head was crowned with what had once been a white felt *sombrero*, now tanned by desert sun, wind, and dirt into a dingy mud-colour; his powerful legs were encased in worn deer-skin breeches tucked into low-topped, broad-soled, well-greased boots; his waist was girt with a rude 'thimble-belt,' in the loops of which were thrust scores of copper cartridges for carbine and pistol; his carbine, and those of all the command, swung in a leather loop athwart the pommel of the saddle; revolvers in all manner of cases hung at the hip, the regulation holster, in most instances, being conspicuous by its absence. Indeed, throughout the entire command the remarkable fact was to be noted that a troop of regular cavalry, taking the field against hostile Indians had discarded pretty much every item of dress or equipment prescribed or furnished by the authorities of the United States, and had supplied themselves with an outfit utterly ununiform, unpicturesque, undeniably slouchy, but not less undeniably appropriate and serviceable. Not a forage-cap was to be seen, not a 'campaign-hat' of the style then prescribed by a board of officers that might have known something of hats, but never could have had an idea on the subject of campaigns. Fancy that black enormity of weighty felt, with flapping brim well-nigh a foot in width, absorbing the fiery heat of an Arizona sun, and concentrating the burning rays upon the cranium of its unhappy wearer! No such head-gear would our troopers suffer in the days when General Crook led them through the cañons and deserts of that inhospitable Territory. Regardless of appearances or style himself, seeking only comfort in his dress, the chief speedily found means to indicate that, in Apache-campaigning at least, it was to be a case of '*inter arma silent leges*' in dead earnest; for, freely translated, the old saw read, 'No red-tape when Indian-fighting.'

Of much of this Lieutenant Billings was only partially informed, and so, as has been said, he was aghast when he marked the utter absence of uniform and the decidedly variegated appearance of his troop. Deerskin, buckskin, canvas, and flannels, leggings, moccasins, and the like, constituted the bill of dress, and old soft felt hats, originally white, the head-gear. If spurs were worn at all, they were of the Mexican variety, easy to kick off, but sure to stay on when wanted. Only two men wore carbine sling-belts, and Mr Billings was almost ready to hunt up his captain and inquire if by any possibility the men could be attempting to 'put up a joke on him,' when the captain himself appeared, looking little if any more like the ideal soldier than his men, and the perfectly satisfied expression on his face as he rode easily around, examining closely the horses of the command, paying especial attention to their feet and the shoes thereof, convinced the lieutenant that all was as it was expected to be, if not as it should be, and he swallowed his surprise and held his peace. Another moment, and Captain Wayne's troop came filing past in column of twos, looking, if anything, rougher than his own.

'You follow right after Wayne,' said Captain Buxton; and with no further formality Mr Billings, in a perfunctory sort of way, wheeled his men to the right by fours, broke into column of twos, and closed up on the leading troop.

Buxton was in high glee on this particular morning in June. He had done very little Indian scouting, had been but moderately successful in what he had undertaken, and now, as luck would have it, the necessity arose for sending something more formidable than a mere detachment down into the Tonto Basin, in search of a powerful band of Apaches who had broken loose from the reservation and were taking refuge in the foothills of the Black Mesa or among the wilds of the Sierra Ancha. As senior captain of the two, Buxton became commander of the entire force,—two well-filled troops of regular cavalry, some thirty Indian allies as scouts, and a goodly-sized train of pack-mules, with its full complement of packers, *cargadors*, and blacksmiths. He fully anticipated a lively fight, possibly a series of them, and a triumphant return to his post, where hereafter he would be looked up to and quoted as an expert and authority on Apache-fighting. He knew just where the hostiles lay, and was going straight to the point to flatten them out forthwith; and so the little command moved off under admirable auspices and in the best of spirits.

It was a four-days' hard march to the locality where Captain Buxton counted on finding his victims; and when on the fourth day, rather tired and not particularly enthusiastic, the command bivouacked along the banks of a mountain-torrent, a safe distance from the supposed location of the Indian stronghold, he sent forward his Apache Mojave allies to make a stealthy reconnoissance, feeling confident that soon after nightfall they would return with the intelligence that the enemy were lazily resting in their 'rancheria,' all unsuspicious of his approach, and that at daybreak he would pounce upon and annihilate them.

Soon after nightfall the scouts did return, but their intelligence was not so gratifying: a small—a *very* small—band of renegades had been encamped in that vicinity some weeks before, but not a 'hostile' or sign of a hostile was to be found. Captain Buxton hardly slept that night, from disappointment and mortification, and when he went the following day to investigate for himself he found that he had been on a false scent from the start, and this made him crabbed. A week's hunt through the mountains resulted in no better luck, and now, having had only fifteen days' rations at the outset, he was most reluctantly and savagely marching homewards to report his failure.

But Mr Billings had enjoyed the entire trip. Sleeping in the open air without other shelter than their blankets afforded, scouting by day in single file over miles of mere game-trails, up hill and down dale through the wildest and most dolefully-picturesque scenery he 'at least' had ever beheld, under frowning cliffs and beetling crags, through dense forests of pine and juniper, through mountain-torrents swollen with the melting snows of the crests so far above them, through cañons, deep, dark, and gloomy, searching ever for traces of the foe they were ordered to find and fight forthwith, Mr Billings and his men, having no responsibility upon their shoulders, were happy and healthy as possible, and consequently in small sympathy with their irate leader.

Every afternoon when they halted beside some one of the hundreds of mountain-brooks that came tumbling down from the gorges of the Black Mesa, the men were required to look carefully at the horses' backs and feet, for mountain Arizona is terrible on shoes, equine or human. This had to be done before the herds were turned out to graze with their guard around them; and often some of the men would get a wisp of straw or a suitable wipe of some kind, and thoroughly rub down their steeds. Strolling about among them, as he always did at this time, our lieutenant had noticed a slim but trimly-built young Irishman whose care of and devotion to his horse it did him good to see. No matter how long the march, how severe the fatigue, that horse was always looked after, his grazing-ground pre-empted by a deftly-thrown picket-pin and lariat which secured to him all the real estate that could be surveyed within the circle of which the pin was the centre and the lariat the radius-vector.

Between horse and master the closest comradeship seemed to exist; the trooper had a way of softly singing or talking to his friend as he rubbed him down, and Mr Billings was struck with the expression and taste with which the little soldier—for he was only five feet five—would render 'Molly Bawn' and 'Kitty Tyrrell.' Except when thus singing or exchanging confidences with his steed, he was strangely silent and reserved; he ate his rations among the other men, yet rarely spoke with them, and he would ride all day through country marvellous for wild beauty and be the only man in the command who did not allow himself to give vent to some expression of astonishment or delight.

'What is that man's name?' asked Mr Billings of the first sergeant one evening.

'O'Grady, sir,' replied the sergeant, with his soldierly salute; and a little later, as Captain Buxton was fretfully complaining to his subaltern of the ill fortune that seemed to overshadow his best efforts, the latter, thinking to cheer him and to divert his attention from his trouble, referred to the troop:

'Why, captain, I don't think I ever saw a finer set of men than you have—anywhere. Now, *there's* a little fellow who strikes me as being a perfect light-cavalry soldier.' And the lieutenant indicated his young Irishman.

'You don't mean O'Grady?' asked the captain in surprise.

'Yes, sir,—the very one.'

'Why, he's the worst man in the troop.'

For a moment Mr Billings knew not what to say. His captain had spoken with absolute harshness and dislike in his tone of the one soldier of all others who seemed to be the most quiet, attentive, and alert of the troop. He had noticed, too, that the sergeants and the men generally, in speaking to O'Grady, were wont to fall into a kindlier tone than usual, and, though they sometimes squabbled among themselves over the choice of patches of grass for their horses, O'Grady's claim was never questioned, much less 'jumped.' Respect for his superior's rank would not permit the lieutenant to argue the matter; but, desiring to know more about the case, he spoke again:

'I am very sorry to hear it. His care of his horse and his quiet ways impressed me so favourably.'

'Oh, yes, d—n him!' broke in Captain Buxton. 'Horses and whiskey are the only things on earth he cares for. As to quiet ways, there isn't a worse devil at large than O'Grady with a few drinks in him. When I came back from two years' recruiting detail he was a sergeant in the troop. I never knew him before, but I soon found he was addicted to drink, and after a while had to 'break' him; and one night when he was raising hell in the quarters, and I ordered him into the dark cell, he turned on me like a tiger. By Jove! if it hadn't been for some of the men he would have killed me,—or I him. He was tried by court-martial, but most of the detail was made up of infantrymen and staff-officers from Crook's head-quarters, and, by—! they didn't seem to think it any sin for a soldier to threaten to cut his captain's heart out, and Crook himself gave me a sort of a rap in his remarks on the case, and—well, they just let O'Grady off scot-free between them, gave him some little fine, and did more harm than good. He's just as surly and insolent now when I speak to him as he was that night when drunk. Here, I'll show you.' And with that Captain Buxton started off towards the herd, Mr Billings obediently following, but feeling vaguely ill at ease. He had never met Captain Buxton before, but letters from his comrades had prepared him for experiences not altogether pleasant. A good soldier in some respects, Captain Buxton bore the reputation of having an almost ungovernable temper, of being at times brutally violent in his language and conduct towards his men, and, worse yet, of bearing ill-concealed malice, and 'nursing his wrath to keep it warm' against such of his enlisted men as had ever ventured to appeal for justice. The captain stopped on reaching the outskirts of the quietly-grazing herd.

'Corporal,' said he to the non-commissioned officer in charge, 'isn't that O'Grady's horse off there to the left?'

'Yes, sir.'

'Go and tell O'Grady to come here.'

The corporal saluted and went off on his errand.

'Now, Mr Billings,' said the captain, 'I have repeatedly given orders that my horses must be side-lined when we are in the hostiles' country. Just come here to the left.' And he walked over towards a handsome, sturdy little California horse of a bright bay colour. 'Here, you see, is O'Grady's horse, and not a side-line: that's his way of obeying orders. More than that, he is never content to have his horse in among the others, but must always get away outside, just where he is most apt to be run off by any Indian sharp and quick enough to dare it. Now, here comes O'Grady. Watch him, if you want to see him in his true light.'

Standing beside his superior, Mr Billings looked towards the approaching trooper, who, with a quick, springy step, advanced to within a few yards of them, then stopped short and, erect and in silence, raised his hand in salute, and with perfectly respectful demeanour looked straight at his captain.

In a voice at once harsh and distinctly audible over the entire bivouac, with frowning brow and angry eyes, Buxton demanded,—

'O'Grady, where are your side-lines?'

'Over with my blankets, sir.'

'Over with your blankets, are they? Why in—, sir, are they

not here on your horse, where they ought to be?' And the captain's voice waxed harsher and louder, and his manner more threatening.

'I understood the captain's orders to be that they need not go on till sunset,' replied the soldier, calmly and respectfully, 'and I don't like to put them on that sore place, sir, until the last moment.'

'Don't like to? No sir, I know d——d well you don't like to obey this or any other order I ever gave, and wherever you find a loop-hole through which to crawl, and you think you can sneak off unpunished, by——, sir, I suppose you will go on disobeying orders. Shut up, sir! not a d——d word!' for tears of mortification were starting to O'Grady's eyes, and with flushing face and trembling lip the soldier stood helplessly before his troop-commander, and was striving to say a word in further explanation.

'Go and get your side-lines at once and bring them here; go at once, sir,' shouted the captain; and with a lump in his throat the trooper saluted, faced about, and walked away.

'He's milder-mannered than usual, d——n him!' said the captain, turning towards his subaltern, who had stood a silent and pained witness of the scene. 'He knows he is in the wrong and has no excuse; but he'll break out yet. Come! step out, you O'Grady!' he yelled after the rapidly-walking soldier. 'Double time, sir. I can't wait here all night.' And Mr Billings noted that silence had fallen on the bivouac so full of soldier-chaff and laughter but a moment before, and that the men of both troops were intently watching the scene already so painful to him.

Obediently O'Grady took up the 'dog-trot' required of him, got his side-lines, and, running back, knelt beside his horse, and with trembling hands adjusted them, during which performance Captain Buxton stood over him, and, in a tone that grew more and more that of a bully as he lashed himself up into a rage, continued his lecture to the man.

The latter finally rose, and, with huge beads of perspiration starting out on his forehead, faced his captain.

'May I say a word, sir?' he asked.

'You may now; but be d—d careful how you say it,' was the reply, with a sneer that would have stung an abject slave into a longing for revenge, and that grated on Mr Billings's nerves in a way that made him clinch his fists and involuntarily grit his teeth. Could it be that O'Grady detected it? One quick, wistful, half-appealing glance flashed from the Irishman's eyes towards the subaltern, and then, with evident effort at composure, but with a voice that trembled with the pent-up sense of wrong and injustice, O'Grady spoke:

'Indeed, sir, I had no thought of neglecting orders. I always care for my horse; but it wasn't sunset when the captain came out—'

'Not sunset!' broke in Buxton, with an outburst of profanity. 'Not sunset! why, it's well-nigh dark now, sir, and every man in the troop had side-lined his horse half an hour ago. D—n your insolence, sir! your excuse is worse than your conduct. Mr Billings, see to it, sir, that this man walks and leads his horse in rear of the troop all the way back to the post. I'll see, by—! whether he can be taught to obey orders.' And with that the captain turned and strode away.

The lieutenant stood for an instant stunned,—simply stunned. Involuntarily he made a step towards O'Grady; their eyes met; but the restraint of discipline was upon both. In that brief meeting of their glances, however, the trooper read a message that was unmistakable.

'Lieutenant—' he said, but stopped abruptly, pointed aloft over the trees to the eastward with his right hand, dashed it across his eyes, and then, with hurried salute and a choking sort of gurgle in his throat, he turned and went back to his comrades.

Mr Billings gazed after the retreating form until it disappeared among the trees by the brook-side; then he turned to see what was the meaning of the soldier's pointing over towards the *mesa* to the east.

Down in the deep valley in which the little command had halted for the night the pall of darkness had indeed begun to settle; the bivouac-fires in the timber threw a lurid glare upon the groups gathering around them for supper, and towards the west the rugged upheavals of the Mazatzal range stood like a black barrier against the glorious hues of a bank of summer cloud. All in the valley spoke of twilight and darkness: the birds were still, the voices of the men subdued. So far as local indications were concerned, it *was*—as Captain Buxton had insisted—almost dark. But square over the gilded tree-tops to the east, stretching for miles and miles to their right and left, blazed a vertical wall of rock crested with scrub-oak and pine, every boulder, every tree, glittering in the radiant light of the invisibly setting sun. O'Grady had *not* disobeyed his orders.

Noting this, Mr Billings proceeded to take a leisurely stroll through the peaceful herd, carefully inspecting each horse as he passed. As a result of his scrutiny, he found that, while most of the horses were already encumbered with their annoying hobble, in 'A' Troop alone there were at least a dozen still unfettered, notably the mounts of the non-commissioned officers and the older soldiers. Like O'Grady, they did not wish to inflict the side-line upon their steeds until the last moment. Unlike O'Grady, they had not been called to account for it.

When Mr Billings was summoned to supper, and he rejoined his brother-officers, it was remarked that he was more taciturn than usual. After that repast had been appreciatively disposed of, and the little group with lighted pipes prepared to spend an hour in chat and contentment, it was observed that Mr Billings did not take part in the general talk, but that he soon rose, and, out of ear-shot of the officers' camp-fire, paced restlessly up and down, with his head bent forward, evidently plunged in thought.

By and by the half-dozen broke up and sought their blankets. Captain Buxton, somewhat mollified by a good supper, was about rolling into his 'Navajo,' when Mr Billings stepped up:

'Captain, may I ask for information as to the side-line order? After you left this evening, I found that there must be some misunderstanding about it.'

'How so?' said Buxton, shortly.

'In this, captain;' and Mr Billings spoke very calmly and distinctly. 'The first sergeant, several other non-commissioned officers and men,—more than a dozen, I should say,—did not side-line their horses until half an hour after you spoke to O'Grady, and the first sergeant assured me, when I called him to account for it, that your orders were that it should be done at sunset.'

'Well, by—! it was after sunset—at least it was getting mighty dark—when I sent for that black-guard O'Grady,' said Buxton, impetuously, 'and there is no excuse for the rest of them.'

'It was beginning to grow dark down in this deep valley, I know, sir; but the tree-tops were in a broad glare of sunlight while we were at the herd, and those cliffs for half an hour longer.'

'Well, Mr Billings, I don't propose to have any hair-splitting in the management of my troop,' said the captain, manifestly nettled. 'It was practically sunset to us when the light began to grow dim, and my men know it well enough.' And with that he rolled over and turned his back to his subaltern.

Disregarding the broad hint to leave, Mr Billings again spoke:

'Is it your wish, sir, that any punishment should be imposed on the men who were equally in fault with O'Grady?'

Buxton muttered something unintelligible from under his blankets.

'I did not understand you, sir,' said the lieutenant, very civilly.

Buxton savagely propped himself up on one elbow, and blurted out,—

'No, Mr Billings! no! When I want a man punished I'll give the order myself, sir.'

'And is it still your wish, sir, that I make O'Grady walk the rest of the way?'

For a moment Buxton hesitated; his better nature struggled to assert itself and induce him to undo the injustice of his order; but the 'cad' in his disposition, the weakness of his character, prevailed. It would never do to let his lieutenant get the upper hand of him, he argued, and so the reply came, and came angrily.

'Yes, of course; he deserves it anyhow, by—! and it'll do him good.'

Without another word Mr Billings turned on his heel and left him.

The command returned to garrison, shaved its stubbly beard of two weeks' growth, and resumed its uniform and the routine duties of the post. Three days only had it been back when Mr Billings, marching on as officer of the day, and receiving the prisoners from his predecessor, was startled to hear the list of names wound up with 'O'Grady,' and when that name was called there was no response.

The old officer of the day looked up inquiringly: 'Where is O'Grady, sergeant?'

'In the cell, sir, unable to come out.'

'O'Grady was confined by Captain Buxton's order late last night,' said Captain Wayne, 'and I fancy the poor fellow has been drinking heavily this time.'

A few minutes after, the reliefs being told off, the prisoners sent out to work, and the officers of the day, new and old, having made their reports to the commanding officer, Mr Billings returned to the guard-house, and, directing his sergeant to accompany him, proceeded to make a deliberate inspection of the premises. The guard-room itself was neat, clean, and dry; the garrison prison-room was well ventilated, and tidy as such rooms ever can be made; the

Indian prison-room, despite the fact that it was empty and every shutter was thrown wide open to the breeze, had that indefinable, suffocating odour which continued aboriginal occupancy will give to any apartment; but it was the cells Mr Billings desired to see, and the sergeant led him to a row of heavily-barred doors of rough unplaned timber, with a little grating in each, and from one of these gratings there peered forth a pair of feverishly-glittering eyes, and a face, not bloated and flushed, as with recent and heavy potations, but white, haggard, twitching, and a husky voice in piteous appeal addressed the sergeant:

'Oh, for God's sake, Billy, get me something, or it'll kill me!'

'Hush, O'Grady,' said the sergeant: 'here's the officer of the day.'

Mr Billings took one look at the wan face only dimly visible in that prison-light, for the poor little man shrank back as he recognized the form of his lieutenant:

'Open that door, sergeant.'

With alacrity the order was obeyed, and the heavy door swung back upon its hinges.

'O'Grady,' said the officer of the day, in a tone gentle as that he would have employed in speaking to a woman, 'come out here to me. I'm afraid you are sick.'

Shaking, trembling, twitching in every limb, with wild, dilated eyes and almost palsied step, O'Grady came out.

'Look to him a moment, sergeant,' said Mr Billings, and, bending low, he stepped into the cell. The atmosphere was stifling, and in another instant he backed out into the hall-way. 'Sergeant, was it by the commanding officer's order that O'Grady was put in there?'

'No, sir; Captain Buxton's.'

'See that he is not returned there during my tour, unless the orders come from Major Stannard. Bring O'Grady into the prison-room.'

Here in the purer air and brighter light he looked carefully over the poor fellow, as the latter stood before him quivering from head to foot and hiding his face in his shaking hands. Then the lieutenant took him gently by the arm and led him to a bunk:

'O'Grady, man, lie down here. I'm going to get something that will help you. Tell me one thing: how long had you been drinking before you were confined?'

'About forty-eight hours, sir, off and on.'

'How long since you ate anything?'

'I don't know, sir; not for two days, I think.'

'Well, try and lie still. I'm coming back to you in a very few minutes.'

And with that Mr Billings strode from the room, leaving O'Grady, dazed, wonder-stricken, gazing stupidly after him.

The lieutenant went straight to his quarters, took a goodly-sized goblet from the painted pine sideboard, and with practised hand proceeded to mix therein a beverage in which granulated sugar, Angostura bitters, and a few drops of lime-juice entered as minor ingredients, and the coldest of spring-water and a brimming measure of whiskey as constituents of greater quality and quantity. Filling with this mixture a small leather-covered flask, and stowing it away within the breast-pocket of his blouse, he returned to the guard-house, musing as he went, '"If this be treason," said Patrick Henry, "make the most of it." If this be conduct prejudicial, etc., say I, do your d—dest. That man would be in the horrors of jim-jams in half an hour more if it were not for this.' And so saying to himself, he entered the prison-room, called to the sergeant to bring him some cold water, and then approached O'Grady, who rose unsteadily and strove to stand attention, but the effort was too much, and again he covered his face with his arms, and threw himself in utter misery at the foot of the bunk.

Mr Billings drew the flask from his pocket, and, touching O'Grady's shoulder, caused him to raise his head:

'Drink this, my lad. I would not give it to you at another time, but you need it now.'

Eagerly it was seized, eagerly drained, and then, after he had swallowed a long draught of the water, O'Grady slowly rose to his feet, looking, with eyes rapidly softening and losing their wild glare, upon the young officer who stood before him. Once or twice he passed his hands across his forehead, as though to sweep away the cobwebs that pressed upon his brain, but for a moment he did not essay a word. Little by little the colour crept back to his cheek; and, noting this, Mr Billings smiled very quietly, and said, 'Now, O'Grady, lie down; you will be able to sleep now until the men come in at noon; then you shall have another drink, and you'll be able to eat what I send you. If you cannot sleep, call the sergeant of the guard; or if you want anything, I'll come to you.'

Then, with tears starting to his eyes, the soldier found words: 'I thank the lieutenant. If I live a thousand years, sir, this will never be forgotten,—never, sir! I'd have gone crazy without your help, sir.'

Mr Billings held out his hand, and, taking that of his prisoner, gave it a cordial grip: 'That's all right, O'Grady. Try to sleep now, and we'll pull you through. Good-by, for the present.' And, with a heart lighter, somehow, than it had been of late, the lieutenant left.

At noon that day, when the prisoners came in from labour and the officer's of the day inspected their general condition before permitting them to go to their dinner, the sergeant of the guard informed him that O'Grady had slept quietly almost all the morning, but was then awake and feeling very much better, though still weak and nervous.

'Do you think he can walk over to my quarters?' asked Mr Billings.

'He will try it, sir, or anything the lieutenant wants him to try.'

'Then send him over in about ten minutes.'

Home once more, Mr Billings started a tiny blaze in his oil-stove, and soon had a kettle of water boiling merrily. Sharp to time a member of the guard tapped at the door, and, on being bidden 'Come in,' entered, ushering in O'Grady; but meantime, by the aid of a little pot of meat-juice and some cayenne pepper, a glass of hot soup or beef-tea had been prepared, and, with some dainty slices of potted chicken and the accompaniments of a cup of fragrant tea and some ship-biscuit, was in readiness on a little table in the back room.

Telling the sentinel to remain in the shade on the piazza, the lieutenant proceeded first to make O'Grady sit down in a big wicker arm-chair, for the man in his broken condition was well-nigh exhausted by his walk across the glaring parade in the heat of an Arizona noonday sun. Then he mixed and administered the counterpart of the beverage he had given his prisoner-patient in the morning, only in point of potency it was an evident falling off, but sufficient for the purpose, and in a few minutes O'Grady was able to swallow his breakfast with evident relish, meekly and unhesitatingly obeying every suggestion of his superior.

His breakfast finished, O'Grady was then conducted into a cool, darkened apartment, a back room in the lieutenant's quarters.

'Now, pull off your boots and outer clothing, man, spread yourself on that bed, and go to sleep, if you can. If you can't, and you want to read, there are books and papers on that shelf; pin up the blanket on the window, and you'll have light enough. You shall not be disturbed, and I know you won't attempt to leave.'

'Indeed, sir, I won't,' began O'Grady, eagerly; but the lieutenant had vanished, closing the door after him, and a minute later the soldier had thrown himself upon the cool, white bed, and was crying like a tired child.

Three or four weeks after this incident, to the small regret of his troop and the politely-veiled indifference of the commissioned element of the garrison, Captain Buxton concluded to avail himself of a long-deferred 'leave,' and turned over his company property to Mr Billings in a condition that rendered it necessary for him to do a thing that 'ground' him, so to speak: he had to ask several favours of his lieutenant, between whom and himself there had been no cordiality since the episode of the bivouac, and an open rupture since Mr Billings's somewhat eventful tour as officer of the day, which has just been described.

It appeared that O'Grady had been absent from no duty (there were no drills in that scorching June weather), but that, yielding to the advice of his comrades, who knew that he had eaten nothing for two days and was drinking steadily into a condition that would speedily bring punishment upon him, he had asked permission to be sent to the hospital, where, while he could get no liquor, there would be no danger attendant upon his sudden stop of all stimulant. The first sergeant carried his request with the sick-book to Captain Buxton, O'Grady meantime managing to take two or three more pulls at the bottle, and Buxton, instead of sending him to the hospital, sent for him, inspected him, and did what he had no earthly authority to do, directed the sergeant of the guard to confine him at once in the dark cell.

'It will be no punishment as he is now,' said Buxton to himself, 'but it will be hell when he wakes.'

And so it had been; and far worse it probably would have been but for Mr Billings's merciful interference.

Expecting to find his victim in a condition bordering upon the abject and ready to beg for mercy at any sacrifice of pluck or pride, Buxton had gone to the guard-house soon after retreat and told the sergeant that he desired to see O'Grady, if the man was fit to come out.

What was his surprise when the soldier stepped forth in his trimmest undress uniform, erect and steady, and stood unflinchingly before him!—a day's rest and quiet, a warm bath, wholesome and palatable food, careful nursing, and the kind treatment he had received having brought him round with a sudden turn that he himself could hardly understand.

'How is this?' thundered Buxton. 'I ordered you kept in the dark cell.'

'The officer of the day ordered him released, sir,' said the sergeant of the guard.

And Buxton, choking with rage, stormed into the mess-room, where the younger officers were at dinner, and, regardless of the time, place, or surroundings, opened at once upon his subaltern:

'Mr Billings, by whose authority did you release O'Grady from the dark cell?'

Mr Billings calmly applied his napkin to his moustache, and then as calmly replied, 'By my own, Captain Buxton.'

'By—! sir, you exceeded your authority.'

'Not at all, captain; on the contrary, you exceeded yours.'

At this Buxton flew into a rage that seemed to deprive him of all control over his language. Oaths and imprecations poured from his lips; he raved at Billings, despite the efforts of the officers to quiet him, despite the adjutant's threat to report his language at once to the commanding officer.

Mr Billings paid no attention whatever to his accusations, but went on eating his dinner with an appearance of serenity that only added fuel to his captain's fire. Two or three officers rose and left the table in disgust, and just how far the thing might have gone cannot be accurately told, for in less than three minutes there came a quick, bounding step on the piazza, the clank and rattle of a sabre, and the adjutant fairly sprang back into the room:

'Captain Buxton, you will go at once to your quarters in close arrest, by order of Major Stannard.'

Buxton knew his colonel and that little fire-eater of an

adjutant too well to hesitate an instant. Muttering imprecations on everybody, he went.

The next morning, O'Grady was released and returned to duty. Two days later, after a long and private interview with his commanding officer, Captain Buxton appeared with him at the officers' mess at dinner-time, made a formal and complete apology to Lieutenant Billings for his offensive language, and to the mess generally for his misconduct; and so the affair blew over; and, soon after, Buxton left, and Mr Billings became commander of Troop 'A.'

And now, whatever might have been his reputation as to sobriety before, Private O'Grady became a marked man for every soldierly virtue. Week after week he was to be seen every fourth or fifth day, when his guard tour came, reporting to the commanding officer for duty as 'orderly,' the nattiest, trimmest soldier on the detail.

'I always said,' remarked Captain Wayne, 'that Buxton alone was responsible for that man's downfall; and this proves it. O'Grady has all the instincts of a gentleman about him, and now that he has a gentleman over him he is himself again.'

One night, after retreat-parade, there was cheering and jubilee in the quarters of Troop 'A.' Corporal Quinn had been discharged by expiration of term of service, and Private O'Grady was decorated with his chevrons. When October came, the company muster-roll showed that he had won back his old grade; and the garrison knew no better soldier, no more intelligent, temperate, trustworthy non-commissioned officer, than Sergeant O'Grady. In some way or other the story of the treatment resorted to by his amateur medical officer had leaked out. Whether faulty in theory or not, it was crowned with the verdict of success in practice; and, with the strong sense of humour which pervades all organizations wherein the Celt is represented as a component part, Mr Billings had been lovingly dubbed 'Doctor' by his men, and there was one of their number who would have gone through fire and water for him.

One night some herdsmen from up the valley galloped wildly into the post. The Apaches had swooped down, run off their cattle, killed one of the cowboys, and scared off the rest. At daybreak the next morning Lieutenant Billings, with Troop 'A' and about a dozen Indian scouts, was on the trail, with orders to pursue, recapture the cattle, and punish the marauders.

To his disgust, Mr Billings found that his allies were not of the tribes who had served with him in previous expeditions. All the trusty Apache Mojaves and Hualpais were off with other commands in distant parts of the Territory. He had to take just what the agent could give him at the reservation,—some Apache Yumas, who were total strangers to him. Within forty-eight hours four had deserted and gone back; the others proved worthless as trailers, doubtless intentionally, and had it not been for the keen eye of Sergeant O'Grady it would have been impossible to keep up the pursuit by night; but keep it up they did, and just at sunset, one sharp autumn evening, away up in the mountains, the advance caught sight of the cattle grazing along the shores of a placid little lake, and, in less time than it takes to write it, Mr Billings and his command tore down upon the quarry, and, leaving a few men to 'round up' the herd, were soon engaged in a lively running fight with the fleeing Apaches which lasted until dark, when the trumpet sounded the recall, and, with horses somewhat blown, but no casualties of importance, the command reassembled and marched back to the grazing-ground by the lake. Here a hearty supper was served out, the horses were rested, then given a good 'feed' of barley, and at ten o'clock Mr Billings with his second lieutenant and some twenty men pushed ahead in the direction taken by the Indians, leaving the rest of the men under experienced non-commissioned officers to drive the cattle back to the valley.

That night the conduct of the Apache Yuma scouts was incomprehensible. Nothing would induce them to go ahead or out on the flanks; they cowered about the rear of column, yet declared that the enemy could not be hereabouts. At two in the morning Mr Billings found himself well through a pass in the mountains, high peaks rising to his right and left, and a broad valley in front. Here he gave the order to unsaddle and camp for the night.

At daybreak all were again on the alert: the search for the trail was resumed. Again the Indians refused to go out without the troops; but the men themselves found the tracks of Tonto moccasins along the bed of a little stream purling through the cañon, and presently indications that they had made the ascent of the mountain to the south. Leaving a guard with his horses and pack-mules, the lieutenant ordered up his men, and soon the little command was silently picking its way through rock and boulder, scrub-oak and tangled juniper and pine. Rougher and steeper grew the ascent; more and more the Indians cowered, huddling together in rear of the soldiers. Twice Mr Billings signalled a halt, and, with his sergeants, fairly drove the scouts up to the front and ordered them to hunt for signs. In vain they protested, 'No sign,—no Tonto here,' their very looks belied them, and the young commander ordered the search to be continued. In their eagerness the men soon leaped ahead of the wretched allies, and the latter fell back in the same huddled group as before.

After half an hour of this sort of work, the party came suddenly upon a point whence it was possible to see much of the face of the mountain they were scaling. Cautioning his men to keep within the concealment afforded by the thick timber, Mr Billings and his comrade-lieutenant crept forward and made a brief reconnoissance. It was evident at a glance that the farther they went the steeper grew the ascent and the more tangled the low shrubbery, for it was little better, until, near the summit, trees and underbrush, and herbage of every description, seemed to cease entirely, and a vertical cliff of jagged rocks stood sentinel at the crest, and stretched east and west the entire length of the face of the mountain.

'By Jove, Billings! if they are on top of that it will be a nasty place to rout them out of,' observed the junior.

'I'm going to find out where they are, anyhow,' replied the other. 'Now those infernal Yumas have *got* to scout, whether they want to or not. You stay here with the men, ready to come the instant I send or signal.'

In vain the junior officer protested against being left behind; he was directed to send a small party to see if there were an easier way up the hill-side farther to the west, but to keep the main body there in readiness to move whichever way they might be required. Then, with Sergeant O'Grady and the reluctant Indians, Mr Billings pushed up to the left front, and was soon out of sight of his command. For fifteen minutes he drove his scouts, dispersed in skirmish order, ahead of him, but incessantly they sneaked behind rocks and trees out of his sight; twice he caught them trying to drop back, and at last, losing all patience, he sprang forward, saying, 'Then *come* on, you whelps, if you cannot lead,' and he and the sergeant hurried ahead. Then the Yumas huddled together again and slowly followed.

Fifteen minutes more, and Mr Billings found himself standing on the edge of a broad shelf of the mountain,—a shelf covered with huge boulders of rock tumbled there by storm and tempest, riven by lightning-stroke or the slow disintegration of nature from the bare, glaring, precipitous ledge he had marked from below. East and west it seemed to stretch, forbidding and inaccessible. Turning to the sergeant, Mr Billings directed him to make his way off to the right and see if there were any possibility of finding a path to the summit; then looking back down the side, and marking his Indians cowering under the trees some fifty yards away, he signalled 'come up,' and was about moving farther to his left to explore the shelf, when something went whizzing past his head, and, embedding itself in a stunted oak behind him, shook and quivered with the shock,—a Tonto arrow. Only an instant did he see it, photographed as by electricity upon the retina, when with a sharp stinging pang and whirring 'whist' and thud a second arrow, better aimed, tore through the flesh and muscles just at the outer corner of his left eye, and glanced away down the hill. With one spring he gained the edge of the shelf, and shouted to the scouts to come on. Even as he did so, bang! bang! went the reports of two rifles among the rocks, and, as with one accord, the Apache Yumas turned tail and rushed back down the hill, leaving him alone in the midst of hidden foes. Stung by the arrow, bleeding, but not seriously hurt, he crouched behind a rock, with carbine at ready, eagerly looking for the first sign of an enemy. The whiz of another arrow from the left drew his eyes thither, and quick as a flash his weapon leaped to his shoulder, the rocks rang with its report, and one of the two swarthy forms he saw among the boulders tumbled over out of sight; but even as he threw back his piece to reload, a rattling volley greeted him, the carbine dropped to the ground, a strange, numbed sensation had seized his shoulder, and his right arm, shattered by a rifle-bullet, hung dangling by the flesh, while the blood gushed forth in a torrent.

Defenceless, he sprang back to the edge; there was nothing for it now but to run until he could meet his men. Well he knew they would be tearing up the mountain to the rescue. Could he hold out till then? Behind him with shout and yells came the Apaches, arrow and bullet whistling over his head; before him lay the steep descent,—jagged rocks, thick, tangled bushes: it was a desperate chance; but he tried it, leaping from rock to rock, holding his helpless arm in his left hand; then his foot slipped: he plunged heavily forward; quickly the nerves threw out their signal for support to the muscles of the shattered member, but its work was done, its usefulness destroyed. Missing its support, he plunged heavily forward, and went crashing down among the rocks eight or ten feet below, cutting a jagged gash in his forehead, while the blood rained down into his eyes and blinded him; but he struggled up and on a few yards more; then another fall, and, well-nigh senseless, utterly exhausted, he lay groping for his revolver,—it had fallen from its case. Then—all was over.

Not yet; not yet. His ear catches the sound of a voice he knows well,—a rich, ringing, Hibernian voice it is: 'Lieutenant, *lieutenant*! *Where* are ye?' and he has strength enough to call, 'This way, sergeant, this way,' and in another moment O'Grady, with blended anguish and gratitude in his face, is bending over him. 'Oh, thank God you're not kilt, sir!' (for when excited O'Grady *would* relapse into the brogue); 'but are ye much hurt?'

'Badly, sergeant, since I can't fight another round.'

'Then put your arm round my neck, sir,' and in a second the little Patlander has him on his brawny back. But with only one arm by which to steady himself, the other hanging loose, the torture is inexpressible, for O'Grady is now bounding down the hill, leaping like a goat from rock to rock, while the Apaches with savage yells come tearing after them. Twice, pausing, O'Grady lays his lieutenant down in the shelter of some large boulder, and, facing about, sends shot after shot up the hill, checking the pursuit and driving the cowardly footpads to cover. Once he gives vent to a genuine Kilkenny 'hurroo' as a tall Apache drops his rifle and plunges head foremost among the rocks with his hands convulsively clasped to his breast. Then the sergeant once more picks up his wounded comrade, despite pleas, orders, or imprecations, and rushes on.

'I cannot stand it, O'Grady. Go and save yourself. You *must* do it. I *order* you to do it.' Every instant the shots and arrows whiz closer, but the sergeant never winces, and at last, panting, breathless, having carried his chief full three hundred yards down the rugged slope, he gives out entirely, but with a gasp of delight points down among the trees:

'Here come the boys, sir.'

Another moment, and the soldiers are rushing up the rocks beside them, their carbines ringing like merry music through the frosty air, and the Apaches are scattering in every direction.

'Old man, are you much hurt?' is the whispered inquiry his brother-officer can barely gasp for want of breath, and, reassured by the faint grin on Mr Billings's face, and a barely audible 'Arm busted,—that's all; pitch in and use them up,' he pushes on with his men.

In ten minutes the affair is ended. The Indians have been swept away like chaff; the field and the wounded they have abandoned are in the hands of the troopers; the young commander's life is saved; and then, and for long after, the hero of the day is Buxton's *bête noire*, 'the worst man in the troop.'

37

THE FATE OF 'NANA SAHIB'S ENGLISHMAN'

Archibald Forbes

One fine evening in September 1856, young Mr Kidson entered Escobel Castle by the great front door, and was hurrying across the hall on his way to the passage leading to his own apartments, when his worthy old mother, who had seen from her parlour window her son approach the house, ran out into the hall to meet him in a state of great agitation. It was little wonder that the aspect the young man presented excited the good creature's maternal emotion. The region around his right optic was so puffed and inflamed as to give the surest promise of a black eye of the first magnitude in the course of a few hours; to say that his nose was simply 'bashed' is very inadequately to describe the condition of that feature; his lower lip was split and streaming with blood; and he carried in his left hand a couple of front teeth which had been forcibly dislodged from their normal position in his upper jaw. He was bareheaded, and he carried on his clothes enough red clay to constitute him an eligible investment on the part of an enterprising brickmaker. 'Guid be here, my ain laddie!' wailed the poor mother in her unmitigated Glasgow Doric, 'what's come tae you? Wha has massacred my son this fearsome bloodthirsty gait?' 'Oh, hang it!' was the genial youth's sole acknowledgment of the maternal grief and sympathy, as, dodging her outstretched arms, he slunk to his rooms and rang vehemently for hot water and a raw beef-steak.

Young Mr Kidson's parents were brand-new rich Glasgow folks, who in their old age of vast wealth had recently bought the Highland estate of Escobel, in the hope to gratify Mr Kidson senior's ambition to gain social recognition as a country gentleman and to become the founder of a family, an aspiration in which he received but feeble assistance from his simple old wife, who had a tender corner in her memory for the Guse-Dubs in which she was born. Their only son, the hero of the puffed eye and the 'bashed' nose, had been ignominiously sent down from Oxford while yet a freshman. At present he was supposed to be doing a little desultory reading in view of entering the army; in reality he was spending most of his time in boozing with grooms and gamekeepers in a low shebeen. A downright bad lot, this young Mr Kidson, of whom, in the nature of things, nothing but evil could come.

While he was skulking into the privacy of his 'den,' an extremely pretty girl was sobbing convulsively on the breast of a stalwart fair-haired young fellow, whose eyes were flashing wrath, whose face still had an angry flush, and the knuckles of whose right hand were cut open, the blood trickling unheeded down the weeping girl's white dress. She, Mary Fraser, was the daughter of the clergyman of the parish; the young man, by name Sholto Mackenzie, was the orphan nephew of the old laird of Kinspiel, a small hill-property on the mountain slope. The two were sweethearts, and small chance was there of their ever being anything more. For Kinspiel was strictly entailed, and the old laird, who was so ill that he might die any day, had a son who had sons of his own, and was in no position, if he had the will, to help on his dead sister's manchild. Mary Fraser and Sholto Mackenzie had trysted to meet this evening in the accustomed pine glade on the edge of the heather. The girl was there before the time. Young Mr Kidson, listlessly smoking as he lounged on a turf bank, caught a glimpse of her dress through the trees, and promptly bore down on her. There was a slight acquaintance, and she returned his greeting, supposing that he would pass on. But he did not—on the contrary, he waxed fluent in coarse flatteries, and suddenly grasping the girl in his arms was making strenuous efforts to snatch kisses from her, undeterred by her struggles and shrieks. At this crisis Sholto Mackenzie, hearing the cries, came running up at the top of his speed. Young Mr Kidson, fancying himself a bit as a man who could use his fists, had not the poor grace to run away. While the girl leant half fainting against a tree there was a brief pugilistic encounter between the young men, as the issue of which Mr Kidson was disabused of a misconception, and presented the aspect which a few minutes later brought tribulation to his mother. As he carried himself and his damages off, he muttered through his pulped lips with a fierce oath that the day would come when his antagonist should rue the evening's work. Whereat the antagonist laughed contemptuously, and addressed himself to the pleasant task of calming and consoling his agitated sweetheart.

Before the grouse season closed the old laird of Kinspiel was a dead man, and there was no longer a home for Sholto Mackenzie in the quaint old crow-stepped house in the upland glen among the bracken. What career was open to the penniless young fellow? He had no interest for a cadetship, and that Indian service in which so many men of his race have earned name and fame was not for him. In those days there was no Manitoba, no ranching in Texas or Wyoming; the Cape gave no opportunities, the Argentine was not yet a resort for English youth of enterprise, and he had not money enough to take him to the Australian gold-diggings or to the sheep-runs of New Zealand. He saw no resource but to offer himself to the Queen's service in the capacity of a private soldier, in the hope that education, good conduct, and fervent zeal would bring him promotion and perhaps distinction. By the advice of a local pensioner he journeyed to

London and betook himself to the metropolitan recruiting centre in Charles Street, Westminster. No Sergeants Kite now patrol that thoroughfare in quest of lawful prey; nay, the little street with its twin public-house headquarters is itself a thing of the past. About the centre of the long wooden shanty recently built for the purposes of the census, stood the old 'Hampshire Hog,' with its villainous *rendezvous* in the rear; nearer the Park on the opposite side, just where is now the door of the India Office, the 'Cheshire Cheese' reared its frowsy front. In the days I am writing of, recruits accepted or had foisted on them the 'Queen's Shilling,' received a bounty, gave themselves for twenty-four years' service, and were escorted by a staff-sergeant to their respective regiments. Now there is neither Queen's shilling nor bounty, and the recruit, furnished with a travelling warrant, is his own escort to Ballincollig or Fort George. What scenes had dingy Charles Street witnessed in its day! How much sin and sorrow; too late remorse, too late forgiveness! In many a British household has Charles Street been cursed with bitter curses; yet has it not been, in a sense, the cradle of heroes? It sent to battle the men whose blood dyed the sward of the Balaclava valley; it fed the trenches of Sebastopol; it was the sieve through whose meshes passed the staunch warriors who stormed Delhi and who defended Lucknow, who bled and conquered at Sobraon and Goojerat.

Sholto Mackenzie had eaten Queen Victoria's rations for some six months, had been dismissed recruits' drill, and become a duty soldier, when the order was issued that the '30th Light,' the regiment into which he had enlisted, was to go out for its turn of service in India, and of course the young soldier went with his regiment. Those were the days before big Indian troopships and the Suez Canal; reinforcements for India went out round the Cape. Sholto's troop was accompanied by two married women who were on the strength of the regiment. Nowadays the soldier's wife adorns her room in the married quarters with cheap Liberty hangings, and walks out in French boots and kid gloves. Mrs Macgregor and Mrs Malony lived each her married life and reared her family in a bunk in the corner of the troop-room of which she had the 'looking after.' Such a life seems one of sheer abomination and barbarism, does it not? Yet the arrangement had the surprising effect, in most instances, of bringing about a certain decency, self-restraint, and genuinely human feeling alike in the men and the married woman of the room. Neither Mrs Macgregor nor Mrs Malony had ever been abroad before; and both evinced a strong propensity to take with them copious mementoes of their native land. Mrs Macgregor, honest woman, had manifested that concentrativeness which is a feature in the character of the nation to which, as her name indicated, she belonged. She had packed into a great piece of canvas sheeting a certain feather-bed, which, as an heirloom from her remote ancestors, she was fond of boasting of when the other matrons were fain to sew together a couple of regimental palliasse covers, and stuff the same with straw. In the capacious bosom of this family relic she had stowed a variety of minor articles, among which were a wash-hand jug of some primeval earthenware, a hoary whisky decanter—which, trust Mrs Macgregor, was quite empty—a cradle, sundry volumes of Gaelic literature, and a small assortment of cooking utensils. Over those collected properties stood grimly watchful the tall, gaunt woman with the grey eye, the Roman nose, and the cautious taciturnity. Of another stamp was Mrs Malony, a little, slatternly, pock-marked Irishwoman. Her normal condition was that of a nursing-mother—nobody could remember the time when Biddy Malony had not a brat hanging at that bosom of hers which she was wont partially to conceal by an old red woollen kerchief. Biddy was a merry soul, spite of many a trial and many a cross—always ready with a flash of Irish humour, just as ready as she always was for a glass of gin. She had not attempted the methodical packing of her goods and chattels, but had bundled them together anyhow in a chaotic state. Her great difficulty was her inability to perform the difficult operation of carrying her belongings 'in her head,' and after she had pitchforked into the baggage-van a quantity of incongruous *débris*, she was still in a bewildered way questing after a wicker bird-cage and 'a few other little throifles.'

Embarking along with his comrades and reaching the main deck of the troopship, Sholto found the two ladies already there—Mrs Macgregor grimly defiant, not to say fierce, in consequence of a request just made to her by a sailor for a glass of grog; Mrs Malony in a semi-hysterical state, having lost a shoe, a wash-tub, and, she much feared, one of the young Malonys. Matters were improved, however, when Sholto found the young bog-trotter snugly squatted in the cows' manger. The shoe was gone hopelessly, having fallen into the water when its wearer was mounting the gangway; and Mrs Malony happily remembered that she had made a present of the missing wash-tub to a 'green-grosher's lady' in the town of embarkation.

Sholto had been made lance-corporal soon after the troopship sailed, and served in that rank during the long voyage with so much credit that when the regiment reached Bangalore the colonel of the 30th Light gave him the second stripe, so that he was full corporal in less than a year after he had enlisted. During a turn of guard duty about three months after he joined at Bangalore, he happened to hear it mentioned in the guard-room that a new officer—a cornet—had arrived that day, and had been posted to the vacancy in the troop to which Sholto belonged. The new-comer's name was not stated, and beyond a cursory hope that he would turn out a good and smart officer, Corporal Mackenzie gave no further heed to the matter. Late the same night, he was relieving the sentry on the mess-house post when the merry party of officers broke up. Laughing and chatting they came out under the verandah, a little more noisy than usual, no doubt because of the customary 'footing' in champagne paid by the new arrival. As they passed Sholto, a voice caught his ear—an unfamiliar voice, yet that stirred in him an angry memory; and as the officers lounged past him in the moonlight, he gazed into the group with earnest inquisitiveness. Arm and arm between two subalterns, his face inflamed with drink, his mouth full of slang, rolled the man he had thrashed among the Scottish pines. As he grinned his horse-laugh Sholto discerned the vacuum in his upper teeth which his fist had made that evening; and now this man was his officer. The eyes of the two met, and Kidson gave a sudden start and seemed about to speak, but controlling the impulse, he smiled a silent smile, the triumphant insolence of which stung Sholto bitterly. Verily his enemy was his master; and Sholto read the man's nature too truly not to be sure that he would forgo no jot of the sweet revenge of humiliation.

Very soon the orderly sergeant of the troop fell unwell, and Sholto had to take up his duty, one detail of which was to carry the order-book round to the bungalows of the troop-officers for their information. This duty entailed on Sholto the disagreeable necessity of a daily interview with Mr Kidson. That officer took the opportunity of throwing every imaginable slight on the corporal, but was careful not to give warrant for any specific complaint. But it was very bitter to be kept standing at attention for some ten minutes at a time, orderly book in hand, until Mr Kidson thought fit to lay aside his book, or to desist from pulling his terrier's ears. Often the cornet was in his bedroom; and while waiting for his appearance Sholto noticed how ostentatiously careless his officer was as to his valuables—a handful of money or a gold watch and chain left lying on the table amid spurs and gloves and soda-water bottles.

The morning after an exceptionally long wait for Mr Kidson's emergence from his bedroom, Sholto was returning from the horse lines when the regimental sergeant-major met him and ordered him to his room under arrest. In utter bewilderment he begged for some explanation, but without success. When he reached his cot, he casually noticed that his box was open and the lock damaged, but he was too disturbed to give heed to this circumstance. Presently a sergeant came and escorted him to the orderly room. Here he found the colonel sitting in the windsor arm-chair with the discipline book open before him, the adjutant standing behind him, and on the flank Mr Kidson and the sergeant-major of his own troop. The colonel, if a stern, was a just man; and in a grave tone he expressed his concern that so heinous a charge should come against a young soldier of character hitherto so creditable. Sholto replied that he had not the remotest idea what the nature of the charge was. The old chief shot a keen glance at him as he spoke—

'Corporal Mackenzie, you are accused of stealing a gold watch and chain, the property of Mr Kidson. What have you to say to this charge?'

The lad's head swam, and for a moment he thought he was going to faint. Then the blood came back to his heart and flushed up into his face as he looked the colonel straight between the eyes and answered—

'It is a wicked falsehood, sir!'

'Then of course you deny it?'

'I do, sir, if it were the last word I had to say on earth!'

'Mr Kidson,' said the old soldier in a dry business tone, 'will you state what you know about this matter?'

Thus enjoined, Kidson briefly and with a certain nervous glibness stated that after Corporal Mackenzie had left his quarters on the previous afternoon, he had missed his watch and chain. That morning he had renewed the search unsuccessfully. He had previous suspicions of Corporal Mackenzie having from time to time stolen money from off his table. He had reported the matter to his troop sergeant-major, who had at once searched

Corporal Mackenzie's kit, with what result the sergeant-major would himself state.

The sergeant-major for his part had only to testify that having been spoken to by Mr Kidson on the subject of his loss, he had taken another sergeant-major with him, and searched Corporal Mackenzie's box, where he had found the missing watch and chain, which he had at once handed to the adjutant, who now held it.

The evidence was strong enough to hang a man.

'Corporal Mackenzie,' said the colonel, with some concern, 'the case seems very clear. What you have to say, if anything, you must say elsewhere. It is my duty to send you back for a district court-martial.'

Sholto was confined in a room adjacent to the quarter-guard for a few days, when he was brought before the court-martial, which heard the evidence against the prisoner, to whom then was given the opportunity to cross-examine the witnesses. But the president would not allow interrogations tending to establish animus on Mr Kidson's part against the prisoner, and finally poor Sholto lost his temper, and exclaimed with passion—

'Your permission to cross-examine is nothing better than a farce!'

'Perhaps,' retorted the president, with a grim smile,—'perhaps you may not think the punishment which will probably befall you a farce!'

Sholto's defence was in a sentence—the assertion of his complete innocence. He had known Mr Kidson in other days, he said, when as yet both were civilians, and they had parted in bad blood.

A member of the court demanded that Mr Kidson should have the opportunity of contradicting this assertion, if in his power to do so; whereupon that officer emphatically swore that to his knowledge he had never seen Corporal Mackenzie in his life before he joined the 30th Light there in Bangalore. So Sholto was put back to wait for many days while the finding of the court-martial was being submitted to the Commander-in-Chief.

One evening Mick Sullivan his comrade brought him his tea as usual—the good fellow never would let the mat-boy carry his chum his meals. He stood looking at Sholto for a while with a strange concern in his honest face; and then he broke silence—

'Sholto, me lad, it's me heart is sore for you this day. Yer coort-martial will be read out to-morrow morning! Aye, and—and'—his voice sank into a whisper—'the farrier-major has got the ordhers for to rig the thriangles. It's to be flogged ye are, my poor fellow!'

Sholto sent his chum away abruptly; he could not talk, he could hardly think; all he could do was to wish himself dead and spared this unutterable shame. Death came not, but instead the morning; and with the morning came Mick with a copious dose of brandy, which he entreated his comrade to drink, for it would 'stun the pain.' 'Every fellow,' he argued, 'primed himself so before a flogging, and why shouldn't he?'

But Sholto refused to fortify himself with Dutch courage; and then poor Mick produced his last evidence of affection in the shape of a leaden bullet which he had beaten flat, and which held tight between the teeth, he knew from personal experience, was a great help in enabling a fellow to resist 'hollerin' out.'

Presently the escort fell in and marched the prisoner to the riding-school. Sholto found there two troops of the regiment drawn up, in front of them a knot of officers, among whom he noticed Mr Kidson, and in front of them again the colonel, with the court-martial documents in his hand. The lad's eye took in the doctor, the farriers—each with his cat—and the triangle rigged against the wall under the gallery. The sergeant of the escort ordered him to take two paces to the front, remove his cap, and stand at attention. And so he stood, outwardly calm, waiting for his sentence.

'Proceedings of a district court-martial'—the colonel began, reading in a loud voice from the scroll in his hand. To Sholto the document seemed interminable. At last the end came. 'The Court, having considered the evidence brought before it, finds the prisoner, No. 420, Corporal Sholto Mackenzie, G troop, Thirtieth Light Dragoons, guilty of the said charge of theft, and does hereby sentence the said prisoner to be reduced to the rank and pay of a private dragoon'—here the colonel paused for a moment and then added—'and further to undergo the punishment of fifty lashes.'

The regimental sergeant-major strode up to Sholto, with a penknife ripped the gold lace corporal stripes from the arm of his jacket, and threw them down on the tan. Then the colonel's stern cold voice uttered the word 'Strip.' There was a little momentary bustle, and then Sholto was half hanging, half standing, lashed by the wrists and ankles to the triangles, while the farrier-major stood measuring his distance, fingering the whip-cords of his 'cat,' and waiting for the word 'Begin'!

Suddenly a wild shriek pealed through the great building from the gallery above the head of the man fastened up there to be flogged.

'Arrah musha, colonel dear!' followed in shrill accents—'for the love of the Holy Jasus and the blissed Vargin, hould yer hand, and spare an innocent man! I tell ye he's as innocent as the babe unborn, and it's mesilf, Bridget Malony, an honest married woman on the strength, that can pruve that same! Ochone, colonel dear, listen to me, won't yez?'

All eyes were concentrated on the little gallery. It was a sort of gazebo, built out from the wall at the height of about ten feet, and the only access to it was from outside. Bending eagerly over the rail, attired in nothing but a petticoat and a chemise, her hair streaming wildly over her shoulders, and with a round bare place like a tonsure on the crown of her head, which gave her a most extraordinary appearance, was visible Mrs Malony. She had been struck down by a sunstroke the day Sholto was put under arrest, and had been in hospital ever since.

The general opinion was that the good woman was crazy: but Mrs Malony knew her own mind—she had something to say, and she was determined to say it. She had just finished her wild appeal to the colonel, when she cast a hurried glance over her shoulder, and then, indifferently clad as she was, nimbly climbed over the rail, and dropped upon the tan. At that moment a couple of nurses rushed into the balcony, but they were too late. Mrs Malony had got the 'flure'; straight up to the colonel she ran on her bare feet, and broke out again into vehement speech.

'I swear to yer honner the corporal is as innocent as my little Terence, what should be at his mother's breasht this moment. He is, so help me God! There is the rapscallion uv a conspirator,' she yelled, pointing a long, bare, skinny arm at Mr Kidson; 'there is his white-livered tool!'—and up went the other arm like a danger-signal pointing to the sergeant-major. 'Hear me shpake, sor,' cried the woman, 'and sure am I ye'll belave me!'

'Nonsense,' said the chief, 'you are mad or drunk, woman! Here, take her away!' and he beckoned to the nurses.

But the major, a Scotsman, intervened.

'At least hear her story,' he argued; 'there must be some reason in all this fervour of hers. I know the woman; she is no liar.'

'Well, what have you to say, Mrs Malony?' said the colonel.

'One moment, sir!' interposed the major, and there passed a few words in an undertone between him and the colonel—then the latter spoke aloud.

'Mr James,' said he, addressing the adjutant, 'take Mr Kidson outside and remain there with him, and you, Sergeant-Major Norris, take charge of Sergeant-Major Hope. Mr James, you will see that the two are kept apart.'

And then Mrs Malony gained her point and was allowed to tell her story. She had been 'doing for' Mr Kidson, she said, ever since he joined. The day before Sholto was put under arrest, when she was in the lumber-room of Mr Kidson's bungalow, she overheard the plot concocted between him and the sergeant-major. Early next morning, when the regiment was out at 'watering order,' she had watched Sergeant-Major Hope go to Corporal Mackenzie's cot, pick the lock of his trunk, take out his holdall, and therein place Mr Kidson's watch and chain. An hour later, when she was on her way to the bungalow of the 'praste' to ask 'his riverence's' advice as to what she should do, she received a sunstroke, and was insensible for several days. When she recovered consciousness she had forgotten everything that happened for a day or more before her accident until that morning, when she happened to hear the attendants gossiping amongst themselves that Corporal Mackenzie was to be flogged that day for stealing Mr Kidson's watch and chain. Then everything flashed vividly back into her memory, and she had made her escape from the hospital and reached the scene just in time.

Mrs Malony spoke with amazing volubility, and the telling of her story did not occupy more time than a few minutes. When she was done, and stood silent, panting and weeping, the colonel turned to the sergeant of the guard and ordered the prisoner to be unfastened and marched back to the guard-room. While Mrs Malony had been speaking, nobody had noticed Sholto, and when they went to cut him loose, they found that he had fainted. The parade was dismissed; and the colonel, the major, and the adjutant adjourned to the orderly room. Mr Kidson was ordered to be brought in. He met Mrs Malony's accusation with a flat and contemptuous denial, desiring with some insolence in his tone to know whether the colonel could think it proper to take the word of a crazy Irish barrack-room slut before that of an officer and a gentleman. 'That depends on circumstances, and whether I happen to accept your definitions,' was the colonel's dry comment, as he formally put Mr Kidson under arrest, and having ordered him to his quarters, called for the sergeant-major to be brought in. This man was a poor faint-hearted rascal. He was ghastly pale, and his knees trembled as he flinched under the colonel's searching eye. On cross-examination he broke down altogether, and at length, with many protestations of remorse, confessed the whole truth, and that Mr Kidson had bribed him to co-operate in the scheme to ruin Corporal Mackenzie. This wretched accomplice was in his turn sent away into close arrest, and Mr Kidson was re-summoned into the orderly room and informed that his sergeant-major had confessed everything.

The two field-officers were fain to avert from the regiment the horrible scandal, even at the cost of some frustration of justice. The option was given to Kidson of standing a court-martial, or of sending in the resignation of his commission within an hour and quitting the station before the day was out. Then and there the shameless blackguard wrote out the document, made an insolent sweeping salaam all round, mounted his tat, and rode off to his bungalow. As he was crossing the parade-ground he encountered Sholto Mackenzie, who had just been released by the colonel's orders, leaving the guard-room a free man and surrounded by a knot of troop-mates, conspicuous among whom was Mick Sullivan, half mad with delight. As Kidson passed the group with a baleful scowl, the trammels of discipline snapped for once, and a burst of groans and hooting made him quicken his pace, lest worse things should befall. In two hours more the disgraced man was clear of the cantonment.

In the previous article it has been told how in the early days of the great mutiny Mick Sullivan and his comrade were transmogrified from cavalrymen into members of that gallant regiment the Ross-shire Buffs—the old 78th Highlanders—and did good service in the 'little fighting column' at the head of which Havelock fought his way up country from Allahabad to

Cawnpore. It was on the afternoon of Havelock's first fight, the sharp action of Futtehpore, that Sholto Mackenzie and Mick Sullivan were lying down in the shade of a tree waiting for the baggage to come up. Futtehpore town had been carried by a rush, and there had been some hand-to-hand fighting in the streets— for the mutinied Sepoys dodged about among the houses and had to be driven out. There was a delay in following up the fugitives; for a waggon-load of rupees had been upset in the principal street and the temptation of the silver caused the soldiers to dally, while others straggled in search of food and drink.

Meanwhile the mutineer cavalry rallied beyond the town. Palliser's Irregulars were sent forward to disperse the formation, followed by such men of our infantry as could hastily be mustered. Among those who went forward was Sholto Mackenzie. Palliser's native troopers were half-hearted and hung back when their chief charged the Sepoy horse, with the result that Palliser was dashed from his horse, and would have been cut to pieces but for the devotion of his ressaldar, who lost his own life in saving that of his leader.

'Did you notice,' said Sholto to his comrade as they rested, 'the squadron leader of the Pandy Cavalry that handled Palliser's fellows so roughly out yonder?'

'Bedad, an' I did not!' replied Sullivan. 'Every divil av thim was uglier than the other, an' it's their own mothers should be ashamed to own the biling av thim!'

'Look here, Mick,' said Sholto, 'I'll take my oath I saw that dog Kidson to-day, in command of the Pandy Squadron!'

'Kidson!' ejaculated Sullivan in the wildest astonishment. 'It's dhramin' ye are! Sure Kidson must be either prowlin' somewhere in Madras, or else on his road home to England!'

'I tell you I am as sure I saw him to-day as I am that I see you now. It was he who dismounted Palliser and cut down the ressaldar. I am convinced it was he and none other!'

'Well, if you're so sure as that, it's no use to conthradick ye. Plase the saints, ye may get a close chance at him soon, and then—Lord pity him!'

Mick's aspiration was fulfilled. The 'close chance' came to Sholto a few days later, in the heart of the battle of Cawnpore. The Highlanders had rolled up the Sepoy flank by a bayonet charge, had shattered their centre, and captured the village on which it rested. The mutineer infantry of the left and centre were in full rout, their retreat covered by a strong body of native cavalry which showed a very determined front.

Sholto and his comrade were close together in the ranks of the Ross-shire Buffs, when the former suddenly grasped the latter's arm, and in a low earnest voice asked—

'Mick, do you see that officer in charge of the covering squadron of the Pandies?'

Sullivan gazed long and intently, and then burst out—

'By the holy poker, it's that treacherous blackguard Kidson!'

'Right, Mick, and I must get at him somehow!'

'Wid all my heart, chum, but it's aisier said than done, just now, at any rate. You must mark time, and trust to luck!'

Just then Barrow came galloping up at the head of his handful of horsemen, and besought the chief to let him go at the mutineer sowars. But Havelock shook his head, for Barrow's strength all told was but eighteen sabres. But a little later Beatson, the Adjutant-General, who, stricken with cholera and unable to sit his horse, had come up to the front on a gun-carriage, saw an opportunity after the General had ridden away, and took it on himself to give Barrow leave to attack. The flank of the grenadier company of the Highlanders, where Sholto stood, was close to Beatson's gun-carriage, in rear of which his horse was led, and a sudden thought struck the young fellow. Stepping forward with carried rifle, he told Captain Beatson that he was a cavalry soldier, and noticing the led horse, begged eagerly to be allowed to mount it and join the charge for which the volunteer cavalry were preparing.

'Up with you, my man!' said poor dying Beatson. 'Here, you shall have my sword, and I don't want it back clean, remember!'

Sholto was in the saddle with a spring, and made the nineteenth man under Barrow's command; a mixed lot, but full of pluck to a man. As he formed up on the flank, there reached his ears honest Mick's cheery advice—

'Now, Sholto, me dear lad, keep yer sword-hand up and yer bridle-hand down, an' remimber ye reprisint the honour an' glory of the ould 30th Light!'

Barrow threw away his cigar, gathered up his reins, and with a shout of 'Charge!' that might have given the word of command to a brigade, rammed his spurs into his horse's flank and went off at score, his little band close on his heels. Hard on the captain's flank galloped Sholto Mackenzie, a red spot on each cheek, his teeth hard set, his blazing eyes never swerving from the face of one man of that seething mass on which they were riding. 'Give 'em the point, lads!' roared Barrow, as he skewered a havildar and then drove right in among them. The white-faced man with the black moustache, who was Sholto's mark, rather shirked out of the *mêlée* when he saw it was to be close quarters; but Mackenzie, looking neither to the right nor to the left, with his bridle-hand well down, and Beatson's sword in full play, drove his way at length within weapon's length of the other.

'Now, liar and perjurer!' he hissed from between his teeth, 'if you are not coward as well, stand up to me and let us fight it out!'

Kidson's answer was a lurid scowl and a pistol bullet, which just grazed Sholto's temple. Lifting his horse with his bridle-hand, and striking its flanks with his spurless heels, the latter sent his sword-point straight at Kidson's throat. The thrust would have gone through and out at the further side, but that the sword-point struck some concealed protection and was shivered up to the hilt. The renegade Briton smiled a baleful smile as he brought his weapon from guard to point, as if the other was at his mercy. But this was not so; with a shout Sholto tightened the curb-rein till his horse reared straight on end, striking it as it rose with the shattered sword hilt. The maddened animal plunged forward, receiving in his chest the point of Kidson's sword; and Sholto on the instant bending forward fastened a deadly grip on the other's throat. The impetus hurled both of them to the ground, and now, down among the horses' feet, the close-locked strife swaying and churning above them, their struggle unto the death was wrought out. Kidson struggled like a madman; he bit, he kicked, he fought with an almost superhuman fury; but the resolute grip of the avenger never slackened on his throat. Sholto held on with his right hand, groping about with his left for some weapon wherewith to end the contest. At length his grasp closed on the hilt of a dropped sword;—and a moment later it was all over with the man whom the survivors of Havelock's Ironsides speak of with scorn and disgust to this day by the name of 'Nana Sahib's Englishman.'

38

A BAFFLED AMBUSCADE

Ambrose Bierce

Connecting Readyville and Woodbury was a good, hard turnpike nine or ten miles long. Readyville was an outpost of the Federal army at Murfreesboro; Woodbury had the same relation to the Confederate army at Tullahoma. For months after the big battle at Stone River these outposts were in constant quarrel, most of the trouble occurring, naturally, on the turnpike mentioned, between detachments of cavalry. Sometimes the infantry and artillery took a hand in the game by way of showing their good-will.

One night a squadron of Federal horse commanded by Major Seidel, a gallant and skillful officer, moved out from Readyville on an uncommonly hazardous enterprise requiring secrecy, caution and silence.

Passing the infantry pickets, the detachment soon afterwards approached two cavalry videttes staring hard into the darkness ahead. There should have been three.

'Where is your other man?' said the major. 'I ordered Dunning to be here to-night.'

'He rode forward, sir,' the man replied. 'There was a little firing afterwards, but it was a long way to the front.'

'It was against orders and against sense for Dunning to do that,' said the officer, obviously vexed. 'Why did he ride forward?'

'Don't know, sir; he seemed mighty restless. Guess he was skeered.'

When this remarkable reasoner and his companion had been

absorbed into the expeditionary force, it resumed its advance. Conversation was forbidden; arms and accouterments were denied the right to rattle. The horses' tramping was all that could be heard and the movement was slow in order to have as little as possible of that. It was after midnight and pretty dark, although there was a bit of moon somewhere behind the masses of cloud.

Two or three miles along, the head of the column approached a dense forest of cedars bordering the road on both sides. The major commanded a halt by merely halting, and, evidently himself a bit 'skeered,' rode on alone to reconnoiter. He was followed, however, by his adjutant and three troopers, who remained a little distance behind and, unseen by him, saw all that occurred.

After riding about a hundred yards towards the forest, the major suddenly and sharply reined in his horse and sat motionless in the saddle. Near the side of the road, in a little open space and hardly ten paces away, stood the figure of a man, dimly visible and as motionless as he. The major's first feeling was that of satisfaction in having left his cavalcade behind; if this were an enemy and should escape he would have little to report. The expedition was as yet undetected.

Some dark object was dimly discernible at the man's feet; the officer could not make it out. With the instinct of the true cavalryman and a particular indisposition to the discharge of firearms, he drew his saber. The man on foot made no movement in answer to the challenge. The situation was tense and a bit dramatic. Suddenly the moon burst through a rift in the clouds and, himself in the shadow of a group of great oaks, the horseman saw the footman clearly, in a patch of white light. It was Trooper Dunning, unarmed and bareheaded. The object at his feet resolved itself into a dead horse, and at a right angle across the animal's neck lay a dead man, face upwards in the moonlight.

'Dunning has had the fight of his life,' thought the major, and was about to ride forward. Dunning raised his hand, motioning him back with a gesture of warning; then, lowering the arm, he pointed to the place where the road lost itself in the blackness of the cedar forest.

The major understood, and turning his horse rode back to the little group that had followed him and was already moving to the rear in fear of his displeasure, and so returned to the head of his command.

'Dunning is just ahead there,' he said to the captain of his leading company. 'He has killed his man and will have something to report.'

Right patiently they waited, sabers drawn, but Dunning did not come. In an hour the day broke and the whole force moved cautiously forward, its commander not altogether satisfied with his faith in Private Dunning. The expedition had failed, but something remained to be done.

In the little open space off the road they found the fallen horse. At a right angle across the animal's neck face upwards, a bullet in the brain, lay the body of Trooper Dunning, stiff as a statue, hours dead.

Examination disclosed abundant evidence that within a half-hour the cedar forest had been occupied by a strong force of Confederate infantry—an ambuscade.

39

WAR

Jack London

He was a young man, not more than twenty-four or five, and he might have sat his horse with the careless grace of his youth had he not been so catlike and tense. His black eyes roved everywhere, catching the movements of twigs and branches where small birds hopped, questing ever onwards through the changing vistas of trees and brush, and returning always to the clumps of undergrowth on either side. And as he watched, so did he listen, though he rode on in silence, save for the boom of heavy guns from far to the west. This had been sounding monotonously in his ears for hours, and only its cessation would have aroused his notice. For he had business closer to hand. Across his saddle-bow was balanced a carbine.

So tensely was he strung, that a bunch of quail, exploding into flight from under his horse's nose, startled him to such an extent that automatically, instantly, he had reined in and fetched the carbine half-way to his shoulder. He grinned sheepishly, recovered himself, and rode on. So tense was he, so bent upon the work he had to do, that the sweat stung his eyes unwiped, and unheeded rolled down his nose and spattered his saddle pommel. The band of his cavalryman's hat was fresh-stained with sweat. The roan horse under him was likewise wet. It was high noon of a breathless day of heat. Even the birds and squirrels did not dare the sun, but sheltered in shady hiding places among the trees.

Man and horse were littered with leaves and dusted with yellow pollen, for the open was ventured no more than was compulsory. They kept to the brush and trees, and invariably the man halted and peered out before crossing a dry glade or naked stretch of upland pasturage. He worked always to the north, though his way was devious, and it was from the north that he seemed most to apprehend that for which he was looking. He was no coward, but his courage was only that of the average civilized man, and he was looking to live, not die.

Up a small hillside he followed a cowpath through such dense scrub that he was forced to dismount and lead his horse. But when the path swung around to the west, he abandoned it and headed to the north again along the oak-covered top of the ridge.

The ridge ended in a steep descent—so steep that he zigzagged back and forth across the face of the slope, sliding and stumbling among the dead leaves and matted vines and keeping a watchful eye on the horse above that threatened to fall down upon him. The sweat ran from him, and the pollen-dust, settling pungently in mouth and nostrils, increased his thirst. Try as he would, nevertheless the descent was noisy, and frequently he stopped, panting in the dry heat and listening for any warning from beneath.

At the bottom he came out on a flat, so densely forested that he could not make out its extent. Here the character of the woods changed, and he was able to remount. Instead of the twisted hillside oaks, tall straight trees, big-trunked and prosperous, rose from the damp fat soil. Only here and there were thickets, easily avoided, while he encountered winding, park-like glades where the cattle had pastured in the days before war had run them off.

His progress was more rapid now, as he came down into the valley, and at the end of half an hour he halted at an ancient rail fence on the edge of a clearing. He did not like the openness of it, yet his path lay across to the fringe of trees that marked the banks of the stream. It was a mere quarter of a mile across that open, but the thought of venturing out in it was repugnant. A rifle, a score of them, a thousand, might lurk in that fringe by the stream.

Twice he essayed to start, and twice he paused. He was appalled by his own loneliness. The pulse of war that beat from the west suggested the companionship of battling thousands; here was naught but silence, and himself, and possible death-dealing bullets from a myriad ambushes. And yet his task was to find what he feared to find. He must go on, and on, till somewhere, some time, he encountered another man, or other men, from the other side, scouting, as he was scouting, to make report, as he must make report, of having come in touch.

Changing his mind, he skirted inside the woods for a distance, and again peeped forth. This time, in the middle of the clearing, he saw a small farmhouse. There were no signs of life. No smoke curled from the chimney, not a barnyard fowl clucked and strutted. The kitchen door stood open, and he gazed so long and hard into the black aperture that it seemed almost that a farmer's wife must emerge at any moment.

He licked the pollen and dust from his dry lips, stiffened himself, mind and body, and rode out into the blazing sunshine. Nothing stirred. He went on past the house, and approached the wall of trees and bushes by the river's bank. One thought persisted maddeningly. It was of the crash into his body of a high-velocity bullet. It made him feel very fragile and defenseless, and he crouched lower in the saddle.

Tethering his horse in the edge of the wood, he continued a hundred yards on foot till he came to the stream. Twenty feet wide it was, without perceptible current, cool and inviting, and he was very thirsty. But he waited inside his screen of leafage, his eyes fixed on the screen on the opposite side. To make the wait endurable, he sat down, his carbine resting on his knees. The minutes passed, and slowly his tenseness relaxed. At last he decided there was no danger; but just as he prepared to part the bushes and bend down to the water, a movement among the opposite bushes caught his eye.

It might be a bird. But he waited. Again there was an agitation of the bushes, and then, so suddenly that it almost startled a cry from him, the bushes parted and a face peered out. It was a face covered with several weeks' growth of ginger-coloured beard. The eyes were blue and wide apart, with laughter-wrinkles in the corners that showed despite the tired and anxious expression of the whole face.

All this he could see with microscopic clearness, for the distance was no more than twenty feet. And all this he saw in such brief time, that he saw it as he lifted his carbine to his shoulder. He glanced along the sights, and knew that he was gazing upon a man who was as good as dead. It was impossible to miss at such point blank range.

But he did not shoot. Slowly he lowered the carbine and watched. A hand, clutching a water-bottle, became visible and the ginger beard bent downwards to fill the bottle. He could hear the gurgle of the water. Then arm and bottle and ginger beard disappeared behind the closing bushes. A long time he waited, when, with thirst unslaked, he crept back to his horse, rode slowly across the sun-washed clearing, and passed into the shelter of the woods beyond.

II

Another day, hot and breathless. A deserted farmhouse, large, with many outbuildings and an orchard, standing in a clearing. From the woods, on a roan horse, carbine across pommel, rode the young man with the quick black eyes. He breathed with relief as he gained the house. That a fight had taken place here earlier in the season was evident. Clips and empty cartridges, tarnished with verdigris, lay on the ground, which, while wet, had been torn up by the hoofs of horses. Hard by the kitchen garden were graves, tagged and numbered. From the oak tree by the kitchen door, in tattered, weather-beaten garments, hung the bodies of two men. The faces, shriveled and defaced, bore no likeness to the faces of men. The roan horse snorted beneath them, and the rider caressed and soothed it and tied it farther away.

Entering the house, he found the interior a wreck. He trod on empty cartridges as he walked from room to room to reconnoiter from the windows. Men had camped and slept everywhere, and on the floor of one room he came upon stains unmistakable where the wounded had been laid down.

Again outside, he led the horse around behind the barn and invaded the orchard. A dozen trees were burdened with ripe apples. He filled his pockets, eating while he picked. Then a thought came to him, and he glanced at the sun, calculating the time of his return to camp. He pulled off his shirt, tying the sleeves and making a bag. This he proceeded to fill with apples.

As he was about to mount his horse, the animal suddenly pricked up its ears. The man, too, listened, and heard, faintly, the thud of hoofs on soft earth. He crept to the corner of the barn and peered out. A dozen mounted men, strung out loosely, approaching from the opposite side of the clearing, were only a matter of a hundred yards or so away. They rode on to the house. Some dismounted, while others remained in the saddle as an earnest that their stay would be short. They seemed to be holding a council, for he could hear them talking excitedly in the detested tongue of the alien invader. The time passed, but they seemed unable to reach a decision. He put the carbine away in its boot, mounted, and waited impatiently, balancing the shirt of apples on the pommel.

He heard footsteps approaching, and drove his spurs so fiercely into the roan as to force a surprised groan from the animal as it leaped forward. At the corner of the barn he saw the intruder, a mere boy of nineteen or twenty for all of his uniform, jump back to escape being run down. At the same moment the roan swerved, and its rider caught a glimpse of the aroused men by the house. Some were springing from their horses, and he could see the rifles going to their shoulders. He passed the kitchen door and the dried corpses swinging in the shade, compelling his foes to run around the front of the house. A rifle cracked, and a second, but he was going fast, leaning forward, low in the saddle, one hand clutching the shirt of apples, the other guiding the horse.

The top bar of the fence was four feet high, but he knew his roan and leaped it at full career to the accompaniment of several scattered shots. Eight hundred yards straight away were the woods, and the roan was covering the distance with mighty strides. Every man was now firing. They were pumping their guns so rapidly that he no longer heard individual shots. A bullet went through his hat, but he was unaware, though he did know when another tore through the apples on the pommel. And he winced and ducked even lower when a third bullet, fired low, struck a stone between his horse's legs and ricochetted off through the air, buzzing and humming like some incredible insect.

The shots died down as the magazines were emptied, until, quickly, there was no more shooting. The young man was elated. Through that astonishing fusillade he had come unscathed. He glanced back. Yes, they had emptied their magazines. He could see several reloading. Others were running back behind the house for their horses. As he looked, two already mounted, came back into view around the corner, riding hard. And at the same moment, he saw the man with the unmistakable ginger beard kneel down on the ground, level his gun, and coolly take his time for the long shot.

The young man threw his spurs into the horse, crouched very low, and swerved in his flight in order to distract the other's aim. And still the shot did not come. With each jump of the horse, the woods sprang nearer. They were only two hundred yards away, and still the shot was delayed.

And then he heard it, the last thing he was to hear, for he was dead ere he hit the ground in the long crashing fall from the saddle. And they, watching at the house, saw him fall, saw his body bounce when it struck the earth, and saw the burst of red-cheeked apples that rolled about him. They laughed at the unexpected eruption of apples, and clapped their hands in applause of the long shot by the man with the ginger beard.

40

AN EPISODE OF WAR

Stephen Crane

The lieutenant's rubber blanket lay on the ground, and upon it he had poured the company's supply of coffee. Corporals and other representatives of the grimy and hot-throated men who lined the breastwork had come for each squad's portion.

The lieutenant was frowning and serious at this task of division. His lips pursed as he drew with his sword various crevices in the heap, until brown squares of coffee, astoundingly equal in size, appeared on the blanket. He was on the verge of a great triumph in mathematics, and the corporals were thronging forward, each to reap a little square, when suddenly the lieutenant cried out and looked quickly at a man near him as if he suspected it was a case of personal assault. The others cried out also when they saw blood upon the lieutenant's sleeve.

He had winced like a man stung, swayed dangerously, and then straightened. The sound of his hoarse breathing was plainly audible. He looked sadly, mystically, over the breastwork at the green face of a wood, where now were many puffs of white smoke. During this moment the men about him gazed statue-like and silent, astonished and awed by this catastrophe which happened when catastrophes were not expected—when they had leisure to observe it.

As the lieutenant stared at the wood, they too swung their heads, so that for another instant all hands, still silent, contemplated the distant forest as if their minds were fixed upon the mystery of a bullet's journey.

The officer had, of course, been compelled to take his sword into his left hand. He did not hold it by the hilt. He gripped it at the middle of the blade, awkwardly. Turning his eyes from the wood, he looked at the sword as he held it there, and seemed puzzled as to what to do with it. In short, this weapon had of a sudden become a stange thing to him. He looked at it in a kind of stupefaction, as if he had been endowed with a trident, a scepter, or a spade.

Finally he tried to sheathe it. To sheathe a sword held by the left hand, at the middle of the blade, in a scabbard hung at the left hip, is a feat worthy of a sawdust ring. This wounded officer engaged in a desperate struggle with the sword and the wobbling scabbard, and during the time of it he breathed like a wrestler.

But at this instant the men, spectators, awoke from their stone-like poses and crowded forward sympathetically. The orderly-sergeant took the sword and tenderly placed it in the scabbard. At the time, he leaned nervously backwards, and did not allow even his finger to brush the body of the lieutenant. A wound gives stange dignity to him who bears it. Well men shy from this new and terrible majesty. It is as if the wounded man's hand is upon the curtain which hangs before the revelations of all existence—the meaning of ants, potentates, wars, cities, sunshine, snow, a feather dropped from a bird's wing; and the power of it sheds radiance upon a bloody form, and makes the other men understand sometimes that they are little. His comrades look at him with large eyes thoughtfully. Moreover, they fear vaguely that the weight of a finger upon him might send him headlong, precipitate the tragedy, hurl him at once into the dim, grey unknown. And so the orderly-sergeant, while sheathing the sword, leaned nervously backwards.

There were others who proffered assistance. One timidly presented his shoulder and asked the lieutenant if he cared to lean upon it, but the latter waved him away mournfully. He wore the

AN EPISODE OF WAR • 425

look of one who knows he is the victim of a terrible disease and understands his helplessness. He again stared over the breastwork at the forest, and then, turning, went slowly rearwards. He held his right wrist tenderly in his left hand as if the wounded arm was made of brittle glass.

And the men in silence stared at the woods, then at the departing lieutenant; then at the wood, then at the lieutenant.

As the wounded officer passed from the line of battle, he was enabled to see many things which as a participant in the fight were unknown to him. He saw a general on a black horse gazing over the lines of blue infantry at the green woods which veiled his problems. An aide galloped furiously, dragged his horse suddenly to a halt, saluted, and presented a paper. It was, for a wonder, precisely like an historical painting.

To the rear of the general and his staff a group, composed of a bugler, two or three orderlies, and the bearer of the corps standard, all upon maniacal horses, were working like slaves to hold their ground, preserve their respectful interval, while the shells boomed in the air about them, and caused their chargers to make furious quivering leaps.

A battery, a tumultuous and shining mass, was swirling towards the right. The wild thud of hoofs, the cries of the riders, shouting blame and praise, menace and encouragement, and, last, the roar of the wheels, the slant of the glistening guns, brought the lieutenant to an intent pause. The battery swept in curves that stirred the heart; it made halts as dramatic as the crash of a wave on the rocks, and when it fled onwards this aggregation of wheels, levers, motors had a beautiful unity, as if it were a missile. The sound of it was a war chorus that reached into the depths of man's emotion.

The lieutenant, still holding his arm as if it were of glass, stood watching this battery until all detail of it were lost, save the figures of the riders, which rose and fell and waved lashes over the black mass.

Later, he turned his eyes towards the battle, where the shooting sometimes crackled like bush-fires, sometimes sputtered with exasperating irregularity, and sometimes reverberated like the thunder. He saw the smoke rolling upwards and saw crowds of men who ran and cheered, or stood and blazed away at the inscrutable distance.

He came upon some some stragglers, and they told him how to find the field hospital. They described its exact location. In fact, these men, no longer having part in the battle, knew more of it than the others. They told the performance of every corps, every division, the opinion of every general. The lieutenant, carrying his wounded arm rearwards, looked upon them with wonder.

At the roadside a brigade was making coffee and buzzing with talk like a girl's boarding school. Several officers came out to him and inquired concerning things of which he knew nothing. One, seeing his arm, began to scold. 'Why, man, that's no way to do. You want to fix that thing.' He appropriated the lieutenant and the lieutenant's wound. He cut the sleeve and laid bare the arm, every nerve of which softly fluttered under his touch. He bound his handkerchief over the wound, scolding away in the meantime. His tone allowed one to think that he was in the habit of being wounded every day. The lieutenant hung his head, feeling, in this presence, that he did not know how to be correctly wounded.

The low white tents of the hospital were grouped around an old schoolhouse. There was here a singular commotion. In the foreground two ambulances interlocked wheels in the deep mud. The drivers were tossing the blame of it back and forth, gesticulating and berating, while from the ambulances, both crammed with wounded, there came an occasional groan. An interminable crowd of bandaged men were coming and going. Great numbers sat under the trees nursing heads or arms or legs. There was a dispute of some kind raging on the steps of the schoolhouse. Sitting with his back against a tree a man with a face as grey as a new army blanket was serenely smoking a corncob pipe. The lieutenant wished to rush forward and inform him that he was dying.

A busy surgeon was passing near the lieutenant. 'Good morning,' he said, with a friendly smile. Then he caught sight of the lieutenant's arm, and his face at once changed. 'Well, let's have a look at it.' He seemed possessed suddenly of a great contempt for the lieutenant. This wound evidently placed the latter on a very low social plane. The doctor cried out impatiently: 'What mutton-head had tied it up that way anyhow?'

The lieutenant answered, 'Oh a man.'

When the wound was disclosed the doctor fingered it disdainfully. 'Humph,' he said. 'You come along with me and I'll 'tend to you.' His voice contained the same scorn as if he were saying: 'You will have to go to jail.'

The lieutenant had been very meek, but now his face flushed, and he looked into the doctor's eyes. 'I guess I won't have it amputated,' he said.

'Nonsense, man! Nonsense! Nonsense!' cried the doctor. 'Come along, now. I won't amputate it. Come along. Don't be a baby.'

'Let go of me,' said the lieutenant, holding back wrathfully, his glance fixed upon the door of the old school house, as sinister to him as the portals of death.

And this is the story of how the lieutenant lost his arm. When he reached home, his sisters, his mother, his wife, sobbed for a long time at the sight of the flat sleeve. 'Oh, well,' he said, standing shamefaced amid these tears, 'I don't suppose it matters so much as all that.'

41

THE GENTLEMAN PRIVATE OF THE 'SKILAMALINKS'

Archibald Forbes

It was in the autumn of the year 1856 that a squadron of that gallant Light Cavalry Regiment familiarly known as the 'Skilamalinks' crossed Sheffield Moor, rode down Snighill, and proceeded along the valley of the dirty Don to the old cavalry barracks in the angle made by the divagation of the upper and lower Western roads. The 'Skilamalinks' had followed Cardigan in that glorious, crazy gallop up the long valley of Balaclava, and when the eventful twenty-five minutes were over, their gallant array had dwindled to a weak troop, in which there was scarcely a scatheless man and horse. The bitter winter on the Chersonese had yet further thinned the handful that had escaped the Russian cross-fire, and there was a time when the 'Skilamalinks' could barely furnish for duty a weak picket. But when the cruel winter ended, reinforcements came pouring in so freely that before the battle of the Tchernaya the regiment was near its full strength. It had returned to England, dismounted, early in 1856, had spent the summer in south of Ireland quarters, engaged in reorganization and breaking in the remounts which had been sent to it, and in the autumn it had got the route for Yorkshire, headquarters at York, with out-quarters at Sheffield, and, if I remember rightly, at Leeds. Captain Jolliffe, the senior captain of the regiment, was in command of the Sheffield squadron, and it was as a lance-corporal in that fine soldier's troop that I, No.

420, Arthur Fraser, rode into the cramped little barrack-yard at the fork of the roads. My moustache is snow-white now, and, as I walk, I limp a bit from the Cossack lance-thrust through the calf of the leg which is my souvenir of the memorable Light Cavalry charge; but when I dismounted in the Sheffield barrack-yard thirty-five years ago, there was not in Queen Victoria's army, although I say it, a more strapping young fellow than Lance-Corporal Arthur Fraser, of A troop in the 'Skilamalink' Hussars.

It is many a long year since I last saw the dense smoke under whose pall Sheffield breathes hard over its grindstones, and no doubt there are many changes in the dingy, rough, cordial town. When I last soldiered there our quarters were in the fine new barracks, a mile beyond the ramshackle old structure at the fork of the roads. The young soldiers took delight in the airy spaciousness of the former, whose front looks across to the public-house famous in my day for the tenpenny ale one glass of which made a fellow garrulous, and whose flank overhangs the beautiful valley which has long since recovered from the devastation wrought by the bursting of the great dam high up in its throat; but the old soldiers still nourished pleasant memories of the cramped old quarters nearer to the heart of the town. For aught I know, those may have been demolished long ago, and the Sheffielder of to-day may know them no more; but when our out-marching squadron on its way to Norwich last rode along the lower road towards Snighill, we oldsters looked rightwards at the dingy tiled roofs, and at the little windows of what had been our troop-rooms, but which were now let out to civilian inhabitants who cultivated scrawny geraniums and reluctant fuchsias in stumpy little window-boxes. And as I gazed my heart swelled and the water came into my eyes, for the scene recalled the memory of a tragic occurrence which had for years cast a gloom on my life.

Most people are aware that nowadays no inconsiderable

number of young gentlemen are serving in the ranks of the army. These are mostly men with a specific aim. They are fellows who have failed to get into the service as officers either through the front door of Sandhurst, or through the easier side door of the Militia. So they enlist, work hard, and keep steady, while their connections meanwhile are exciting all the influence in their power to further their promotion to commissioned rank. But it is not so generally known that in the old purchase days there was quite a considerable leaven of gentle-manhood in the ranks, without any such specific anxiety for promotion as actuates the gentleman-ranker of to-day. The gentleman-ranker of the old days—so far back as the Peninsular War he was common enough in the army—for the most part enlisted because he had come to grief in some fashion or other. Nowadays, a fellow who has done this has many resources other than the ranks. You find him in the Australian bush, in a mining camp of the Western States, in a Florida orange garden, on a ranche in Texas, or in the 'fertile belt' out beyond Winnipeg. He may be prospecting in the Transvaal or galloping after steers in the Argentine. I have shaken the hand—and a deuced greasy hand it was—of a broken baronet doing duty as cook in a New Zealand timber-cutting camp, and have had a hackman at Portage la Prairie who was the son of a noble marquis, and had himself a courtesy title. For the broken gentleman of the Crimean war time there were no such opportunities of obscurity and possible redemption. The alternatives for him were utter blackguardism or the ranks of the army. When he chose the latter he invariably went for cavalry, ignorant or regardless of the harder work devolving on that arm; and almost invariably it was a light cavalry regiment in which he enrolled himself—always under a false name. The 'Skilamalinks' were a favourite corps with gentlemen recruits under a cloud. Its chief was proud of this preference, and showed kindness to the waifs of good family. In my day they were invariably posted to A troop, which Captain Jolliffe ruled so kindly and yet so firmly, and which went in the regiment by the name of 'the Gentlemen's Troop.' When possible the gentlemen were always quartered together in the same troop-room, and were on their honour to behave creditably and show a good example in every respect. There were twelve of us, I remember, in one of those low-roofed attics above the stables in the old cavalry barracks of Sheffield. The corporal in charge of the room was the son of a great squire and M.P.; his mother the daughter of a Scotch marquis.

My chum was a stalwart and handsome young fellow, who had joined on the same day I became a 'Skilamalink.' He was reticent as to his antecedents; but he had confided to me that he had held a commission in an Indian native cavalry regiment, had come a mucker over high play at Simla, could not bring himself to face his mother (who was the widow of a clergyman of small means), had thrown up his commission, come home, and had 'listed for 'the Skilamalinks' at the old 'Hampshire Hog' in Charles Street, Westminster, on the very day he landed. As we rode back together from out the hell of slaughter on the morning of Balaclava, Charlie Johnstone (of course a 'purser's' name) had killed the Cossack who had speared me, and cut down another who was in the act of skewering me from behind. Farther up the valley I believe I saved his life when the cannon-shot that bowled over his horse broke his leg, and when, lame though I was, I managed to carry him on my back up to the cover of Brandling's battery on the Causeway Ridge. So you may believe we were friends and comrades, and had a love for each other 'passing the love of woman.'

My chum was not a very social person, although always on perfectly good terms with his comrades of the 'gentlemen's' barrack-room. He had frequent accesses of gloom, caused, I assumed, by the sudden shipwreck he had made of a career that must have been very promising, for he was a man of strong intellect, highly accomplished, a fine linguist, and well versed in military history and the science of war. When the shadow fell upon him, he used to spend much of his time in the stable with his mare. She was rather a notable animal. Desperately wounded as she was in the retreat from the Balaclava Charge, she had pulled herself together, reached the rallying-place of the Light Brigade, and formed up on the flank of the troop to which she belonged. She had recovered from her injuries with extraordinary rapidity, and had withstood with singular fortitude the hardships and starvation of the terrible winter; and she now among all troop horses in the regiment was the only survivor of the famous Charge. The dreadful Crimean winter had left its mark upon her. Before that evil time her nature had been gentle, and her paces smooth and easy. But during the worst of it, too weak to stand, she had long lain embedded in frozen mud and snow. She had risen, indeed, out of this misery, and had regained strength and shapeliness, but ever after she was the roughest trotter in the regiment. And with the ease of her paces had gone, too, the mare's temper. She had become a vicious and dangerous savage, to approach which was unsafe for any one save only the trooper who had ridden her in the Charge, to whom she was uniformly gentle and affectionate. Johnstone would sit by her for hours at a time on the manger at her head, or on the hanging bale by her side, talking in low tones to the old jade, and she listened to him for all the world as if she understood him, which, indeed, I am sure, he more than believed that she did.

Christmas Day in the army is the great festival of the year. The preparations for its adequate celebration are commenced days in advance. I hear—but I do not know whether it is true—that the cost of the Christmas dinner is now defrayed out of the canteen fund. But in our day—at all events in the cavalry regiments—the captain of each troop took, and was proud to take, that obligation upon himself as regarded his own men. There used to be quite a little ceremony about the matter. Some ten days in advance the troop sergeant-major would go round the barrack-rooms, and make a little speech in each room. 'Men,' he would say, striking an attitude, 'our worthy captain has commissioned me to inform you that he will have great pleasure in having the men of his troop eat their Christmas dinner at his expense, and that he will also contribute towards the celebration of the day half a gallon of stout per man, which he regards as an adequate allowance if his men, as he anxiously desires, are to keep reasonably sober, and not discredit him and themselves by getting drunk.' Cheers would follow this intimation, and a sarcastic old soldier might interject the remark, 'The captain don't know, Sergeant-Major, how strong A troop heads are. We could drink a gallon per man, and never turn a hair!' Whereunto the honest sergeant-major would retort, 'Ah, Lucas, we know what a power of suction you have without showing the drink, but remember it's not a fortnight since when you were walking pack-drill for being as drunk as a boiled owl.' Lucas thus suppressed, the sergeant-major would proceed: 'Now, men, take a day or two to make your minds up what you prefer for dinner—geese, turkeys, roast pork, veal—whatever delicacies of the season you may fancy, and then let the orderly corporal know your choice, so that he may give the order in good time. The materials for the plum-pudding—they are—of course you know.'

Then the artistic genius of the room would betake himself to mural decorations, representations in colours of the banners of the regiment, the captain's coat-of-arms, such legends as 'A Merry Christmas to all!' 'Long life to our worthy Captain!' 'The 'Skilamalinks' take the right of the line!' and so forth. Adjacent plantations are harried of Christmas trees, holly, and mistletoe, and each room becomes an evergreen bower. Christmas Eve is the period of busy labour, skill and triumph on the part of the pudding-compounder, whose satellites pick raisins of their stones, chop the lemon-peel, and heroically refrain from taking surreptitious sips of the brandy destined to invigorate the pudding. Volunteers are ready with their clean towels to serve as pudding-cloths, and then a procession marches to the cookhouse, where the puddings are consigned to the copper over which the conscientious compounder holds his long vigil. It is a pleasant time when on Christmas Day the bountiful fare is spread on the barrack-room table, and when the captain goes round the rooms, and says a few genial words to the men standing at attention while they listen. Then the oldest soldier, nudged by his mates, takes one pace to his front, halts, comes to preternaturally rigid attention, and shoots out the words, 'Captain Jolliffe, sir'—then stammers painfully for the space of about a minute, and finally blurts out—'wish to thank you, sir—most liberal dinner, stout, sir—drink your health, sir—proud of our captain, sir—wish you and yours Merry Christmas and many of 'em!' 'Same to you, men,' replies the captain—genially tastes the stout which the cheekiest man tenders him in a stoneware soup basin, and with, mayhap, the words 'Be merry but be wise' clanks out of the room, followed by a cheer.

The inmates of the 'Gentlemen's Room,' it was always understood, preferred not to be beholden to their captain for their Christmas dinner. They were not indeed bloated plutocrats, but most of them had their pittance of army pay supplemented by remittances from home, some stated, some occasional; and some little expenditure was made in modest amenities. They luxuriated, for instance, in tablecloths, and in cups and saucers in lieu of the rough stoneware basins supplied to the other barrack-rooms by the contractor for the mess-table refuse. But although the gentlemen chose to be independent in regard to the Christmas dinner, they were glad to accept in the spirit in which it was tendered the dozen of wine which Captain Jolliffe sent over from the officers' mess with his compliments and the good wishes of the season. We had dined, and had formed a wide circle round the cheerful fire as we sat over the captain's wine, whose array of bottles was marshalled on the table which we encircled—we were drinking the Château Margaux out of teacups, I remember—when all at once there was a timid little knock at the door. 'Come in!' cried Corporal Hayward; the door opened, and there entered into the barrack-room a handsome white-haired lady, with scared, wistful eyes, and a worn face the expression of which had for me something vaguely familiar. She was in a state of manifest agitation, and for the moment, as she stood catching her breath as if to keep down the sobs that were rising in her throat, she was unable to utter articulate sounds.

We all rose to our feet, opening our circle. With high-bred courtesy and genuine concern, Corporal Hayward hastened to her side, and led her to the chair which he had vacated—the only one in the room. Then in a measure she regained her composure, and asked, still rather flutteringly—

'Is this what is called "The Gentlemen's Room?"'

'The fellows call it so,' replied Hayward, 'but we make no pretensions.'

'The corporal of the guard sent me here,' said the lady, 'as the likeliest place—' and then she burst into tears and broke down.

'Likeliest place for what, madam?' inquired Hayward, with sympathy and concern in his accents.

'I—I am searching for my lost son,' she answered through her tears, 'for the only son of his mother, and she a widow.'

'Pray tell me his name,' said Hayward.

'Josceline L'Estrange,' replied the lady more firmly, 'twenty-three years of age, tall, slight, with light wavy hair, and blue eyes. My boy! my boy!' and the sobs came again thick and fast.

'There is no man of that name among us, or indeed in the regiment. But men do not always enlist in their own names. Look around you—but, no, I am sure your son cannot be one of us, else long before now he would have been on his knees before you!'

The lady scanned face after face in vain. Hayward undertook that she might be present at muster parade on the following morning, so that she might have the opportunity of seeing every man in the regiment. This gentleness, and the concern of all of us, seemed to soothe her; she sat quiet and silent with folded hands. Jack Dalrymple—I saw him the other day on the box of his drag at the parade of the Coaching Club—boiled some water in a pannikin and made the lady a cup of tea. As she sipped it, she began to talk—to tell us the story of her lost son.

He had been for two years in India, a subaltern in one of the Company's native cavalry regiments. She had not heard from him for several months when, in the late autumn of '53, she read in an Anglo-Indian newspaper that he had resigned his commission. Greatly distressed, she wrote out to one of his brother-officers begging for tidings of him. The reply came that he had got into a scrape in which there was nothing dishonourable, but which had ruined him financially, that he had persisted in throwing up his commission and returning to England, intending, so his comrade stated, to enlist in one of the Queen's light cavalry regiments in time to take part in the war with Russia which he had assured himself was impending. Before those tidings reached England, the light cavalry brigade had already sailed for the East; but the poor mother had gone to London and devoted herself to inquiries among the recruiting sergeants in Charles Street, Westminster. One of the fraternity had professed to recognize the son by the description given by the mother, and from the circumstance that the former had told him he had been an officer in the Company's native cavalry; but since the old sergeant had forgotten the name of the intending recruit and did not recollect in what regiment he had enlisted, the quest had run to ground. After the return of the brigade to England on the termination of the Crimean War, the mother had been searching without result among the regiments of it quartered in the South-country stations, and it was finally, on the advice of a Lancer major, who had recently exchanged from the 'Skilamalinks,' that she should visit Captain Jolliffe's troop in that regiment, since in it there was an exceptional number of gentlemen rankers, that she had come to Sheffield. And now, she piteously said, her last hope seemed dead; she would search no further, but go home and die, the light of her life gone out.

Hayward, tender and anxious as he was, did not dare to speak words to her that might inspire her with false hope. But it had been growing upon me, as she told her simple mournful story, that I had the power to do more than inspire her with hope—to give her, in very truth, the sweet joy of its realization. Stronger and more strong had grown my conviction, as I listened to her, that my chum was none other than her lost son. Everything of his life that he had confided to me—and to me alone—tallied closely with the story related by the white-haired lady sitting in Hayward's windsor-chair. Soon after dinner he had become silent and abstracted, and presently he had risen and left us. But I knew perfectly well where to find my poor brooding comrade—up in the stall alongside that vicious old chestnut jade which had carried him through Russian cannon-fire and Cossack spears on the sad, glorious day of Balaclava.

I had only to descend the staircase and go a little way to the left, to reach the door of the stable in which was old 'Termagant's' stall. Before I threw open the door, indeed before I reached it, I heard an unwonted din of hoofs clattering on the cobblestones, of vicious kicks against bales and pillar-posts, of scared snortings and squealing. The usually quiet troop horses I found infected with a wild delirium of mingled fury and panic, as the sweat poured down their flanks, and as they snuffed a strange fresh odour which pervaded the stable. I called my chum; there was no answer. No; but in the farthest stall I found him—found him down among the infernal hoofs of that vicious old hell-jade, the chestnut of the Balaclava Charge. She had trodden him almost into pulp. The odour which was maddening the other horses was the smell of his blood. She was kneeling on his chest with her forelegs. She was off the short jib, and was tearing pieces off his face and skull with her cursed long yellow fangs.

The sight whirled me into a reckless fury. I dashed at her head, caught her hard by the nose, half stunned her with swinging blows from the horse-log that sent her bloody tusks down her throat as she came at me, forced her back into the gangway, and fastened her up in a spare stall. Then, dodging her final vicious lash out, I ran to where my comrade lay. No one could have recognized him; hardly in the crushed, torn, and bleeding mass could there be discerned aught of human being. Yet he was not quite dead. I felt the last beats of his heart, and it seemed to me that he tried in vain to speak ere his shattered head fell back over my knee. I laid him quietly down, ran under the window of our room, and called for Hayward.

He came down. We went into the stable together where my comrade's remains lay, and I told him I was sure that the dead man was the old lady's son. He went across the barrack-yard to Captain Jolliffe's quarters, and told him of the double tragedy of this Christmas afternoon. His wife put her bonnet on, went with her husband to the 'Gentlemen's Room,' and carried the white-haired lady with her to her own quarters, her guest for the night. Four of us took a table-slab off its trestles, and on it carried the mangled corpse to the little hospital in the corner of the barrack-yard, Captain Jolliffe accompanying us. There was no need to send in a hurry for the civilian doctor who had medical charge of the detachment. We gently cut the clothing off the wrecked form, and straightened the mangled limbs. Then my assurance became doubly sure. On the crushed chest, yet itself intact, hung by a ribbon round the neck a locket containing a miniature of the white-haired lady who had come to the 'Gentlemen's Room' in search of her son. It was her likeness to him that from the first had made her face seem familiar to me, although I did not grasp the resemblance until she was telling her story.

The woful task fell to Mrs Jolliffe of breaking to the poor mother the grievous tidings that she had found her son only to lose him for ever in the grave. But God in His mercy averted the blow. The Captain's wife began the duty devolved on her by showing to the mother, without a word, the locket and the miniature. The poor woman devoured it with eager eyes, made a futile clutch at the trinket she recognized: her arms fell, she heaved one quick, sudden sigh, and fell back dead in her armchair. We knew afterwards she had been suffering from advanced heart disease.

Friends came to carry home to the Wiltshire village the dead mother and son. Captain Jolliffe went to be present at the funeral of the gentleman private of his troop, who had been a good soldier in war-time and peace-time; and he took Hayward and myself with him that we might lay our comrade's head in the grave. There was no Dead March in *Saul* to which to keep the measured time as the little procession wended its way under the gaunt elm-trees to the rural churchyard, nor did any firing-party ring out the triple volley over the soldier's corpse; but there lay on his coffin the sabre whose edge his country's enemies had felt, and from under the busbies of hussar-comrades tears dropped on his coffin as it lay in the open grave.

42

A WAY YOU'LL NEVER BE

Ernest Hemingway

The attack had gone across the field, been held up by machine-gun fire from the sunken road and from the group of farm houses, encountered no resistance in the town, and reached the bank of the river. Coming along the road on a bicycle, getting off to push the machine when the surface of the road became too broken, Nicholas Adams saw what had happened by the position of the dead.

They lay alone or in clumps in the high grass of the field and along the road, their pockets out, and over them were flies and around each body or group of bodies were the scattered papers.

In the grass and the grain, beside the road, and in some places scattered over the road, there was much material: a field kitchen, it must have come over when things were going well; many of the calf-skin-covered haversacks, stick bombs, helmets, rifles, sometimes one butt up, the bayonet stuck in the dirt, they had dug quite a little at the last; stick bombs, helmets, rifles, intrenching tools, ammunition boxes, star-shell pistols, their shells scattered about, medical kits, gas masks, empty gas-mask cans, a squat, tripodded machine gun in a nest of empty shells, full belts protruding from the boxes, the water-cooling can empty and on its side, the breech block gone, the crew in odd positions, and around them, in the grass, more of the typical papers.

There were mass prayer books, group postcards showing the machine-gun unit standing in ranked and ruddy cheerfulness as in a football picture for a college annual; now they were humped and swollen in the grass; propaganda postcards showing a soldier in Austrian uniform bending a woman backwards over a bed; the figures were impressionistically drawn; very attractively depicted and had nothing in common with actual rape in which the woman's skirts are pulled over her head to smother her, one comrade sometimes sitting upon the head. There were many of these inciting cards which had evidently been issued just before the offensive. Now they were scattered with the smutty postcards, photographic; the small photographs of village girls by village photographers, the occasional pictures of children, and the letters, letters, letters. There was always much paper about the dead and the débris of this attack was no exception.

These were new dead and no one had bothered with anything but their pockets. Our own dead, or what he thought of, still, as our own dead, were surprisingly few, Nick noticed. Their coats had been opened too and their pockets were out, and they showed, by their positions, the manner and the skill of the attack. The hot weather had swollen them all alike regardless of nationality.

The town had evidently been defended, at the last, from the line of the sunken road and there had been few or no Austrians to fall back into it. There were only three bodies in the street and they looked to have been killed running. The houses of the town were broken by the shelling and the street had much rubble of plaster and mortar and there were broken beams, broken tiles, and many holes, some of them yellow-edged from the mustard gas. There were many pieces of shell, and shrapnel balls were scattered in the rubble. There was no one in the town at all.

Nick Adams had seen no one since he had left Fornaci, although, riding along the road through the over-foliaged country, he had seen guns hidden under screens of mulberry leaves to the left of the road, noticing them by the heatwaves in the air above the leaves where the sun hit the metal. Now he went on through the town, surprised to find it deserted, and came out on the low road beneath the bank of the river. Leaving the town there was a bare open space where the road slanted down and he could see the placid reach of the river and the low curve of the opposite bank and the whitened, sun-baked mud where the Austrians had dug. It was all very lush and over-green since he had seen it last and becoming historical had made no change in this, the lower river.

The battalion was along the bank to the left. There was a series of holes in the top of the bank with a few men in them. Nick noticed where the machine guns were posted and the signal rockets in their racks. The men in the holes in the side of the bank were sleeping. No one challenged. He went on and as he came around a turn in the mud bank a young second lieutenant with a stubble of beard and red-rimmed, very blood-shot eyes pointed a pistol at him.

'Who are you?'

Nick told him.

'How do I know this?'

Nick showed him the tessera with photograph and identification and the seal of the third army. He took hold of it.

'I will keep this.'

'You will not,' Nick said. 'Give me back the card and put your gun away. There. In the holster.'

'How am I to know who you are?'

'The tessera tells you.'

'And if the tessera is false? Give me that card.'

'Don't be a fool,' Nick said cheerfully. 'Take me to your company commander.'

'I should send you to battalion headquarters.'

'All right,' said Nick. 'Listen, do you know the Captain Paravicini? The tall one with the small moustache who was an architect and speaks English?'

'You know him?'

'A little.'

'What company does he command?'

'The second.'

'He is commanding the battalion.'

'Good,' said Nick. He was relieved to know that Para was all right. 'Let us go to the battalion.'

As Nick had left the edge of the town three shrapnel had burst high and to the right over one of the wrecked houses and since then there had been no shelling. But the face of this officer looked like the face of a man during a bombardment. There was the same tightness and the voice did not sound natural. His pistol made Nick nervous.

'Put it away,' he said. 'There's the whole river between them and you.'

'If I thought you were a spy I would shoot you now,' the second lieutenant said.

'Come on,' said Nick. 'Let us go to the battalion.' This officer made him very nervous.

The Captain Paravicini, acting major, thinner and more English looking than ever, rose when Nick saluted from behind the table in the dugout that was battalion headquarters.

'Hello,' he said. 'I didn't know you. What are you doing in that uniform?'

'They've put me in it.'

'I am very glad to see you, Nicolo.'

'Right. You look well. How was the show?'

'We made a very fine attack. Truly. A very fine attack. I will show you. Look.'

He showed on the map how the attack had gone.

'I came from Fornaci,' Nick said. 'I could see how it had been. It was very good.'

'It was extraordinary. Altogether extraordinary. Are you attached to the regiment?'

'No. I am supposed to move around and let them see the uniform.'

'How odd.'

'If they see one American uniform that is supposed to make them believe others are coming.'

'But how will they know it is an American uniform?'

'You will tell them.'

'Oh. Yes, I see. I will send a corporal with you to show you about and you will make a tour of the lines.'

'Like a bloody politician,' Nick said.

'You would be much more distinguished in civilian clothes. They are what is really distinguished.'

'With a homburg hat,' said Nick.

'Or with a very furry fedora.'

'I'm supposed to have my pockets full of cigarettes and postal cards and such things,' Nick said. 'I should have a musette full of chocolate. These I should distribute with a kind word and a pat on the back. But there weren't any cigarettes and postcards and no chocolate. So they said to circulate around anyway.'

'I'm sure your appearance will be very heartening to the troops.'

'I wish you wouldn't,' Nick said. 'I feel badly enough about it as it is. In principle, I would have brought you a bottle of brandy.'

'In principle,' Para said and smiled, for the first time, showing yellowed teeth. 'Such a beautiful expression. Would you like some Grappa?'

'No, thank you,' Nick said.

'It hasn't any ether in it.'

'I can taste that still,' Nick remembered suddenly and completely.

'You know I never knew you were drunk until you started talking coming back in the camions.'

'I was stinking in every attack,' Nick said.

'I can't do it,' Para said. 'I took it in the first show, the very first show, and it only made me very upset and then frightfully thirsty.'

'You don't need it.'

'You're much braver in an attack than I am.'

'No,' Nick said. 'I know how I am and I prefer to get stinking. I'm not ashamed of it.'

'I've never seen you drunk.'

'No?' said Nick. 'Never? Not when we rode from Mestre to Portogrande that night and I wanted to go to sleep and used the bicycle for a blanket and pulled it up under my chin?'

'That wasn't in the lines.'

'Let's not talk about how I am,' Nick said. 'It's a subject I know too much about to want to think about it any more.'

'You might as well stay here a while,' Paravicini said. 'You can take a nap if you like. They didn't do much to this in the bombardment. It's too hot to go out yet.'

'I suppose there is no hurry.'

'How are you really?'

'I'm fine. I'm perfectly all right.'

'No. I mean really.'

'I'm all right. I can't sleep without a light of some sort. That's all I have now.'

'I said it should have been trepanned. I'm no doctor but I know that.'

'Well, they thought it was better to have it absorb, and that's what I got. What's the matter? I don't seem crazy to you, do I?'

'You seem in top-hole shape.'

'It's a hell of a nuisance once they've had you certified as nutty,' Nick said. 'No one ever has any confidence in you again.'

'I would take a nap, Nicolo,' Paravicini said. 'This isn't battalion headquarters as we used to know it. We're just waiting to be pulled out. You oughtn't to go out in the heat now—it's silly. Use that bunk.'

'I might just lie down,' Nick said.

Nick lay on the bunk. He was very disappointed that he felt this way and more disappointed, even, that it was so obvious to Captain Paravicini. This was not as large a dugout as the one where that platoon of the class of 1899, just out at the front, got hysterics during the bombardment before the attack, and Para had had him walk them two at a time outside to show them nothing would happen, he wearing his own chin strap tight across his mouth to keep his lips quiet. Knowing they could not hold it when they took it. Knowing it was all a bloody balls—If he can't stop crying, break his nose to give him something else to think about. I'd shoot one but it's too late now. They'd all be worse. Break his nose. They've put it back to five-twenty. We've only got four minutes more. Break that other silly bugger's nose and kick his silly ass out of here. Do you think they'll go over? If they don't, shoot two and try to scoop the others out some way. Keep behind them, sergeant. It's no use to walk ahead and find there's nothing coming behind you. Bail them out as you go. What a bloody balls. All right. That's right. Then, looking at the watch, in that quiet tone, that valuable quiet tone, 'Savoia.' Making it cold, no time to get it, he couldn't find his own after the cave-in, one whole end had caved in; it was that started them; making it cold up that slope the only time he hadn't done it stinking. And after they came back the teleferica house burned, it seemed, and some of the wounded got down four days later and some did not get down, but we went up and we went back and we came down—we always came down. And there was Gaby Delys, oddly enough, with feathers on; you called me baby doll a year ago tadada you said that I was rather nice to know tadada with feathers on, with feathers off, the great Gaby, and my name's Harry Pilcer, too, we used to step out of the far side of the taxis when it got steep going up the hill and he could see that hill every night when he dreamed with Sacré

Coeur, blown white, like a soap bubble. Sometimes his girl was there and sometimes she was with some one else and he could not understand that, but those were the nights the river ran so much wider and stiller than it should and outside of Fossalta there was a low house painted yellow with willows all around it and a low stable and there was a canal, and he had been there a thousand times and never seen it, but there it was every night as plain as the hill, only it frightened him. That house meant more than anything and every night he had it. That was what he needed but it frightened him especially when the boat lay there quietly in the willows on the canal, but the banks weren't like this river. It was all lower, as it was at Portogrande, where they had seen them come wallowing across the flooded ground holding the rifles high until they fell with them in the water. Who ordered that one? If it didn't get so damned mixed up he could follow it all right. That was why he noticed everything in such detail to keep it all straight so he would know just where he was, but suddenly it confused without reason as now, he lying in a bunk at battalion headquarters, with Para commanding a battalion and he in a bloody American uniform. He sat up and looked around; they all watching him. Para was gone out. He lay down again.

The Paris part came earlier and he was not frightened of it except when she had gone off with some one else and the fear that they might take the same driver twice. That was what frightened about that. Never about the front. He never dreamed about the front now any more but what frightened him so that he could not get rid of it was that long yellow house and the different width of the river. Now he was back here at the river, he had gone through that same town, and there was no house. Nor was the river that way. Then where did he go each night and what was the peril, and why would he wake, soaking wet, more frightened than he had ever been in a bombardment, because of a house and a long stable and a canal?

He sat up, swung his legs carefully down; they stiffened any time they were out straight for long; returned the stares of the adjutant, the signallers and the two runners by the door and put on his cloth-covered trench helmet.

'I regret the absence of the chocolate, the postal-cards and cigarettes,' he said. 'I am, however, wearing the uniform.'

'The major is coming back at once,' the adjutant said. In that army an adjutant is not a commissioned officer.

'The uniform is not very correct,' Nick told them. 'But it gives you the idea. There will be several millions of Americans here shortly.'

'Do you think they will send Americans down here?' asked the adjutant.

'Oh, absolutely. Americans twice as large as myself, healthy, with clean hearts, sleep at night, never been wounded, never been blown up, never had their heads caved in, never been scared, don't drink, faithful to the girls they left behind them, many of them never had crabs, wonderful chaps. You'll see.'

'Are you an Italian?' asked the adjutant.

'No, American. Look at the uniform. Spagnolini made it but it's not quite correct.'

'A North or South American?'

'North,' said Nick. He felt it coming on now. He would quiet down.

'But you speak Italian.'

'Why not? Do you mind if I speak Italian? Haven't I a right to speak Italian?'

'You have Italian medals.'

'Just the ribbons and the papers. The medals come later. Or you give them to people to keep and the people go away; or they are lost with your baggage. You can purchase others in Milan. It is the papers that are of importance. You must not feel badly about them. You will have some yourself if you stay at the front long enough.'

'I am a veteran of the Iritrea campaign,' said the adjutant stiffly. 'I fought in Tripoli.'

'It's quite something to have met you,' Nick put out his hand. 'Those must have been trying days. I noticed the ribbons. Were you, by any chance, on the Carso?'

'I have just been called up for this war. My class was too old.'

'At one time I was under the age limit,' Nick said. 'But now I am reformed out of the war.'

'But why are you here now?'

'I am demonstrating the American uniform,' Nick said. 'Don't you think it is very significant? It is a little tight in the collar but soon you will see untold millions wearing this uniform swarming like locusts. The grasshopper, you know, what we call the grasshopper in America, is really a locust. The true grasshopper is small and green and comparatively feeble. You must not, however, make a confusion with the seven-year locust or cicada which emits a peculiar sustained sound which at the moment I cannot recall. I try to recall it but I cannot. I can almost hear it and then it is quite gone. You will pardon me if I break off our conversation?'

'See if you can find the major,' the adjutant said to one of the two runners. 'I can see you have been wounded,' he said to Nick.

'In various places,' Nick said. 'If you are interested in scars I can show you some very interesting ones but I would rather talk about grasshoppers. What we call grasshoppers that is; and what are, really, locusts. These insects at one time played a very important part in my life. It might interest you and you can look at the uniform while I am talking.'

The adjutant made a motion with his hand to the second runner who went out.

'Fix your eyes on the uniform. Spagnolini made it, you know.

You might as well look, too,' Nick said to the signallers. 'I really have no rank. We're under the American consul. It's perfectly all right for you to look. You can stare, if you like. I will tell you about the American locust. We always preferred one that we called the medium-brown. They last the best in the water and fish prefer them. The larger ones that fly making a noise somewhat similar to that produced by a rattlesnake rattling his rattlers, a very dry sound, have vivid coloured wings, some are bright red, others yellow barred with black, but their wings go to pieces in the water and they make a very blowsy bait, while the medium-brown is a plump, compact, succulent hopper that I can recommend as far as one may well recommend something you gentlemen will probably never encounter. But I must insist that you will never gather a sufficient supply of these insects for a day's fishing by pursuing them with your hands or trying to hit them with a hat. That is sheer nonsense and a useless waste of time. I repeat, gentlemen, that you will get nowhere at it. The correct procedure, and one which should be taught all young officers at every small-arms course if I had anything to say about it, and who knows but what I will have, is the employment of a seine or net made of common mosquito netting. Two officers holding this length of netting at alternate ends, or let us say one at each end, stoop, hold the bottom extremity of the net in one hand and the top extremity in the other and run into the wind. The hoppers, flying with the wind, fly against the length of netting and are imprisoned in its folds. It is no trick at all to catch a very great quantity indeed, and no officer, in my opinion, should be without a length of mosquito netting suitable for the improvisation of one of these grasshopper seines. I hope I have made myself clear, gentlemen. Are there any questions? If there is anything in the course you do not understand please ask questions. Speak up. None? Then I would like to close on this note. In the words of that great soldier and gentleman, Sir

Henry Wilson: Gentlemen, either you must govern or you must be governed. Let me repeat it. Gentlemen, there is one thing I would like to have you remember. One thing I would like you to take with you as you leave this room. Gentlemen, either you must govern—or you must be governed. That is all, gentlemen. Good-day.'

He removed his cloth-covered helmet, put it on again and, stooping, went out the low entrance of the dugout. Para, accompanied by the two runners, was coming down the line of the sunken road. It was very hot in the sun and Nick removed the helmet.

'There ought to be a system for wetting these things,' he said. 'I shall wet this one in the river.' He started up the bank.

'Nicolo,' Paravicini called. 'Nicolo. Where are you going?'

'I don't really have to go.' Nick came down the slope, holding the helmet in his hands. 'They're a damned nuisance wet or dry. Do you wear yours all the time?'

'All the time,' said Para. 'It's making me bald. Come inside.'

Inside Para told him to sit down.

'You know they're absolutely no damned good,' Nick said. 'I remember when they were a comfort when we first had them, but I've seen them full of brains too many times.'

'Nicolo,' Para said. 'I think you should go back. I think it would be better if you didn't come up to the line until you had those supplies. There's nothing here for you to do. If you move around, even with something worth giving away, the men will group and that invites shelling. I won't have it.'

'I know it's silly,' Nick said. 'It wasn't my idea. I heard the brigade was here so I thought I would see you or some one else I knew. I could have gone to Zenzon or to San Dona. I'd like to go to San Dona to see the bridge again.'

'I won't have you circulating around to no purpose,' Captain Paravicini said.

'All right,' said Nick. He felt it coming on again.

'You understand?'

'Of course,' said Nick. He was trying to hold it in.

'Anything of that sort should be done at night.'

'Naturally,' said Nick. He knew he could not stop it now.

'You see, I am commanding the battalion,' Para said.

'And why shouldn't you be?' Nick said. Here it came. 'You can read and write, can't you?'

'Yes,' said Para gently.

'The trouble is you have a damned small battalion to command. As soon as it gets to strength again they'll give you back your company. Why don't they bury the dead? I've seen them now. I don't care about seeing them again. They can bury them any time as far as I'm concerned and it would be much better for you. You'll all get bloody sick.'

'Where did you leave your bicycle?'

'Inside the last house.'

'Do you think it will be all right?'

'Don't worry,' Nick said. 'I'll go in a little while.'

'Lie down a little while, Nicolo.'

'All right.'

He shut his eyes, and in place of the man with the beard who looked at him over the sights of the rifle, quite calmly before squeezing off, the white flash and clublike impact, on his knees, hot-sweet choking, coughing it onto the rock while they went past him, he saw a long, yellow house with a low stable and the river much wider than it was and stiller. 'Christ,' he said, 'I might as well go.'

He stood up.

'I'm going, Para,' he said. 'I'll ride back now in the afternoon. If any supplies have come I'll bring them down tonight. If not I'll come at night when I have something to bring.'

'It is still hot to ride,' Captain Paravicini said.

'You don't need to worry,' Nick said. 'I'm all right now for quite a while. I had one then but it was easy. They're getting much better. I can tell when I'm going to have one because I talk so much.'

'I'll send a runner with you.'

'I'd rather you didn't. I know the way.'

'You'll be back soon?'

'Absolutely.'

'Let me send—'

'No,' said Nick. 'As a mark of confidence.'

'Well, Ciaou then.'

'Ciaou,' said Nick. He started back along the sunken road towards where he had left the bicycle. In the afternoon the road would be shady once he had passed the canal. Beyond that there were trees on both sides that had not been shelled at all. It was on that stretch that, marching, they had once passed the Terza Savoia cavalry regiment riding in the snow with their lances. The horses' breath made plumes in the cold air. No, that was somewhere else. Where was that?

'I'd better get to that damned bicycle,' Nick said to himself. 'I don't want to lose the way to Fornaci.'

43

THE FLY

Katherine Mansfield

'Y'are very snug in here,' piped old Mr Woodifield, and he peered out of the great, green leather armchair by his friend the boss's desk as a baby peers out of its pram. His talk was over; it was time for him to be off. But he did not want to go. Since he had retired, since his...stroke, the wife and the girls kept him boxed up in the house every day of the week except Tuesday. On Tuesday he was dressed and brushed and allowed to cut back to the City for the day. Though what he did there the wife and girls couldn't imagine. Made a nuisance of himself to his friends, they supposed... Well, perhaps so. All the same, we cling to our last pleasures as the tree clings to its last leaves. So there sat old Woodifield, smoking a cigar and staring almost greedily at the boss, who rolled in his office chair, stout, rosy, five years older than he, and still going strong, still at the helm. It did one good to see him. Wistfully, admiringly, the old voice added, 'It's snug in here, upon my word!'

'Yes, it's comfortable enough,' agreed the boss, and he flipped the Financial Times with a paper-knife. As a matter of fact he was proud of his room; he liked to have it admired, especially by old Woodifield. It gave him a feeling of deep, solid satisfaction to be planted there in the midst of it in full view of that frail old figure in the muffler.

'I've had it done up lately,' he explained, as he had explained for the past—how many?— weeks. 'New carpet,' and he pointed to the bright red carpet with a pattern of large white rings. 'New furniture,' and he nodded towards the massive bookcase and the table with legs like twisted treacle. 'Electric heating!' He waved almost exultantly towards the five transparent, pearly sausages glowing so softly in the tilted copper pan.

But he did not draw old Woodifield's attention to the photograph over the table of a grave-looking boy in uniform standing in one of those spectral photographers' parks with photographers' storm-clouds behind him. It was not new. It had been there for over six years.

'There was something I wanted to tell you,' said old Woodifield, and his eyes grew dim remembering. 'Now what was it? I had it in my mind when I started out this morning.' His hands began to tremble, and patches of red showed above his beard.

Poor old chap, he's on his last pins, thought the boss. And, feeling kindly, he winked at the old man, and said jokingly, 'I tell you what. I've got a little drop of something here that'll do you good before you go out into the cold again. It's beautiful stuff. It wouldn't hurt a child.' He took a key off his watch-chain, unlocked a cupboard below his desk, and drew forth a dark, squat bottle. 'That's the medicine,' said he. 'And the man from whom I got it told me on the strict Q.T. it came from the cellars at Windsor Cassel.'

Old Woodifield's mouth fell open at the sight. He couldn't have looked more surprised if the boss had produced a rabbit.

'It's whisky, ain't it?' he piped, feebly.

The boss turned the bottle and lovingly showed him the label. Whisky it was.

'D'you know,' said he, peering up at the boss wonderingly, 'they won't let me touch it at home.' And he looked as though he was going to cry.

'Ah, that's where we know a bit more than the ladies,' cried the boss, swooping across for two tumblers that stood on the table with the water-bottle, and pouring a generous finger into each. 'Drink it down. It'll do you good. And don't put any water with it. It's sacrilege to tamper with stuff like this. Ah!' He tossed off his, pulled out his handkerchief, hastily wiped his moustaches, and cocked an eye at old Woodifield, who was rolling his in his chaps.

The old man swallowed, was silent a moment, and then said faintly, 'It's nutty!'

But it warmed him; it crept into his chill old brain—he remembered.

'That was it,' he said, heaving himself out of his chair. 'I thought you'd like to know. The girls were in Belgium last week having a look at poor Reggie's grave, and they happened to come across your boy's. They're quite near each other, it seems.'

Old Woodifield paused, but the boss made no reply. Only a quiver in his eyelids showed that he heard.

'The girls were delighted with the way the place is kept,' piped the old voice. 'Beautifully looked after. Couldn't be better if they were at home. You've not been across, have yer?'

'No, no!' For various reasons the boss had not been across.

'There's miles of it,' quavered old Woodifield, 'and it's all as neat as a garden. Flowers growing on all the graves. Nice broad paths.' It was plain from his voice how much he liked a nice broad path.

The pause came again. Then the old man brightened wonderfully.

'D'you know what the hotel made the girls pay for a pot of jam?' he piped. 'Ten-francs! Robbery, I call it. It was a little pot, so Gertrude says, no bigger than a half-crown. And she hadn't taken more than a spoonful when they charged her ten francs. Gertrude brought the pot away with her to teach 'em a lesson. Quite right, too; it's trading on our feelings. They think because we're over there having a look round we're ready to pay anything.

That's what it is.' And he turned towards the door.

'Quite right, quite right!' cried the boss, though what was quite right he hadn't the least idea. He came round by his desk, followed the shuffling footsteps to the door, and saw the old fellow out. Woodifield was gone.

For a long moment the boss stayed, staring at nothing, while the grey-haired office messenger, watching him, dodged in and out of his cubby hole like a dog that expects to be taken for a run. Then: 'I'll see nobody for half an hour, Macey,' said the boss. 'Understand? Nobody at all.'

'Very good, sir.'

The door shut, the firm heavy steps recrossed the bright carpet, the fat body plumped down in the spring chair, and leaning forward, the boss covered his face with his hands. He wanted, he intended, he had arranged to weep...

It had been a terrible shock to him when old Woodifield sprang that remark upon him about the boy's grave. It was exactly as though the earth had opened and he had seen the boy lying there with Woodifield's girls staring down at him. For it was strange. Although over six years had passed away, the boss never thought of the boy except as lying unchanged, unblemished in his uniform, asleep for ever. 'My son!' groaned the boss. But no tears came yet. In the past, in the first months and even years after the boy's death, he had only to say those words to be overcome by such grief that nothing short of a violent fit of weeping could relieve him. Time, he had declared then, he had told everybody, could make no difference. Other men perhaps might recover, might live their loss down, but not he. How was it possible? His boy was an only son. Ever since his birth the boss had worked at building up this business for him; it had no other meaning if it was not for the boy. Life itself had come to have no other meaning. How on earth could he have slaved, denied himself, kept going all those years without the promise for ever before him of the boy's stepping into his shoes and carrying on where he left off?

And that promise had been so near being fulfilled. The boy had been in the office learning the ropes for a year before the war. Every morning they had started off together; they had come back by the same train. And what congratulations he had received as the boy's father! No wonder; he had taken to it marvellously. As to his popularity with the staff, every man jack of them down to old Macey couldn't make enough of the boy. And he wasn't in the least spoilt. No, he was just his bright, natural self, with the right word for everybody, with that boyish look and his habit of saying, 'Simply splendid!'

But all that was over and done with as though it never had been. The day had come when Macey had handed him the telegram that brought the whole place crashing about his head. 'Deeply regret to inform you...' And he had left the office a broken man, with his life in ruins.

Six years ago, six years... How quickly time passed! It might have happened yesterday. The boss took his hands from his face; he was puzzled. Something seemed to be wrong with him. He wasn't feeling as he wanted to feel. He decided to get up and have a look at the boy's photograph. But it wasn't a favourite photograph of his; the expression was unnatural. It was cold, even stern-looking. The boy had never looked like that.

At that moment the boss noticed that a fly had fallen into his broad inkpot, and was trying feebly but desperately to clamber out again. Help! help! said those struggling legs. But the sides of the inkpot were wet and slippery; it fell back again and began to swim. The boss took up a pen, picked the fly out of the ink, and shook it on to a piece of blotting-paper. For a fraction of a second it lay still on the dark patch that oozed round it. Then the front legs waved, took hold, and, pulling its small, sodden body up it began the immense task of cleaning the ink from its wings. Over and under, over and under, went a leg along a wing, as the stone goes over and under the scythe. Then there was a pause, while the fly, seeming to stand on the tips of its toes, tried to expand first one wing and then the other. It succeeded at last, and, sitting down, it began, like a minute cat, to clean its face. Now one could imagine that the little front legs rubbed against each other lightly, joyfully. The horrible danger was over; it had escaped; it was ready for life again.

But just then the boss had an idea. He plunged his pen back into the ink, leaned his thick wrist on the blotting paper, and as the fly tried its wings down came a great heavy blot. What would it make of that? What indeed! The little beggar seemed absolutely cowed, stunned, and afraid to move because of what would happen next. But then, as if painfully, it dragged itself forward. The front legs waved, caught hold, and, more slowly this time, the task began from the beginning.

He's a plucky little devil, thought the boss, and he felt a real admiration for the fly's courage. That was the way to tackle things; that was the right spirit. Never say die; it was only a question of... But the fly had again finished its laborious task, and the boss had just time to refill his pen, to shake fair and square on the new-cleaned body yet another dark drop. What about it this time? A painful moment of suspense followed. But behold, the front legs were again waving ; the boss felt a rush of relief. He leaned over the fly and said to it tenderly, 'You artful little b...' And he actually had the brilliant notion of breathing on it to help the drying process. All the same, there was something timid and weak about its efforts now, and the boss decided that this time should be the last, as he dipped the pen deep into the inkpot.

It was. The last blot fell on the soaked blotting-paper, and the draggled fly lay in it and did not stir. The back legs were stuck to the body; the front legs were not to be seen.

'Come on,' said the boss. 'Look sharp!' And he stirred it with his pen—in vain. Nothing happened or was likely to happen. The fly was dead.

The boss lifted the corpse on the end of the paper-knife and flung it into the waste-paper basket. But such a grinding feeling of wretchedness seized him that he felt positively frightened. He started forward and pressed the bell for Macey.

'Bring me some fresh blotting-paper,' he said, sternly, 'and look sharp about it.' And while the old dog padded away he fell to wondering what it was he had been thinking about before. What was it? It was... He took out his handkerchief and passed it inside his collar. For the life of him he could not remember.

44

DALYRIMPLE GOES WRONG

F. Scott Fitzgerald

I

In the millennium an educational genius will write a book to be given to every young man on the date of his disillusion. This work will have the flavour of Montaigne's essays and Samuel Butler's note-books—and a little of Tolstoi and Marcus Aurelius. It will be neither cheerful nor pleasant but will contain numerous passages of striking humour. Since first-class minds never believe anything very strongly until they've experienced it, its value will be purely relative...all people over thirty will refer to it as 'depressing.'

This prelude belongs to the story of a young man who lived, as you and I do, before the book.

II

The generation which numbered Bryan Dalyrimple drifted out of adolescence to a mighty fan-fare of trumpets. Bryan played the star in an affair which included a Lewis gun and a nine-day romp behind the retreating German lines, so luck triumphant or sentiment rampant awarded him a row of medals and on his arrival in the States he was told that he was second in importance only to General Pershing and Sergeant York. This was a lot of fun. The governor of his State, a stray congressman, and a citizens' committee gave him enormous smiles and 'By God, Sirs' on the dock at Hoboken; there were newspaper reporters and photographers who said 'would you mind' and 'if you could just'; and back in his home town there were old ladies, the rims of whose eyes grew red as they talked to him, and girls who hadn't remembered him so well since his father's business went blah! in nineteen-twelve.

But when the shouting died he realized that for a month he had been the house guest of the mayor, that he had only fourteen dollars in the world and that 'the name that will live forever in the annals and legends of this State' was already living there very quietly and obscurely.

One morning he lay late in bed and just outside his door he heard the up-stairs maid talking to the cook. The up-stairs maid said that Mrs Hawkins, the mayor's wife, had been trying for a week to hint Dalyrimple out of the house. He left at eleven o'clock in intolerable confusion, asking that his trunk be sent to Mrs Beebe's boarding-house.

Dalyrimple was twenty-three and he had never worked. His father had given him two years at the State University and passed away about the time of his son's nine-day romp, leaving behind him some mid-Victorian furniture and a thin packet of folded paper that turned out to be grocery bills. Young Dalyrimple had very keen grey eyes, a mind that delighted the army psychological examiners, a trick of having read it—whatever it was—some time before, and a cool hand in a hot situation. But these things did not save him a final, unresigned sigh when he realized that he had to go to work—right away.

It was early afternoon when he walked into the office of Theron G. Macy, who owned the largest wholesale grocery house in town. Plump, prosperous, wearing a pleasant but quite unhumorous smile, Theron G. Macy greeted him warmly.

'Well—how do, Bryan? What's on your mind?'

To Dalyrimple, straining with his admission, his own words, when they came, sounded like an Arab beggar's whine for alms.

'Why—this question of a job.' ('This question of a job' seemed somehow more clothed than just 'a job.')

'A job?' An almost imperceptible breeze blew across Mr Macy's expression.

'You see, Mr Macy,' continued Dalrymple, 'I feel I'm wasting time. I want to get started at something. I had several chances about a month ago but they all seem to have—gone—'

'Let's see,' interrupted Mr Macy. 'What were they?'

'Well, just at the first the governor said something about a vacancy on his staff. I was sort of counting on that for a while, but I hear he's given it to Allen Gregg, you know, son of G. P. Gregg. He sort of forgot what he said to me—just talking, I guess.'

'You ought to push those things.'

'Then there was that engineering expedition, but they decided they'd have to have a man who knew hydraulics, so they couldn't use me unless I paid my own way.'

'You had just a year at the university?'

'Two. But I didn't take any science or mathematics. Well, the day the battalion paraded, Mr Peter Jordan said something about a vacancy in his store. I went around there to-day and I found he meant a sort of floor-walker—and then you said something one day'—he paused and waited for the older man to take him up, but noting only a minute wince continued—'about a position, so I thought I'd come and see you.'

'There was a position,' confessed Mr Macy reluctantly, 'but since then we've filled it.' He cleared his throat again. 'You've waited quite a while.'

'Yes, I suppose I did. Everybody told me there was no hurry—and I'd had these various offers.'

Mr Macy delivered a paragraph on present-day opportunities which Dalrymple's mind completely skipped.

'Have you had any business experience?'

'I worked on a ranch two summers as a rider.'

'Oh, well,' Mr Macy disparaged this neatly, and then continued: 'What do you think you're worth?'

'I don't know.'

'Well, Bryan, I tell you, I'm willing to strain a point and give you a chance.'

Dalyrimple nodded.

'Your salary won't be much. You'll start by learning the stock. Then you'll come in the office for a while. Then you'll go on the road. When could you begin?'

'How about to-morrow?'

'All right. Report to Mr Hanson in the stock-room. He'll start you off.'

He continued to regard Dalyrimple steadily until the latter, realizing that the interview was over, rose awkwardly.

'Well, Mr Macy, I'm certainly much obliged.'

'That's all right. Glad to help you, Bryan.'

After an irresolute moment, Dalyrimple found himself in the hall. His forehead was covered with perspiration, and the room had not been hot.

'Why the devil did I thank the son of a gun?' he muttered.

III

Next morning Mr Hanson informed him coldly of the necessity of punching the time-clock at seven every morning, and delivered him for instruction into the hands of a fellow worker, one Charley Moore.

Charley was twenty-six, with that faint musk of weakness hanging about him that is often mistaken for the scent of evil. It took no psychological examiner to decide that he had drifted into indulgence and laziness as casually as he had drifted into life, and was to drift out. He was pale and his clothes stank of smoke; he enjoyed burlesque shows, billiards, and Robert Service, and was always looking back upon his last intrigue or forward to his next one. In his youth his taste had run to loud ties, but now it seemed to have faded, like his vitality, and was expressed in pale-lilac four-in-hands and indeterminate grey collars. Charley was listlessly struggling that losing struggle against mental, moral, and physical anaemia that takes place ceaselessly on the lower fringe of the middle classes.

The first morning he stretched himself on a row of cereal cartons and carefully went over the limitations of the Theron G. Macy Company.

'It's a piker organization. My Gosh! Lookit what they give me. I'm quittin' in a coupla months. Hell! Me stay with this bunch!'

The Charley Moores are always going to change jobs next month. They do, once or twice in their careers, after which they sit around comparing their last job with the present one, to the infinite disparagement of the latter.

'What do you get?' asked Dalyrimple curiously.

'Me? I get sixty.' This rather defiantly.

'Did you start at sixty?'

'Me? No, I started at thirty-five. He told me he'd put me on the road after I learned the stock. That's what he tells 'em all.'

'How long've you been here?' asked Dalyrimple with a sinking sensation.

'Me? Four years. My last year, too, you bet your boots.'

Dalyrimple rather resented the presence of the store detective as he resented the time-clock, and he came into contact with him almost immediately through the rule against smoking. This rule was a thorn in his side. He was accustomed to his three or four cigarettes in a morning, and after three days without it he followed Charley Moore by a circuitous route up a flight of back stairs to a little balcony where they indulged in peace. But this was not for long. One day in his second week the detective met him in a nook of the stairs, on his descent, and told him sternly that next time he'd be reported to Mr Macy. Dalyrimple felt like an errant schoolboy.

Unpleasant facts came to his knowledge. There were 'cave-dwellers' in the basement who had worked there for ten or fifteen years at sixty dollars a month, rolling barrels and carrying boxes through damp, cement-walled corridors, lost in that echoing half-darkness between seven and five-thirty and, like himself, compelled several times a month to work until nine at night.

At the end of a month he stood in line and received forty dollars. He pawned a cigarette-case and a pair of field-glasses and managed to live—to eat, sleep, and smoke. It was, however, a narrow scrape; as the ways and means of economy were a closed book to him and the second month brought no increase, he voiced his alarm.

'If you've got a drag with old Macy, maybe he'll raise you,' was Charley's disheartening reply. 'But he didn't raise ME till I'd been here nearly two years.'

'I've got to live,' said Dalyrimple simply. 'I could get more pay as a labourer on the railroad but, Golly, I want to feel I'm where there's a chance to get ahead.'

Charles shook his head sceptically and Mr Macy's answer next day was equally unsatisfactory.

Dalyrimple had gone to the office just before closing time.

'Mr Macy, I'd like to speak to you.'

'Why—yes.' The unhumorous smile appeared. The voice vas faintly resentful.

'I want to speak to you in regard to more salary.'

Mr Macy nodded.

'Well,' he said doubtfully, 'I don't know exactly what you're doing. I'll speak to Mr Hanson.'

He knew exactly what Dalyrimple was doing, and Dalyrimple knew he knew.

'I'm in the stock-room—and, sir, while I'm here I'd like to ask you how much longer I'll have to stay there.'

'Why—I'm not sure exactly. Of course it takes some time to learn the stock.'

'You told me two months when I started.'

'Yes. Well, I'll speak to Mr Hanson.'

Dalyrimple paused irresolute.

'Thank you, sir.'

Two days later he again appeared in the office with the result of a count that had been asked for by Mr Hesse, the bookkeeper. Mr Hesse was engaged and Dalyrimple, waiting, began idly fingering in a ledger on the stenographer's desk.

Half unconsciously he turned a page—he caught sight of his name—it was a salary list:

Dalyrimple
Demming
Donahoe
Everett

His eyes stopped—

Everett. $60

So Tom Everett, Macy's weak-chinned nephew, had started at sixty—and in three weeks he had been out of the packing-room and into the office.

So that was it! He was to sit and see man after man pushed over him: sons, cousins, sons of friends, irrespective of their capabilities, while *he* was cast for a pawn, with 'going on the road' dangled before his eyes—put of with the stock remark: 'I'll see; I'll look into it.' At forty, perhaps, he would be a bookkeeper like old Hesse, tired, listless Hesse with a dull routine for his stint and a dull background of boarding-house conversation.

This was a moment when a genii should have pressed into his hand the book for disillusioned young men. But the book has not been written.

A great protest swelling into revolt surged up in him. Ideas half forgotten, chaotically perceived and assimilated, filled his mind. Get on—that was the rule of life—and that was all. How he did it, didn't matter—but to be Hesse or Charley Moore.

'I won't!' he cried aloud.

The bookkeeper and the stenographers looked up in surprise. 'What?'

For a second Dalyrimple stared—then walked up to the desk.

'Here's that data,' he said brusquely. 'I can't wait any longer.'

Mr Hesse's face expressed surprise.

It didn't matter what he did—just so he got out of this rut. In a dream he stepped from the elevator into the stock-room, and walking to an unused aisle, sat down on a box, covering his face with his hands.

His brain was whirring with the frightful jar of discovering a platitude for himself.

'I've got to get out of this,' he said aloud and then repeated, 'I've got to get out'—and he didn't mean only out of Macy's wholesale house.

When he left at five-thirty it was pouring rain, but he struck off in the opposite direction from his boarding-house, feeling, in the first cool moisture that oozed soggily through his old suit, an odd exultation and freshness. He wanted a world that was like walking through rain, even though he could not see far ahead of him, but fate had put him in the world of Mr Macy's fetid storerooms and corridors. At first merely the overwhelming need of change took him, then half-plans began to formulate in his imagination.

'I'll go East—to a big city—meet people—bigger people—

people who'll help me. Interesting work somewhere. My God, there *must* be.'

With sickening truth it occurred to him that his facility for meeting people was limited. Of all places it was here in his own town that he should be known, was known—famous—before the water of oblivion had rolled over him.

You had to cut corners, that was all. Pull—relationship—wealthy marriages—

For several miles the continued reiteration of this preoccupied him and then he perceived that the rain had become thicker and more opaque in the heavy grey of twilight and that the houses were falling away. The district of full blocks, then of big houses, then of scattering little ones, passed and great sweeps of misty country opened out on both sides. It was hard walking here. The sidewalk had given place to a dirt road, streaked with furious brown rivulets that splashed and squashed around his shoes.

Cutting corners—the words began to fall apart, forming curious phrasings—little illuminated pieces of themselves. They resolved into sentences, each of which had a strangely familiar ring.

Cutting corners meant rejecting the old childhood principles that success came from faithfulness to duty, that evil was necessarily punished or virtue necessarily rewarded—that honest poverty was happier than corrupt riches.

It meant being hard.

This phrase appealed to him and he repeated it over and over. It had to do somehow with Mr Macy and Charley Moore—the attitudes, the methods of each of them.

He stopped and felt his clothes. He was drenched to the skin. He looked about him and, selecting a place in the fence where a tree sheltered it, perched himself there.

In my credulous years—he thought—they told me that evil was a sort of dirty hue, just as definite as a soiled collar, but it seems to me that evil is only a manner of hard luck, or heredity-and-environment, or 'being found out.' It hides in the vacillations of dubs like Charley Moore as certainly as it does in the intolerance of Macy, and if it ever gets much more tangible it becomes merely an arbitrary label to paste on the unpleasant things in other people's lives.

In fact—he concluded—it isn't worth worrying over what's evil and what isn't. Good and evil aren't any standard to me—and they can be a devil of a bad hindrance when I want something. When I want something bad enough, common sense tells me to go and take it—and not get caught.

And then suddenly Dalyrimple knew what he wanted first. He wanted fifteen dollars to pay his overdue board bill.

With a furious energy he jumped from the fence, whipped off his coat, and from its black lining cut with his knife a piece about five inches square. He made two holes near its edge and then fixed it on his face, pulling his hat down to hold it in place. It flapped grotesquely and then dampened and clung to his forehead and cheeks.

Now... The twilight had merged to dripping dusk...black as pitch. He began to walk quickly back towards town, not waiting to remove the mask but watching the road with difficulty through the jagged eye-holes. He was not conscious of any nervousness... the only tension was caused by a desire to do the thing as soon as possible.

He reached the first sidewalk, continued on until he saw a hedge far from any lamp-post, and turned in behind it. Within a minute he heard several series of footsteps—he waited—it was a woman and he held his breath until she passed...and then a man, a labourer. The next passer, he felt, would be what he wanted...the labourer's footfalls died far up the drenched street... other steps grew nears grew suddenly louder.

Dalyrimple braced himself.

'Put up your hands!'

The man stopped, uttered an absurd little grunt, and thrust pudgy arms skywards.

Dalyrimple went through the waistcoat.

'Now, you shrimp,' he said, setting his hand suggestively to his own hip pocket, 'you run, and stamp—loud! If I hear your feet stop I'll put a shot after you!'

Then he stood there in sudden uncontrollable laughter as audibly frightened footsteps scurried away into the night.

After a moment he thrust the roll of bills into his pocket, snatched of his mask, and running quickly across the street, darted down an alley.

IV

Yet, however Dalyrimple justified himself intellectually, he had many bad moments in the weeks immediately following his decision. The tremendous pressure of sentiment and inherited ambition kept raising riot with his attitude. He felt morally lonely.

The noon after his first venture he ate in a little lunch-room with Charley Moore and, watching him unspread the paper, waited for a remark about the hold-up of the day before. But either the hold-up was not mentioned or Charley wasn't interested. He turned listlessly to the sporting sheet, read Doctor Crane's crop of seasoned bromides, took in an editorial on ambition with his mouth slightly ajar, and then skipped to Mutt and Jeff.

Poor Charley—with his faint aura of evil and his mind that refused to focus, playing a lifeless solitaire with cast-off mischief.

Yet Charley belonged on the other side of the fence. In him could be stirred up all the flamings and denunciations of righteousness; he would weep at a stage heroine's lost virtue, he could become lofty and contemptuous at the idea of dishonour.

On my side, thought Dalyrimple, there aren't any resting-places; a man who's a strong criminal is after the weak criminals as well, so it's all guerilla warfare over here.

What will it all do to me? he thought, with a persistent weariness. Will it take the colour out of life with the honour? Will it scatter my courage and dull my mind?—despiritualize me completely—does it mean eventual barrenness, eventual remorse, failure?

With a great surge of anger, he would fling his mind upon the barrier—and stand there with the flashing bayonet of his pride. Other men who broke the laws of justice and charity lied to all the world. He at any rate would not lie to himself. He was more than Byronic now: not the spiritual rebel, Don Juan; not the philosophical rebel, Faust; but a new psychological rebel of his own century—defying the sentimental a priori forms of his own mind—

Happiness was what he wanted—a slowly rising scale of gratifications of the normal appetites—and he had a strong conviction that the materials, if not the inspiration of happiness, could be bought with money.

V

The night came that drew him out upon his second venture, and as he walked the dark street he felt in himself a great resemblance to a cat—a certain supple, swinging litheness. His muscles were rippling smoothly and sleekly under his spare, healthy flesh—he had an absurd desire to bound along the street, to run dodging among trees, to tarn 'cart-wheels' over soft grass.

It was not crisp, but in the air lay a faint suggestion of acerbity, inspirational rather than chilling.

'The moon is down—I have not heard the clock!'

He laughed in delight at the line which an early memory

had endowed with a hushed awesome beauty.

He passed a man and then another a quarter of mile afterwards.

He was on Philmore Street now and it was very dark. He blessed the city council for not having put in new lamp-posts as a recent budget had recommended. Here was the red-brick Sterner residence which marked the beginning of the avenue; here was the Jordon house, the Eisenhaurs', the Dents', the Markhams', the Frasers'; the Hawkins', where he had been a guest; the Willoughbys', the Everett's, colonial and ornate; the little cottage where lived the Watts old maids between the imposing fronts of the Macys' and the Krupstadts'; the Craigs—

Ah...*there*! He paused, wavered violently—far up the street was a blot, a man walking, possibly a policeman. After an eternal second he found himself following the vague, ragged shadow of a lamp-post across a lawn, running bent very low. Then he was standing tense, without breath or need of it, in the shadow of his limestone prey.

Interminably he listened—a mile off a cat howled, a hundred yards away another took up the hymn in a demoniacal snarl, and he felt his heart dip and swoop, acting as shock-absorber for his mind. There were other sounds; the faintest fragment of song far away; strident, gossiping laughter from a back porch diagonally across the alley; and crickets, crickets singing in the patched, patterned, moonlit grass of the yard. Within the house there seemed to lie an ominous silence. He was glad he did not know who lived here.

His slight shiver hardened to steel; the steel softened and his nerves became pliable as leather; gripping his hands he gratefully found them supple, and taking out knife and pliers he went to work on the screen.

So sure was he that he was unobserved that, from the dining-room where in a minute he found himself, he leaned out and carefully pulled the screen up into position, balancing it so it would neither fall by chance nor be a serious obstacle to a sudden exit.

Then he put the open knife in his coat pocket, took out his pocket-flash, and tiptoed around the room.

There was nothing here he could use—the dining-room had never been included in his plans for the town was too small to permit disposing of silver.

As a matter of fact his plans were of the vaguest. He had found that with a mind like his, lucrative in intelligence, intuition, and lightning decision, it was best to have but the skeleton of a campaign. The machine-gun episode had taught him that. And he was afraid that a method preconceived would give him two points of view in a crisis—and two points of view meant wavering.

He stumbled slightly on a chair, held his breath, listened, went on, found the hall, found the stairs, started up; the seventh stair creaked at his step, the ninth, the fourteenth. He was counting them automatically. At the third creak he paused again for over a minute—and in that minute he felt more alone than he had ever felt before. Between the lines on patrol, even when alone, he had had behind him the moral support of half a billion people; now he was alone, pitted against that same moral pressure—a bandit. He had never felt this fear, yet he had never felt this exultation.

The stairs came to an end, a doorway approached; he went in and listened to regular breathing. His feet were economical of steps and his body swayed sometimes at stretching as he felt over the bureau, pocketing all articles which held promise—he could not have enumerated them ten seconds afterwards. He felt on a chair for possible trousers, found soft garments, women's lingerie. The corners of his mouth smiled mechanically.

Another room...the same breathing, enlivened by one ghastly snort that sent his heart again on its tour of his breast. Round object—watch; chain; roll of bills; stick-pins; two rings—

he remembered that he had got rings from the other bureau. He started out winced as a faint glow flashed in front of him, facing him. God!—it was the glow of his own wrist-watch on his outstretched arm.

Down the stairs. He skipped two crumbing steps but found another. He was all right now, practically safe; as he neared the bottom he felt a slight boredom. He reached the dining-room—considered the silver—again decided against it.

Back in his room at the boarding-house he examined the additions to his personal property:

Sixty-five dollars in bills.

A platinum ring with three medium diamonds, worth, probably, about seven hundred dollars. Diamonds were going up.

A cheap gold-plated ring with the initials O.S. and the date inside—'03—probably a class-ring from school. Worth a few dollars. Unsalable.

A red-cloth case containing a set of false teeth.

A silver watch.

A gold chain worth more than the watch.

An empty ring-box.

A little ivory Chinese god—probably a desk ornament.

A dollar and sixty-two cents in small change.

He put the money under his pillow and the other things in the toe of an infantry boot, stuffing a stocking in on top of them. Then for two hours his mind raced like a high-power engine here and there through his life, past and future, through fear and laughter. With a vague, inopportune wish that he were married, he fell into a deep sleep about half past five.

VI

Though the newspaper account of the burglary failed to mention the false teeth, they worried him considerably. The picture of a human waking in the cool dawn and groping for them in vain, of a soft, toothless breakfast, of a strange, hollow, lisping voice calling the police station, of weary, dispirited visits to the dentist, roused a great fatherly pity in him.

Trying to ascertain whether they belonged to a man or a woman, he took them carefully out of the case and held them up near his mouth. He moved his own jaws experimentally; he measured with his fingers; but he failed to decide: they might belong either to a large-mouthed woman or a small-mouthed man.

On a warm impulse he wrapped them in brown paper from the bottom of his army trunk, and printed FALSE TEETH on the package in clumsy pencil letters. Then, the next night, he walked down Philmore Street, and shied the package onto the lawn so that it would be near the door. Next day the paper announced that the police had a clew—they knew that the burglar was in town. However, they didn't mention what the clew was.

VII

At the end of a month 'Burglar Bill of the Silver District' was the nurse-girl's standby for frightening children. Five burglaries were attributed to him, but though Dalyrimple had only committed three, he considered that majority had it and appropriated the title to himself. He had once been seen—'a large bloated creature with the meanest face you ever laid eyes on.' Mrs Henry Coleman, awaking at two o'clock at the beam of an electric torch flashed in her eye, could not have been expected to recognize Bryan Dalyrimple at whom she had waved flags last Fourth of July, and whom she had described as 'not at all the daredevil type, do you think?'

When Dalyrimple kept his imagination at white heat he managed to glorify his own attitude, his emancipation from petty scruples and remorses—but let him once allow his thought to rove unarmoured, great unexpected horrors and depressions would overtake him. Then for reassurance he had to go back to think out the whole thing over again. He found that it was on the whole better to give up considering himself as a rebel. It was more consoling to think of every one else as a fool.

His attitude towards Mr Macy underwent a change. He no longer felt a dim animosity and inferiority in his presence. As his fourth month in the store ended he found himself regarding his employer in a manner that was almost fraternal. He had a vague but very assured conviction that Mr Macy's innermost soul would have abetted and approved. He no longer worried about his future. He had the intention of accumulating several thousand dollars and then clearing out—going east, back to France, down to South America. Half a dozen times in the last two months he had been about to stop work, but a fear of attracting attention to his being in funds prevented him. So he worked on, no longer in listlessness, but with contemptuous amusement.

VIII

Then with astounding suddenness something happened that changed his plans and put an end to his burglaries.

Mr Macy sent for him one afternoon and with a great show of jovial mystery asked him if he had an engagement that night. If he hadn't, would he please call on Mr Alfred J. Fraser at eight o'clock. Dalyrimple's wonder was mingled with uncertainty. He debated with himself whether it were not his cue to take the first train out of town. But an hour's consideration decided him that his fears were unfounded and at eight o'clock he arrived at the big Fraser house in Philmore Avenue.

Mr Fraser was commonly supposed to be the biggest political influence in the city. His brother was Senator Fraser, his son-in-law was Congressman Demming, and his influence, though not wielded in such a way as to make him an objectionable boss, was strong nevertheless.

He had a great, huge face, deep-set eyes, and a barn-door of an upper lip, the melange approaching a worthy climax in a long professional jaw.

During his conversation with Dalyrimple his expression kept starting towards a smile, reached a cheerful optimism, and then receded back to imperturbability.

'How do you do, sir?' he said, holding out his hand. 'Sit down. I suppose you're wondering why I wanted you. Sit down.'

Dalyrimple sat down.

'Mr Dalyrimple, how old are you?'

'I'm twenty-three.'

'You're young. But that doesn't mean you're foolish. Mr Dalyrimple, what I've got to say won't take long. I'm going to make you a proposition. To begin at the beginning, I've been watching you ever since last Fourth of July when you made that speech in response to the loving-cup.'

Dalyrimple murmured disparagingly, but Fraser waved him to silence.

'It was a speech I've remembered. It was a brainy speech, straight from the shoulder, and it got to everybody in that crowd. I know. I've watched crowds for years.' He cleared his throat as if tempted to digress on his knowledge of crowds—then continued. 'But, Mr Dalyrimple, I've seen too many young men who promised brilliantly go to pieces, fail through want of steadiness, too many high-power ideas, and not enough willingness to work. So I waited. I wanted to see what you'd do. I wanted to see if you'd go to work, and if you'd stick to what you started.'

Dalyrimple felt a glow settle over him.

'So,' continued Fraser, 'when Theron Macy told me you'd started down at his place, I kept watching you, and I followed your record through him. The first month I was afraid for awhile. He told me you were getting restless, too good for your job, hinting around for a raise—'

Dalyrimple started.

'—But he said after that you evidently made up your mind to shut up and stick to it. That's the stuff I like in a young man! That's the stuff that wins out. And don't think I don't understand. I know how much harder it was for you after all that silly flattery a lot of old women had been giving you. I know what a fight it must have been—'

Dalyrimple's face was burning brightly. It felt young and strangely ingenuous.

'Dalyrimple, you've got brains and you've got the stuff in you— and that's what I want. I'm going to put you into the State Senate.'

'The *what?*'

'The State Senate. We want a young man who has got brains, but is solid and not a loafer. And when I say State Senate I don't stop there. We're up against it here, Dalyrimple. We've got to get some young men into politics—you know the old blood that's been running on the party ticket year in and year out.'

Dalyrimple licked his lips.

'You'll run me for the State Senate?'

'I'll *put* you in the State Senate.'

Mr Fraser's expression had now reached the point nearest a smile and Dalyrimple in a happy frivolity felt himself urging it mentally on—but it stopped, locked, and slid from him. The barn-door and the jaw were separated by a line strait as a nail. Dalyrimple remembered with an effort that it was a mouth, and talked to it.

'But I'm through,' he said. 'My notoriety's dead. People are fed up with me.'

'Those things,' answered Mr Fraser, 'are mechanical. Linotype is a resuscitator of reputations. Wait till you see the *Herald*, beginning next week—that is if you're with us—that is,' and his voice hardened slightly, 'if you haven't got too many ideas yourself about how things ought to be run.'

'No,' said Dalyrimple, looking him frankly in the eye. 'You'll have to give me a lot of advice at first.'

'Very well. I'll take care of your reputation then. Just keep yourself on the right side of the fence.'

Dalyrimple started at this repetition of a phrase he had thought of so much lately. There was a sudden ring at the door-bell.

'That's Macy now,' observed Fraser, rising. 'I'll go let him in. The servants have gone to bed.'

He left Dalyrimple there in a dream. The world was opening up suddenly—The State Senate, the United States Senate—so life was this after all—cutting corners—common sense, that was the rule. No more foolish risks now unless necessity called—but it was being hard that counted— Never to let remorse or self-reproach lose him a night's sleep—let his life be a sword of courage—there was no payment—all that was drivel—drivel.

He sprang to his feet with clinched hands in a sort of triumph.

'Well, Bryan,' said Mr Macy stepping through the portieres.

The two older men smiled their half-smiles at him.

'Well Bryan,' said Mr Macy again.

Dalyrimple smiled also.

'How do, Mr Macy?'

He wondered if some telepathy between them had made this new appreciation possible—some invisible realization...

Mr Macy held out his hand.

'I'm glad we're to be associated in this scheme—I've been for you all along—especially lately. I'm glad we're to be on the same side of the fence.'

'I want to thank you, sir,' said Dalyrimple simply. He felt a whimsical moisture gathering back of his eyes.

45

THE BOWMEN

Arthur Machen

It was during the Retreat of the Eighty Thousand, and the authority of the Censorship is sufficient excuse for not being more explicit. But it was on the most awful day of that awful time, on the day when ruin and disaster came so near that their shadow fell over London far away; and, without any certain news, the hearts of men failed within them and grew faint; as if the agony of the army in the battlefield had entered into their souls.

On this dreadful day, then, when three hundred thousand men in arms with all their artillery swelled like a flood against the little English company, there was one point above all other points in our battle line that was for a time in awful danger, not merely of defeat, but of utter annihilation. With the permission of the Censorship and of the military expert, this corner may, perhaps, be described as a salient, and if this angle were crushed and broken, then the English force as a whole would be shattered, the Allied left would be turned, and Sedan would inevitably follow.

All the morning the German guns had thundered and shrieked against this corner, and against the thousand or so of men who held it. The men joked at the shells, and found funny names for them, and had bets about them, and greeted them with scraps of music-hall songs. But the shells came on and burst, and tore good Englishmen limb from limb, and tore brother from brother, and as the heat of the day increased so did the fury of that terrific cannonade. There was no help, it seemed. The English artillery was good, but there was not nearly enough of it; it was being steadily battered into scrap iron.

There comes a moment in a storm at sea when people say to one another, 'It is at its worst; it can blow no harder,' and then there is a blast ten times more fierce than any before it. So it was in these British trenches.

There were no stouter hearts in the whole world than the hearts of these men; but even they were appalled as this seven-times-heated hell of the German cannonade fell upon them and overwhelmed them and destroyed them. And at this very moment they saw from their trenches that a tremendous host was moving against their lines. Five hundred of the thousand remained, and as far as they could see the German infantry was pressing on against them, column upon column, a grey world of men, ten thousand of them, as it appeared afterwards.

There was no hope at all. They shook hands, some of them. One man improvised a new version of the battlesong, 'Good-bye, good-bye to Tipperary,' ending with 'And we shan't get there'. And they all went on firing steadily. The officers pointed out that such an opportunity for high-class, fancy shooting might never occur again; the Germans dropped line after line; the Tipperary humourist asked, 'What price Sidney Street?' And the few machine guns did their best. But everybody knew it was of no use. The dead grey bodies lay in companies and battalions, as others came on and on and on, and they swarmed and stirred and advanced from beyond and beyond.

'World without end. Amen,' said one of the British soldiers with some irrelevance as he took aim and fired. And then he remembered—he says he cannot think why or wherefore—a queer vegetarian restaurant in London where he had once or twice eaten eccentric dishes of cutlets made of lentils and nuts that pretended to be steak. On all the plates in this restaurant there was printed a figure of St George in blue, with the motto, Adsit Anglis Sanctus Geogius—May St George be a present help to the

English. This soldier happened to know Latin and other useless things, and now, as he fired at his man in the grey advancing mass—300 yards away—he uttered the pious vegetarian motto. He went on firing to the end, and at last Bill on his right had to clout him cheerfully over the head to make him stop, pointing out as he did so that the King's ammunition cost money and was not lightly to be wasted in drilling funny patterns into dead Germans.

For as the Latin scholar uttered his invocation he felt something between a shudder and an electric shock pass through his body. The roar of the battle died down in his ears to a gentle murmur; instead of it, he says, he heard a great voice and a shout louder than a thunder-peal crying, 'Array, array, array!'

His heart grew hot as a burning coal, it grew cold as ice within him, as it seemed to him that a tumult of voices answered to his summons. He heard, or seemed to hear, thousands shouting: 'St George! St George!'

'Ha! messire; ha! sweet Saint, grant us good deliverance!'

'St George for merry England!'

'Harow! Harow! Monseigneur St George, succour us.'

'Ha! St George! Ha! St George! a long bow and a strong bow.'

'Heaven's Knight, aid us!'

And as the soldier heard these voices he saw before him, beyond the trench, a long line of shapes, with a shining about them. They were like men who drew the bow, and with another shout their cloud of arrows flew singing and tingling through the air towards the German hosts.

The other men in the trench were firing all the while. They had no hope; but they aimed just as if they had been shooting at Bisley. Suddenly one of them lifted up his voice in the plainest English, 'Gawd help us!' he bellowed to the man next to him, 'but we're blooming marvels! Look at those grey...gentlemen, look at them! D'ye see them? They're not going down in dozens, nor in 'undreds; it's thousands, it is. Look! look! there's a regiment gone while I'm talking to ye.'

'Shut it!' the other soldier bellowed, taking aim, 'what are ye gassing about!'

But he gulped with astonishment even as he spoke, for, indeed, the grey men were falling by the thousands. The English could hear the guttural scream of the German officers, the crackle of their revolvers as they shot the reluctant; and still line after line crashed to the earth.

All the while the Latin-bred soldier heard the cry: 'Harow! Harow! Monseigneur, dear saint, quick to our aid! St George help us!'

'High Chevalier, defend us!'

The singing arrows fled so swift and thick that they darkened the air; the heathen horde melted from before them.

'More machine guns!' Bill yelled to Tom.

'Don't hear them,' Tom yelled back. 'But, thank God, anyway; they've got it in the neck.'

In fact, there were ten thousand dead German soldiers left before that salient of the English army, and consequently there was no Sedan. In Germany, a country ruled by scientific principles, the Great General Staff decided that the contemptible English must have employed shells containing an unknown gas of a poisonous nature, as no wounds were discernible on the bodies of the dead German soldiers. But the man who knew what nuts tasted like when they called themselves steak knew also that St George had brought his Agincourt Bowmen to help the English.

46

MARY POSTGATE

Rudyard Kipling

Of Miss Mary Postgate, Lady McCausland wrote that she was 'thoroughly conscientious, tidy, companionable, and ladylike. I am very sorry to part with her, and shall always be interested in her welfare.'

Miss Fowler engaged her on this recommendation, and to her surprise, for she had had experience of companions, found that it was true. Miss Fowler was nearer sixty than fifty at the time, but though she needed care she did not exhaust her attendant's vitality. On the contrary, she gave out, stimulatingly and with reminiscences. Her father had been a minor Court official in the days when the Great Exhibition of 1851 had just set its seal on Civilization made perfect. Some of Miss Fowler's tales, none the less, were not always for the young. Mary was not young, and though her speech was as colourless as her eyes or her hair, she was never shocked. She listened unflinchingly to every one; said at the end, 'How interesting!' or 'How shocking!' as the case might be, and never again referred to it, for she prided herself on a trained mind, which 'did not dwell on these things.' She was, too, a treasure at domestic accounts, for which the village tradesmen, with their weekly books, loved her not. Otherwise she had no enemies; provoked no jealousy even among the plainest; neither gossip nor slander had ever been traced to her; she supplied the odd place at the Rector's or the Doctor's table at half an hour's notice; she was a sort of public aunt to very many small children of the village street, whose parents, while accepting everything, would have been swift to resent what they called 'patronage'; she served on the Village Nursing Committee as Miss Fowler's nominee when Miss Fowler was crippled by rheumatoid arthritis, and came out of six months' fortnightly meetings equally respected by all the cliques.

And when Fate threw Miss Fowler's nephew, an unlovely orphan of eleven, on Miss Fowler's hands, Mary Postgate stood to her share of the business of education as practised in private and public schools. She checked printed clothes-lists, and unitemised bills of extras; wrote to Head and House masters, matrons, nurses and doctors, and grieved or rejoiced over half-term reports. Young Wyndham Fowler repaid her in his holidays by calling her 'Gatepost,' 'Postey,' or 'Packthread,' by thumping her between her narrow shoulders, or by chasing her bleating, round the garden, her large mouth open, her large nose high in air, at a stiff-necked shamble very like a camel's. Later on he filled the house with clamour, argument, and harangues as to his personal needs, likes and dislikes, and the limitations of 'you women,' reducing Mary to tears of physical fatigue, or, when he chose to be humorous, of helpless laughter. At crises, which multiplied as he grew older, she was his ambassadress and his interpretress to Miss Fowler, who had no large sympathy with the young; a vote in his interest at the councils on his future; his sewing-woman, strictly accountable for mislaid boots and garments; always his butt and his slave.

And when he decided to become a solicitor, and had entered an office in London; when his greeting had changed from 'Hullo, Postey, you old beast,' to 'Mornin', Packthread,' there came a war which, unlike all wars that Mary could remember, did not stay decently outside England and in the newspapers, but intruded on the lives of people whom she knew. As she said to Miss Fowler, it was 'most vexatious.' It took the Rector's son who was going into business with his elder brother; it took the Colonel's nephew on the eve of fruit-farming in Canada; it took Mrs Grant's son who, his mother said, was devoted to the ministry; and, very early indeed, it took Wynn Fowler, who announced on a postcard that he had joined the Flying Corps and wanted a cardigan waistcoat.

'He must go, and he must have the waistcoat,' said Miss Fowler. So Mary got the proper-sized needles and wool, while Miss Fowler told the men of her establishment—two gardeners and an odd man, aged sixty—that those who could join the Army had better do so. The gardeners left. Cheape, the odd man, stayed on, and was promoted to the gardener's cottage. The cook, scorning to be limited in luxuries, also left, after a spirited scene with Miss Fowler, and took the housemaid with her. Miss Fowler gazetted Nellie, Cheape's seventeen-year-old daughter, to the vacant post; Mrs Cheape to the rank of cook, with occasional cleaning bouts; and the reduced establishment moved forward smoothly.

Wynn demanded an increase in his allowance. Miss Fowler, who always looked facts in the face, said, 'He must have it. The chances are he won't live long to draw it, and if three hundred makes him happy—'

Wynn was grateful, and came over, in his tight-buttoned uniform, to say so. His training centre was not thirty miles away, and his talk was so technical that it had to be explained by charts of the various types of machines. He gave Mary such a chart.

'And you'd better study it, Postey,' he said. 'You'll be seeing a lot of 'em soon.' So Mary studied the chart, but when Wynn next arrived to swell and exalt himself before his womenfolk, she failed badly in cross-examination, and he rated her as in the old days.

'You *look* more or less like a human being,' he said in his new Service voice. 'You *must* have had a brain at some time in your past. What have you done with it? Where d'you keep it? A sheep would know more than you do, Postey. You're lamentable. You are less use than an empty tin can, you dowey old cassowary.'

'I suppose that's how your superior officer talks to *you*?' said

Miss Fowler from her chair.

'But Postey doesn't mind,' Wynn replied. 'Do you, Packthread?'

'Why? Was Wynn saying anything? I shall get this right next time you come,' she muttered, and knitted her pale brows again over the diagrams of Taubes, Farmans, and Zeppelins.

In a few weeks the mere land and sea battles which she read to Miss Fowler after breakfast passed her like idle breath. Her heart and her interest were high in the air with Wynn, who had finished 'rolling' (whatever that might be) and had gone on from a 'taxi' to a machine more or less his own. One morning it circled over their very chimneys, alighted on Vegg's Heath, almost outside the garden gate, and Wynn came in, blue with cold, shouting for food. He and she drew Miss Fowler's bath-chair, as they had often done, along the Heath foot-path to look at the bi-plane. Mary observed that 'it smelt very badly.'

'Postey, I believe you think with your nose,' said Wynn. 'I know you don't with your mind. Now, what type's that?'

'I'll go and get the chart,' said Mary.

'You're hopeless! You haven't the mental capacity of a white mouse,' he cried, and explained the dials and the sockets for bomb-dropping till it was time to mount and ride the wet clouds once more.

'Ah!' said Mary, as the stinking thing flared upwards. 'Wait till our Flying Corps gets to work! Wynn says it's much safer than in the trenches.'

'I wonder,' said Miss Fowler. 'Tell Cheape to come and tow me home again.'

'It's all downhill. I can do it,' said Mary, 'if you put the brake on.' She laid her lean self against the pushing-bar and home they trundled.

'Now, be careful you aren't heated and catch a chill,' said overdressed Miss Fowler.

'Nothing makes me perspire,' said Mary. As she bumped

the chair under the porch she straightened her long back. The exertion had given her a colour, and the wind had loosened a wisp of hair across her forehead. Miss Fowler glanced at her.

'What do you ever think of, Mary?' she demanded suddenly.

'Oh, Wynn says he wants another three pairs of stockings—as thick as we can make them.'

'Yes. But I mean the things that women think about. Here you are, more than forty—'

'Forty-four,' said truthful Mary.

'Well?'

'Well?' Mary offered Miss Fowler her shoulder as usual.

'And you've been with me ten years now.'

'Let's see,' said Mary. 'Wynn was eleven when he came. He's twenty now, and I came two years before that. It must be eleven.'

'Eleven! And you've never told me anything that matters in all that while. Looking back, it seems to me that *I've* done all the talking.'

'I'm afraid I'm not much of a conversationalist. As Wynn says, I haven't the mind. Let me take your hat.'

Miss Fowler, moving stiffly from the hip, stamped her rubber-tipped stick on the tiled hall floor. 'Mary, aren't you *anything* except a companion? Would you *ever* have been anything except a companion?'

Mary hung up the garden hat on its proper peg. 'No,' she said after consideration. 'I don't imagine I ever should. But I've no imagination, I'm afraid.'

She fetched Miss Fowler her eleven-o'clock glass of Contrexeville.

That was the wet December when it rained six inches to the month, and the women went abroad as little as might be. Wynn's flying chariot visited them several times, and for two mornings (he had warned her by postcard) Mary heard the thresh of his propellers at dawn. The second time she ran to the window, and stared at the whitening sky. A little blur passed overhead. She lifted her lean arms towards it.

That evening at six o'clock there came an announcement in an official envelope that Second Lieutenant W. Fowler had been killed during a trial flight. Death was instantaneous. She read it and carried it to Miss Fowler.

'I never expected anything else,' said Miss Fowler; 'but I'm sorry it happened before he had done anything.'

The room was whirling round Mary Postgate, but she found herself quite steady in the midst of it.

'Yes,' she said. 'It's a great pity he didn't die in action after he had killed somebody.'

'He was killed instantly. That's one comfort,' Miss Fowler went on.

'But Wynn says the shock of a fall kills a man at once—whatever happens to the tanks,' quoted Mary.

The room was coming to rest now. She heard Miss Fowler say impatiently, 'But why can't we cry, Mary?' and herself replying, 'There's nothing to cry for. He has done his duty as much as Mrs Grant's son did.'

'And when he died, *she* came and cried all the morning,' said Miss Fowler. 'This only makes me feel tired—terribly tired. Will you help me to bed, please, Mary?—And I think I'd like the hot-water bottle.'

So Mary helped her and sat beside, talking of Wynn in his riotous youth.

'I believe,' said Miss Fowler suddenly, 'that old people and young people slip from under a stroke like this. The middle-aged feel it most.'

'I expect that's true,' said Mary, rising. 'I'm going to put away the things in his room now. Shall we wear mourning?'

'Certainly not,' said Miss Fowler. 'Except, of course, at the funeral. I can't go. You will. I want you to arrange about his being buried here. What a blessing it didn't happen at Salisbury!'

Every one, from the Authorities of the Flying Corps to the Rector, was most kind and sympathetic. Mary found herself for the moment in a world where bodies were in the habit of being despatched by all sorts of conveyances to all sorts of places. And at the funeral two young men in buttoned-up uniforms stood beside the grave and spoke to her afterwards.

'You're Miss Postgate, aren't you?' said one. 'Fowler told me about you. He was a good chap—a first-class fellow—a great loss.'

'Great loss!' growled his companion. 'We're all awfully sorry.'

'How high did he fall from?' Mary whispered.

'Pretty nearly four thousand feet, I should think, didn't he? You were up that day, Monkey?'

'All of that,' the other child replied. 'My bar made three thousand, and I wasn't as high as him by a lot.'

'Then *that's* all right,' said Mary. 'Thank you very much.'

They moved away as Mrs Grant flung herself weeping on Mary's flat chest, under the lych-gate, and cried, '*I* know how it feels! *I* know how it feels!'

'But both his parents are dead,' Mary returned, as she fended her off. 'Perhaps they've all met by now,' she added vaguely as she escaped towards the coach.

'I've thought of that too,' wailed Mrs Grant; 'but then he'll be practically a stranger to them. Quite embarrassing!'

Mary faithfully reported every detail of the ceremony to Miss Fowler, who, when she described Mrs Grant's outburst, laughed aloud.

'Oh, how Wynn would have enjoyed it! He was always utterly unreliable at funerals. D'you remember—' And they talked of him again, each piecing out the other's gaps. 'And now,' said Miss Fowler, 'we'll pull up the blinds and we'll have a general tidy. That always does us good. Have you seen to Wynn's things?'

'Everything—since he first came,' said Mary. 'He was never

destructive—even with his toys.'

They faced that neat room.

'It can't be natural not to cry,' Mary said at last. 'I'm *so* afraid you'll have a reaction.'

'As I told you, we old people slip from under the stroke. It's you I'm afraid for. Have you cried yet?'

'I can't. It only makes me angry with the Germans.'

'That's sheer waste of vitality,' said Miss Fowler. 'We must live till the war's finished.' She opened a full wardrobe. 'Now, I've been thinking things over. This is my plan. All his civilian clothes can be given away—Belgian refugees, and so on.'

Mary nodded. 'Boots, collars, and gloves?'

'Yes. We don't need to keep anything except his cap and belt.'

'They came back yesterday with his Flying Corps clothes'— Mary pointed to a roll on the little iron bed.

'Ah, but keep his Service things. Some one may be glad of them later. Do you remember his sizes?'

'Five feet eight and a half; thirty-six inches round the chest. But he told me he's just put on an inch and a half. I'll mark it on a label and tie it on his sleeping-bag.'

'So that disposes of *that*,' said Miss Fowler, tapping the palm of one hand with the ringed third finger of the other. 'What waste it all is! We'll get his old school trunk to-morrow and pack his civilian clothes.'

'And the rest?' said Mary. 'His books and pictures and the games and the toys—and—and the rest?'

'My plan is to burn every single thing,' said Miss Fowler. 'Then we shall know where they are and no one can handle them afterwards. What do you think?'

'I think that would be much the best,' said Mary. 'But there's such a lot of them.'

'We'll burn them in the destructor,' said Miss Fowler.

This was an open-air furnace for the consumption of refuse; a little circular four-foot tower of pierced brick over an iron grating. Miss Fowler had noticed the design in a gardening journal years ago, and had had it built at the bottom of the garden. It suited her tidy soul, for it saved unsightly rubbish-heaps, and the ashes lightened the stiff clay soil.

Mary considered for a moment, saw her way clear, and nodded again. They spent the evening putting away well-remembered civilian suits, underclothes that Mary had marked, and the regiments of very gaudy socks and ties. A second trunk was needed, and, after that, a little packing-case, and it was late next day when Cheape and the local carrier lifted them to the cart. The Rector luckily knew of a friend's son, about five feet eight and a half inches high, to whom a complete Flying Corps outfit would be most acceptable, and sent his gardener's son down with a barrow to take delivery of it. The cap was hung up in Miss Fowler's bedroom, the belt in Miss Postgate's; for, as Miss Fowler said, they had no desire to make tea-party talk of them.

'That disposes of *that*,' said Miss Fowler. 'I'll leave the rest to you, Mary. I can't run up and down the garden. You'd better take the big clothes-basket and get Nellie to help you.'

'I shall take the wheel-barrow and do it myself,' said Mary, and for once in her life closed her mouth.

Miss Fowler, in moments of irritation, had called Mary deadly methodical. She put on her oldest waterproof and gardening-hat and her ever-slipping goloshes, for the weather was on the edge of more rain. She gathered fire-lighters from the kitchen, a half-scuttle of coals, and a faggot of brushwood. These she wheeled in the barrow down the mossed paths to the dank little laurel shrubbery where the destructor stood under the drip of three oaks. She climbed the wire fence into the Rector's glebe just behind, and from his tenant's rick pulled two large armfuls of good hay, which she spread neatly on the fire-bars. Next, journey by journey, passing Miss Fowler's white face at the morning-room window each time, she brought down in the towel-covered clothes-basket, on the wheel-barrow, thumbed and used Hentys, Marryats, Levers, Stevensons, Baroness Orczys, Garvices, schoolbooks, and atlases, unrelated piles of the *Motor Cyclist*, the *Light Car*, and catalogues of Olympia Exhibitions; the remnants of a fleet of sailing-ships from ninepenny cutters to a three-guinea yacht; a prep-school dressing-gown; bats from three-and-sixpence to twenty-four shillings; cricket and tennis balls; disintegrated steam and clockwork locomotives with their twisted rails; a grey and red tin model of a submarine; a dumb gramophone and cracked records; golf-clubs that had to be broken across the knee, like his walking-sticks, and an assegai; photographs of private and public school cricket and football elevens, and his O.T.C. on the line of march; kodaks, and film-rolls; some pewters, and one real silver cup, for boxing competitions and Junior Hurdles; sheaves of school photographs; Miss Fowler's photograph; her own which he had borne off in fun and (good care she took not to ask!) had never returned; a playbox with a secret drawer; a load of flannels, belts, and jerseys, and a pair of spiked shoes unearthed in the attic; a packet of all the letters that Miss Fowler and she had ever written to him, kept for some absurd reason through all these years; a five-day attempt at a diary; framed pictures of racing motors in full Brooklands career, and load upon load of undistinguishable wreckage of tool-boxes, rabbit-hutches, electric batteries, tin soldiers, fret-saw outfits, and jig-saw puzzles.

Miss Fowler at the window watched her come and go, and said to herself, 'Mary's an old woman. I never realized it before.'

After lunch she recommended her to rest.

'I'm not in the least tired,' said Mary. 'I've got it all arranged. I'm going to the village at two o'clock for some paraffin. Nellie hasn't enough, and the walk will do me good.'

She made one last quest round the house before she started, and found that she had overlooked nothing. It began to mist as soon as she had skirted Vegg's Heath, where Wynn used to descend—it seemed to her that she could almost hear the beat of his propellers overhead, but there was nothing to see. She hoisted her umbrella and lunged into the blind wet till she had reached the shelter of the empty village. As she came out of Mr Kidd's shop with a bottle full of paraffin in her string shopping-bag, she met Nurse Eden, the village nurse, and fell into talk with her, as usual, about the village children. They were just parting opposite the 'Royal Oak,' when a gun, they fancied, was fired immediately behind the house. It was followed by a child's shriek dying into a wail.

'Accident!' said Nurse Eden promptly, and dashed through the empty bar, followed by Mary. They found Mrs Gerritt, the publican's wife, who could only gasp and point to the yard, where a little cart-lodge was sliding sideways amid a clatter of tiles. Nurse Eden snatched up a sheet drying before the fire, ran out, lifted something from the ground, and flung the sheet round it. The sheet turned scarlet and half her uniform too, as she bore the load into the kitchen. It was little Edna Gerritt, aged nine, whom Mary had known since her perambulator days.

'Am I hurted bad?' Edna asked, and died between Nurse Eden's dripping hands. The sheet fell aside and for an instant, before she could shut her eyes, Mary saw the ripped and shredded body.

'It's a wonder she spoke at all,' said Nurse Eden. 'What in God's name was it?'

'A bomb,' said Mary.

'One o' the Zeppelins?'

'No. An aeroplane. I thought I heard it on the Heath, but I fancied it was one of ours. It must have shut off its engines as it came down. That's why we didn't notice it.'

'The filthy pigs!' said Nurse Eden, all white and shaken. 'See the pickle I'm in! Go and tell Dr Hennis, Miss Postgate.' Nurse looked at the mother, who had dropped face down on the floor. 'She's only in a fit. Turn her over.'

Mary heaved Mrs Gerritt right side up, and hurried off for the doctor. When she told her tale, he asked her to sit down in the surgery till he got her something.

'But I don't need it, I assure you,' said she. 'I don't think it would be wise to tell Miss Fowler about it, do you? Her heart is so irritable in this weather.'

Dr Hennis looked at her admiringly as he packed up his bag.

'No. Don't tell anybody till we're sure,' he said, and hastened to the 'Royal Oak,' while Mary went on with the paraffin. The village behind her was as quiet as usual, for the news had not yet spread. She frowned a little to herself, her large nostrils expanded uglily, and from time to time she muttered a phrase which Wynn, who never restrained himself before his womenfolk, had applied to the enemy. 'Bloody pagans! They *are* bloody pagans. But,' she continued, falling back on the teaching that had made her what she was, 'one mustn't let one's mind dwell on these things.'

Before she reached the house Dr Hennis, who was also a special constable, overtook her in his car.

'Oh, Miss Postgate,' he said, 'I wanted to tell you that that accident at the 'Royal Oak' was due to Gerritt's stable tumbling down. It's been dangerous for a long time. It ought to have been condemned.'

'I thought I heard an explosion too,' said Mary.

'You might have been misled by the beams snapping. I've been looking at 'em. They were dry-rotted through and through. Of course, as they broke, they would make a noise just like a gun.'

'Yes?' said Mary politely.

'Poor little Edna was playing underneath it,' he went on, still holding her with his eyes, 'and that and the tiles cut her to pieces, you see?'

'I saw it,' said Mary, shaking her head. 'I heard it too.'

'Well, we cannot be sure.' Dr Hennis changed his tone completely. 'I know both you and Nurse Eden (I've been speaking to her) are perfectly trustworthy, and I can rely on you not to say anything—yet at least. It is no good to stir up people unless—'

'Oh, I never do—anyhow,' said Mary, and Dr Hennis went on to the county town.

After all, she told herself, it might, just possibly, have been the collapse of the old stable that had done all those things to poor little Edna. She was sorry she had even hinted at other things, but Nurse Eden was discretion itself. By the time she reached home the affair seemed increasingly remote by its very monstrosity. As she came in, Miss Fowler told her that a couple of aeroplanes had passed half an hour ago.

'I thought I heard them,' she replied, 'I'm going down to the garden now. I've got the paraffin.'

'Yes, but—what *have* you got on your boots? They're soaking wet. Change them at once.'

Not only did Mary obey but she wrapped the boots in a newspaper, and put them into the string bag with the bottle. So, armed with the longest kitchen poker, she left.

'It's raining again,' was Miss Fowler's last word, 'but—I know you won't be happy till that's disposed of.'

'It won't take long. I've got everything down there, and I've put the lid on the destructor to keep the wet out.'

The shrubbery was filling with twilight by the time she had completed her arrangements and sprinkled the sacrificial oil. As she lit the match that would burn her heart to ashes, she heard a groan or a grunt behind the dense Portugal laurels.

'Cheape?' she called impatiently, but Cheape, with his ancient lumbago, in his comfortable cottage would be the last man to profane the sanctuary. 'Sheep,' she concluded, and threw in the fusee. The pyre went up in a roar, and the immediate flame hastened night around her.

'How Wynn would have loved this!' she thought, stepping back from the blaze.

By its light she saw, half hidden behind a laurel not five paces away, a bareheaded man sitting very stiffly at the foot of one of the oaks. A broken branch lay across his lap—one booted leg protruding from beneath it. His head moved ceaselessly from side to side, but his body was as still as the tree's trunk. He was dressed—she moved sideways to look more closely—in a uniform something like Wynn's, with a flap buttoned across the chest. For an instant, she had some idea that it might be one of the young flying men she had met at the funeral. But their heads were dark and glossy. This man's was as pale as a baby's, and so closely cropped that she could see the disgusting pinky skin beneath. His lips moved.

'What do you say?' Mary moved towards him and stooped.

'Laty! Laty! Laty!' he muttered, while his hands picked at the dead wet leaves. There was no doubt as to his nationality. It made her so angry that she strode back to the destructor, though it was still too hot to use the poker there. Wynn's books seemed to be catching well. She looked up at the oak behind the man; several of the light upper and two or three rotten lower branches had broken and scattered their rubbish on the shrubbery path. On the lowest fork a helmet with dependent strings, showed like a bird's-nest in the light of a long-tongued flame. Evidently this person had fallen through the tree. Wynn had told her that it was quite possible for people to fall out of aeroplanes. Wynn told her too, that trees were useful things to break an aviator's fall, but in this case the aviator must have been broken or he would have moved from his queer position. He seemed helpless except for his horrible rolling head. On the other hand, she could see a pistol case at his belt—and Mary loathed pistols. Months ago, after reading certain Belgian reports together, she and Miss Fowler had had dealings with one—a huge revolver with flat-nosed bullets, which latter, Wynn said, were forbidden by the rules of war to be used against civilised enemies. 'They're good enough for us,' Miss Fowler had replied. 'Show Mary how it works.' And Wynn, laughing at the mere possibility of any such need, had led the craven winking Mary into the Rector's disused quarry, and had shown her how to fire the terrible machine. It lay now in the top-left-hand drawer of her toilet-table—a memento not included in the burning. Wynn would be pleased to see how she was not afraid.

She slipped up to the house to get it. When she came through the rain, the eyes in the head were alive with expectation. The mouth even tried to smile. But at sight of the revolver its corners went down just like Edna Gerritt's. A tear trickled from one eye, and the head rolled from shoulder to shoulder as though trying to point out something.

'Cassee. Tout cassee,' it whimpered.

'What do you say?' said Mary disgustedly, keeping well to one side, though only the head moved.

'Cassee,' it repeated. 'Che me rends. Le medicin! Toctor!'

'Nein!' said she, bringing all her small German to bear with the big pistol. 'Ich haben der todt Kinder gesehn.'

The head was still. Mary's hand dropped. She had been careful to keep her finger off the trigger for fear of accidents. After a few moments' waiting, she returned to the destructor, where the flames were falling, and churned up Wynn's charring books with the poker. Again the head groaned for the doctor.

'Stop that!' said Mary, and stamped her foot. 'Stop that, you bloody pagan!'

The words came quite smoothly and naturally. They were Wynn's own words, and Wynn was a gentleman who for no consideration on earth would have torn little Edna into those vividly coloured strips and strings. But this thing hunched under the oak-tree had done that thing. It was no question of reading horrors out of newspapers to Miss Fowler. Mary had seen it with her own eyes on the 'Royal Oak' kitchen table. She must not allow her mind to dwell upon it. Now Wynn was dead, and everything connected with him was lumping and rustling and tinkling under her busy poker into red black dust and grey leaves of ash. The thing beneath the oak would die too. Mary had seen death more than once. She came of a family that had a knack of dying under, as she told Miss Fowler, 'most distressing circumstances.' She would stay where she was till she was entirely satisfied that It was dead—dead as dear papa in the late 'eighties; aunt Mary in 'eighty-nine; mamma in 'ninety-one; cousin Dick in 'ninety-five; Lady McCausland's housemaid in 'ninety-nine; Lady McCausland's sister in nineteen hundred and one; Wynn buried five days ago; and Edna Gerritt still waiting for decent earth to hide her. As she thought—her underlip caught up by one faded canine, brows knit and nostrils wide—she wielded the poker with lunges that jarred the grating at the bottom, and careful scrapes round the brick-work above. She looked at her wrist-watch. It was getting on to half-past four, and the rain was coming down in earnest. Tea would be at five. If It did not die before that time, she would be soaked and would have to change. Meantime, and this occupied her, Wynn's things were burning well in spite of the hissing wet, though now and again a book-back with a quite distinguishable title would be heaved up out of the mass. The exercise of stoking had given her a glow which seemed to reach to the marrow of her bones. She hummed—Mary never had a voice—to herself. She had never believed in all those advanced views—though Miss Fowler herself leaned a little that way—of woman's work in the world; but now she saw there was much to be said for them. This, for instance, was *her* work—work which no man, least of all Dr Hennis, would ever have done. A man, at such a crisis, would be what Wynn called a 'sportsman'; would leave everything to fetch help, and would certainly bring It into the house. Now a woman's business was to make a happy home for—for a husband and children. Failing these—it was not a thing one should allow one's mind to dwell upon—but—

'Stop it!' Mary cried once more across the shadows. 'Nein, I tell you! Ich haben der todt Kinder gesehn.'

But it was a fact. A woman who had missed these things could still be useful—more useful than a man in certain respects. She thumped like a pavior through the settling ashes at the secret thrill of it. The rain was damping the fire, but she could feel—it was too dark to see—that her work was done. There was a dull red glow at the bottom of the destructor, not enough to char the wooden lid if she slipped it half over against the driving wet. This arranged, she leaned on the poker and waited, while an increasing rapture laid hold on her. She ceased to think. She gave herself up to feel. Her long pleasure was broken by a sound that she had waited for in agony several times in her life. She leaned forward and listened, smiling. There could be no mistake. She closed her eyes and drank it in. Once it ceased abruptly.

'Go on,' she murmured, half aloud. 'That isn't the end.'

Then the end came very distinctly in a lull between two rain-gusts. Mary Postgate drew her breath short between her teeth and shivered from head to foot. '*That's* all right,' said she contentedly, and went up to the house, where she scandalised the whole routine by taking a luxurious hot bath before tea, and came down looking, as Miss Fowler said when she saw her lying all relaxed on the other sofa, 'quite handsome!'

47

DAGON

H.P. Lovecraft

I am writing this under an appreciable mental strain, since by tonight I shall be no more. Penniless, and at the end of my supply of the drug which alone, makes life endurable, I can bear the torture no longer; and shall cast myself from this garret window into the squalid street below. Do not think from my slavery to morphine that I am a weakling or a degenerate. When you have read these hastily scrawled pages you may guess, though never fully realize, why it is that I must have forgetfulness or death.

It was in one of the most open and least frequented parts of the broad Pacific that the packet of which I was supercargo fell a victim to the German sea-raider. The great war was then at its very beginning, and the ocean forces of the Hun had not completely sunk to their later degradation; so that our vessel was made a legitimate prize, whilst we of her crew were treated with all the fairness and consideration due us as naval prisoners. So liberal, indeed, was the discipline of our captors, that five days after we were taken I managed to escape alone in a small boat with water and provisions for a good length of time.

When I finally found myself adrift and free, I had but little idea of my surroundings. Never a competent navigator, I could only guess vaguely by the sun and stars that I was somewhat south of the equator. Of the longitude I knew nothing, and no island or coastline was in sight. The weather kept fair, and for uncounted days I drifted aimlessly beneath the scorching sun;

waiting either for some passing ship, or to be cast on the shores of some habitable land. But neither ship nor land appeared, and I began to despair in my solitude upon the heaving vastness of unbroken blue.

The change happened whilst I slept. Its details I shall never know; for my slumber, though troubled and dream-infested, was continuous. When at last I awakened, it was to discover myself half sucked into a slimy expanse of hellish black mire which extended about me in monotonous undulations as far as I could see, and in which my boat lay grounded some distance away.

Though one might well imagine that my first sensation would be of wonder at so prodigious and unexpected a transformation of scenery, I was in reality more horrified than astonished; for there was in the air and in the rotting soil a sinister quality which chilled me to the very core. The region was putrid with the carcasses of decaying fish, and of other less describable things which I saw protruding from the nasty mud of the unending plain. Perhaps I should not hope to convey in mere words the unutterable hideousness that can dwell in absolute silence and barren immensity. There was nothing within hearing, and nothing in sight save a vast reach of black slime; yet the very completeness of the stillness and the homogeneity of the landscape oppressed me with a nauseating fear.

The sun was blazing down from a sky which seemed to me almost black in its cloudless cruelty; as though reflecting the inky marsh beneath my feet. As I crawled into the stranded boat I realized that only one theory could explain my position. Through some unprecedented volcanic upheaval, a portion of the ocean floor must have been thrown to the surface, exposing regions which for innumerable millions of years had lain hidden under unfathomable watery depths. So great was the extent of the new land which had risen beneath me, that I could not detect the faintest noise of the surging ocean, strain my ears as I might. Nor were there any sea-fowl to prey upon the dead things.

For several hours I sat thinking or brooding in the boat, which lay upon its side and afforded a slight shade as the sun moved across the heavens. As the day progressed, the ground lost some of its stickiness, and seemed likely to dry sufficiently for travelling purposes in a short time. That night I slept but little, and the next day I made for myself a pack containing food and water, preparatory to an overland journey in search of the vanished sea and possible rescue.

On the third morning I found the soil dry enough to walk upon with ease. The odour of the fish was maddening; but I was too much concerned with graver things to mind so slight an evil, and set out boldly for an unknown goal. All day I forged steadily westward, guided by a far-away hummock which rose higher than any other elevation on the rolling desert. That night I encamped, and on the following day still travelled towards the hummock, though that object seemed scarcely nearer than when I had first espied it. By the fourth evening I attained the base of the mound, which turned out to be much higher than it had appeared from a distance, an intervening valley setting it out in sharper relief from the general surface. Too weary to ascend, I slept in the shadow of the hill.

I know not why my dreams were so wild that night; but ere the waning and fantastically gibbous moon had risen far above the eastern plain, I was awake in a cold perspiration, determined to sleep no more. Such visions as I had experienced were too much for me to endure again. And in the glow of the moon I saw how unwise I had been to travel by day. Without the glare of the parching sun, my journey would have cost me less energy; indeed, I now felt quite able to perform the ascent which had deterred me at sunset. Picking up my pack, I started for the crest of the eminence.

I have said that the unbroken monotony of the rolling plain was a source of vague horror to me; but I think my horror was greater when I gained the summit of the mound and looked down the other side into an immeasurable pit or canyon, whose black recesses the moon had not yet soared high enough to illumine. I felt myself on the edge of the world, peering over the rim into a fathomless chaos of eternal night. Through my terror ran curious reminiscences of *Paradise Lost*, and Satan's hideous climb through the unfashioned realms of darkness.

As the moon climbed higher in the sky, I began to see that the slopes of the valley were not quite so perpendicular as I had imagined. Ledges and outcroppings of rock afforded fairly easy footholds for a descent, whilst after a drop of a few hundred feet, the declivity became very gradual. Urged on by an impulse which I cannot definitely analyse, I scrambled with difficulty down the rocks and stood on the gentler slope beneath, gazing into the Stygian deeps where no light had yet penetrated.

All at once my attention was captured by a vast and singular object on the opposite slope, which rose steeply about a hundred yards ahead of me; an object that gleamed whitely in the newly bestowed rays of the ascending moon. That it was merely a gigantic piece of stone, I soon assured myself; but I was conscious of a distinct impression that its contour and position were not altogether the work of Nature. A closer scrutiny filled me with sensations I cannot express; for despite its enormous magnitude, and its position in an abyss which had yawned at the bottom of the sea since the world was young, I perceived beyond a doubt that the strange object was a well-shaped monolith whose massive bulk had known the workmanship and perhaps the worship of living and thinking creatures.

Dazed and frightened, yet not without a certain thrill of the scientist's or archaeologist's delight, I examined my surroundings more closely. The moon, now near the zenith, shone weirdly and vividly above the towering steeps that hemmed in the chasm, and revealed the fact that a far-flung body of water flowed at the bottom, winding out of sight in both directions, and almost lapping my feet as I stood on the slope. Across the chasm, the wavelets washed the base of the Cyclopean monolith, on whose surface I could now trace both inscriptions and crude sculptures. The writing was in a system of hieroglyphics unknown to me, and unlike anything I had ever seen in books, consisting for the most part of conventionalised aquatic symbols such as fishes, eels, octopi, crustaceans, molluscs, whales and the like. Several characters obviously represented marine things which are unknown to the modern world, but whose decomposing forms I had observed on the ocean-risen plain.

It was the pictorial carving, however, that did most to hold me spellbound. Plainly visible across the intervening water on account of their enormous size was an array of bas-reliefs whose subjects would have excited the envy of a Doré. I think that these things were supposed to depict men—at least, a certain sort of men; though the creatures were shown disporting like fishes in the waters of some marine grotto, or paying homage at some monolithic shrine which appeared to be under the waves as well. Of their faces and forms I dare not speak in detail, for the mere remembrance makes me grow faint. Grotesque beyond the imagination of a Poe or a Bulwer, they were damnably human in general outline despite webbed hands and feet, shockingly wide and flabby lips, glassy, bulging eyes, and other features less pleasant to recall. Curiously enough, they seemed to have been chiselled badly out of proportion with their scenic background; for one of the creatures was shown in the act of killing a whale represented as but little larger than himself. I remarked, as I say, their grotesqueness and strange size; but in a moment decided that they were merely the imaginary gods of some primitive fishing or seafaring tribe; some tribe whose last descendant had perished eras before the first ancestor of the Piltdown or Neanderthal Man was born. Awestruck at this unexpected glimpse into a past beyond the conception of the most daring anthropologist, I stood musing whilst the moon cast queer reflections on the silent channel before me.

Then suddenly I saw it. With only a slight churning to mark its rise to the surface, the thing slid into view above the dark waters. Vast, Polyphemus-like, and loathsome, it darted like a stupendous monster of nightmares to the monolith, about which it flung its gigantic scaly arms, the while it bowed its hideous head and gave vent to certain measured sounds. I think I went mad then.

Of my frantic ascent of the slope and cliff, and of my delirious journey back to the stranded boat, I remember little. I believe I sang a great deal, and laughed oddly when I was unable to sing. I have indistinct recollections of a great storm some time after I reached the boat; at any rate, I knew that I heard peals of thunder and other tones which Nature utters only in her wildest moods.

When I came out of the shadows I was in a San Francisco hospital; brought thither by the captain of the American ship which had picked up my boat in mid-ocean. In my delirium I had said much, but found that my words had been given scant attention. Of any land upheaval in the Pacific, my rescuers knew nothing; nor did I deem it necessary to insist upon a thing which I knew they could not believe. Once I sought out a celebrated ethnologist, and amused him with peculiar questions regarding the ancient Philistine legend of Dagon, the Fish-God; but soon perceiving that he was hopelessly conventional, I did not press my inquiries.

It is at night, especially when the moon is gibbous and waning, that I see the thing. I tried morphine; but the drug has given only transient surcease, and has drawn me into its clutches as a hopeless slave. So now I am to end it all, having written a full account for the information or the contemptuous amusement of my fellow-men. Often I ask myself if it could not all have been a pure phantasm—a mere freak of fever as I lay sun-stricken and raving in the open boat after my escape from the German man-of-war. This I ask myself, but ever does there come before me a hideously vivid vision in reply. I cannot think of the deep sea without shuddering at the nameless things that may at this very moment be crawling and floundering on its slimy bed, worshipping their ancient stone idols and carving their own detestable likenesses on submarine obelisks of water-soaked granite. I dream of a day when they may rise above the billows to drag down in their reeking talons the remnants of puny, war-exhausted mankind—of a day when the land shall sink, and the dark ocean floor shall ascend amidst universal pandemonium.

The end is near. I hear a noise at the door, as of some immense slippery body lumbering against it. It shall not find me. God, that hand! The window! The window!

48

MIXING WAR, ART AND DANCING

Ernest Hemingway

Outside a woman walked along the wet street-lamp lit sidewalk through the sleet and snow.

Inside in the Fine Arts Institute on the sixth floor of the Y.W.C.A. Building, 1020 McGee Street, a merry crowd of soldiers from Camp Funston and Fort Leavenworth fox trotted and one-stepped with girls from the Fine Arts School while a sober faced young man pounded out the latest jazz music as he watched the moving figures. In a corner a private in the signal corps was discussing Whistler with a black haired girl who heartily agreed with him. The private had been a member of the art colony at Chicago before the war was declared.

Three men from Funston were wandering arm in arm along the wall looking at the exhibition of paintings by Kansas City artists. The piano player stopped. The dancers clapped and cheered and he swung into 'The Long, Long Trail Awinding'. An infantry corporal, dancing with a swift moving girl in a red dress, bent his head close to hers and confided something about a girl in Chautauqua, Kas. In the corridor a group of girls surrounded a tow-headed young artilleryman and applauded his imitation of his pal Bill challenging the colonel, who had forgotten the password. The music stopped again and the solemn pianist rose from his stool and walked out into the hall for a drink.

A crowd of men rushed up to the girl in the red dress to plead for the next dance. Outside the woman walked along the wet lamp lit sidewalk.

It was the first dance for soldiers to be given under the auspices of the War Camp Community Service. Forty girls of the art school, chaperoned by Miss Winifred Sexton, secretary of the school and Mrs J.F. Binnie were the hostesses. The idea was formulated by J.P. Robertson of the War Camp Community Service, and announcements were sent to the commandants at Camp Funston and Fort Leavenworth inviting all soldiers on leave. Posters made by the girl students were put up at Leavenworth on the interurb an trains.

The first dance will be followed by others at various clubs and schools throughout the city according to Mr Robertson.

The pianist took his seat again and the soldiers made a dash for partners. In the intermission the soldiers drank to the girls in fruit punch. The girl in red, surrounded by a crowd of men in olive drab, seated herself at the piano, the men and the girls gathered around and sang until midnight. The elevator had stopped running and so the jolly crowd bunched down the six flights of stairs and rushed waiting motor cars. After the last car had gone, the woman walked along the wet sidewalk through the sleet and looked up at the dark windows of the sixth floor.

49

THE LOCKET

Kate Chopin

I

One night in autumn a few men were gathered about a fire on the slope of a hill. They belonged to a small detachment of Confederate forces and were awaiting orders to march. Their grey uniforms were worn beyond the point of shabbiness. One of the men was heating something in a tin cup over the embers. Two were lying at full length a little distance away, while a fourth was trying to decipher a letter and had drawn close to the light. He had unfastened his collar and a good bit of his flannel shirt front.

'What's that you got around your neck, Ned?' asked one of the men lying in the obscurity.

Ned—or Edmond—mechanically fastened another button of his shirt and did not reply. He went on reading his letter.

'Is it your sweet heart's picture?'

''Taint no gal's picture,' offered the man at the fire. He had removed his tin cup and was engaged in stirring its grimy contents with a small stick. 'That's a charm; some kind of hoodoo business that one o' them priests gave him to keep him out o' trouble. I know them Cath'lics. That's how come Frenchy got permoted an never got a scratch sence he's been in the ranks. Hey, French! aint I right?' Edmond looked up absently from his letter.

'What is it?' he asked.

'Aint that a charm you got round your neck?'

'It must be, Nick,' returned Edmond with a smile. 'I don't

know how I could have gone through this year and a half without it.'

The letter had made Edmond heart sick and home sick. He stretched himself on his back and looked straight up at the blinking stars. But he was not thinking of them nor of anything but a certain spring day when the bees were humming in the clematis; when a girl was saying good bye to him. He could see her as she unclasped from her neck the locket which she fastened about his own. It was an old fashioned golden locket bearing miniatures of her father and mother with their names and the date of their marriage. It was her most precious earthly possession. Edmond could feel again the folds of the girl's soft white gown, and see the droop of the angel-sleeves as she circled her fair arms about his neck. Her sweet face, appealing, pathetic, tormented by the pain of parting, appeared before him as vividly as life. He turned over, burying his face in his arm and there he lay, still and motionless.

The profound and treacherous night with its silence and semblance of peace settled upon the camp. He dreamed that the fair Octavie brought him a letter. He had no chair to offer her and was pained and embarrassed at the condition of his garments. He was ashamed of the poor food which comprised the dinner at which he begged her to join them.

He dreamt of a serpent coiling around his throat, and when he strove to grasp it the slimy thing glided away from his clutch. Then his dream was clamour.

'Git your duds! you! Frenchy!' Nick was bellowing in his face. There was what appeared to be a scramble and a rush rather than any regulated movement. The hill side was alive with clatter and motion; with sudden up-springing lights among the pines. In the east the dawn was unfolding out of the darkness. Its glimmer was yet dim in the plain below.

'What's it all about?' wondered a big black bird perched in

the top of the tallest tree. He was an old solitary and a wise one, yet he was not wise enough to guess what it was all about. So all day long he kept blinking and wondering.

The noise reached far out over the plain and across the hills and awoke the little babes that were sleeping in their cradles. The smoke curled up towards the sun and shadowed the plain so that the stupid birds thought it was going to rain; but the wise one knew better.

'They are children playing a game,' thought he. 'I shall know more about it if I watch long enough.'

At the approach of night they had all vanished away with their din and smoke. Then the old bird plumed his feathers. At last he had understood! With a flap of his great, black wings he shot downwards, circling towards the plain.

A man was picking his way across the plain. He was dressed in the garb of a clergyman. His mission was to administer the consolations of religion to any of the prostrate figures in whom there might yet linger a spark of life. A negro accompanied him, bearing a bucket of water and a flask of wine.

There were no wounded here; they had been borne away. But the retreat had been hurried and the vultures and the good Samaritans would have to look to the dead.

There was a soldier—a mere boy—lying with his face to the sky. His hands were clutching the sward on either side and his finger nails were stuffed with earth and bits of grass that he had gathered in his despairing grasp upon life. His musket was gone; he was hatless and his face and clothing were begrimed. Around his neck hung a gold chain and locket. The priest, bending over him, unclasped the chain and removed it from the dead soldier's neck. He had grown used to the terrors of war and could face them unflinchingly; but its pathos, someway, always brought the tears to his old, dim eyes.

The angelus was ringing half a mile away. The priest and the negro knelt and murmured together the evening benediction and a prayer for the dead.

II

The peace and beauty of a spring day had descended upon the earth like a benediction. Along the leafy road which skirted a narrow, tortuous stream in central Louisiana, rumbled an old fashioned cabriolet, much the worse for hard and rough usage over country roads and lanes. The fat, black horses went in a slow, measured trot, notwithstanding constant urging on the part of the fat, black coachman. Within the vehicle were seated the fair Octavie and her old friend and neighbour, Judge Pillier, who had come to take her for a morning drive.

Octavie wore a plain black dress, severe in its simplicity. A narrow belt held it at the waist and the sleeves were gathered into close fitting wristbands. She had discarded her hoopskirt and appeared not unlike a nun. Beneath the folds of her bodice nestled the old locket. She never displayed it now. It had returned to her sanctified in her eyes; made precious as material things sometimes are by being forever identified with a significant moment of one's existence.

A hundred times she had read over the letter with which the locket had come back to her. No later than that morning she had again pored over it. As she sat beside the window, smoothing the letter out upon her knee, heavy and spiced odours stole in to her with the songs of birds and the humming of insects in the air.

She was so young and the world was so beautiful that there came over her a sense of unreality as she read again and again the priest's letter. He told of that autumn day drawing to its close, with the gold and the red fading out of the west, and the night gathering its shadows to cover the faces of the dead. Oh! She could not believe that one of those dead was her own! with visage uplifted to the grey sky in an agony of supplication. A spasm of resistance and rebellion seized and swept over her. Why was the spring here with its flowers and its seductive breath if he was dead! Why was she here! What further had she to do with life and the living!

Octavie had experienced many such moments of despair, but a blessed resignation had never failed to follow, and it fell then upon her like a mantle and enveloped her.

'I shall grow old and quiet and sad like poor Aunt Tavie,' she murmured to herself as she folded the letter and replaced it in the secretary. Already she gave herself a little demure air like her Aunt Tavie. She walked with a slow glide in unconscious imitation of Mademoiselle Tavie whom some youthful affliction had robbed of earthly compensation while leaving her in possession of youth's illusions.

As she sat in the old cabriolet beside the father of her dead lover, again there came to Octavie the terrible sense of loss which had assailed her so often before. The soul of her youth clamoured for its rights; for a share in the world's glory and exultation. She leaned back and drew her veil a little closer about her face. It was an old black veil of her Aunt Tavie's. A whiff of dust from the road had blown in and she wiped her cheeks and her eyes with her soft, white handkerchief, a homemade handkerchief, fabricated from one of her old fine muslin petticoats.

'Will you do me the favour, Octavie,' requested the judge in the courteous tone which he never abandoned, 'to remove that veil which you wear. It seems out of harmony, someway, with the beauty and promise of the day.'

The young girl obediently yielded to her old companion's wish and unpinning the cumbersome, sombre drapery from her bonnet, folded it neatly and laid it upon the seat in front of her.

'Ah! that is better; far better!' he said in a tone expressing unbounded relief. 'Never put it on again, dear.' Octavie felt a little hurt; as if he wished to debar her from share and parcel in the burden of affliction which had been placed upon all of them. Again she drew forth the old muslin handkerchief.

They had left the big road and turned into a level plain which had formerly been an old meadow. There were clumps of thorn trees here and there, gorgeous in their spring radiance. Some cattle were grazing off in the distance in spots where the grass was tall and luscious. At the far end of the meadow was the towering lilac hedge, skirting the lane that led to Judge Pillier's house, and the scent of its heavy blossoms met them like a soft and tender embrace of welcome.

As they neared the house the old gentleman placed an arm around the girl's shoulders and turning her face up to him he said: 'Do you not think that on a day like this, miracles might happen? When the whole earth is vibrant with life, does it not seem to you, Octavie, that heaven might for once relent and give us back our dead?' He spoke very low, advisedly, and impressively. In his voice was an old quaver which was not habitual and there was agitation in every line of his visage. She gazed at him with eyes that were full of supplication and a certain terror of joy.

They had been driving through the lane with the towering hedge on one side and the open meadow on the other. The horses had somewhat quickened their lazy pace. As they turned into the avenue leading to the house, a whole choir of feathered songsters fluted a sudden torrent of melodious greeting from their leafy hiding places.

Octavie felt as if she had passed into a stage of existence which was like a dream, more poignant and real than life. There was the old grey house with its sloping eaves. Amid the blur of green, and dimly, she saw familiar faces and heard voices as if they came from far across the fields, and Edmond was holding her. Her dead Edmond; her living Edmond, and she felt the beating of his heart against her and the agonizing rapture of his kisses striving to awake her. It was as if the spirit of life and the awakening spring had given back the soul to her youth and bade her rejoice.

It was many hours later that Octavie drew the locket from her bosom and looked at Edmond with a questioning appeal in her glance.

'It was the night before an engagement,' he said. 'In the hurry of the encounter, and the retreat next day, I never missed it till the fight was over. I thought of course I had lost it in the heat of the struggle, but it was stolen.'

'Stolen,' she shuddered, and thought of the dead soldier with his face uplifted to the sky in an agony of supplication.

Edmond said nothing; but he thought of his messmate; the one who had lain far back in the shadow; the one who had said nothing.

50

TWO FRIENDS

Guy de Maupassant

Besieged Paris was in the throes of famine. Even the sparrows on the roofs and the rats in the sewers were growing scarce. People were eating anything they could get.

As Monsieur Morissot, watchmaker by profession and idler for the nonce, was strolling along the boulevard one bright January morning, his hands in his trousers pockets and stomach empty, he suddenly came face to face with an acquaintance—Monsieur Sauvage, a fishing chum.

Before the war broke out Morissot had been in the habit, every Sunday morning, of setting forth with a bamboo rod in his hand and a tin box on his back. He took the Argenteuil train, got out at Colombes, and walked thence to the Ile Marante. The moment he arrived at this place of his dreams he began fishing, and fished till nightfall.

Every Sunday he met in this very spot Monsieur Sauvage, a stout, jolly, little man, a draper in the Rue Notre Dame de Lorette, and also an ardent fisherman. They often spent half the day side by side, rod in hand and feet dangling over the water, and a warm friendship had sprung up between the two.

Some days they did not speak; at other times they chatted; but they understood each other perfectly without the aid of words, having similar tastes and feelings.

In the spring, about ten o'clock in the morning, when the early sun caused a light mist to float on the water and gently warmed the backs of the two enthusiastic anglers, Morissot would occasionally remark to his neighbour:

'My, but it's pleasant here.'

To which the other would reply:

'I can't imagine anything better!'

And these few words sufficed to make them understand and appreciate each other.

In the autumn, towards the close of day, when the setting sun shed a blood-red glow over the western sky, and the reflection of the crimson clouds tinged the whole river with red, brought a glow to the faces of the two friends, and gilded the trees, whose leaves were already turning at the first chill touch of winter, Monsieur Sauvage would sometimes smile at Morissot, and say:

'What a glorious spectacle!'

And Morissot would answer, without taking his eyes from his float:

'This is much better than the boulevard, isn't it?'

As soon as they recognized each other they shook hands cordially, affected at the thought of meeting under such changed circumstances.

Monsieur Sauvage, with a sigh, murmured:

'These are sad times!'

Morissot shook his head mournfully.

'And such weather! This is the first fine day of the year.'

The sky was, in fact, of a bright, cloudless blue.

They walked along, side by side, reflective and sad.

'And to think of the fishing!' said Morissot. 'What good times we used to have!'

'When shall we be able to fish again?' asked Monsieur Sauvage.

They entered a small cafe and took an absinthe together, then resumed their walk along the pavement.

Morissot stopped suddenly.

'Shall we have another absinthe?' he said.

'If you like,' agreed Monsieur Sauvage.

And they entered another wine shop.

They were quite unsteady when they came out, owing to the effect of the alcohol on their empty stomachs. It was a fine, mild day, and a gentle breeze fanned their faces.

The fresh air completed the effect of the alcohol on Monsieur Sauvage. He stopped suddenly, saying:

'Suppose we go there?'

'Where?'

'Fishing.'

'But where?'

'Why, to the old place. The French outposts are close to Colombes. I know Colonel Dumoulin, and we shall easily get leave to pass.'

Morissot trembled with desire.

'Very well. I agree.'

And they separated, to fetch their rods and lines.

An hour later they were walking side by side on the highroad. Presently they reached the villa occupied by the colonel. He smiled at their request, and granted it. They resumed their walk, furnished with a password.

Soon they left the outposts behind them, made their way through deserted Colombes, and found themselves on the outskirts of the small vineyards which border the Seine. It was about eleven o'clock.

Before them lay the village of Argenteuil, apparently lifeless. The heights of Orgement and Sannois dominated the landscape. The great plain, extending as far as Nanterre, was empty, quite empty-a waste of dun-coloured soil and bare cherry trees.

Monsieur Sauvage, pointing to the heights, murmured:

'The Prussians are up yonder!'

And the sight of the deserted country filled the two friends with vague misgivings.

The Prussians! They had never seen them as yet, but they had felt their presence in the neighbourhood of Paris for months past—ruining France, pillaging, massacring, starving them. And a kind of superstitious terror mingled with the hatred they already felt towards this unknown, victorious nation.

'Suppose we were to meet any of them?' said Morissot.

'We'd offer them some fish,' replied Monsieur Sauvage, with that Parisian light-heartedness which nothing can wholly quench.

Still, they hesitated to show themselves in the open country, overawed by the utter silence which reigned around them.

At last Monsieur Sauvage said boldly:

'Come, we'll make a start; only let us be careful!'

And they made their way through one of the vineyards, bent double, creeping along beneath the cover afforded by the vines, with eye and ear alert.

A strip of bare ground remained to be crossed before they could gain the river bank. They ran across this, and, as soon as they were at the water's edge, concealed themselves among the dry reeds.

Morissot placed his ear to the ground, to ascertain, if possible, whether footsteps were coming their way. He heard nothing. They seemed to be utterly alone.

Their confidence was restored, and they began to fish.

Before them the deserted Ile Marante hid them from the farther shore. The little restaurant was closed, and looked as if it had been deserted for years.

Monsieur Sauvage caught the first gudgeon, Monsieur Morissot the second, and almost every moment one or other raised his line with a little, glittering, silvery fish wriggling at the end; they were having excellent sport.

They slipped their catch gently into a close-meshed bag lying at their feet; they were filled with joy—the joy of once more indulging in a pastime of which they had long been deprived.

The sun poured its rays on their backs; they no longer heard anything or thought of anything. They ignored the rest of the world; they were fishing.

But suddenly a rumbling sound, which seemed to come from the bowels of the earth, shook the ground beneath them: the cannon were resuming their thunder.

Morissot turned his head and could see towards the left, beyond the banks of the river, the formidable outline of Mont-Valerien, from whose summit arose a white puff of smoke.

The next instant a second puff followed the first, and in a few moments a fresh detonation made the earth tremble.

Others followed, and minute by minute the mountain gave forth its deadly breath and a white puff of smoke, which rose slowly into the peaceful heaven and floated above the summit of the cliff.

Monsieur Sauvage shrugged his shoulders.

'They are at it again!' he said.

Morissot, who was anxiously watching his float bobbing up and down, was suddenly seized with the angry impatience of a peaceful man towards the madmen who were firing thus, and remarked indignantly:

'What fools they are to kill one another like that!'

'They're worse than animals,' replied Monsieur Sauvage.

And Morissot, who had just caught a bleak, declared:

'And to think that it will be just the same so long as there are governments!'

'The Republic would not have declared war,' interposed Monsieur Sauvage.

Morissot interrupted him:

'Under a king we have foreign wars; under a republic we have civil war.'

And the two began placidly discussing political problems with the sound common sense of peaceful, matter-of-fact citizens—agreeing on one point: that they would never be free. And Mont-Valerien thundered ceaselessly, demolishing the houses of the French with its cannon balls, grinding lives of men to powder, destroying many a dream, many a cherished hope, many a prospective happiness; ruthlessly causing endless woe and suffering in the hearts of wives, of daughters, of mothers, in other lands.

'Such is life!' declared Monsieur Sauvage.

'Say, rather, such is death!' replied Morissot, laughing.

But they suddenly trembled with alarm at the sound of footsteps behind them, and, turning round, they perceived close at hand four tall, bearded men, dressed after the manner of livery servants and wearing flat caps on their heads. They were covering the two anglers with their rifles.

The rods slipped from their owners' grasp and floated away down the river.

In the space of a few seconds they were seized, bound, thrown into a boat, and taken across to the Ile Marante.

And behind the house they had thought deserted were about a score of German soldiers.

A shaggy-looking giant, who was bestriding a chair and smoking a long clay pipe, addressed them in excellent French with the words:

'Well, gentlemen, have you had good luck with your fishing?'

Then a soldier deposited at the officer's feet the bag full of fish, which he had taken care to bring away. The Prussian smiled.

'Not bad, I see. But we have something else to talk about. Listen to me, and don't be alarmed:

'You must know that, in my eyes, you are two spies sent to reconnoitre me and my movements. Naturally, I capture you and I shoot you. You pretended to be fishing, the better to disguise your real errand. You have fallen into my hands, and must take the consequences. Such is war.

'But as you came here through the outposts you must have a password for your return. Tell me that password and I will let you go.'

The two friends, pale as death, stood silently side by side, a slight fluttering of the hands alone betraying their emotion.

'No one will ever know,' continued the officer. 'You will return peacefully to your homes, and the secret will disappear with you. If you refuse, it means death—instant death. Choose!'

They stood motionless, and did not open their lips.

The Prussian, perfectly calm, went on, with hand outstretched towards the river:

'Just think that in five minutes you will be at the bottom of that water. In five minutes! You have relations, I presume?'

Mont-Valerien still thundered.

The two fishermen remained silent. The German turned and gave an order in his own language. Then he moved his chair a little way off, that he might not be so near the prisoners, and a dozen men stepped forward, rifle in hand, and took up a position, twenty paces off.

'I give you one minute,' said the officer; 'not a second longer.'

Then he rose quickly, went over to the two Frenchmen, took Morissot by the arm, led him a short distance off, and said in a low voice:

'Quick! the password! Your friend will know nothing. I will pretend to relent.'

Morissot answered not a word.

Then the Prussian took Monsieur Sauvage aside in like manner, and made him the same proposal.

Monsieur Sauvage made no reply.

Again they stood side by side.

The officer issued his orders; the soldiers raised their rifles.

Then by chance Morissot's eyes fell on the bag full of gudgeon lying in the grass a few feet from him.

A ray of sunlight made the still quivering fish glisten like silver. And Morissot's heart sank. Despite his efforts at self-control his eyes filled with tears.

'Good-by, Monsieur Sauvage,' he faltered.

'Good-by, Monsieur Morissot,' replied Sauvage.

They shook hands, trembling from head to foot with a dread beyond their mastery.

The officer cried:

'Fire!'

The twelve shots were as one.

Monsieur Sauvage fell forward instantaneously. Morissot, being the taller, swayed slightly and fell across his friend with face turned skywards and blood oozing from a rent in the breast of his coat.

The German issued fresh orders.

His men dispersed, and presently returned with ropes and large stones, which they attached to the feet of the two friends; then they carried them to the river bank.

Mont-Valerien, its summit now enshrouded in smoke, still continued to thunder.

Two soldiers took Morissot by the head and the feet; two others did the same with Sauvage. The bodies, swung lustily by strong hands, were cast to a distance, and, describing a curve, fell feet foremost into the stream.

The water splashed high, foamed, eddied, then grew calm; tiny waves lapped the shore.

A few streaks of blood flecked the surface of the river.

The officer, calm throughout, remarked, with grim humour:

'It's the fishes' turn now!'

Then he retraced his way to the house.

Suddenly he caught sight of the net full of gudgeons, lying forgotten in the grass. He picked it up, examined it, smiled, and called:

'Wilhelm!'

A white-aproned soldier responded to the summons, and the Prussian, tossing him the catch of the two murdered men, said:

'Have these fish fried for me at once, while they are still alive; they'll make a tasty dish.'

Then he resumed his pipe.